DESTINED DAWN

HANNAH HAZE

FOREWORD

This book is a 'why choose' romance with one female main character and several love interests. There are groups scenes in this book as well as talk of contraception and pregnancy. There are scenes that some readers may find uncomfortable including death, violence and gore. For more detailed content warnings, please visit my website.

If you spot any typos in this book, please drop me a line so I can make it right: hannahhazewrites@gmail.com (Or just drop me an email anyway. I love to chat!).

PROLOGUE

B ronwyn

Twenty years ago

"Take her."

My sister shakes her head violently, fixing me with a steely glare, even though silent tears race down her cheeks and drip off her chin.

I peer down into my daughter's sleeping face. So serene, so peaceful, unaware of all the danger and chaos that exists in this world. My battered heart breaks that little bit more.

"Please Mabel," I beg, unable to drag my eyes from my daughter's face. She is so beautiful, so perfect, from the miniature nails on each of her tiny fingers to each long dark lash that rests against the curve of her delicate cheek. My heart aches. I don't want to hand her to my sister any more than she wants to take her from me.

But what choice do I have?

"Don't ask me to, Bronwyn. Please don't ask me to," she whispers.

"You're the only person I can trust. The only person I know will keep her safe."

"She needs you. Her mother."

My spine straightens and I look up to meet the watery eyes of my sister.

"I've told you. My days are numbered. What use does Rhianna have with a dead mother?" My sister winces, shaking her head again. But she doesn't argue with me about what I've seen. We both know by now that my dreams do not lie. They show me the future and the future is my death.

We can bemoan and bitch about it until we're blue in the face, until we've driven ourselves mad. But the future can't be changed – not something like this – no matter what those who have used my powers may believe. The future is coming no matter what.

"And if you don't take her, think who will."

"Caspian?" she says. "He would keep her safe."

I gaze back down at my daughter. I can see him in her features. The dark hue of her hair, the structure of her small face. I am there too. In the color of her eyes, in the fairness of her skin. She is the perfect amalgamation of us both.

"He wouldn't," I say.

"Surely, he will come and–"

"Mabel! There is no time! Take her. Take her now and hide her. Please, before it is too late."

"He's her father. He would keep her safe. He is far more

powerful than I am. He has a whole army, for goodness' sake, Bronwyn."

Now I shake my head. How can I tell my sister the truth? She has always been so adamant when it comes to the things she believes in. She sees the world in black and white. For her, there is no gray. She has never wavered. She is strong. How can I admit I have been seduced by – that I have fallen for – a man I know is not good? That I suspected this about him, but turned my face away from the truth and loved him anyway.

"The only person she is safe with is you." With the remaining part of my heart shattering into a million pieces, I hold the baby out to her. It takes all my strength, the act almost physically impossible, my arms not wanting to give her away. Bile sloshes in my stomach, burning all along my throat, and I force back the tears bubbling in the corner of my eyes. If I crack now, my sister will never take my daughter from me.

"I have seen it," I whisper to her, almost afraid to utter the words out loud. "She is the girl from the Fourth Prophecy."

"The prophecy?" Mabel says, her nose crinkling in the way it does when she's confused. "But that prophecy is unclear and—"

"It doesn't matter. It puts her in danger, Mabel, so much danger. They will come. They will come for her – you know they will. Either to destroy her or to attempt to steal her powers."

"Steal her powers?" Mabel says in alarm. "Have you seen that?"

I hold my sister's gaze. "You must keep her hidden. Keep her safe ... please ..."

"But even from Caspian? From her own father?"

"Yes, Mabel," I snap. "Especially her own father."

My sister considers my face. Goodness knows what she must think. Goodness knows how many questions she must have about what has passed between me and the Black Prince. But my sister is stoic and unshakeable. She keeps her curiosity to herself. It's why I trust her with Rhianna's life.

And her silence is for the best. How would I ever explain it? The Black Prince – leader of the so-called dark forces in the West, our mortal enemy – the man we have been fighting these past years. He disarmed me completely. Made me fall so hopelessly in love with him. Made me believe all his promises, all his visions for the future – a future of peace, of no more war, of no more fighting.

I have been such a fool.

My daughter snuffles in her sleep, her tiny nose wrinkling.

I have made mistakes, but I can make amends now, make amends by ensuring Rhianna is protected.

"But how?" my sister says. "How will I do it? I'm no seer. I have no special powers. Surely, there is someone better equipped to care for her than me."

I shake my head adamantly. "There isn't."

My sister peers down into the sleeping face of my daughter, and her face lights up with affection. There is no one but me who loves Rhianna as much as Mabel does.

She lifts her arms, the tears now flowing freely from her eyes, and carefully, I lay my daughter in her hold. I am trusting her with the most precious thing I have in the world and though I know that my child is safer with her than she is with me, I have to force myself not to scream and snatch her right back.

"What if I can't? What if I fail?" my sister asks. "What if I fail you, Bronwyn?"

"You won't. You are stronger than me." Better than me too. She always said I was too trusting, too quick to follow my heart and not my head. Not this time. This time, I ignore my broken heart. "And I will always be here. We all will. You can always call on us for help."

I stroke my finger down the face of my daughter, her skin so soft, so new, so fragile, like the petals of a flower. Not yet blemished by the sun, ravished by the wind, marked by time.

"What will I tell her?" Mabel asks.

"What?" I say, too mesmerized by my daughter's face – a face I am committing to memory – every line, every color, every expression, every sound, even the milky smell of her. I will remember it all. I will think of it when the final blow hits. My last thought will be of her. This beautiful, precious creature.

"When she's older, Bronwyn? Old enough to know, to understand? What should I tell her?"

I press my lips to my daughter's warm forehead, inhaling the scent of her one last time. "Tell her that I love her. That I love her so, so much. And that I will always be close by."

1

R^{hi}

"WHAT MEMORIES?" Tristan asks, swinging his gaze from me to Stone as we glare at each other across the bedroom.

"The ones locked inside her head," Azlan says. "We tried to open them once before, but it caused Rhianna too much pain. We had to abort."

"Why are there memories locked inside your head?" Spencer asks.

I shrug. Exactly. Why? Stone has always believed they were locked away to protect me from them, and while that may be true, I think they may hold answers, clues as to why I – a girl from nowhere, a nobody, a no one – has been plucked by fate and bound to these five men. Men more powerful, knowledgeable, and resourceful than I am.

Stone stares at me over the length of the bedroom and I know him well enough to read the expression on his face, even if — unlike him — I can't read the thoughts in his head. He doesn't want to do it. He doesn't want to search through those memories again. He hasn't changed his mind on this.

"It's a bad idea," he says, "and look what yesterday's bad idea cost us."

"It didn't cost us anything. We're all here," I say. "We're all safe, alive."

He turns his head to glare at the assassin. "Just."

"You think they're going to help in some way?" Spencer asks me.

"I don't know," I say honestly. "But maybe and if so, I don't want to miss out on a source of information that might give us answers."

"This is all based on the premise that you think fate is a logical force," Stone says, sounding more like his professor-self than he usually does, "and not a random one. The forces that have bound us together may be little more than chance. There may be no other reason for it."

"You don't really believe that," I tell him.

"I'm not obnoxious enough to pretend I do understand these things, Miss Blackwaters."

"Bullshit," Tristan says, "Rhi is right. Fate rarely binds people together and when it does, it has a purpose."

Stone turns his steely gaze on him next. "And what do you think that purpose is, Kennedy?"

Tristan pauses for a moment, then says with conviction: "To remove my father from power and restore democracy to the republic." Renzo cackles. "What?" Tristan challenges. He's not used to being laughed at.

"Restore democracy?" Renzo sneers. "What fucking democracy?"

What follows is a load of bickering and I lie back against

the cushion and watch all the mayhem unfold, escalating in Azlan having to grab Tristan by the back of his shirt to stop him swinging for Renzo.

Yeah, maybe it was chaos and chance that brought us together, because it's been precisely ten minutes in the same room together before one mate has threatened to kill another.

I scramble off the bed, hooking Pip under my arm as I do, and head towards the door.

"Where are you going?" Azlan calls after me.

"To get some breakfast," I tell him, slamming the door behind me.

The air in the hallway is cool. I hug Pip closer to my body, despite his attempt to wriggle free, and descend the staircase, entering the empty kitchen a minute later. I'm assuming Winnie and Trent are still in bed and an unusual feeling of jealousy spirals through my stomach. That's where I'd like to be – with any one of my mates – and yet that feels impossible. Six of us? How on earth is that going to work? I almost feel envious of Winnie and her one boyfriend. I'm not sure I'm cut out for five.

Placing Pip on the floor, I step towards the window, wrapping my arms around myself and watching the winter sun play across the prairie and the spindly grass sway in the wind. I'm so lost in my thoughts, I don't hear Stone enter until he's standing right beside me at the window.

"I'll do it," he says. "I don't like it, but, fuck it, I seem incapable of refusing you anything, Rhianna Blackwaters, so if it's what you really want, I will help you."

I turn from the window and look up into his unusually serious face. I smile at him, resting my hand against his chest.

"Do you ever wish it was just the two of us?" I ask him quietly.

"Do I ever wish I had you all to myself and didn't have to share you with four other ... fairly average-looking men?"

I hit him on the arm. "Yes."

"Nah," he says.

"Oh," I say, a little disappointed by his answer.

He grins at me. "Miss Blackwaters, you are smarter than that. Of course, I wish I had you all to myself. As well as wishing all your clothes would miraculously disappear and that we got locked in our bedroom for eternity with no escape and an endless supply of fine dining and good wine. Unfortunately, what we wish for isn't always possible and I'm more than content with what I have. Azlan is my best friend and I'm happy to share you with him, and as for the others ..."

"As for the others ...?"

"We'll work it out." He examines my face. "Why? Do you wish it was just us two? I'm flattered you'd pick me as your favorite."

"I don't have a favorite," I say sternly. I don't want to give my mates any more reasons to fight. Also, it's the truth. When I stand back and consider it, I really don't have a favorite. Each of my fated mates is different and unique in their own way, and I like each one of them for that reason. Even Renzo. Even Spencer.

"Sure, you don't," Stone says with a wink.

"I don't."

"Hmmm," he pulls me towards him, "I bet I could think of some ways to ensure I am top of your list."

"I can think of one," I say, crawling my fingers up his chest.

"Really?" His eyes darken.

"Yes," I say, reaching up onto my tiptoes so I can whisper into his ear. "Help me search those memories."

He laughs, his chest rumbling beneath my palms.

"You're such a brat."

"Stone?"

"Fuck, yes, I'll do it," he says, shaking his head at me. "But this is the last time, okay? The last time I agree to one of your stupid plans."

"It's not stupid. I know my aunt. I know she'd leave me something and I've looked everywhere else."

This time, he nods. "I actually agree with you. I think she has too. But it might not be the answer to the question you have. How could she have known you'd end up bonded to five fated mates?"

"Four," I correct him.

"I've seen the way he looks at you," Stone mutters. "It's only a matter of time."

"My mom was a seer, Stone. Maybe she saw all this. Maybe my aunt knew what was going to happen. Maybe she knew what was in store for us."

Stone scrubs his fingers through his beard, then tugs me a little closer. "I'm not sure I want to see the future."

"Phoenix Stone," I say with a smile hovering on my lips, "are you afraid?"

Stone always seems so damn sure of himself. It's hard to believe he could be afraid of anything at all.

"Yes, I'm afraid," he says deadly seriously. "Very afraid of losing you. I've – we've – already come close to that happening far too many times."

I can't deny that, and that fear resides inside me too. I'm not afraid to die. I suspect I've spent my entire life skirting close to death. When it's there, hovering at your shoulder the entire time, you get used to it. It doesn't seem so scary. But the thought of losing Stone ... of losing any of them ...

"So don't you see?" I tell him. "Understanding the past, maybe gaining a glimpse of the future, could help us. It could help keep all of us safe."

He sighs. I know I haven't convinced him. I also know he's familiar with me enough now to understand how stubborn I am. I'm not backing down on this.

"Okay," he says, "breakfast first and then we'll do it."

"Do it? He really can't keep his hands off you, can he, little rabbit?" Renzo says, striding into the kitchen with the others behind him.

"He was talking about the memories," I mutter.

Stone raises an eyebrow at me as if to challenge that assumption.

I pinch his arm and then busy myself boiling eggs that Azlan managed to pick up on his journey back to the mansion yesterday.

Breakfast turns out to be a lot less awkward than I expected.

Azlan and Tristan talk quietly with one another at one end of the table while Renzo tries to strike up a conversation with Stone; although the topic he chooses – the best way to snap a man's neck – definitely isn't to Stone's taste. It leaves me and Spencer together at the other end of the table (Winnie and Trent yet to reappear).

"This is really fucking weird," Spencer says, scooping out the contents of his fourth egg. It seems he barely ate while imprisoned and I wasn't blind to the tears in the corner of his eyes when I placed the first egg down in front of him, with a warning to them all that this isn't some Snow White and the Seven Dwarves situation and I won't be cooking and cleaning for them.

Spencer stuffs the egg into his mouth and chews.

"What's weird?" I ask, cradling a warm cup of coffee in both my hands.

"This," he says, gesturing to us all with his spoon. "I never expected to be in some grand, decrepit house in the middle of nowhere with Tris, the man in black, Professor Stone, an assassin and you. It's pretty surreal."

"I guess so." I sip my drink. "You miss your dueling buddies? You miss all those cheerleaders?"

He places his spoon down on the table and swallows. "No, no, I don't."

I roll my eyes. Spencer lived for all that adulation, so did Tristan.

"What?" he says. "It's true. They've shown their true colors – their prejudice and bigotry – and I don't miss them one bit."

"You didn't notice their prejudice and bigotry in their treatment towards me?"

"No," he says honestly, "I guess I didn't."

I consider his words. I'm kind of grateful he's owned up to that and not tried to defend his behavior or somehow justify it.

"And I'd much rather be here with you than anywhere else," he adds.

"Because I make good eggs," I say, pointing to the half-full shell.

"They are good. Not too runny, not overdone."

"It comes with keeping chickens. You end up cooking and eating a lot of eggs."

"You kept chickens?" he says, picking up his spoon again.

"Yep, it's harder than it looks. You have to keep them happy or they won't lay. They seemed to like listening to a

bit of '50s rock'n'roll best. I used to have to sing to them."
Spencer chuckles. "We used to grow our own vegetables too
– without the use of magic. We couldn't afford to use it too
often in case anyone noticed we were magicals."

"Shit," he says, "I can't imagine not being able to use my
magic. I get kind of scratchy if I haven't used it in a while."
He scrapes the last of the egg from the shell. "Why were you
hiding? You never told me."

I know enough about my past, about my mom and
maybe even my dad, to have my suspicions, but I want to
know for sure.

"I don't know," I say honestly. "But I think it's time we
found out once and for all."

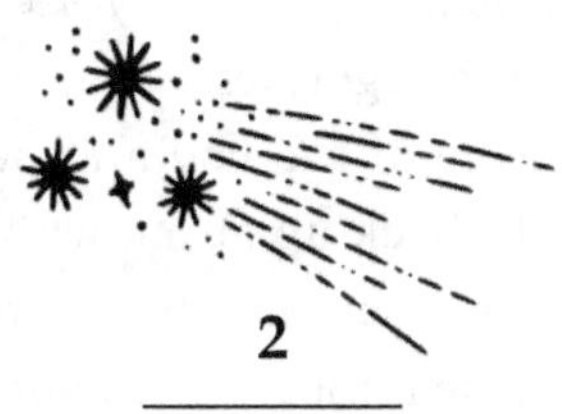

2

S tone

I LEAD her back up to the bedroom, the other four men following behind us, Renzo Barone practically breathing down my neck. He seems to want to make friends. At least that's what I think the monologue at breakfast about snapping necks was all about. Either that or he's sizing me up, working out the best way to kill me.

I grip Rhi's elbow a little tighter and pick up our pace, creating a little distance between me and the assassin.

In the bedroom, I tell her to lie down on the mattress.

"Are the theatrics really required?" she asks, climbing up onto the bed and lying down flat on her back. "I feel like you're going to measure me out for a coffin."

"I think it's best if we do this somewhere comfortable." I crack my knuckles, remembering the last time; how she'd flailed and writhed around on the hard floor. This time it could be worse, more violent – who the fuck knows – and I don't want her injuring herself. Not physically, anyway. The emotional damage heading her way seems inevitable and yet she wants to do this regardless.

I hover by the side of the bed and peer down into her face. She stares right back up at me with those honey eyes and it's easy to forget everyone else in the room. She's so damn beautiful – I take it for granted. But every so often, I'm struck by it all over again.

"Stone?" she says, knocking me out of my trance.

"You're sure about this, sweetheart?" I whisper to her.

She nods, resting her hands on her stomach.

"I trust you, Stone." And stars, I wish she wouldn't say that. I'm not reliable. I'm not someone a girl like her should put her trust in. "I know you'll look after me."

I place my palm on her forehead and then bend down to kiss her lips – unable to help myself. She tastes of butter and coffee, her lips soft and wet.

Reluctantly, I pull away, sigh, and close my eyes, letting my mind wander into hers. There's no barrier there today. She lets me stride right in, like I used to when we first met, her thoughts and her mind completely clear to me, like an open book ready for me to leaf through the pages.

Right there on the surface, I find my own face staring back at me, and then I glide through her whirring thoughts – her eagerness to learn the truth, her concerns about the five men bound to her, her fears about the future. I'd like to linger here, understand her better, but it's an invasion into her privacy and the longer I stray into her mind, the more dangerous it is for her.

I sink deeper into her mind, through her more recent memories, images of me, of Azlan, of the others, racing past my eyes, past her older memories of the house, of the pig, of her aunt, and then I'm there again, back at the box.

We already unlocked it and let out all those memories, but since then Rhi has suppressed them, driven them back inside that box, to protect herself.

I feel my body tauten, my hands balling into fists.

I don't want to do this and yet here I am again, doing something I disagree with because this woman has a way of weaving me around her little finger. Stars, I'm a fool, a fool for her. But I made her a promise. Not just to help her with this, but to be by her side for life.

I brace myself. Then I tug off the lid of the box. It comes away with more ease this time and immediately the memories surge out, colors and images streaming past my eyes. Rhi tenses beneath me, but she's stronger than she was before, more battle-hardened and fully aware of what to expect. Her mind rings with resilience and determination. She won't let the dark memories suck her down, she won't let them drag her into their depths.

I filter through the memories. There are the dreams and the memories of her and her aunt — the memories that terrorized her before. Memories of men chasing them, of hiding away, of her aunt taking beatings, and worse, from the men who came for them.

My nails sink deeper into my flesh. They endured so much — she endured so much. If I ever, ever get my hands on those men, I'll smash them into smithereens. I'll feed them to Spencer's fucking beast.

But I'm allowing myself to be distracted. We didn't come here for these memories – for the memories her aunt locked away to keep her safe. We came for answers.

There are more memories here, older ones, fainter, less vivid, memories from when Rhi was only small, her mind still learning and understanding. Memories of dreams again, dreams of the future and I've no doubt now – no doubt at all – that once upon a time Rhianna possessed the gift to see the future, to dream of it. Just like her mom.

Is that what her aunt was protecting her from? She'd seen what had happened to her sister. She didn't want the same fate to befall her niece. So she found a way to make those dreams stop and she locked away all knowledge of them in Rhianna's mind.

I'm about to pull out. I've already stayed in Rhi's mind long enough. But then something catches my attention. A memory lurking at the bottom of the box. A memory unlike the others. A bright golden color not steeped in red like so many of Rhi's other memories. No, this is different. This isn't Rhi's memory at all. It's someone else's. Someone else's memory hidden away in Rhi's mind.

Rhi was right. The answers were here all along.

I take a hold of that alien memory – one that doesn't belong here – and I wrench it from my mate's mind.

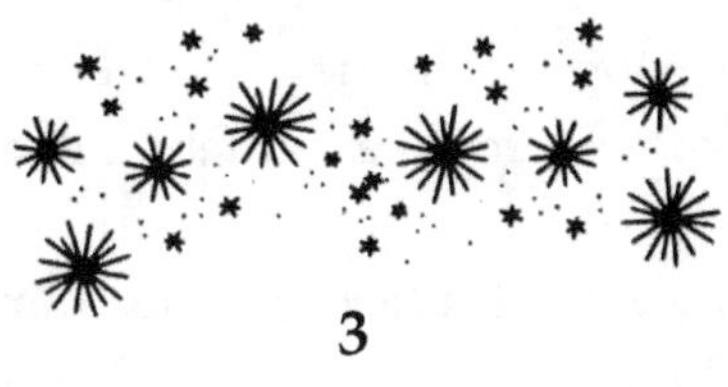

3

———

R^{hi}

THROUGH THE HAZE of bad memories, I see a small ball of golden light hovering inches above my nose and behind it, Stone's face, his brow furrowed, his light blue eyes intense.

"What is it?" I say with gritted teeth as the dark memories threaten to drag me into their midst.

"A memory," he says, from what sounds like far, far away. "Someone else's memory in your mind."

It takes me a moment to process his words, my attention diverted by the black clouds swirling in my mind.

"This is what we need, Rhi," he says, squeezing my hand. "The rest doesn't matter. You can let them go. Lock them away again."

But is that the right thing to do? These memories are dark and terrifying, but over the last few weeks, I've faced many dark and terrifying things. These memories don't seem nearly as bad as they once did, not in comparison. I am no longer afraid of them. They are a part of me. They are my history. They have made me who I am as much as the good and the happy memories have. Hiding them away, refusing to acknowledge their existence, doesn't seem right anymore.

I have to accept them, accept who I am. As soon as I make this realization, they don't seem to have the power they once did. They sink back down into my mind, dissolving away with the other memories residing in my head – and I focus back up at that strange golden ball.

"Can you tell who put it there?" Azlan asks from the end of the bed as I watch the ball spin, its surface shifting like drifting clouds.

"No, I don't think we will know that until Rhi looks inside. Something I think Rhi ought to do in private." My eyes flick away from the golden ball and to Stone instead. "It was put there for you, sweetheart, and we don't know why."

"I don't think we should have secrets from each other," I say. "They've only caused us harm."

"Perhaps," Azlan says, "but Phoenix is right–"

"He actually admits it for once," Stone mutters.

"–this is yours, something personal. Something you ought to look at alone. You can tell us afterwards what's inside."

"What if it's something bad?" Renzo says, eyeing the ball with mistrust.

"It's okay, I can handle it," I tell him, because I know I can. Hell, if I can handle Renzo, I can probably handle just about anything.

Carefully, I roll up to sit, the ball continuing to hover right in front of my face.

"How do I open it?" I ask Stone.

"Just allow it into your mind." He squeezes my shoulder. "Come find us afterwards." Then he ushers the others out of the room, practically shoving Renzo through the doorway, the assassin continuing to stare at the strange ball menacingly until the door slams shut.

And then I'm alone and I suddenly don't feel so brave without those five strong men around me. I remind myself that I was alone for a long time before they showed up and I survived just fine. Plus, despite what Renzo may think, I am with Stone on this one. I think this memory is here to help me.

I cross my legs and focus my eyes on the shimmering gold, allowing the memory to drift into my mind, until the gold is shining somewhere inside my head, lighting it up with its brightness. But as quickly as it gleams, it fades and in its place is my aunt's face, staring back at me.

She's younger than she was, her fair hair braided around her head, the locket resting against her clavicle, fewer lines on her pale skin.

"Rhi," she says. And I'd forgotten how much I'd missed her voice, even though I've heard it so many times in my memories, in moments where I forget. Now I'm hearing it again, the soft yet firm tone of her voice; it has a sob catching in my throat.

"Aunty," I whisper. But she can't hear me. She isn't really here. This is a memory, a recording, a message from the past. And I realize I'm not looking into her face, I'm looking at her reflection.

"Darling, Rhi." She smiles and I remember that smile. Like a reward. Always forthcoming when I'd done something to make her proud.

I bunch my hands in the bed sheets. I can feel my body shaking. She has something to tell me and what if I don't like it? What if Renzo's correct and it isn't something I want to hear?

"If you're watching this now, then you are as bright, as tenacious, as wonderful as I always suspected." The smile falters, her voice cracking slightly as she speaks. "And I am no longer here to help you, my darling. I'm sorry. Sorry if I let you down, sorry I can't be there with you. And I am sorry that there are things I kept hidden from you when I was there with you. Know I did it for your safety. Everything I've ever done was to keep you from harm." She nods, composing herself. "I'm sure you have a lot of questions."

She swallows and then she tells me about my mom, about how she was a talented seer who dreamed of the future, of how those in power learned of her gift and took her away from her family, of how they used her in their ongoing battles for power and dominance. I know all this – from the pieces I've puzzled together, it's nothing new – and yet I sit there entranced, listening to my aunt tell the story, reading the pain on her face when she describes how my mom was torn away from those she loved, how she was used and abused.

And then my aunt turns to the subject of me.

"Rhi," she says, "your mom was a powerful weapon, and I guess it was inevitable that the fight would turn eventually to possessing that weapon." She meets my eyes through time and through space. "Bronwyn was taken by forces from the West – kidnapped. She fell in love with your father while she was being held there. She had you and for a time they were happy together. But it didn't last, and all I know is that she reappeared on my doorstep with you in her arms and begged me to take you. To keep you hidden from everyone – the authorities, the chancellor, even your father."

My aunt is quiet as if she foretold I'd need a moment to gather my thoughts, to process this all.

My dad was a magical from the West. I was conceived while my mom was being held captive there, and then she fled with me.

I think of what Renzo told me, of who he believes my dad to be. Is that right? Did my mom fall for the Black Prince? And if she did, why did she leave him? Why did she beg my aunt to keep me hidden?

"Your mom loved you so very much, Rhi," my aunt continues, and a lone tear trickles down her cheek. "And I love you too, my darling, as if you were my own. You are so very precious, so perfect, so wonderful. It breaks my heart every day that she didn't get the opportunity to see the amazing person you're turning out to be. But I know she'd be proud of you, just as I am."

She reaches out to touch the plane of the mirror, her reflected hand coming to meet it so that her fingers touch their twin, but it's me she's reaching out to touch, to tuck my hair behind my ear like she always used to do and stroke my cheek.

"Wherever you are now, my darling, whatever it is you're doing, know you are your mother's daughter, my daughter too. You are enough, you are strong. You are loved."

I think that will be it. That she's told me everything there is for me to know, that the memory will fade and I'll be left here alone on the bed.

It doesn't.

She fixes me with her steely gaze.

"Rhi, there's more. Bronwyn had a vision about you, about your future."

I sit up a little straighter on the bed. This is it. The truth.

Something, if I'm honest with myself, I've suspected right from the moment I learned my mom could read the future.

"You are the girl from the Fourth Prophecy, Rhianna. Your mother foresaw it."

I stare at my aunt's face. I don't know what that means.

"I had to keep you safe, my darling, protect you. Because Bronwyn was right: they came looking for you. She said they would. That some would want to destroy you and some would want to use your powers for their own means. It's why I hid you away and it's why ..." she leans closer to the mirror as if she wants to whisper the next part to me, "your dreams, Rhi, they didn't simply stop, I stopped them. I suppressed your powers. Please forgive me, but they tormented you so much, and you were so young, so frightened by them. They were such a danger to you. I found a way, and I stopped them."

I stare at her, thinking of all those years I never dreamed, how they plagued me when I was little and then they'd stopped, just like that. I never questioned it before. How strange that was. To never dream. No dreams at all, not until recently, not until the last few days. Then I'd had those dreams that offered me a glimpse of the future.

And then I know, before she says the words, before she tells me the truth.

I know.

Pip.

My dreams came back when Pip was unwell.

Pip.

I hadn't even noticed he was here in the room with me, because he always is, always by my side, my ever faithful companion. He stares at me from the end of the bed, head raised, clever eyes observing me.

And I know.

"Pip," I say as the woman in the memory playing out inside my head says his name too. Both of us saying his name together.

His snout wrinkles.

"I'm sure you've figured out by now that he is no ordinary pig." She smiles at me and through her face I see the outline of my ever dependable pet. "Pip is your familiar. He's here to help you, Rhianna. Here to stop your dreams. To ..." she hesitates, "repress that darker magic I sense running through your veins. He's here until you need him. Here to help protect you. But ..." The smile slides off her face and a sense of unease brews in my stomach.

I shake my head. I don't know what's coming next, and yet I sense I am not going to like it. I shake my head in frustration.

"One day," my aunt continues, "there's going to come a time – a time when you're ready to meet the destiny your mother foretold, when you'll need to call on all your powers – and then you'll need to let him go. To let all of us go." I stare at her, dazed. "Rhianna, the only way to release your full powers, will be to let Pip go."

I shift my gaze to my faithful, dependable pet, sitting there watching me.

There are a lot of things I am willing to do, that I am prepared to risk or sacrifice. Bonding with five men. Flying on the back of a dragon. Fighting magicals far more powerful than I am.

But give Pip up?

Never.

I'm never going to do that. And frankly, I can't see why I'd ever need to. I'm already stronger than I was. With each bonding to one of my fated mates, the magic in my veins has soared. I don't need any more magic. I don't need the ability to see the future. I need Pip.

My aunt's still talking but I don't hear any more of the words. Instead, I reach for Pip and drag him onto my lap, snuggling my face against the top of his soft head as he squeaks at me.

How did I never see it? How did I never realize?

A pig that never ages. Who seems to understand me. Who's there whenever I need him.

The answers were there right in front of my very nose the entire time.

"It's okay," I tell him. "It's okay. I won't ever let you go."

A sudden anger flares through my stomach. How could she even suggest such a thing? She left me. So did my mom. My dad. All the people who should have been here to care for and protect me – all those who were meant to love me. Not Pip. He's been here through thick and thin. The only one I've ever been able to depend on.

The anger grows. Why did she make this all so hard? Secret memories in my head? Lockets that could have protected me? Knives with secret histories? She could have told me all this. Face to face. Let me ask all my questions.

She didn't. She left me struggling and all alone, barely hanging on.

A voice in my head protests. The illness took her suddenly. She had no time.

But I don't care. There was plenty of time. All those years together, all those long, lonely nights. And she chose never to tell me a thing.

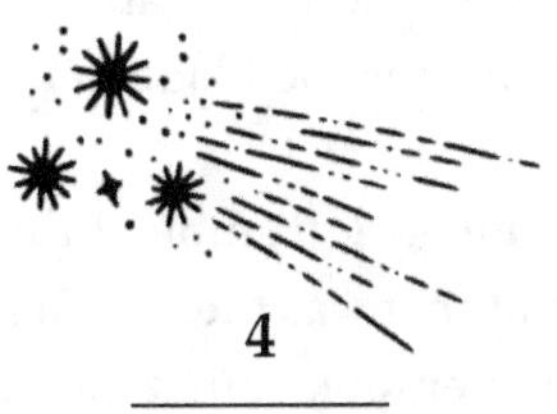

4

R enzo

I don't like people.

I don't like the way they smell. I don't like the weird noises they make. And I don't like the space they take up.

Mostly I like being on my own.

The only exception is my little rabbit. I like the way she smells. The way she tastes. And fuck, I love the sounds she makes. Especially when she's coming. Or when she's really mad and her magic makes that dark and dangerous hissing sound. Yeah, I really love that.

Everyone else can go to hell and I'll happily send them there myself.

But I'm not allowed to kill her other fated mates. I have to be *nice* to them instead.

How the fuck am I meant to do that? Especially when

they refuse to stand within a meter of me, like I have the plague and it's catching.

I spin my knife around in irritation and the others look at me as the light catches the blade and flashes across their faces.

"It's taking too long," I grumble. I thought the professor was smart. I thought that was the fucking point. But it seems dumb to me letting her look at that memory all on her lonesome, especially when we don't know what it is. I don't like it.

I pocket the knife and march to the door. Behind me, the others call out to stop but nothing could stop me. Nothing at all. I race up the stairs anyway, just in case one of the fuckers gets it into their heads to try, and on the landing I nearly collide with my little rabbit, little man hugged tightly to her chest like a kid might clutch its teddy bear.

(Fuck, I think I had one of those once. Plucked off its eyes and pulled out its stuffing, hung him from the ceiling by his foot and used him as target practice. Yeah, we had fun me and him).

I examine her face, trying to search for clues. What did she learn? Was it good? Or was it bad?

Thunder rages all over her face and her magic is doing that angry thing I love. In fact, it's so furious I can almost taste it, crackling on the end of my tongue.

"I don't want to talk about it," she snaps, "and I'm not–"

"Sure," I say. It's of no importance to me. Those other dudes can pull their hair out worrying over shit that's going to come to pass whether we know about it or not. I'm just happy to be here. With her. With my bond pulsating in my gut and my cock ... "Wanna fuck instead?"

She tilts her head to one side, that angry line deep

between her brows, her eyes hissing. I'm pretty certain she's considering it – my blood heating – but then the little man goes and butts his snout in, snorting at us both. I glare at him. I thought he was on my side.

"We're bonded mates now," I remind him, "it's what we're meant to do."

"And when do you ever do what you're meant to do?" she hisses like I'm the one she's mad at.

"I'm very good at taking orders," I inform her, thinking of all those people I killed because Lowsky instructed me to. "Wanna give me an order? Wanna order me onto my knees and lick your pussy?"

She glares at me and for one moment, I think she's going to slap me real hard around the face. I grin at the prospect. Fuck that would be fun.

Instead, she drops the pig on his trotters, and pushes me hard on the chest. She's half my size. Her efforts are feeble. I stay exactly where I'm standing, the grin on my face grows wider.

"You're such a shithead," she growls.

"Am I?" I say. I thought offering to lick out her pussy was considered a nice thing to do. "You don't want me to eat you out?"

"I'm angry!" she says. "And all you can think about is sex!"

"Little rabbit," I say, lowering my head to meet those angry eyes, the way she's looking at me driving my cock wild. "All I can *ever* think about is fucking you."

"That's so … that's so … selfish!"

"Is it?" I stalk closer to her.

"Yes!"

I take another pace towards her, and she huffs and takes

a step away. The side of my mouth lifts in a half smile. I like this game.

I keep walking towards her and she keeps right on walking away, still scowling at me, until she hits the wall.

I have her trapped. I lean against the wall, my hands on either side of her head.

"If you're angry, little rabbit, you can use me to release that anger."

"I'm not using you for anything!" she cries, attempting to push me away.

"Even if I want you to?" I say, my voice heavy with lust. "Even if I really, really want you to?" I lean in further and nip at her throat and she drums her fists against my chest. "Yeah, baby, just like that. I'll be your punching bag anytime you need me to be."

She growls in frustration and then she's hitting me harder, punching against my body. It's not like I'm being hit by several pounds of solid muscle, but it's her and she's angry and it's stirring that dark magic inside her and, fuck, I love it.

I suck hard on her neck, hard enough to bruise, and she struggles at my t-shirt, trying in all her frustration to rip the thing off me.

"Touch me, little rabbit," I beg her. "Touch me."

"I really hate you," she mutters with no conviction whatsoever and I take her hands in mine and place them under my shirt, flat against my skin. Fuck, I love it when she touches me, her magic sparking all over my skin.

"What's wrong, little rabbit?" I croon to her, sinking her nails deep into my flesh. "What's made you so mad? Was it that memory?"

I drag her nails down my chest, the pain sharp in my skin and delicious. I groan.

"I'm so fucking angry at her," she says and with that frown on her face, she leans down and swipes her tongue right along the scratch marks she's just made on my chest.

It's too fucking much. Too ... fucking ... much!

When my little rabbit turns feral so do I.

I lift her up and walk her straight into the nearest bedroom. Her legs curl around my waist, her core presses right up and personal against my cock, and she winds her arms around my neck and drags my mouth against hers. She kisses me deep and hard and angry as I walk her to the bed.

"Going to fuck you now, little rabbit," I tell her because my everlasting patience has finally run dry and I have no more fucks to give. If she says no now, it won't matter. I'm having her anyway.

Fortunately, that ain't a problem. This little rabbit is so desperate for my cock she's rubbing herself against me, making those whiny little noises in her throat.

I've spent a lot of time considering all the ways I can fuck her. There are countless ways. I'm fucking spoiled for choice. But I decide how I want her is on her knees.

I place her down on her feet and she yanks off her clothes, her eyes still thundering. And then there's skin, so much skin, all pink and unmarked and untainted. Two full tits, two pert nipples. Curves and curves.

I want to suck every inch of her, cover her in bruises from my mouth. Little gifts just for her.

I reach my hand over my head, grip my shirt and pull it off. She watches me with that scowl as I undo my belt, pull down my zipper and lose my jeans.

I kiss her again, encouraging her to scrape her nails up my back, over my shoulders and into my scalp. Then I push her down onto the mattress and climb on top of her. She scowls right up at me but she doesn't tell me to stop, doesn't scream and make a fuss like girls do.

"Protection," she says firmly.

I groan but before I can stop her, she's already casting a spell, and it looks like we're using it whether I like it or not.

Next, she grabs my ass with her hands, little claws piercing my fucking skin, and practically drags my cock inside her.

And I'm not fighting that, am I? It's everything I've been dreaming of – my cock sinking into her pussy like it's where it belongs.

She's all tight and warm and mewls like a kitten as I penetrate her, the flames in her eyes extinguishing as they roll back in their sockets.

"Fuck, yeah, little rabbit, you like that? You like my cock inside of you?"

"No talking," she tells me, rocking her hips below me, cunt squeezing the living daylights out of me, threatening to kill me all over again.

I pry her fingers from my ass and clamp my hands around her wrists, pinning them to the bed above her head.

"You are a bossy little thing when you want to be. I fucking love it, little rabbit. But let's be clear, I'm going to talk to you all I want while I fuck you because there's some important stuff you have to know. Like how fucking good your pussy feels around my cock." I grind into her, real slow, even though this is most definitely killing me. I'm more of a wham bam thank you ma'am kinda dude. Get my kicks, get out of there. But I like playing with her. It's like playing with – or what some call torturing – a victim right before you end them. Only better. A thousand million times better.

Her face gets all grouchy again. Beads of sweat dribble down between her bouncing tits.

"More," she demands, frowning at me.

I bend low, lick at that sweat. Then I bite her nipple. Not hard enough to draw blood, but hard enough to make her scream, all needy and desperate.

"Gonna be *nice* and say please, little rabbit."

She struggles underneath me. "If you're not going to–"

I fuck her hard, like my life depends on it, pounding her until my brow is damp with sweat and my arms give way. I'm flat on top of her, pressing her down into the bed and she yanks her hands from my grip and wraps her arms tight around me, holding me so close I can feel her heart thrashing around in her chest, our damp skin sliding against one another.

"Renzo," she mutters right by my ear, saying my name like it's heavenly or something.

"Yeah, little rabbit, I got you. Going to make it all better now."

I reach between our bodies and rub at that stiff little nub of hers as I fuck and fuck and fuck – and then she's coming, her cunt squeezing me so hard a million stars explode across my vision and she yanks the orgasm straight through my body.

I groan and grunt like an animal, pumping her full of my spunk, as I lose my rhythm, as I lose everything. Something sparks in my brain. Short circuits. And the next moment, we're on the hard floor, then out in the hallway, then in the fucking bathroom and finally back in the bed.

"Wh-what happened?" she asks, still shaking underneath me.

"We fucked," I say, licking more of that sweat from her skin. Then I scurry down her body, the sheets all damp and tangled and pry her legs wide open. Her pussy's all swollen, but it's not bloody, not sore. Funny, but I'm pleased about it.

Blood is usually the icing on the cake. But this cake was sweet enough. Sweet enough to rot every one of my teeth. Bloodied icing would have ruined it all.

"You feel better now, little rabbit?" I ask her.

"Yes." She sighs, all content sounding, as I stroke my fingers carefully through her folds.

"Gonna tell me why you got all worked up and angry like that? Was it the memory?"

I feel her body stiffen slightly so I jam my fingers right up inside her, making her hips lift up off the mattress. She's all warm and sticky with me inside. Just like she ought to be.

"Yes and no," she says reluctantly.

So I find that spot inside her, thinking I can loosen her tongue. I massage it with my fingers and soon she's panting again, her hands scrabbling for purchase in the sheets as she lifts one of her legs and hooks it over my shoulder. I nip her soft thigh.

"What was it? What was the memory?"

"My ... a ... a ... a... aunt," she mutters, struggling to get her words out, her eyes screwed up tight, "it was a message, she left me a message."

"And what did it say?" I ask her, pressing my thumb to her clit.

She ignores my question, that line forming on her brow again. "Why did she make everything so difficult? Why didn't she tell me the truth from the start? Why didn't she trust me?"

I stroke inside her and circle her clit and slowly that line melts away and her body relaxes.

"What was the message?" I ask her again.

She bites down on her lip, her hips rising. She's on the cusp of coming.

"My mom had a vision," she says, her voice all tight now

as I wind her higher. "She had a vision," she says, core suddenly taut. I give her more, tip her over the edge, straight into ecstasy. "That I am the girl in the Fourth Prophecy," she murmurs as she comes.

I freeze, my fingers ceasing their busy work.

The Fourth Prophecy? What the fuck is that?

5

Rhi

AZLAN SLIDES A CUP of strong coffee in front of me.

"Want to tell us what you saw, sweetheart?" he asks.

I stare down at the black liquid, feeling seven pairs of eyes assessing me.

It took me a lot of arguing with Renzo to escape his arms and make it down here into the kitchen where the others were waiting. He finally got me into bed with him and he didn't want to let me go. He wanted to interrogate me about the message from my aunt. That or mess around some more.

But I knew the others would be dying with curiosity downstairs and it felt like a conversation that we should have together.

"The memory belonged to my aunt. I was right all along. She left a message for me."

Tristan shifts on his seat. "What did she say in this message?"

"She confirmed my mom was a seer. And she said my mom had a vision about me."

The room is quiet and I can hear eight hearts beat in unison.

"Did she tell you what your mom saw?"

I nod my head and pull a face. "My mom saw that I was the girl from the Fourth Prophecy and that is why I had to be kept hidden. To keep me safe." I glance up at them all, that anger threatening to boil away inside me again. "I mean what does that even mean? More fucking riddles!"

"The *Fourth* Prophecy?" Azlan asks, peering towards his friend.

I frown. Let me guess. They all know about this prophecy and I'm the only one who doesn't. Sur-fucking-prise.

"Do you know of any prophecy, Phoenix?"

The professor strokes his beard. "There are several prophecies. Only one I can think of relates to a woman."

"Humph," I snort. Why does that not surprise me?

"The prophecy is unclear, though – its interpretation open to debate. Scholars have argued as to its meaning for centuries."

This time Winnie snorts. "It is not. It's really obvious what it means."

Stone rolls his eyes. "In that case, please feel free to enlighten us, Miss Wence? What have other learned scholars missed that is so blatantly obvious?"

"You're all clever people," she glances at Renzo, "well, most of you." He shrugs. "I think you all know what the prophecy means."

"I don't even know about some fucking prophecy," Spencer mumbles.

"Me neither," I say.

"There were six prophecies collected during ancient times, preserved and guarded. Three, it is said, have already been fulfilled. Three remain. Of those, only one relates to a woman. It foretells the second coming of Queen Æðelflæd."

"According to Miss Wence."

I shake my head. "What do you mean?"

Stone sighs. "There is a belief among some that Queen Æðelflæd and her fated mates weren't simply fairytale figures, that they were real magicals, that their story was true. And there are some who believe that she will return with her mates one day to reclaim her crown."

"And you think that's me?" I say, pointing to my chest.

"Yes," Winnie says, nodding her head.

"We don't even know that's what the prophecy means," Stone mutters.

"What exactly did your mom see?" Azlan asks me.

"My aunt didn't say exactly." I chew the inside of my cheek, thoughts spinning in my head. "She just said my mom saw that I would prove to be the girl in the Fourth Prophecy and that would put me in danger."

"Of course it fucking would," Tristan says, standing suddenly so that his chair tumbles to the floor. "My dad already considers you a threat just because there are rumors about you. If he learns you're some girl from a prophecy, he's going to be determined to eliminate you. He won't stop until he's hunted you down."

"Because you are destined to change things for us all, Rhi," Winnie says with such certainty it scares me.

"By becoming some queen?" I say, laughing. "I'm no leader. Winnie, you can't be serious?"

"I am, Rhi. You're different. Special. You know you are."

"So are you, Winnie."

My friend smiles at me. "Not in the same way, bestie, and you know that."

"Nonsense, you're smart and talented and–"

"I can't wield crimson magic–"

"I bet you could learn."

"–I've never predicted the future."

"Those dreams were vague and misleading and–"

"I don't have five powerful fated mates by my side."

I shake my head, still unconvinced by the idea. "What does this prophecy say exactly?"

I glance at Winnie whose cheeks pinken. I turn my gaze to Stone. He opens his mouth, pauses, then shuts it again.

I frown at them both. "Don't you know?"

"No," Stone says, giving me a hard stare, "I do not have all six of the ancient prophecies committed to memory."

"She doesn't want all six, Prof., just one," Renzo points out.

Stone inhales and exhales slowly.

"Winnie?" I ask.

"I never read the actual original text, just papers about the supposed interpretations."

Stone buries his face in his hands like Winnie just admitted to some hideous crime. "How many times have I told you students to always read the original?"

"Can we look it up on the internet?" I ask, peering towards Trent.

"The internet's been severely restricted by the Lord Protector, Rhi," he tells me. "Only the most basic of functions are operating right now and all websites, except the authorities', have been barred."

"Great," I say. "So my aunt says I'm some girl from this

prophecy but we have no idea what the hell that actually means."

"I'm telling you–" Winnie begins but I stare her down.

"Where exactly can we find these prophecies?"

"What?" Stone mutters.

"Where are these prophecies kept? If there's one written down about me, I'd like to read it for myself. See what is actually written about my fate."

"You promised me no more crazy ideas," he says darkly.

"No," I say, "you said that. I made no such promise."

Stone glares at me.

"The ancient prophecies are kept in the Albany convent," Tristan says. "On the Gray Isle."

"Right, so how do we get there?"

"We're not going to the Gray Isle," Azlan says sternly.

"I am," I say, staring him down. "So you can either come with me or not."

"It's too dangerous," he argues.

"You said staying here for too long would be dangerous. That we'd have to move soon enough. Why not move there?"

"There's a price on your head. If anyone spots you–"

"There was a price on my head before, remember?" I say, pointing at Renzo. "I'm not afraid."

Azlan folds his arms and shakes his head.

"What? Are there ninja nuns at this convent or something?"

"No, the convent's been empty for the last century," Stone tells me.

"Empty? These supposed prophecies are being kept somewhere unguarded?"

"People are superstitious about moving them. Besides which, the convent is surrounded by treacherous waters–"

"Haunted waters," Tristan clarifies.

"The journey there is too risky. Someone could spot you," Azlan adds again.

I cross my arms over my chest and stare them all down. Azlan's jaw hardens. It's obviously going to take all my powers of persuasion to convince them that this is what we have to do. But I'm determined and Stone is right – I need to read that prophecy with my own eyes.

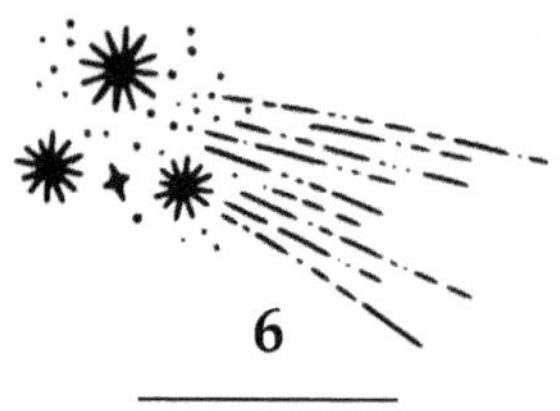

6

S pencer

I'M NOT AS HEALED as I think I am, because all the chatter, all the noise, is making my head ache. Or maybe it's all the thoughts now clattering around in my head.

Are they right? Was Rhi born to be some powerful magical, foreseen in some ancient prophecy? And are we destined to help her?

Am *I* destined to help her? A werebeast? What use would I be?

As the others continue to argue around me, I slouch out of the kitchen and into the quiet hallway, dust particles floating in the air, the silence soothing.

I'm stiff from all those hours chained to a dungeon wall. I roll out my shoulders, lift my hands above my head, stretching my unused muscles and as I do, the beast rumbles inside me. He wants to be let out – he's demanding it, scraping at the constraints of my insides. He's been just as cooped up, just as restricted as I have. It's only fair that I release him.

I glance towards the doorway.

Is it safe? I may have argued that the beast would never harm Rhianna, but I can't know that for sure. And am I prepared to take that risk?

Hell, no, I'm not. Even if it causes me pain. Even if it has the beast spitting and snarling inside me.

I close my eyes, fighting him as he tries to break free.

"Spencer?"

My eyelids flick open and I meet the honey eyes of my fated mate.

The bond inside me spirals and the beast quietens.

"Are you okay?" She steps towards me and places her hand on my arm. I don't deserve her touch but I relish it anyway. It feels divine against my skin. After all that violence, all that cruelty, the tenderness of her touch is enough to send the beast purring.

I never liked to be touched before. But now I think I'd crawl over hot coals to have her touch me like this.

"Spencer?" she says again.

I consider lying to her. But hiding the truth from her was foolish. It meant I wasn't there to protect her when I should have been. I won't make that mistake again. Even if it costs me distance between us.

"I need to change," I tell her. Her brows knit together. She doesn't understand. "I've spent too long in my human form. I need to let my beast out."

"Oh, I didn't realize that was how it worked."

"Yeah," I say, unable to help from smiling at her. "The longer I remain in human form, the harder it is to control him."

"So, were you secretly changing into a beast the entire time we were at the academy?"

I shake my head. "I was taking pills to help control things but ..." I rub my hand over my head, feeling fucking foolish. "Then you came along and drove my beast into a frenzy and it got a whole lot harder to control him."

She rolls her eyes like I'm exaggerating.

"It's true. He's pretty darn obsessed with you."

She steps closer to me, lowering her voice. "He said some stuff to me," her cheeks pinken, "about wanting to devour me."

Inwardly I groan. Fuck, yes, I'd like to devour her too.

"Erm, I don't think he wants to eat you, Rhianna. In fact, I think he wants to eat you out."

She swallows. "That is pretty ..." Revolting? Disgusting? Sick? Yeah, I know what we are. "Intimidating," she says.

The beast scrabbles inside my body and I flinch.

"Is it hurting you?"

I grimace, trying to force a smile onto my face. "It's fine. Nothing I can't handle."

"If it's causing you pain, Spencer, you should let him out."

I shake my head. "It's too dangerous."

"For me?"

"Yes, and for them," I say, gesturing my head towards the kitchen. "I can't control him."

"You really think he'd hurt me, that he'd hurt them too?"

I mull this question over. Inside me, the beast snarls at me, insulted I'd even consider the possibility. "I don't know," I say, earning myself a stab of pain from the beast within me.

"I can look after myself, Spencer," she tells me, lifting her chin in that damn infuriating act of defiance.

"The beast is powerful."

"So am I, remember?" she says with a huge dollop of sarcasm. "I'm the girl from some prophecy."

"But pretty damn hopeless at self defense."

She pouts. "I was starting to get better at it before you left."

"Yeah," I admit. "You were. Maybe we should resume those lessons." Because I'd really, really like to get my hands on her again. The beast practically drools at the prospect.

"I'd like that."

The beast strains against his fleshy confines, desperate to break free, and I curl in on myself, straining with all my might to keep him contained.

"Spencer, this is stupid. Let him out." I pry open my eyes. "I don't like seeing you in pain like this."

"Fine," I say, uncurling myself and striding towards the door. Maybe this is my best chance to let him out. Who knows if we'll still be here in 24 hours, who knows if I'll have another chance? And here, I can lose myself in the prairie land, get myself as far away from Rhi and the others as possible, then I can transform and hope the beast doesn't come charging straight back here to pounce on her.

When I reach the front door, I halt, realizing Rhianna is standing right behind me.

"What are you doing?"

"Coming with you."

What the fuck? Is she insane? The house is safe – for now – fortified and hidden by the spells the others have cast. Stepping outside is dangerous; stepping outside with a werebeast is crazy.

I go to tell her all that but she beats me to it.

"I want to see. I want to watch you transform."

I stare at her. She is crazy. Totally crazy.

"Why would you want to do that?"

"I'm … curious."

My mouth falls open.

"You know curiosity killed the cat?"

"Spencer, you're my fated mate and you've kept this part of you hidden from me. I want to see it. I want to understand."

"It's not pretty, Rhianna," I say. It's agony to endure the morphing of my body, bones snapping and reforming, skin straining and stretching. I remember the first time I saw my dad transform. I must have been really small, barely able to walk. He'd lost control and changed in front of me and the sight of it had left me screaming in terror, unable to sleep for weeks despite my mother's reassurance that it was just papa, that he was okay.

Do I want to give Rhi another reason to shun me?

She shrugs. "I think the beast is kind of pretty."

I laugh because that definitely is the craziest shit I've ever heard. Not that the beast seems to agree, in fact, I can feel him puffing up with pride at the compliment.

"Pretty? Most people wouldn't consider a werebeast pretty."

"I'm not most people."

And ain't that the truth.

I try changing tactics. "The others will kill me if they find out I let you anywhere near the beast."

"That isn't how this is going to work. You – all of you – don't get to say what I can and can't do." And there's that lift of the chin again, the hard stare, informing me just how determined she is.

I stare right back at her. I don't like this idea – it scares me shitless – but it also turns me the fuck on. The fact she, my mate, wants to see this. Wants to see me in all my raw brutality. It's irresistible, especially when the beast wants it too.

"Okay," I say, "okay. But we need to be careful." I glance towards the kitchen where the conversation is continuing. "You need to keep your distance and if–"

"If the beast tries anything I don't like, I'll blast him straight to hell," she says with a grin.

"Fine, let's go." I take her hand in mine and pull her through the doorway. On the path, she hesitates, her eyes scanning the landscape.

"You think someone's here?" I ask her, pausing too.

"No, I'd be able to sense them if they were."

I huff in amusement. "You're a tracker."

"Uh huh."

I'm not even surprised.

"Right then, let's go."

We step out into what once was the front yard of the mansion with its overgrown hedgerows and flowerbeds, and stop in front of the crumbling wall.

"This is where you wait," I instruct her.

"Wait? Where are you going?"

"Far away from you."

She grips my hand. "No, Spencer. You do it here in front of me."

"That isn't what we agreed. We need distance between us to keep you safe and–"

And it's too late. The beast has had enough. He wants this girl just as badly as I do and he's tired of waiting.

I snatch my hand from her, stumbling as best I can away from her as my body begins to change, and the vision of her face, frowning with concentration, fades away as I'm plunged into the darkness.

7

R^{hi}

SPENCER FALLS to his hands and knees right in front of me and his body begins to jerk and jolt like he's being hit by a thousand volts of electricity.

He's right. It isn't pretty. In fact, it's really difficult to watch as his body stretches and alters in front of me, his bones crunching and snapping. It looks like agony, like torture, and I swallow down a gasp, my hands flying to cover my mouth.

Soon his body is almost twice the size it was and his face has lengthened and changed, great teeth crowd along his jaw and thick dark fur sprouts all over his skin as his clothes rip and fall away.

It continues for several minutes, though feels like a lifetime, and then it's a huge wolf-like creature that crouches in front of me, no longer Spencer. In fact, all traces of the boy I know are gone, until the great beast swings his head upwards and its eyes meet mine. A deep chestnut color, glowing in the light. They're Spencer's eyes and I wonder if he's in there, somewhere, watching us.

The last time the beast and I met I was frozen with fear. This time I'm not afraid. I know what he is. I know who he is. And I wasn't lying, he is beautiful in a strange and powerful could-crush-your-skull-in-his-jaws kind of way.

The beast's eyes flicker over my form and then it staggers up onto its hind legs, stretching up tall and towering above me. It shakes its head, then its neck, shoulders and back, and the dark fur ruffles along its spine as if caught in the wind. It uncurls its paws, the claws on the ends of its fingers razor sharp, and then it flings back its head and howls up into the sky. The sound both beautiful and pitiful.

"Shhh," I mutter. "Do you want the others to come rushing out here and causing a fuss?"

The beast lowers its chin slowly and catches me in its penetrating stare.

"Little mate," he purrs, and it's like before. I'm unsure if I hear his words with my ears or whether the words are spoken inside my head, like Stone has done in the past. He cocks his head, his ears twitching.

"Rhianna," I tell him.

"Rhianna," he says slowly, his tongue unfurling from his jaws and sliding along his teeth as if he's caressing every syllable of my name. Then he falls back down onto his four legs, his head level with mine. He paces closer, sniffing the air around me.

"Your scent." He takes a deep inhale, his brown eyes rolling backwards in their sockets. "In all the years, it has not changed. I have missed you."

I take a step away from him. I don't know what I was

expecting when I came face to face again with Spencer's beast. Maybe a repeat of last time. Not this. His words make no sense and yet they stir an unease in my bond. My hands stray to my belly automatically.

The beast's gaze drops to my stomach too.

"You are yet to bond with the boy. Yet to lie with him. Why not? He is strong, virile. He would stuff you full and make you dissolve into pleasure." The beast growls, and his eyes flash with heat. "Why have you not sealed the bond?"

I kind of want to tell him that it's none of his damn business. But I guess it is.

"It's ... difficult," I say instead.

"Difficult? You are fated mates. Destined to be together. There is nothing difficult about it."

I scoff. That may have been true if Spencer had welcomed me with open arms. Instead, he stuffed me into a locker, refused to teach me self defense and then left all together.

"The boy is young and sometimes foolish," the beast says, stepping so close, his whiskers brush against my face and his breath whistles over my skin. "He has made mistakes."

He smells like Spencer and I realize for the first time how distinct his scent is, powerful and deep and bold.

"But he finds it hard to resist you." The beast nuzzles his muzzle under my chin and my heart leaps into my throat, my magic sizzling at the ends of my fingertips. Is this safe?

I told Spencer I could take care of myself, but the beast is far bigger than I remember and up close I can see how powerful he is too. My magic is strong – stronger than it ever was – but would it be strong enough to stop a werebeast?

"You are so young, so soft, so beautiful," he croons, the tip of the beast's tongue lapping over the point where my pulse beats in my throat. "Just as you always were, little mate."

And I don't know what possesses me – if I'm just really stupid or the tenor of his voice, low and lulling, has me in a trance – but I lift my hands and stroke my fingers through the dark fur on his head. It's thick and luscious and soft to the touch and the beast responds, closing his eyes and purring with pleasure.

"I am yours to command, little mate. Your faithful mutt."

"Don't say that word," I mutter.

"Yes," he says, "he doesn't like it either. He is ashamed of what we are, afraid of it."

"He shouldn't be," I tell him.

"No," he says. "You must make him understand that."

"I'm not sure I can make Spencer Moreau do anything," I say with a huff, reaching to stroke the mane of fur on his neck, his body vibrating as he purrs with satisfaction, a vibration I feel in my chest and my bond.

"The boy would do anything for you." The beast slides his long tongue up my throat. "He is as infatuated with you as I am."

I move around him, continuing to comb my fingers through his fur and then, because I definitely have lost my mind, bury my face in his fur and rest my body weight against his huge frame. Is it strange that his presence is somehow comforting, reassuring? At the academy I saw this beast smash through five men at once. I saw him tear them to pieces. I saw him lick the blood from his jaw.

But is he any worse than Renzo? Any worse than Azlan? They are all killers. All monsters in their own way. Even Stone and Tristan have acted cruelly more times than not. I can't pretend my fated mates are nice, gentle types. I'm not sure I can even pretend that they are good men.

Then again, I'm not sure good men are what I need. Or what I want. I have a taste for monsters now. And if my mom is correct, and others are going to come for me, like they came for her, maybe monsters are exactly what I need to protect me.

We stand there, the beast and I, for some time, my head buried in his soft fur, my mind lost to my thoughts, until finally he says, "I need to move now, little mate, to run." He stands back up on his hind legs looking more humanoid than wolf. "Do you wish to come with me?"

"With you?" I say, laughing. "I don't think I could keep up."

"I will allow you to mount me. To ride me."

"Erm ..." I say.

"Are you afraid?"

"No," I say, squaring my shoulders. "It's just it seems ... are you sure?"

"Little mate," the beast says, his eyes flashing again. "You can ride me any time you like." His lips curl into a smirk. "Any way you wish."

I swallow, trying damn hard not to look at the huge object that hangs between his legs. That is just ... that is just ...

I shake my head. "Another time." I take a step backward.

"Little mate, I will not hurt you."

He lifts his arm, offering me his great paw, the claws long and sharp.

And Spencer was right, one of these days my curiosity is going to get me killed. Maybe that day will be today, but damn it. Riding a dragon was one of the most amazing things I've ever done. Am I really going to turn down the chance to ride a werebeast?

Yeah, silly question. Of course, I'm not.

I slide my hand into his paw and he curls his fingers – or are they toes – around it and tugs me closer. Then he bends one leg, kneeling down.

"Climb onto my back then, little one, wrap your legs tightly around my waist and your arms tightly around my neck."

I follow his instruction, feeling solid, packed muscle beneath his fur as I cling onto him.

He stands, lifting me high above the ground, and rests his paws on my thighs gripping them tightly.

Then he throws back his head, like he did before, howling up towards the winter sky, drops down onto his four paws and takes off across the prairie land.

He runs so quickly, the landscape around me blurs into one long flash of color and the wind whips through my hair and plasters it flat against my head.

I lower my head so my chin rests against his neck, and screw up my eyes. Beneath me his muscles ripple and lurch, working hard as he thunders across the land. It's not as smooth, not as magical, as riding the dragon, but it's damn exhilarating, like riding a fast motorbike, only the engine humming beneath my thighs is alive. He takes us right over the brow of the hill in the distance, through long grass that brushes against my legs, until, when I turn my head, I can no longer see the mansion behind us.

When we hit a stream, gurgling with water, he takes a hard left, his back paws scrabbling on the earth, and then he's speeding along the bank. I watch as a flock of small birds shoot up into the sky, disturbed by our presence, and a small fish leaps from the water, its scales glistening like jewels.

The beast's skin is hot beneath me and his fur begins to dampen with sweat. But he doesn't stop. On and on he runs.

Only finally coming to an abrupt halt at the outcrop of dense trees.

"There," he whispers, motioning with his head and I peer through the gloom of the trees. A stag, grazing on the short grass beneath the branches, a magnificent pair of white antlers balancing on the crown of his head. The beast lowers his body until he's lying flat in the tall grass and I slide off his back.

"You're going to hunt him?" I ask and the beast growls quietly in response. "You can't," I insist. "He's too beautiful."

The beast's chestnut eyes flick to mine and he looks at me with curiosity.

"You think only beautiful things deserve to live?"

My brow crinkles and I shake my head. "No, I think every creature deserves to live, beautiful or not."

"And cruel creatures? Malicious creatures? Do they deserve to live?"

"Nature is cruel." I saw it often enough, raising the chickens, tending our vegetable plot.

"Doesn't the hunter deserve to eat?" the beast asks, his eyes focusing back on the oblivious stag.

"You're not hunting him for food."

"But it's in my nature. Would you deny me my nature?"

I turn my head away. Life was easy before. All I had to worry about was whether the chickens had laid any eggs that day, whether I could spare a tin from the larder, whether I had enough to eat. I didn't have to worry about wrong or right. My head didn't ring continually with these complicated decisions.

This is his nature. To kill. Who am I to demand he changes? Should I not accept him as he is?

"I don't know," I admit in the end. The beast stalks

forward. I close my eyes. I've seen so many people die now. You'd think I'd be used to it.

But then I hear the thundering of hooves and when I open my eyes, I see the stag cantering away.

"He caught a hint of our scents," the beast says, watching him go.

I let out the breath I was holding and lie out in the grass beside the beast. The cold air nips at my nose but the beast radiates heat and I snuggle closer to him to keep warm. He rolls onto his side, bending his elbow and resting his head on his paw. He peers down at me and then lifts his other paw and drags a claw softly – barely hard enough for me to feel it – down my cheek.

"I hope we will have other moments like this, little mate."

I open my mouth to reply, but he rolls away from me and his body jerks and jolts like Spencer's did earlier. Only this time, the fur retracts, his frame shrinks and his muzzle contracts, until it's Spencer lying on the cold earth beside me.

A very fucking naked Spencer.

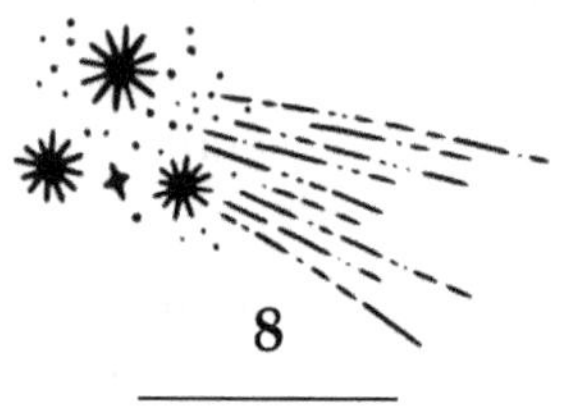

8

S pencer

I OPEN my eyes and look up into a creamy blue sky. Beneath me the earth is hard and the air is bitingly cold.

Where the hell am I?

"Spencer?" I turn my head to the left and find Rhi lying beside me, long prairie grass caging us in.

Her cheeks are a little pink and she's trying real hard to keep her eyes trained on my face. I lower my hands and cover my junk.

"What happened?" I ask.

"I spoke with the beast, and then he took me on a run." She smiles at me. "We're miles from the house."

"And it's freezing," I say, shivering against the cold.

"Is he always this thoughtless?" she says.

"You have no fucking idea," I say, rolling my eyes. We should stand up, and start walking back to the mansion. It's only going to get colder. But there's something tantalizing about lying out here with her, hidden away from everything and everyone. I wonder if he planned it that way. "What did he say to you?"

"Lots of things." She doesn't move. It seems she is as happy to lie here as I am.

"Like ..." I prompt.

"He says you're ashamed of what you are. That you're ashamed of him."

I sigh. "I'm not ... ashamed."

"Really?"

"You have no idea what it's like to lose control, to have no memory of where you've been or what you've done. No idea if you've fucked up, or hurt someone or ..."

"Spencer," she says. "I understand."

I nod. "I met another werebeast. He was locked in the cell with me. Before then, I'd never met another were outside my family. I liked him." I shrug my shoulders. "I don't know, he made me feel better about myself even when those bastards were telling me I was nothing but scum."

"I don't think you should be ashamed. You're a hell of a lot better than they are."

"Am I?" I say, staring into her eyes.

"Well, the beast thinks you're an idiot."

"Fucking charming. He's the one who's left me in the middle of nowhere, in the middle of winter, without any clothes."

Rhianna giggles and the sound has my stomach spinning. I've always liked that sound and I want to make it my mission to make her laugh as often as I can. No more tears because of me.

"It does leave you in rather a pickle."

"It does leave *you* with rather an eyeful," I say winking at her, and letting my biceps flex.

"I've seen it all before, remember? In the locker room?"

"Not this up close and personal, though."

Now she rolls her eyes. "Congratulations, you have a very beautiful body, Spencer Moreau."

"Yours is pretty damn beautiful too, Rhianna Blackwaters."

She snorts and I nearly screw everything up by making some pig joke. Instead, I bite my tongue.

"It is," I say. "Your tits, your hips, your ass." My eyes flicker all over her, soaking her up. "Oh fuck, your ass."

Despite the cold, this conversation, her proximity, the way her eyes can't help but flick over my body too, has my cock stiffening under my hands.

I lean a little closer. "Why do you think I refused to teach you properly?"

"Because you're an asshole?"

"Because it gave me an excuse to put my hands all over your body."

"Ahhh, because you're a pervert."

I laugh. "Guilty as fucking charged, Rhianna Blackwaters."

She rolls over onto her stomach, kicking up her heels and snapping a piece of grass from the ground, winding it around her fingers.

"Do you ..." she looks up at me through her eyelashes, "do you still want to put your hands on me?"

I glance down at my hands, and my stiff cock beneath them. "What do you think, Rhianna?"

"I think you're not answering the question."

With one hand still covering – pretty badly – my cock, I reach over with the other and give her ass a hard squeeze, groaning as I do. "Yes, I want to put my hands on you. On every damn inch of you."

I glide my hand over her rump, caressing her waist and stroking up her back and her shoulder, then I cradle her jaw and, rolling towards her, I kiss her mouth.

It's still freaking freezing, I can't feel my toes and my balls are aching, but I can feel her lips, soft and warm and hungry.

I slide my hand back down her body as I kiss her mouth, sucking on her lips and her tongue, until I reach her ass. I squeeze it again, then give it a little slap, something that has her moaning into my mouth. My cock twitches beneath my hand.

"Such a nice ass," I whisper.

If she were any other girl, I'd already be pulling her towards me, grinding my cock against her, and stripping off her clothes.

But I fucked things up with Rhianna and I know I have to go slow. Besides which, I want to. I want to savor the moment. This girl has four other men fighting for her attention and I want to bask in being with her while I can.

I massage her butt, squeezing first one cheek between my fingers and then the other. She's wearing yoga pants, the material is slippery, stretchy and thin and it means I can caress her better. I slip my palm right over her ass and in between her legs, stroking along the seam of the pants with my fingertips, feeling the plump lips of her pussy beneath.

She moans again and bites my bottom lip and I give her ass another playful spank.

Then I do it again stroking between her legs, giving her a little friction, before I withdraw my hand and pet her ass. Soon her breath changes. Less mellow, more needy and I wonder if I could get her off this way, make her come.

"You need to put your fingers in her pussy. That's what she really likes."

I jump about a mile off the ground and beside me Rhi does the same.

Then I snatch up to sit and find Renzo Barone sitting in the grass just beyond our feet, chewing a blade of grass.

"What the fuck?" I say. "How long have you been there?" He winks at me. "You've just been sitting there watching us make out?"

He spits the blade of grass onto the ground. "It's funny, I've never been one of those dudes who likes watching girls with other dudes … or other girls," he adds. "Never got off on porn. It's fucking dull. But," his eyes seem to light up, "the idea of watching her with one of you. Of watching you make her fall apart, of watching you fuck her …" He shudders.

"So why the hell did you just interrupt us?" I growl as Rhi rolls up to sit as well, the three of us now sitting in a circle in the grass together like we're at playgroup.

"It was getting boring. You were taking too long. You needed to stuff your fingers inside her pussy and make her come. That's the best fucking bit."

"I was taking my time," I say through gritted teeth, very tempted to crash my fist against this dude's face.

"I am here, you know," Rhi says with irritation.

"Yeah, you are," Barone says, grinning at her, his eyes dark with lust. "Wanna lie back down and let him finger you while I watch, little rabbit?"

Her eyes flick from me to him and back again. Then she flips forward onto her knees and shuffles towards me in the grass. She rests her hand against my cheek and then kisses me. A long deep, slow kiss. I reach for her, to drag her right up against me, already forgetting we have company, but she shuffles away from me and towards him, and by the time my eyes are open again, she's kissing him, that same slow deep kiss.

He does the exact same thing I did, attempting to hook his arm around her waist and drag her to him. But she's up on her feet and brushing off dirt from her backside.

"Come on," she says. "It's freezing out here, and I didn't go to all that effort to save you, Spencer Moreau, just so you could go and die of hypothermia."

She begins to walk in the direction of the mansion.

I glare at the assassin and he winks again.

"Never mind. Next time," he says, jumping up and I stumble up too, following after my mate as I shiver against the cold, clutching my disappointed cock.

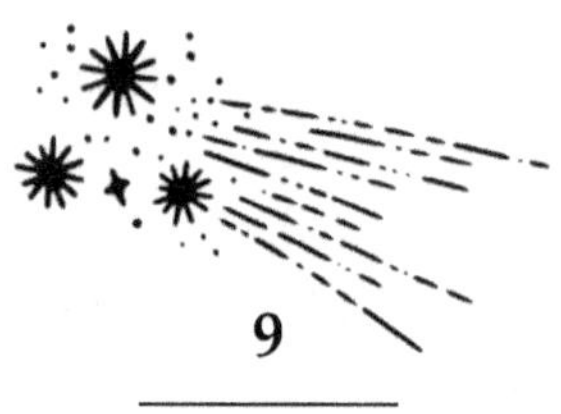

9

T ristan

THE FRONT DOOR swings open and Rhi comes marching through, stamping her feet and blowing on her fingers.

"Jeez, it's so cold out there," she says, walking straight past me in the direction of the warm kitchen.

Renzo Barone follows right after her, whistling under his breath and swinging his arms. And after him comes my friend, completely naked and shivering violently. He slams the door behind him and we're quiet until the assassin disappears into the kitchen.

"What the hell happened to you?" I ask. "Did he steal your clothes?"

"No," he says, looking so pissed off I doubt whether that's the truth. "I went for a run."

"Without clothes? Without shoes?"

"I had to let the beast out. It was getting unbearable." He

glares at me, his brow furrowed.

"What did I do?" I ask, pointing to my chest.

"Just get it over and done with, will you?"

"Get what over and done with?"

"The lecture about how stupid I am, how dangerous it is to let the beast anywhere near Rhianna."

Now it's my time to frown. "You said he wasn't a danger to her."

"Yeah, but none of you seem to agree with that."

"If you say he's not a danger, I believe you. Anyway," I say, glancing at the kitchen door, "she looked perfectly fine. You're the one who looks worse for wear."

"I'm going to light a fire," he says, stomping into one of the empty rooms that leads off the hallway, this one looking like some sort of parlor. He walks straight up to the fireplace, swiping a blanket that covers one of the old-fashioned couches as he passes and wrapping it around his shoulders. The grill is stacked with old rotten logs and he flings his magic at them. Immediately, flames leap up into the air, and he holds out his hands, groaning in relief.

"I'm so fucking cold I thought my balls were going to freeze solid and snap off."

"Talking of blue balls ..." I say, coming to stand next to him and digging my hands into my pockets, searching for an old joint and coming up empty. "Have you ... you know ... with Rhianna?"

"She's pretty angry with me," he says, bending and flexing his stiff fingers.

"I'm not sure that's stopped you in the past. A hate-fuck can be pretty damn hot."

"This is different. She's different. And you know it."

"Yeah," I admit. I guess I do. I lay my hand on his shoulder. I know it's bullshit, but I can't help it, I'm feeling pretty smug that I've fucked her and he hasn't. I also feel a little sorry for the dude. It must suck knowing everyone else is getting a piece of the girl and he isn't. "She'll come around, pal. It's just a matter of time."

"Yeah, she's already beginning to. In fact, if freaking Barone hadn't interrupted us ..."

I snatch my hand away. All my sympathy vanishing in an instant.

I've had Piglet once. Just once. And though it was fucking mind blowing, it was also rushed, quick, and not nearly enough. I want more of her. A lot more.

I've decided I'm going in search of her to get me some more, turning my back on my friend, when Spencer says, "What do you think about that memory? Do you believe it, Tris?"

I stare down at the faded rug beneath my feet and watch as a woodlouse struggle across the thick threads.

"I think ..." My shoulders tighten. "I think my dad won't rest until he has her in his grasp, until he has all of us. There are already rumors swirling about Rhi and he spent a lot of his time trying to get the truth from me. It won't matter if we sail across the ocean, or rocket off to some distant planet; if he sees her as a threat, he's going to come for us. Which means, it's down to one thing and one thing only: us or him. And frankly, I'd much rather it was us."

"You think we should make the initial strike?"

I stroke my chin. It was always our preferred gameplay when we dueled as a team. Get in that early strike, take them by surprise, weaken them right from the start. Could it work in this situation?

"We're vastly outnumbered. But I can't help the feeling that fate has thrown us together for a reason and I'm beginning to suspect that reason is to protect Rhi."

Spencer lowers his voice. "You really think we could work with those others?" His face distorts with disgust. "With Barone?"

"He helped to rescue us, Spencer. They worked together to do that."

"Yeah, but their stupid fucking plan nearly blew up in their faces."

"Mine to rescue you didn't fare much better, did it?"

Spencer stares at me, then tips his head back and laughs. And relief floods through my body. I've been worried about him, worried the stay in that damn awful cell had broken him somehow. At times he's always been a grumpy asshole, but mostly he isn't. Most of the time he's upbeat, fun to be around. I haven't seen much of that side of him over the last 24 hours. But hearing him laugh, that deep bellyful Spencer laugh, is a relief. He's going to be okay.

"It was fucking cocky as hell," Spencer chuckles.

I scrub my hand through the locks of my hair sheepishly. "Yeah, it was. And I'm ..." I meet his eyes, "I'm sorry about what happened to your friend."

He nods his head. "I wonder how many of my kind will be left by the time your dad is through."

"Which is why I'm sure that premonition Rhi's mom saw is correct. My dad is a sadistic, power-hungry bastard. He'll want Rhianna's powers. We have to stop him."

I LEAVE Spencer warming up by the fire and go in search of Rhianna. I find her up in the main bedroom, curled up on the window seat with her friend and her pig. They're whispering and giggling together but it all stops when I enter.

"Were you talking about me?" I ask, leaning against one of the posts of the bed.

"We were talking about girl's stuff," Winnie says, "things that are none of your business."

I eye them both. Why do I suspect Rhi was giving her friend a lowdown about what happened between the two of us right after she drained the drugs from my body?

Thinking about what happened between us has me wanting to walk her friend out of the room so I can throw Piglet down on the bed.

My eyes lock with Rhi's and my bond pulsates in my stomach. The bond is new and it wants us together.

"Okay guys, I get the hint," Winnie says, ducking her head down and collecting the pig up into her arms. "I'm leaving, okay."

"Wh-what?" Rhi says, struggling to drag her eyes away from me. "You don't have to go."

"Pip and I are clearly in the way here." The pig squeaks in protest. "They want to tear each other's clothes off, Pip, and we *are* in the way." Winnie scuttles away towards the door and Rhi makes a lunge for her, missing. In the doorway, her friend waves at us.

"Have fun." And then she shuts the door.

"Is she always so blunt?" I ask, swinging my gaze back around toward Rhianna and finding her charging towards me.

At first I fling my hands up to protect myself, assuming I must have done something wrong and am going to meet her wrath. But instead of pelting me with angry magic, she pushes me hard against my chest. It takes me by surprise and I fall back onto the mattress, the girl crawling on top of me immediately and straddling my lap.

I still don't know what the hell is going on, but when she

reaches for the hem of her sweater and pulls it over her head along with her top, I get a fair idea.

"Fuck," I mutter looking up at her perched on top of me in only her bra and her pants. "Going to take that off for me too, little Piglet?"

"You have to stop calling me that."

"Not a chance."

"Then, no, I won't," she says, sticking out her bottom lip in a pout.

I take a tight hold of her waist and flip her over onto her back, caging my body over hers.

"Then I'll just have to do it myself." I smirk at her and then I take the lacy material of the bra cup between my teeth, about to tug it down. Then I stop, spitting the thing out.

"Where the hell did you get underwear like this?" The bra is made from a combination of silk and lace. Real silk and real lace. Expensive and damn sexy.

"Azlan."

"Remind me to thank him," I mutter, before I take the material back between my teeth and yank it down, exposing her stiff pink nipple. "Hello there," I say, making her giggle, "nice to meet you." I pinch the nipple between my teeth making her squeak and her back arch so that she pushes her tit up into my mouth.

I moan, licking my tongue around the velvety skin and then sucking on it. This time she squirms beneath me, grinding her core against my hardening cock.

I yank away the other cup of her bra, rubbing the pad of my thumb over her left nipple as I continue to kiss the right, and she scrabbles at my shirt.

"This needs to come off," she says. I peer up at her and she grins at me. Then her magic sparks in the air and my shirt is gone, her hands gliding down my chest and taking a hold of my belt buckle.

She's needy and she wants this. But it was too fast before. I want this to last.

"Slow down, Piglet," I tell her.

She makes a little whimper in her throat that tells me she doesn't like that idea.

I push up onto my hands and peer down at her.

"Wh-wh-what are you doing?" she says, attempting to hook her hands around my neck and drag me back down towards her.

"Taking my fucking time with you." I peer into her eyes and then I let my gaze meander over her face, down her throat, lingering at her breasts and down her flat belly. A flush sweeps across her body, trailing after my gaze.

"So fucking beautiful."

She squirms again. This girl can't take a compliment. And I have a feeling I'm partly to blame for that.

"You don't believe me?"

"Oh, I believe you. I'd just really like you to stop looking and start ... you know."

I lift an eyebrow. "No, I don't. You want me to start ...?" She frowns at me. And I wrestle my face into a deadly serious expression. "What do you want me to do, Piglet?"

She raises up onto her elbows. "I want you to stop calling me that."

I nod slowly. "I'll give that some thought." I go to move off the bed.

"Wait!" she cries, and makes a grab for me, her elbows flying from under her, so she lands flat on her back, with me on top of her, pinning her down with my weight.

"Was there something else?"

"Are you going to make me beg? Is that what this is? I

suppose the great Tristan Kennedy is used to having girls beg him to fuck them?"

"Ahhh so that's what you want, huh?" I say, nipping at her earlobe. "You want me to fuck you." I grind my hips into her and she moans. "You don't have to beg. You just have to ask."

I lift my head so my face is hovering directly above hers, so I can see all the golden shades of her eyes.

"You're an asshole."

"Are you trying to seduce me into bed?" She glares at me and I grind into her again, making her bottom lip quiver. "Is it so hard to say it, Rhianna?" I say, earnestly, my ego punctured. "So hard to admit you want me?"

"Yes," she says, just as earnestly, scraping her fingernails against my scalp. "I'm scared that I'm a fool for sleeping with you – for wanting you – after everything you did to me."

I nod. She still doesn't trust me. I still have to make it up to her. And I'm going to start right now.

I kiss her mouth. Then her throat, then her right breast and her left, sliding down her body, kissing her belly button, then lower, shimmying her pants and her underwear down her legs as I kiss the soft curls between her thighs and then her pussy lips.

"I thought we'd agreed you were going to fuck me," she says, rising up on her elbows again, to peer down at me.

"We did, did we?" I say, smirking and then I part her legs open, gazing down at her, all bare and exposed, all pink and wet, and bury my face right into her pussy.

10

R^{hi}

Tristan Kennedy pins my legs apart and proves to me he's just as talented at this as he is at everything else he does. I assume that's from all the damn practice he's been doing.

In fact, I can't get the image of him fucking that other girl out of my head. Or all the other images of girls draped over him, touching him, rubbing up against him.

Jealousy spikes in my bond and I push his head away with my hands.

"What's wrong?" he says, with genuine concern, his mouth all sloppy with spit and my arousal.

"How many other girls have you done this with exactly?"

"What?" he says, frowning and looking confused.

"How many other girls have there been?"

He lowers his mouth back down to my pussy and gives my clit a hard flick with his tongue. The action sends electricity spiraling straight through my core and I jolt on the bed.

"Are you slut-shaming me, Rhianna Blackwaters?"

My cheeks burn. Perhaps I am being unreasonable but I can't help it.

"You slept with other girls even though you knew I was your fated mate." He opens his mouth, most probably to deny it, so I add quickly, "I saw you remember."

He groans. "We weren't together back then."

"It still hurt," I admit in a whisper. "It still hurts now."

"And I'm sorry. I'm sorry for all the times I've been a massive dickhead and hurt you, Piglet. Because I'm crazy about you and I did some stupidly crazy things at the beginning. But that girl you saw me with, she was the last one."

"What do you mean?"

"I haven't slept with anyone since her."

I scowl at him with suspicion. "Why?"

"I didn't want to. The only girl I wanted to be with was you."

I shake my head. "You expect me to believe that, Tristan? I've seen how girls throw themselves at you."

"I wasn't interested. I didn't want anyone else. I wanted you." He lowers his mouth back down to my pussy and drags his tongue slowly through my folds, like he's savoring the taste of me, every single molecule. "And you were worth the wait. You're fucking delicious." He closes his eyes and groans. "A girl never tasted this good before."

I drop back down flat on the mattress. I think he's probably exaggerating. Telling me things he thinks I want to hear. But soon I can't focus on my thoughts anymore because what he's doing to me fries my brain, spinning his tongue around and around my clit until I'm dizzy, panting and begging for release. He doesn't give it to me, though, he takes me right to the edge, right to the brink, of an orgasm, my hips lifting, my spine arching, my core tensing, and then he pulls away.

"You think I've ever wanted to do this to anyone else? Take my time? Pleasure them? Make them feel this good? I never cared about any girl enough to bother, Rhi. I was only concerned with what was in it for me. But with you ..." I'm panting, my hands tight fists in the bed sheets, "I want to make you feel so damn good. I want to take you to fucking heaven and back. I want you to forgive me." He presses his wet tongue to my clit and starts the process again, winding, achingly slow, around my clit, barely touching me, then increasing the speed and the pressure, licking me harder, licking me faster, until every nerve in my body is alight and I'm so close, so damn close, so so ...

He stops.

I squeal in frustration, my body damp with sweat, my pussy so wet I must be making a mess of the bed sheets.

"Hmmm, I could stay here forever just doing this. I could die right between your thighs and die a happy man. It smells so good, it tastes so good, it feels so good." He strokes his fingertips lightly through my folds, and then kisses my clit. "Your pussy is better than anyone else's. It's the queen of pussies. I'm going to worship it whenever I fucking can."

A remark like that would usually have me snorting or sniggering. But the bond between us shimmers and I can feel his honesty and earnestness shining there. It takes me aback. He really means it. Truly means it.

"Then, please Tristan, for the love of– please, please make me come."

He's gazing, entranced, at my pussy like it's a rare diamond or a masterful piece of art.

"Tristan!" I whine and slowly he lowers his mouth back

down, kissing my clit again, this time with more force, more passion, more reverence. He sucks and licks and flicks at me, my whole pussy inside his mouth and this time he gives me no respite, no moments to recover.

And my body responds, squirming and jolting on the mattress, as he holds me down. It's too much, too much, all my senses alive at once. I try to push his head away, but he simply continues, forcing the orgasm right from my core, so it rips through me, blasting away all sound and sight and making every nerve sing with ecstasy.

"Tristan!" I cry out as the fierce wave of pleasure whips me away. When I open my eyes, he's on top of me again, stroking damp hair from my face.

"Okay?" he asks me, searching my eyes. "Was it good?"

I sigh, my body still floating in bliss.

"Oh my stars," I mutter.

He smirks with satisfaction and I can't help giggling.

"What?" he says, that smirk fading.

"The cockiness is never too far away."

"Not cocky, confident, assertive," he says, kissing my cheek. "But it was good, right? Really good?"

"You really need me to massage your ego?"

"I want to know if you enjoyed it."

"It was good, really, really good."

He gives me that smirk again and heaven help me that does something to my insides.

I push at his chest, forcing him to roll over onto his back and then I climb on top of him, unbuckling his belt and tugging down the zipper of his fly. Then I'm freeing his cock.

"Do you have protection or do you want to do the barrier spell?" I ask him.

His eyes glint. "Barrier spell." He whispers the words, his

magic flaring around us and then he's gripping his cock and helping to line me up.

I pause, inhaling as I meet his gaze, and then I slide down onto his cock, our eyes locked together the entire time.

"Shit, that's ..." he mutters, the tension melting from his face. "Shit!"

I keep going, all the way until I bottom out and then I rest my hand on his thighs behind me and grind in circles on his cock.

"Fuck," he moans, "fuck. You look unreal, Rhi, fucking unreal."

He reaches up and squeezes my tit.

My idea was to torture him just like he did to me, take him to the brink and then take it all away. Wind him up and up. Then stop. But his cock inside me feels too good and I don't have the willpower or the self control. I start off slow and considered, but soon I'm bouncing up and down on him like something possessed, my magic sparking in the air around us and his doing the same too.

I'm still sensitive and I come again quickly, screaming so loudly I'm sure everyone else in this mansion must hear, and then Tristan Kennedy does something surprising. He rolls up to sit so our faces are hovering just millimeters apart, he wraps his arms around me, stroking his hands up and down my back, brushing my hair away from my face, kissing my mouth and my neck. Worshiping me all over again.

When I come a third time, he comes with me, holding me tight against his body, so tight I can feel the thud of his heart, nuzzling into my neck, whispering words of affection that make my heart swell.

We stay like that for several minutes: him buried inside

me, me perched on his lap, just kissing and caressing each other.

"I've never done it bare backed like this before," he admits, "it feels fucking amazing. I can feel all of you."

"You haven't?" I say, surprised by yet another of Tristan Kennedy's revelations, and also confused because didn't we …

I snap up straight, the realization hitting me square between the eyes.

"Before," I gasp.

"What?" he murmurs, sucking on my neck.

"When we did it before, back at your house. Tristan – we didn't use … did you cast a barrier spell then too?"

I don't know why I'm asking. I know he didn't, but there's a little bubble of hope residing in my chest that maybe he did and I was just so caught up in the moment that I didn't notice.

But then he's snapping up straight too, a look of horror in his eyes, and that bubble well and truly pops.

"No, shit, Rhi, no, I was … it was … shit." We stare at each other. "I'm clean," he says. "I've always used protection."

"I know but …"

"It's a small chance," he says, not sounding half as confident as he usually does.

"We're fated mates. Are you sure the chance is that small? Because I'm really not ready for–"

"Me neither. We're on the fucking run! My dad will be looking for us." He tugs at his fair hair. "There has to be a way … something you can take …"

"Winnie will know," I say, hopping straight off him and scuttling off the bed.

"You're going to ask her now?"

"The sooner the better," I say, already sliding my panties

up my legs. I don't bother with a bra, I tug my hoodie over my head and then my pants up my legs and head straight for the door.

"Winnie?" I yell right from the landing. I am so lucky to have this girl. Because I seem to land myself in trouble left, right and center and without her I'd probably be dead in a ditch right now. In fact, I would most definitely be. "Winnie?" I yell again.

"Rhianna?" Azlan calls from somewhere on the ground floor. "Is everything all right?"

I ignore him. "Winnie?" I cry.

One of the bedroom doors snaps open and Winnie sticks her head out. Her braids have been unwound, her mascara's smudged and her cheeks are flushed.

"I'm kind of in the middle of something here, Rhi," she says.

"Winnie," I say and I'm sure there must be panic written all over my face because she ducks back into the room and then emerges again a minute later, dressed in Trent's jeans, her t-shirt – on back to front.

"Winnie," I say, grabbing her hands and not commenting on her appearance. I doubt I look any more respectable.

"What the hell is wrong? Did he do something–" Her eyes swivel towards the master bedroom.

"No, Winnie, no, but I screwed up. I screwed up big time."

Footsteps sound below and I know my other mates are going to come up here and cause a fuss any minute now so I pull Winnie into one of the unused bedrooms, shut the door and lock it with my magic. Precisely a minute later, the door knob starts rattling but I ignore it and drag Winnie to the other side of the room.

"What's going on, Rhi?" Winnie asks, concern etched across her face.

"We didn't use protection," I blurt out. I wince, ready for the Winnie lecture. She doesn't say a word, just nods calmly. "It was the first time, back at the Kennedy house. I guess we just got so carried away in the moment that we didn't think and–"

"Rhi," Winnie says, laying her palms on my shoulders and fixing her gaze with mine. "Breathe." I take a deep inhale and exhale. "Well done. And again." I repeat the action. "Now let's get some things clear. Did he, you know, inside you?" I nod. "Right, well, there's something we can brew that can deal with the risk of pregnancy." I wince again at the words. "Let me see ... how many days out are we ... yes, we should be fine." I let out a sigh of relief. "There's not a lot I can do about potential STIs, though," she says, with a look of apology, "you'd need to go to the clinic for that."

"Oh, that's not a problem. He says he's clean."

Winnie blurts out a snort. Then gives me another apologetic look. "Sorry, Rhi, it's just it's Tristan, and he's ..."

"A massive man-whore?" I say. Winnie swallows. "He says he always used protection before."

"Let's hope he's telling the truth."

"He is," I say firmly, "I could feel it through the bond." I slump down on the bed. "Is this potion going to be disgusting? Or ... hurt?" I grimace. Then bury my face in my hands. "I'm such an idiot, Winnie."

Winnie pinches my arm. "Don't be so dramatic, Rhi. You think you're the first woman to mess up their contraception? Saskia used to brew this potion for a fair price back at the academy – she was making a fortune. I mean you could get it for free from the matron but a lot of girls didn't like going to her about it and–"

"Really?" I say, peeking at Winnie through my fingers.

"Rhi, I had to take it myself two weeks ago, when things got a bit," she waggles her eyebrows "and the condom broke."

"Shit," I say. "I thought those things were indestructible."

"Not always. It depends what you're doing." She grabs my elbow and pulls me back onto my feet. "Come on, we'd better go brew it. The sooner you take it, the more effective it will be."

"You're saying it's not 100% effective!" I say in alarm.

"It will be. I'll make sure of it. We have enough man-babies running around after you. We don't need an actual baby."

I nod my head in agreement, then peer down at my stomach. A baby is not something I'd ever ever considered. I was always too consumed with how to make it through to the next day; I didn't have a chance to think any further into the future. I'd never pictured myself with a family – a husband and a baby. Since the arrival of five fated mates that scenario seems even less likely.

"No, I don't want a baby. Not now, anyway. I mean maybe one day way, way in the future. Is it crazy to even think like that, Winnie? I have four men bonded to me. It's not like we could ever be a conventional family. Not to mention the fact that a very powerful man would probably like me dead – or at least chained to a wall."

"You have every right to want to be happy, to want a family, Rhi. We all do." I smile at her and kiss her cheek.

"Is that what you want, Winnie?"

"I don't know – maybe a long time in the future too. I'd like to do stuff first. Study more."

"Winnie," I say, "has this potion – the one you're going to brew – been around for a long time?"

"Yep, hundreds of years, why?"

"So, if I were the result of ... a mishap or," I swallow, "something much much worse–"

"Your aunt said your mom and dad were in love, Rhi."

"But if I were unplanned, my mom could have used this potion to stop her from getting pregnant. But she didn't. She must have chosen to have me."

I guess I've never expressed that out loud before. But all my life I've wondered. Why did she give me up? Was it to keep me safe? Because she was unable to care for me?

Or was it because she didn't want me?

Now I think I have my answer.

My vision swims with tears.

"She wanted me. My mom wanted to keep me."

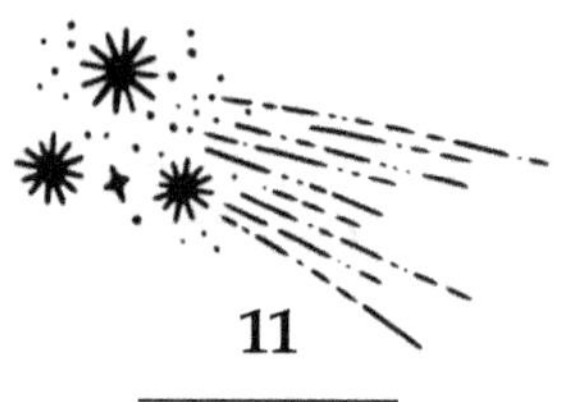

11

A zlan

I'VE SPREAD a large map across the kitchen table, ringing the Gray Isle and the Albany Convent, plotting a route I think we could take safely. I mark it with notes as Phoenix skips through the different radio stations trying to piece information together.

Every now and again, there is another announcement, endless announcements upon announcements. New restrictions the Lord Protector is implementing on the movements and liberty of the people. New laws he will be introducing, including the imprisonment of all weres and emergency powers he can use against the republic's enemies. Plus constant reminders to the public about the fugitives on the run – enemies of the state. Huge rewards are offered for information that results in the capture of any unregistered, illegals or fugitives. I've heard the announcement many times over by now and yet every time it still has the ability to make my blood run cold.

Rhianna's powers have already grown in the time I've known her, they are continuing to grow now. Christopher Kennedy has had a glimpse of those powers and if he's worked out what we have – that Rhi is the girl in the prophecy – he's going to want her dead.

As another of the announcements fades away, I throw my pen down on the table.

"She isn't safe here in the republic, Phoenix. Traveling to the Gray Isle will be even more dangerous – traveling across the country without being spotted, impossible. We're wasting time. We should be formulating a plan. Getting the hell out of here."

Phoenix slams his palm on the radio and the thing falls silent. "She's already spent the majority of her life running and hiding. Is that how you want her to spend the rest of it too?"

"No, I just don't see a scenario where we take my uncle on and walk away alive."

"Even if her mom was right and she's the girl from the prophecy?"

"He has an army, powerful supporters. There's no way we can defeat him. No way we can stay in the republic and keep Rhi safe."

"Stone's right." I turn and find Rhianna hovering with Winnie in the doorway. "I'm not running anymore, Azlan. I can't. Being on the run ..." She shakes her head. "All five of you would hate it. You'd come to resent me for it."

"I wouldn't."

Rhi strides into the room, stopping in front of me and resting her palm on my chest.

"You would, Azlan. And maybe I'd come to resent you for forcing me into that situation."

I appeal to Winnie. Rhianna trusts her judgment and opinion. "What do you think, Winnie? Aren't we better getting Rhi away to safety?"

"I don't think that's her fate," she says. "I don't think that's your fate either."

"Fate isn't some cast-iron force written in stone," I say, jaw tightening. "We can choose our own path. And I'd like to choose the path where Rhianna is safe."

"Safe, but always looking over my shoulder, always moving from one place to the next, never knowing who to trust. It's no way to live, Azlan. So, please, let's do it my way. Let's go read this prophecy, understand exactly what we're facing and then our choices will be better informed."

"Don't let him fool you, sweetheart," Phoenix says, "he's already plotted a route out to the Gray Isle."

"You have?" she asks me with a smile.

"Yes," I say grumpily. "We'll pack up and leave tomorrow. In the evening. It will be safer to travel at night."

"Thank you, Azlan," she says, balancing up onto her toes to kiss my cheek.

Then she turns back to her friend and together they start pulling out pots and pans and raiding the supply of herbs in the pantry.

I leave them to it, assuming they're cooking dinner and return to the map, double-checking my route, ensuring it bypasses any towns or likely checkpoints. It's roundabout and I'm yet to work out how we will actually make the journey. We only have one car.

After a while, a strange odor fills the kitchen, tickling at my nose and I peer over my shoulder. Rhi and Winnie are crowded around a bubbling pot on the stove.

"What are you doing?" I ask, and both of them leap about a meter into the air. I stride over and lean over the pot, taking a look at the concoction inside. It looks like a potion. "What's that?"

Winnie slams the lid on the pot. "Girl's stuff."

"Not dinner then."

Rhi places one hand on her hip. "I already told you, don't expect me to cook for you just because–"

"I'm teasing you. I'll cook. I'd like us all to have dinner together."

Rhi tips her head to one side, then nods. "I'd like that too."

I walk through to the larder to see what I can find, keeping an ear out for Winnie and Rhi's conversation, curious about the girly stuff potion they're brewing.

"It doesn't look like very much," Rhi comments.

"It's not," Winnie answers. "Enough for one dose. But ideally you should take a second tomorrow morning. Sorry, Rhi, but there just wasn't enough Cloudpuff in the stores."

Cloudpuff? What the hell is that used for again? It rings a bell. I wish I'd paid better attention in my damn potion lessons. I'll have to ask Phoenix later, although, despite being an actual professor, he seems to know as much about potions as I do.

"If this is some potion to make your hair shinier or teeth whiter," Phoenix says from the table, obviously also curious about what the girls are up to, "you don't need it, you're perfect as you are."

"Duh," Winnie says, "obviously."

"Then what is it f–"

Rhi ignores him.

"Cloudpuff?" she says. "I saw some growing outside in

the prairie. I can get some more in the morning and we can brew a second batch."

I pull beef out of the freezer, and the last tins of tomatoes and a packet of pasta in the stores. We've already eaten our way through much of the food that was being kept here. By tomorrow evening there won't be enough to feed us all which means we'd have to move on anyway or go find some more food. Both of which would place us in danger.

I carry my finds back into the kitchen in time to see Rhi sipping whatever the two girls have brewed, pulling a face of disgust as she does.

"Are you going to tell me what the hell that is?" I ask, using my magic to thaw the frozen meat before breaking it up into a frying pan. Rhi shakes her head. "I thought we were doing honesty now."

"We are. And I will tell you. Just not right now," she says, peeking at Trent who has taken a second radio to pieces, the parts strewn across the kitchen table.

"And what are you doing?" I ask him as the meat begins to sizzle.

"Erm," the boy says as he twists two wires together, "seeing if I can make a handheld receiver." He reads the puzzlement on Rhi's face. "Walkie-talkies."

"You can do that from that?" I ask.

"He's some kind of gadget genius," Rhi tells me, placing her empty mug on the side and coming to stand next to me. I pull her in front of me, wrapping my arms around her and resting my chin on her shoulder as I stir the cooking meat.

It almost feels domestic, kind of perfect, cooking together as if we were any other ordinary couple, any normal family. As if we didn't have fate hanging over our heads and the Lord Protector determined to hunt us down.

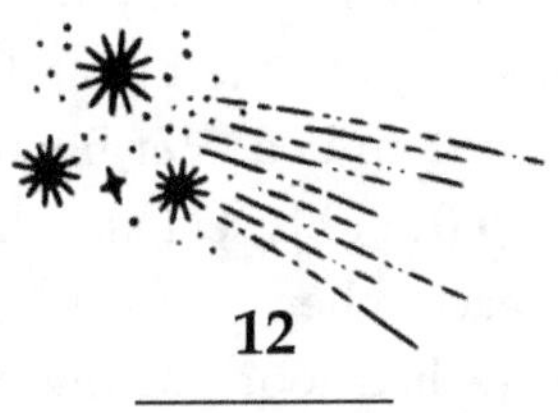

12

S tone

Azlan serves dinner an hour later, all of us sitting around the kitchen table, a motley crew of people that shouldn't belong together but somehow do.

An assassin who wrestles his spaghetti like it's something alive, stabbing and poking at it with his fork. The Lord Protector's son himself, who seems to have acquired a large love bite since this morning (does that have anything to do with the potion Rhi and Winnie were brewing – Cloudpuff? It definitely rings a damn bell). And a werebeast.

Not to mention one grumpy-assed enforcer and a washed-out professor.

Definitely a motley crew.

Which is probably why the conversation isn't exactly flowing. It stops and starts, jumping from one topic to another – avoiding the one we're all really thinking about. If it weren't for Winnie and Trent, we'd probably be arguing by now, possibly wrestling each other across the table.

I'm guessing Miss Wence finally tires of the tension in the room because she gives one big and clearly fake yawn and says she's heading to bed. Her boyfriend immediately and eagerly leaps up from his seat and then it's just the rest of us left staring at each other.

"Are we going to bed too?" Barone asks with obvious hope in his voice, tossing his fork onto his empty plate.

Rhi gives him a hard look, the kind I remember my mom used to give me when I wasn't behaving myself. The assassin grins at her and then slinks away from the table.

"Should we be worried?" Spencer asks, watching as Barone slips from the room.

"No," Rhi says, biting her thumb in a way that suggests to me she's not sure of that.

We don't have long to contemplate what the psycho is up to though. He returns after only a few minutes, a bottle of ancient-looking liquor in one hand, and six shot glasses balancing in the other. He slams them down on the table.

"If we're not going to fuck, we can at least have fun."

"I don't like your kind of fun," Azlan growls. And considering this morning's monologue about neck snapping, I have to agree.

"Right!" The assassin laughs. "Because a man who is as good at killing as you are, can't possibly hate it."

"We're not killing anyone," Rhi says. "Maybe we should just go to bed," she mutters.

"To fuck?" Barone asks eagerly, making my hackles rise.

"To sleep!"

"Nah, that's no fun." He twists the lid off the liquor bottle and lifts the neck to his nose, taking a sharp sniff. "Fuck me, that's strong," he says, blinking.

He slops the bottle over and lets the clear liquid drizzle into each of the glasses, spilling half of it over the tabletop. Then he rights the bottle and slides a glass to each of us. I glare down at mine.

"There's no way in hell I'm touching that stuff," Azlan growls.

I dip my little finger into the liquid, half expecting to see my skin sizzle off. When it doesn't, I dip my finger in my mouth and suck. A sickly alcohol mixture hits my tongue. "It's not half bad," I confirm.

"You don't know what the hell is in it and we could be attacked at any moment," Azlan says, ever the fucking soldier. "We need all our faculties working."

Barone tips the shot straight into his mouth, swallows and slams his glass on the table. "My faculties," he says, "have never worked." He slaps a load more liquid into the glass.

"Fuck it," I mutter, knocking back my own shot. Immediately, a warm sensation swims through my body and some of the tension I've been carrying ever since the academy was attacked leaves my shoulders.

I wipe at my teary eyes, focusing back in on those around us. Rhi's shot glass is half way to her mouth.

"Miss Blackwaters," I warn her, "you know you can't hold your drink." She glares at me and swallows the thing in one go. It leaves her coughing and spluttering and I shake my head. "What did I tell you?"

She gives me the finger and reaches for her water glass.

"So you're going to sit here and get wasted?" Azlan says with obvious disapproval.

"We could fuck instead, but little rabbit doesn't want to do that. Probably on account of all the fucking she did earlier."

Rhi chokes on her water and I give Tristan Kennedy the stink eye. We all know what they were doing earlier. We heard it loud and clear.

"We could make things more interesting," Spencer says, spinning his untouched glass in his fingers.

"More interesting, how?" Rhi asks, her eyes already a little squiffy.

"We could play 'never have I ever'."

Azlan folds his arms over his chest, his biceps bulging in annoyance. "I left school a long time ago."

"I've never played it," Barone says, his glass already empty again.

"Me neither," Rhi says.

"We're not playing 'never have I ever'," I say, in my teacher voice.

"It might be a good way of getting to know each other better," Rhi says.

"You only think that, Miss Blackwaters, because you've never played it."

Rhi turns her gaze away from me and towards Spencer. "How do we play?"

"We take turns to make a statement – something like, never have I ever played a drinking game. If you have done the thing, you drink your drink. If you haven't, you leave it untouched."

"This is immature and stupid," Azlan says.

"It sounds like fun. And I think we deserve a little bit of fun. Things have been … intense," Rhi says, glancing first at Barone, then Spencer and then Tristan. My gaze travels around that little circle and I get a fair idea how my mate has been spending her time today. "Can I go first?" Rhi asks. Spencer nods. "Hmmm." She taps her fingers on the table. "Never have I ever watched porn."

I groan. "That is so lame, sweetheart. If you're going to insist on playing this game, at least make the questions interesting."

She stares me square in the eye. "Have you?"

I swear and down my drink. Everyone else does too – which is hardly fucking surprising. What human hasn't?

Rhianna and Barone apparently.

"Bullshit," I say to him. Rhi had barely any internet connection growing up. But Barone? He's male with a pulse. Of course he's fucking watched porn.

"Not my thing," he says shrugging.

"Not even snuff?" I ask darkly. He smirks at me.

"What's that?" Rhi asks.

I change the subject. "Never have I ever made myself come thinking of someone else in this room." I grin at her.

Rhi smirks right back at me and swallows her drink. From the corner of my eye, I see Tristan hesitate and do the same.

"Fuck, yeah, who, little rabbit? Who were you thinking about?"

She leans across the table, picks up the bottle and pours herself another shot.

"Don't you think you've had enough?" Azlan says, grabbing her wrist.

"No," she says, snatching her hand free. "And this is fun."

"My go," Barone says. He takes the bottle from Rhi's hands. "Never have I ever flayed someone alive." He spins his gaze around the group hopefully. Nobody drinks. He shakes his head and downs his own.

"You really are a sick fuck," Spencer mutters.

"I've seen you rip a man's throat out, Spencer Moreau," the assassin says, something dangerous in his tone.

"I have another one." Rhi snatches the bottle off him. "Never have I ever been in love."

It's clear she says it to try and diffuse the tension in the room. It has the opposite effect. Suddenly everyone is looking uncomfortable, like this is a far worse question and love a far dirtier word than murder and torture.

"Oh, come on," she says, as her cheeks pinken. "Nobody? Nobody's been in love?"

Azlan reaches for his glass and silently drinks the contents.

"Who?" Rhi asks, her tone suddenly sharp. And this is why I didn't want to play this game. It never ends well.

"I'm in love now," he says, refolding his arms, "with you."

"That wasn't the question, asshole," I mutter. "She asked if you'd been in love before."

"Then no, I haven't."

Rhi relaxes.

"I have one," Spencer says. "Never have I ever had a threesome."

"Jeez," I say, "where are all the easing-us-in questions like never have I ever jumped out of a plane?"

"With or without a parachute?" Renzo asks.

"If you'd jumped out of a plane without a parachute you'd be dead."

"Would I?" he says, looking down at his body as if to check it's still there.

"Can we get back to my question?" Spencer says.

"What was it?"

"Threesome."

Yep, I was right, this game is less about getting to know each other and more about digging for information about one another. And Spencer's definitely digging; his eyes glued on Rhi waiting for her response.

She knocks back her drink, as do I, Azlan and Tristan. The assassin whistles.

"Fuck, yes, little rabbit. I love how bad you are."

Tristan looks at his friend, the glass still full in his hand. "You never have?" he says, sounding genuinely surprised. "Girls at the academy seemed to think the best way of climbing into my bed was if there were two of them."

Rhi, swaying ever so slightly on her seat, glares daggers at him; her usual inhibitions definitely impeded.

Tristan leans back in his chair with that usual nonplussed expression. "Piglet, I'm not the only one." He points at me and Azlan.

"Yes, but their threesome was with me!" she blurts out and I decide I won't be informing her that that particular threesome wasn't my first, although I'm pretty sure it was Azlan's.

"So you are happy to be shared?" the assassin says, leaning forward on his seat, his eyes darker than ever.

"Clearly, she is," Spencer says, scowling at me and my friend.

"How many times have you done it?" Tristan asks, the bored expression gone and the interest clear on his face. "The three of you?"

"Once," Rhi hiccups and covers her mouth, "and a half."

"And did you enjoy it?" Tristan asks next, leaning forward on his seat.

"I think we should all go get some sleep," Azlan says, pushing back his chair.

"Nah," Spencer shakes his head, "things are just getting interesting."

"Piglet, did you enjoy being shared?" Tristan repeats.

Rhi's honey eyes spin over us all. "Yes," she says honestly.

"We wouldn't have done it otherwise," Azlan says in a grump. "We're not into making girls do stuff they don't like." He glares at Barone and then his cousin.

Tristan ignores him. "You think you'd like to do it again?"

"We have important matters to be considering. Our safety – Rhi's in particular – for one. Your dick and–"

"Yes," Rhi says, meeting Tristan's gaze, all fire and heat, "I liked it. I liked it a lot."

Tristan licks his lips like her words are something delicious and I can't help but groan; the memory of that afternoon still emblazoned in my memory, scorching hot and erotic.

"You've drunk too much," Azlan says to her, and she twists her head and gives him that bratty glare that drives me wild.

"I haven't. He asked me a question and I answered. I'm not ashamed of what we did. I'm not ashamed of liking it. I'm not ashamed of wanting more." Barone slides her another shot, winking at Azlan as he does, but Rhi leaves it untouched. "Let's be real here. I have five fated mates – all of you. You know how strong the attraction is, how forcefully I'm pulled towards you, how forcefully, you're pulled towards me. You must know it's the same with the others. And if you have a problem with that, Azlan, then maybe it's better we discuss it now."

"I don't have a problem with it."

"No jealousy?" she says.

He crosses his arms again. "No!" he says defiantly, then caves under her scrutinizing glare. "A little."

"The jealousy is a downside to this ... situation," his cousin says, "but it's balanced by a hell of a lot of upsides."

"Such as?" Rhi asks.

"Being with you," he says, "sharing you with your other mates."

"Watching you get fucked," Barone adds.

"Yeah," Tristan says, the room as quiet as a priest's cupboard, the confessions coming thick and fast now. "I'd find that hot. I've never had a threesome with another dude before but I like the idea."

"Azlan?" Rhi asks.

"I don't like the idea of you sleeping with him," he says, jerking his chin towards the assassin.

"Too late!" the assassin says, sitting back in his chair and folding his arms over his chest.

The rest of us all spin our gazes in Rhi's direction.

"Seriously?" I say. Then I frown. "Did he force you, sweetheart?"

"No!" she cries, swaying slightly in her seat.

"I don't know how you can trust him," Azlan mutters.

"I'm not going to hurt her," the assassin says.

"I'm sorry if I don't take your word for that."

"He's not, Azlan," Rhi says. "I trust him on this. You need to trust him too."

"He just told us he flayed someone alive."

"I like making her happy," Barone says with such simplicity I can't help believing him. "And I made her really, really happy."

"Well," I say, letting out a puff of air, "I'm glad we cleared that up."

Rhi giggles, the laughter coming thicker and faster when she takes in Azlan's grumpy stance. The girl has definitely had too much to drink.

"Isn't it a good thing that I'm okay with this?" she asks him. She stands up from her seat, stumbling a little before she regains her balance. Then she tiptoes over to him, wrapping her arms around him. "Especially as it seems we're going to be stuck together for the foreseeable future."

I rub at my beard. She's not wrong. Being together – all of us – even these other men, even Barone, has a contentment humming in my bond like nothing I've ever experienced before. I'm in no doubt that together is how we are meant to be and if I'm struggling to keep my hands off Rhi, the others must be too. Better that we navigate our way around this strange set up, than fight it. Better we find a way that leaves us all happy – especially Rhi.

"I just want you to be happy," Azlan says, as if reading my thoughts, "happy and safe."

"I am happy," she says, smiling at him, "happier than I've ever been – safer than I've ever felt – which is pretty surreal considering the leader of this country wants me dead."

"I won't let that happen," he says.

"*We* won't let that happen," Tristan adds.

Rhi balances up on her tiptoes and kisses my friend. A gentle kiss that expresses her gratitude but deepens as the minutes pass. I watch them together, concluding that Barone and Tristan are both right, watching her with one of her mates is hot. Surprisingly so.

She pulls away from Azlan and then she tiptoes over to me next, swaying again, her eyes slightly out of focus. She bends down to kiss me like she kissed him, her hands tangled in my hair. The others watch us, electricity sizzling in the air and in my veins.

Just as the kiss has my heart pumping blood down south, she steps back and walks over to Barone. He pulls her into his lap and kisses her hard on the mouth. I'm rolling my eyes, unsurprised that Barone would be greedy like that, taking more than the rest of us, but then he sets her back on her feet and she heads to Tristan next. He watches her come, his emerald-green eyes darkening to olive. He takes a hold of her waist, positioning her between his legs as she kisses him too. The electricity and magic vibrating in the air is so violent now it's sparking.

After a moment, she rests her hand flat on his chest and pushes him away and then she's turning to Spencer. His eyes seem to flash and I wonder if the beast is in there somewhere, watching as their mate stalks towards them. He kisses her, hands traveling all over her body hungrily and then she's pulling away from him too.

Her eyelids are heavy with a mixture of lust and alcohol. She bites her bottom lip between her teeth. I snag a flicker of her thoughts. Definitely impaired.

"And now I really am going to bed," she says, attempting to walk seductively towards the door and tripping over her own feet.

I catch her with my arm and she lands in my lap. "I think that's a good idea, sweetheart."

"Are you going to come with me?" she asks, "all of you?"

Barone goes to answer her, but I beat him to it.

"Not tonight, sweetheart. I think you've had a little too much to drink." She opens her mouth to argue with me and a hiccup pops out instead. "Exactly. Probably best you go sleep this off."

"This is what I want," she says, her eyes struggling to focus on my face.

"Oh, I'm sure it is," I say, this conversation sucker-punching me good and proper. "But it's probably a decision best made when you're sober."

She leans and whispers in my ear, thinking she's keeping her next words between me and her when really she's so loud we all hear. "But I might not be brave enough to do this when I'm sober."

"Rhi," I say, "you're the bravest person I know. And I know him." I jerk my thumb in Azlan's direction. Then I gather her up in my arms and carry her out of the room.

I expect her to kick up a fuss like she usually does when she doesn't get her own way. Instead, she snuggles into me, resting her head against my shoulder, and she's out cold by the time I've reached the top of the stairs.

I lay her in the bed and then stir her, forcing her to drink a whole glass of water before I let her nuzzle down under the covers and drift away.

Then I get the hell out of there. In the dining room the others are still sitting there in a stunned silence, nursing their drinks. I pour myself another and knock it back.

"Shit," I mutter to myself, knowing that, even if it was the right thing to do, I just turned down one hell of an opportunity.

An opportunity, given our current circumstances, may never come around again.

13

R^{hi}

I WAKE to Pip nudging my cheek with his snout, my head pounding.

I groan and drag open my eyes.

It's morning, gray light visible around the gaps in the ancient curtains.

"Are you hungry again?" I ask Pip, tickling his ears. He definitely seems to be making up for not eating all those days he was ill. "Come on then, let's go find you some food."

And me some water. Lots of water. And possibly painkillers as well.

In the kitchen I find Winnie, already starting to brew the second dose of my potion.

"Are you the only one up?" I ask, stretching my arms above my head as I stagger towards her.

"Uh huh." She gives me a sly smile. "I think I wore Trent

out last night. He's dead to the world. I'm assuming you did the same to those mates of yours. I've not heard a peep from them this morning."

I shake my head. "Nope." I rub my temples and run the faucet. "I drank too much and got put to bed like a naughty schoolgirl."

Winnie drops her wooden spoon into the mixture and looks at me.

"But they joined you in bed, right?"

"As far as I am aware," I say, glugging down water, "no, I slept alone. That's if you don't count Pip." I point to my pet who is now snuffling down the remains of spaghetti bolognese Azlan left out for him.

Winnie gapes at me like I lost my marbles. She rests her hand on my forehead. "Are you sick? Or simply mad?"

"Neither."

"Five hot men – all clearly wanting to rip your clothes off. Why didn't you take advantage of that?"

"I tried. I got nervous. And I drank too much."

"Why?"

"Because five, Winnie, five!"

"I admit it is rather a lot."

"Yeah, you don't say." Pip squeaks from the floor and I can't help thinking he's on my side on this one. "It's intimidating. Hence the need for alcohol."

"So you don't want to be sleeping with all of them? I mean, it's fine if you don't, obviously. I'm just sort of surprised. I thought the fated mate bond made your mate kind of irresistible."

"Well, yeah, it does. And I'm not saying I don't, it's just …"

"Complicated."

"Yep."

"One thing I've learned from hanging out with you, Rhi, is that nothing in your life is ever straightforward. But one thing I've also seen is that you always find a way through."

"They say they're not going to be jealous, Winnie," I say lowering my voice as my eyes dart to the door, "they even say they'd like to share me."

"Shit, Rhi, that is seriously hot."

"But the practicalities, Winnie. You know those guys. I can't see how they aren't going to get jealous ... and violent."

"I think you'd be surprised. And in the fairytale of Queen Æðelflæd–"

"Woah, Winnie, that fairytale is for kids. There is nothing in there about their bedroom antics."

"Exactly, in the children's versions there aren't, but in the adult version–"

"That's a fairytale, Winnie. Probably written by some horny dude with too vivid an imagination. This is real life."

Winnie lays her hand on my shoulder. "They are crazy about you, Rhi. You have no idea how crazy. They were sort of unhinged when you went missing. Hell, the man in black went charging straight into the Wolves of Night compound, all guns blazing, because he thought they were holding you captive. I think you'll find a way to make this work. You're destined to be together – literally destined."

I nod, because I agree with her. More and more, as my story unfolds, I'm beginning to trust in fate, to let her take me where I need to go. And these men, as crazy as it may seem, are important to me and I can't imagine letting any of them go. Which means I'm going to have to find a way to make it work between us all. Especially in the bedroom.

Pip bumps his snout against my ankle and licks the exposed skin.

There's something else I've been wanting to ask my best friend.

"Winnie, what do you know about familiars?"

Winnie's eyes narrow and then she peers down at Pip.

"Is this a general question or do you want to know for a specific reason?"

"General," I squeak, sounding nowhere near convincing.

Winnie rolls her eyes at me. "We're talking about Pip, right?"

"I honestly don't know. Familiars are meant to protect magicals from danger, aren't they? And while I love Pip to bits and he's a great friend and everything," I shrug, "he hasn't exactly stopped me from landing in trouble."

Pip snorts in an outraged manner and Winnie laughs.

"Yeah, he's not exactly the best guard dog but I still love him to bits."

"Me too."

Winnie picks up the wooden spoon and stirs the potion.

"They say familiars are spirits that take an animal form – occasionally a human one," she says.

"Like a ghost?"

"I don't know. It's not really my area of expertise. And I think the practice of familiars died out long ago."

We both look down at Pip who is now chewing on my shoelace. When the lace tickles the back of his throat, he gags and spits it out.

"Charming," I mutter.

"We still need that Cloudpuff," Winnie says. "Do you remember where you saw it?"

"Yes," I say, "I'll go fetch some now. I could do with some fresh air."

"Alone?" Winnie says as I head towards the door, Pip trotting alongside me.

"No, Pip's coming too."

"I don't think that's a good–" Winnie calls after me, but I've already grabbed my coat and am out the door.

A walk on my own out here in the empty landscape might be just what I need to stop my head from pounding and line my thoughts in order. And not just about my mates but about my mom's vision too. My mates seem to think her vision was correct, that what she saw is already playing out. Christopher Kennedy will come for me. He won't stop until he's destroyed me. But there's this niggling feeling inside me that that isn't it. That we've misunderstood, missed something. And I can't shift it.

The winter sun creeps over the horizon as Pip and I walk away from the mansion and across the fields, heading in the direction the beast took me yesterday. The sky turns slowly gray above us and the air bitterly cold. I peer down at my pig wondering if I should have insisted he wore that cardigan Winnie found him.

I haven't told anyone else about what else my aunt revealed. About Pip. About having to let him go. Because that isn't happening and I'm scared that if I tell them about that part, they'll insist that I have to. And then we really are going to fall out.

"Are you cold?" I ask him.

He snorts, shaking out his body and trotting on ahead of me. In the distance I can see the tall stalks of Cloudpuff growing beside a ditch. I plunge my cold hands deeper into my jacket pockets, crunching them into fists and picking up my pace. I only need a couple of the giant plants but the stalks are thicker than I realized and when I fail to snap them in half, I'm forced to use my magic to sear through the woody stems. I lay the first stalk, with its small white winter flowers, across my lap, and tackle another. I'm half way through slicing the stalk when something niggles at the periphery of my awareness.

Magicals.

I snap up my head and peer out towards the horizon. The sky is covered in a thick blanket of cloud and the light is murky but I swear I can see movement – the tiniest dot of movement out there.

Automatically, I clutch my aunt's locket, resting against my clavicle, thanking my lucky stars I was sensible enough to wear it.

Pip's snuffling in among the tall plants, his nose wet with dew. I hiss his name and beckon him close, remaining in my crouched position as I watch that dot, my senses primed that way too.

The dot grows bigger and bigger, multiplying into two, three dots, and soon it's clear those dots are people. Three people, one dressed in the long dark cloak of an enforcer.

Friends or enemies? I don't know. But I need to warn the others.

There's someone coming! I yell out in my mind and then through my bond, hoping one of my mates will be up by now and might hear me. Then I pick up Pip and start sprinting back towards the house. No magic comes hurtling over my head, no sign at all that I've been seen, and when I reach the crumbling wall that marks the boundary of the garden belonging to the old mansion, I meet Azlan striding quickly my way.

I grab his arm.

"You'll be seen," I hiss at him, twisting my head to search for the magicals – one woman, one man and the enforcer still walking this way.

"They can't see us," Azlan whispers, also peering that

way. "There's a shield around the house which makes it invisible to others. But they can hear us, smell us."

"Do you know who they are?"

"Silas," he says, stepping in front of me. "He was with me when we found this house."

"Is he a friend?"

Azlan's eyes narrow. "I can't be sure."

I hug Pip closer to my chest, whispering at him to be quiet and we stand there and watch the three people walk straight towards us, pausing several yards before the perimeter of the wall. This close I notice a difference about the enforcer's cloak. On the front a crest has been sewn onto the fabric – made from scarlet thread. The other woman and man wear similar emblems pinned to their long winter coats. A closed fist.

I don't know what it means. It's not something I've ever seen before, but it has Azlan frowning.

"There's nothing here," the woman says, swinging her gaze right over us, her eyes not seeing us at all.

"There was. The old mansion was right here. I made a note of its position and I remember that dip and those trees." The enforcer takes a step forward, narrowing his eyes and staring right at us. I hold my breath. "Something's not right here."

"Could be a shield," the woman says, flinging back her arm and firing a bolt of magic right at us.

I gasp and flinch, but the bolt smacks against something unseen in the sky, sparks and shatters to the ground, singeing the grass.

"Did you hear that?" the woman says, her eyes alert and I curse myself for being so dumb.

"Yes, a shield," the enforcer says, lifting his hand as if he's feeling the air for magic.

Azlan grabs my elbow and holds it tight.

The enforcer takes another step forward and I feel Azlan's body grow tense.

"It could be a decoy," the other man says.

"No, those were werebeast prints we saw down by the stream. They're here."

I step closer to Azlan, my blood running cold.

"Azlan!" the enforcer yells. "I know you're there. I know this is your magic and I know you have the girl. Hand her over now and no one will be hurt."

I glance towards my mate, who in turn glares at his former colleague.

When there's no reply, the woman and man fling more magic at the shield, but once again it holds, their magic falling down to the ground.

"It's no use," the enforcer hisses to the other two. "This is Azlan Kennedy. We won't be able to break through his magic. We'll have to come back with reinforcements – with the Lord Protector himself."

The woman doesn't seem convinced. She steps forward, arms raised, until she hits something invisible in front of her, yards from where we stand. She feels along it with her palms, her nose twitching.

"I can smell something cooking."

I peer back to the house.

Azlan takes a step forward, his entire body rigid and alert.

The enforcer steps forward too, so he's standing next to the woman. They're so close I can see the color of their eyes. Hers a brown, his a cool blue, staring straight at me, making me shiver.

"I know you're there, Azlan," he whispers. "And I know you know just how foolish this is. The girl's a menace, a danger, a threat to our country. So make sure you're on the right side of history and hand her in – before you're forced to."

Azlan's broad shoulders rise and fall but he doesn't move, and he doesn't say a word.

The other enforcer shakes his head as if he's disappointed, then he turns to the others.

"It's fine," he says. "They're not going anywhere. There's no escape – nowhere to go – and reinforcements will be here before nightfall."

Azlan spins me around and marches me back to the house.

"Shouldn't we take them out – stop them from calling for those reinforcements?" I hiss at Azlan before he shoves me through the door.

Azlan shakes his head. "It's not possible. If they don't check in, then reinforcements will come looking for them anyway. Either way, they're coming and we're leaving. Right now."

14

R^{hi}

"Get your things," Azlan says, marching towards the stairs and calling Stone's name.

I hurry into the kitchen, the Cloudpuff still in my hand.

"What's wrong?" Winnie asks, registering my face as she looks up from the table where she's sitting on Trent's lap, sipping tea.

"There's someone here."

"Who?"

"An enforcer and two others – magicals who work for Christopher Kennedy. They were looking for us." Winnie leaps up from Trent's lap, spilling most of her tea in the process. "It's okay," I tell her. "They can't get through the shield, but they think they've found us. They've called in for reinforcements. Azlan says we have to leave."

Winnie's face pales and she stands dumbstruck.

"Winnie, the potion."

"Is there time?" she says, glancing at the Cloudpuff in my fist.

"We're going to have to make time."

Winnie nods and turns to Trent.

"Will you pack up our stuff? I mean there isn't much, just the–"

"I'm on it Winnie. You help Rhi."

When he's out of the kitchen, I ask Winnie if she told Trent what we were brewing.

"No, of course not and he didn't pry."

I smile at her. "He is the best."

"Yep," she says. "I know you have five extremely hot dudes and I only have one but mine is far better."

"Hmmm," I say and Winnie laughs, plucking the Cloudpuff from my hands and beginning to grate the stalks.

It's only a few minutes later that I'm drinking another dose of the potion and everyone else is back in the kitchen.

"Where are we going?" Spencer asks when we're all gathered.

Several of us speak at once.

I shake my head at all the suggestions. "We're going to the Albany convent," I say firmly.

"The Albany convent," Tristan says, "are you crazy? We're still sticking to that plan?"

"Of course, we are. Nothing's changed. They're still after us. Like they were yesterday. Like they are today."

"It's too dangerous," Tristan says.

"It's not," I say. "Your dad and everyone else thinks I'm out here and the last place they'll expect me to turn up is at the Albany Convent. We can sneak in, search for that prophecy and then leave."

Everyone starts telling me how stupid this plan is. Everyone but Stone.

"Rhi's right," he says, which is a sentence I never expected to hear fall from Professor Stone's mouth. "We need to see that prophecy. We need to understand what it really says. All we have is second-hand garbled bullshit. We need the truth."

His best friend considers him. "You truly believe it will help?"

"Those prophecies aren't some two-bit fortune-telling hack crap, Azlan. Over the centuries, they've been proven to be accurate. If there is one about Rhianna, we need to see it."

"Okay, then," Azlan says. "Stone and I will head to the convent. The rest of you will go to the Mulhony caves and we'll meet you there."

I shake my head vehemently. "We're stronger together and we're not splitting up again. Ever. Winnie and Trent will go to the Mulhony caves. The rest of us are going to the convent."

"You think I'm going to agree to being left behind?" Winnie says.

"Winnie," I say, "this is my battle – our battle," I add, pointing to my mates, "not yours. You've already done enough. Go to the caves with Trent and wait for us there." She shakes her head as adamantly as I had done. "Winnie, we need your brains and Trent's expertise intact. Please."

Winnie glances at her boyfriend, then caves. "Okay, but only if you promise to take one of these," she presses one of the radios Trent was building yesterday into my hands, "so we can keep in contact. Plus, you'd better come back and–"

"We will," I say firmly.

"This is all good and well," Spencer says, looking

anxiously towards the door, "except, how are we getting out of here?"

My shoulders slump.

"It's a good question," I admit. "Azlan?" I know he spent most of yesterday poring over his map. I also know there's an enforcer and two others standing guard outside the property, Winnie's car isn't big enough to fit all of us inside and the last time Renzo tried to transport so many people it nearly killed him.

"Silas and the others are no problem," Azlan says in a way that leaves me in no doubt.

"But we can't walk all the way to the Gray Isle," Spencer insists. "It would take us forever and Kennedy's forces would catch up with us."

"Barone," Stone says.

"Will not be transporting us," I say. "It's too dangerous."

"I'll do it," he says.

"You won't," I say firmly.

"What would you suggest instead then?" Stone asks.

But I have no ideas.

None at all.

"Erm," Trent says, scratching his head. "There are some broomsticks in the attic."

Stone bursts out laughing but Renzo's eyes light up like a kid's on their birthday and he runs from the room.

I know I'm missing something,

"Broomsticks?" I say to Winnie. "I'm assuming this is relevant somehow."

"Broomsticks, Rhi. It's how magicals got around back in the olden days."

"Really? I thought that was more fairytale bullshit stuff."

"No, I mean it wasn't super common. It's a pretty dangerous method of travel and so most magicals were happy enough to stick with horses and coaches. Then the steam train and the motorcar came along and the practice of broomstick flying pretty much died out."

"Because it's girly as shit," Spencer scoffs.

Winnie fixes him with her most penetrating stare. "Do you have a problem with 'girly shit', Spencer Moreau?"

Spencer's gaze drops to the floor. "Errr, no."

"They also banned broomstick travel," Trent pipes up, "for being dangerous. It's not like a broomstick comes with a seatbelt or an airbag."

"But you think we could use them to take us to the Albany convent?" I ask Trent.

"It was just an observation," he mutters, glancing at Azlan.

"Do any of you actually know how to fly a broomstick?" I ask the others.

Azlan, Stone and Spencer all scoff, like the idea of any of them climbing onto a broomstick is the silliest thing ever considered. Obviously far too girly for such big burly men like them. I roll my eyes. But both Trent and Winnie nod and after a pause Tristan does too.

"Even though it's illegal?" I say, raising an eyebrow at Winnie.

"We used to do it behind my mom's back," Winnie confesses. "We used to steal the broom, take it out back and bewitch it, take turns to have a ride. It's really not as dangerous as Trent is making out."

"That's because you're really, really good at magic, Winnie," Trent says, smiling at her. "We could never get our broomstick under control. It used to kick us off like a bucking bronco! That's how I broke my arm when I was ten – although I told my mom and dad I fell out of a tree."

"And you used to do this too?" I ask Tristan, surprised.

Tristan Kennedy is all about looking cool. Riding broomsticks doesn't seem to fit his image.

"Sometimes, when I was bored," he says while Spencer gapes at him like his best friend just confessed to having three dicks. "It's not that hard."

Trent meets my eye. "It is. Those two are just ..." He shrugs just as Renzo returns with his arms full of broomsticks. Ancient-looking broomsticks made from twigs and sticks tied together with string that must be about to disintegrate.

"There are more up in the attic," he says, dumping them on the ground. "Along with lots of other weird shit. The people who lived here were freaky."

I reach down and pick one up, the handle had been sanded down and polished and despite the advent of time, is still smooth to the touch. The broom is also lighter than I expected it to be, so light I can almost feel its buoyancy.

"How do I make it work?" I ask Tristan.

"You heard Trent," Azlan says. "Broom flying is dangerous."

"So is staying in this mansion," I snipe, "and do you have any better ideas?"

Azlan considers this question. "No," he admits, "I don't."

I turn back to Tristan. He sweeps his hand through his hair uncomfortably and takes a step forward.

"Broomsticks are female," he says.

"Of course they are," Winnie says, her voice dripping with sarcasm. "Because housework is women's work."

"I didn't make the rules. They just are, okay?"

"Really?" Trent says. "I never noticed that."

"No offense," Tristan says, wrapping his hand around mine, "but that's probably why you could never stay on. You need to ask her permission to ride her."

Spencer sniggers but I can tell Tristan is serious about this.

"And how do I do that?"

"Hmmm," he groans, "it's just something I knew how to do. I don't know how to explain it." He closes his eyes, his magic humming in the air, and the end of the broomstick lifts off the ground, the entire thing hovering two feet from the floorboards.

I test my weight against the broom, it gives a little, but remains in the air as if it's floating on water.

"Give it a try," Tristan tells me.

I rest my backside against the trunk of the broom and when I'm sitting on it, I lift my feet carefully from the ground. The broomstick supports my weight perfectly but I have to grip the handle tightly, working my core to remain balanced on the skinny piece of wood.

I grin. Renzo is wrestling with a broomstick in a corner, the thing hissing and writhing at him and Spencer is struggling to get another broom to lift from the ground.

"How do I make it go?"

"With your magic."

I huff. Why is that the answer to everything?

I let my magic curl around the broom, sensing like I had with the dragon, that it has a magic of its own, a sleepy dormant magic that's only just emerging and awakening. I go on instinct, my magic coiling and curling into this old magic, until the broom is vibrating beneath me.

Forward, I say in my head and the broom shoots across the room, leaving me hanging on for dear life.

"Stop!" I yell and the broom comes to a screeching halt, sending me hurtling forward to the floor.

Tristan offers me a hand and helps me up to my feet.

"We're finding another way," Azlan says.

"It was my first go. Give me a chance!" I jump back on the broom and try again, this time urging the broom forward more slowly. I glide forward, swinging to the left when I ask it to and then to the right, circling the room and stopping right in front of Azlan.

"Looks like we've found our way to the Gray Isle."

"Will it be any quicker than walking?" Stone asks skeptically.

"These things can go really fast if you let them," Trent says. "I mean not as fast as Winnie's car, but a lot faster than walking or traveling by most normal forms of transport."

"I really don't understand why people stopped using them?" I say.

"On account of the falling off and smashing their skulls open," Azlan harrumphs.

I admit that doesn't sound like much fun, but neither does falling back into the hands of Christopher Kennedy.

Winnie, Trent and Tristan spend the next few minutes showing the others how to make their brooms work and how to ride them. Renzo brims with enthusiasm. The others less so, grumbling and bitching the entire time. Once they have them working though, Stone seems a little more on board with the idea, especially when he manages to do an impressive swerve around the room. Spencer and Azlan – the biggest of our group – do look slightly ridiculous hunched over their brooms, like giant grizzly bears clinging to the teeniest, tiniest of branches, but tough shit. Escaping Chistopher Kennedy's clutches is worth a little dented pride.

Once we're all confident enough, Winnie goes over some safety precautions, suggesting we all use our magic to lock ourselves to our brooms, refrain from any crazy maneuvers (she directs this comment towards Renzo) and remembering to listen to our broom.

"It knows better than you do how to fly," she says.

"So how are we going to do this?" I ask. "As soon as we pass through the shield, we'll be seen."

"We'll leave out the back. That will put some distance between them and us before we're spotted."

"Pip?" I say.

We all glance down at my pet who for once has been sitting patiently without complaint while the rest of us have been playing with our broomsticks.

"I can't see little man sitting good and proper on the back of your broom," Renzo says and I have to agree. Pip has never had a great sense of balance or acrobatics.

"Want me to knock him out?" Azlan asks.

I peer down at Pip with a look of sympathy.

"Sorry Pip," I say. He stands up alarmed about to snort at me but in the next moment, Azlan waves his arms, and Pip slumps to the floor.

"I'll put him in my rucksack," Renzo offers.

I scoop Pip up and hand him over.

"Okay, but, you heard Winnie, no fancy tricks. Our aim is to get there in one piece as quickly as possible."

"And when we get there, how exactly are we getting into the convent?" Spencer asks. "Isn't the convent on the Gray Isle? That place is surrounded by haunted waters. You know there'll be–"

"Haunted places are not so bad," Tristan says with an unconvincing shrug. "Trekking through the Haunted Forest is how I left the academy a few days ago."

"Okay," I say, squaring my shoulders and taking a deep inhale. This is probably as stupid as our last plan to rescue Spencer. Then again all my plans seem pretty stupid and yet somehow – despite the odds – they work out. I just have to trust in myself and these five men. We'll make this work. We'll find a way. "Let's go."

We stride through the old mansion to the room at the back of the house. It's long and grand and I assume it was used for parties and dancing. Glass doors line its back wall and I can almost imagine all those fancy gentlemen and ladies spilling out onto the terrace with a drink in hand.

Stone unlocks one of the doors; a cold wind sweeping in immediately and sending the usual ghostly dust spiraling up into the air. We step out onto the terrace. There's an old dried-up fountain and several large plant pots, cracked and broken. The carcass of a dead bird lies sprawled across the old paving stones, the fine bones of its wings as white as the clouds above our heads.

I hope it's not an omen, a sign.

"We're heading north," Azlan says, pointing up into the sky. "You'll all follow me. Winnie, Trent, you'll need to head east about an hour into our journey. Then it's straight from there to the coast. You'll hit the caves when you hit the sea."

Winnie nods.

"We'll meet you there later, once we've read the prophecy," I confirm.

"Everybody happy?" Azlan asks.

Spencer snorts, clearly anything but happy.

"What happens if we get separated?" Tristan asks.

"We won't," I say adamantly.

"It's better to be prepared."

"If you're separated from the group, head for the beach across from the Gray Isle and wait for the others there."

"And if they don't turn up?"

"There's the bond," I say, "we can feel each other through the bond."

Spencer fidgets on his feet and I know why. The bond between us isn't sealed. I can't feel him like I can feel the others. That connection isn't cemented. I almost feel guilty about it, but we're not there yet and so it's just the way it's going to have to be.

"Let's go," I say, fearing we've already wasted too much time.

My broom obeys my magic, rising from the ground and I sit on the polished wood, gripping the handle. Then I kick off from the ground and soar up into the clouded sky.

It takes a moment for the enforcer and his companions to spot us. There's a shout from below us and then magic streams towards us like bright fireworks. We dodge and weave between them and plunge our way up into the thick cloud. The magic stops. They can't see us anymore. They've lost us.

I let out an exhale and shake the hair from my face, counting those around me just to be sure we have everyone here.

"You still have Pip?" I call out to Renzo.

"Yep," he answers, patting the rucksack on his back.

Then I grip the handle of my broom and dip my head.

We made it.

Somehow, by the skin of our teeth, we made it again. I just pray our luck will last.

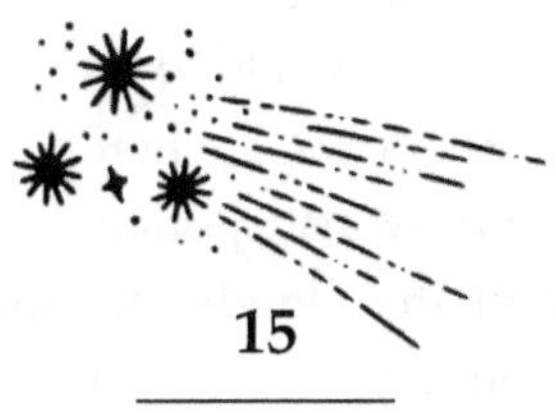

15

S pencer

I'M PERCHED on the smallest piece of wood known to man, clinging on for dear life as the thing vibrates and shakes beneath me. I swear any minute the thing is going to fling me off. It's the most fucking uncomfortable method of transport I've ever experienced, certainly not designed for big people like me.

Rhi on the other hand, she's loving it, whooping and squealing as she glides through the air, her long dark hair streaming out behind her, her eyes bright with excitement and her cheeks all flushed.

That crazy motherfucker Barone seems equally at home, turning somersaults and doing loop-de-loops even though he's carrying the pig and it earns him a lecture from Rhi every time.

I take my right hand from the handle, the broom

wobbling violently beneath me, and swipe the sweat quickly from my eyes, before clutching the wood in both hands again. Then I squint into the distance. Not that I can see a thing. We're flying above the cloud layer so we can't be seen from below. It worked a treat when we left the mansion. Kennedy's men had only just spotted us before we plunged into the wet mist of the clouds and they'd lost us. Sure, they'd fired at us anyway. One bolt sailing mighty close below my feet, but we got away nonetheless and have been flying for four hours straight now.

"How about a break?" I yell at the man in black. My fucking backside is beginning to cramp and I swear my palms are blistering.

"No point," he yells back, "we'll be there in another twenty minutes."

I shake my head in disbelief, regretting the action almost immediately as the broom teeters to one side.

"Fuck." We must be traveling at some fucking speed. No wonder my face feels like it's been stretched to twice its size. I work my jaw and soon Azlan is signaling for us to stop. We hover above the clouds, the moisture catching the rays of sunshine and painting fine rainbows beneath our feet.

"The convent is somewhere beneath us," Azlan says. "I'm going to descend and see where exactly we are, check out what I can see."

"No." Rhi shakes her head, her broom somehow remaining perfectly still even with that motion. "You're gigantic, Azlan. Someone will notice you swooping about in the sky – you look more like a flying gorilla than a bird."

"Thanks," he says, flatly.

"I'll go," she continues, "I'm less noticeable and besides, I have my cloaker." She points to the locket hanging around her neck. "No one will see me."

She doesn't wait for any one of us to argue. Instead, she dives straight through the cloud, disappearing into its misty depths and then it's the five of us, looking like the biggest bunch of dorks on earth.

"I fucking hate this thing," I say as the broom begins to vibrate, rattling my bones and making the beast inside me growl.

"Really, man?" Barone says, sitting with his arms folded over his chest, not holding the broom at all. "I fucking love it."

"I just want to get my feet on solid ground," I hiss, wrestling with the handle again.

Rhi soars back through the cloud, her face covered in a fine layer of moisture. She licks her lips and dries her eyes with the sleeve of her coat.

"We're right above the beach," she says, "the convent's some distance away across the sea and on the isle. I can't see anyone obviously on the lookout. I think we're safe to go down and land on the isle."

"Land on the isle?" Stone shakes his head. "The only way into the convent is via the water, there's a passageway that leads right into the heart of the building."

"Okay, let's head down to the beach then," Rhi says.

Once again, she doesn't wait for a response, dipping down into the cloud and forcing us all to follow.

As soon as my feet touch the soft sand, I fling the broom away and nearly drop to my knees, tempted to kiss the damp ground. If I can help it, I'm never ever flying on one of those damn ridiculous things again.

Behind us the sea crashes onto the shore, the roar loud in our ears, and a thick mist hovers above the water. In the distance we see the craggy isle, emerging from the shifting fog and the outline of the convent built into the gray rock.

Stone's right. There's no obvious place to land. And the convent windows, all long narrow slots carved into the stone, are too narrow to fly through.

"Any ideas?" Stone asks.

"A boat?" Barone suggests.

"Great idea, genius," Stone scoffs, "but where do you intend to get one of those?"

"Over there?" the assassin says, pointing up the beach where the sand is dry and tall spindly weeds are determined to claim the land. Huddled among them is an old wooden rowing boat.

"It probably has a hole," Stone mutters, but Rhi's already striding that way, peering into its hull.

"Looks good to me," she says, pulling the rope tied to its bow from the sand and beginning to tug on it. We all rush to help her, each taking a grip of the rope and heaving the boat over the sand and down towards the shore. The boat bobs as it hits the waves, salty spray slapping our faces and the cold water making my legs ache. The waves become higher, thrashing ferociously around us as we plow further into the depths and soon my clothes are soaked through and my teeth chattering.

"Get in the boat!" someone yells as another wave crashes over my head and then we're all scrabbling inside, the thing rocking violently and threatening to throw us out.

We use our magic to propel the boat forward, eyes stinging with salt, boat rocking up over the waves and slapping back down. For a moment I think we'll never make it past the surf but somehow we do and then we're floating in flat water, a freezing mist crawling in around us.

"Keep your magic active and alert," Tristan says, waving his hand through the impenetrable fog. "There are things out here, I can feel it."

I peer into the gloomy depths of the mist. A few weeks ago I'd have laughed at such bullshit. I never believed the tales of spirits and ghouls lurking about in forests and other supposedly haunted places. But then, I also didn't believe in dragons. I certainly thought they no longer existed. Now I'm prepared to give anything the benefit of the doubt.

As we sail deeper into the mist, the temperature seems to drop by several degrees and it was already a cold day. We use our magic to dry our clothes out but Rhi still shivers and we all pull our coats more firmly around our bodies, Barone lifting the collar of his leather jacket.

The sea is a lifeless gray color, the seabed lost within its depths and the water remains still and calm around us, despite the constant roar of the waves on the shore.

The mist becomes denser as we drive the boat further, so dense I struggle to see Stone sitting right in front of me or Barone behind me. I can hear his heavy breath though, the slight wheeze in his throat, plus the splash of the boat as it cuts through the water, until the density of the fog seems to swallow all the sound, muffling it completely and the darkness is so oppressive, all the color leeches from the place. No ghouls though. No spirits. Although, I swear I can feel the crackling of something dark and magical just out of sight, watching us, observing us.

I let my own magic flow strongly through my body, bold and aggressive, challenging whatever's out there, and maybe it is that that holds it at bay, keeps it away.

I start to relax.

I should know better. Hasn't dueling taught me that? You can never fucking relax. That's when you're at your weakest. That's when they come for you.

The boat slows.

"You hear that?" Tristan asks from the front of the boat and we all strain our ears.

It's that whistling sound, that wheeze in Renzo's lungs. Except it isn't in his lungs. It's somewhere else in among the mists, whining, pleading. I strain my ears even harder, because I swear, goddamn I swear, it sounds just like ... just like ...

"Aunt?" Rhi calls out.

But it wasn't. I swear it was my brother. Calling to me. Begging me to come play. Like we used to. Racing through the trees, chasing one another, rolling around in the dirt.

It can't be real. It can't be. And yet, it sounds like him, just like him, so much so that the breath catches in my lungs and my magic wanes, fades.

My brother's isn't the only voice I hear. I hear my Maman's voice too and my Papa's and the were's, Jacob, from that cell. I see their faces peering at me from under the surface of the water. Their eyes filled with sadness, and the mist crowds around me, closer and closer like the walls of that cell. The memory of all that pain returning to my body.

"Spence!" my brother calls out.

And then he's there right beneath the surface, the water rippling and distorting his perfect face. But he's there. Right there, reaching up towards me, promising to save me.

All I have to do is take his hand.

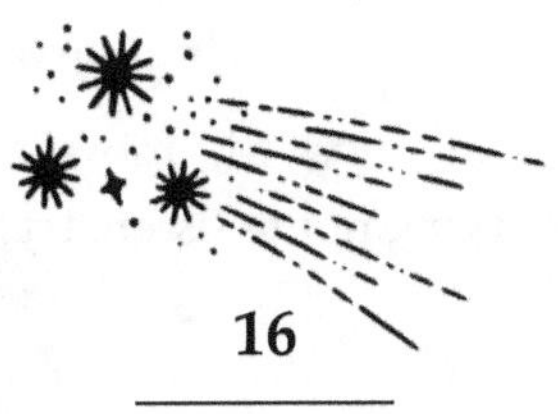

16

zlan

"It's not real!" I shout across the strange sounds ringing in the mist. "We need to keep moving. It's not real."

Although it sounds real. So very real. Like she's just there, hovering somewhere unseen in the mist. All I'd have to do is follow that voice and I'd find her.

I'd forgotten her voice. Soft, gentle, soothing. It's been so long since I heard it, so long since she kissed my cheek and stroked my head. It slices right through my heart, all that pain I've kept suppressed deep deep down inside me, rising to the surface.

I miss her. I miss her so very much.

I strain to hear what she's saying, what she's telling me.

But my mother's isn't the only voice I hear. There are others too. Drowning out her words. Taunting me. Men I've killed. Lives I've taken.

They swoop closer, sharp fingers scraping at my flesh, angry faces sneering and hissing at me.

I screw my eyes shut.

It isn't real.

I shove the boat forward, moving it more quickly through the water, trying not to listen, trying not to hear.

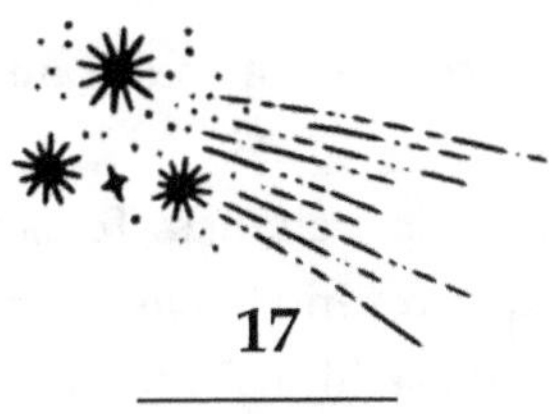

17

S tone

THE MIST IS SUFFOCATING, pressing on my lungs, sinking into my throat, blindfolding the light from my eyes.

But I can hear. Fuck, can I hear. All the voices from long ago. Friends I lost as a kid on the street. Comrades who died in battles at the front. People who've passed from my life. Their voices whirl in the mist, rising and falling like some sick chorus.

And buried among them, a deep voice, a voice that stirs forgotten memories from long ago. A man's voice. One that sounds just like my own.

My dad's.

"Pops?" I stutter.

But my own voice is drowned out in the swell of voices. I swing my head around, searching for him. I don't care if this is a chimera. I don't care if it's all an illusion.

I want to see him. I want to see him one last time.

The voices gurgle and I know they're right there, waiting for me below the surface. I grip the side of the boat, lean right over until my face hits the cold water, and it floods into my nose and my mouth.

It's my chance. My one chance. To say all the things I've always wanted to say to him. To ask him all the questions I've always wanted to ask him. To tell him that I'm trying to be a man that would make him proud.

I tip further into the water, the voices welcoming me towards them. And then a large hand claps down onto my shoulder and drags me back into the boat.

Azlan.

18

R^{hi}

"It isn't real!" Azlan calls out.

And I know he's right. We were warned these waters were haunted and Tristan explained what might lurk out here in the mist.

It doesn't matter.

The voice that calls me is so vivid, so alive, so real. My heart won't accept it as a fake. It just won't.

"Aunt," I whisper back to her as she calls my name through the mist, just like she'd call me back into the house in the evenings. "Are you there?"

She laughs, and I can see her face, her head thrown back, her mouth pulled wide in a smile, her eyes alight.

"Come back," I urge, "come back to me."

I was so mad at her, so angry. All of this could have been

so much easier if only she'd told me the truth, if only she'd explained.

All of those emotions fade now and all that remains is a hungry ache in the pit of my stomach, a longing that hurts so much.

It's been so hard with her gone. So lonely. So difficult. I miss her every single day. I just want her back. Back with me now.

As if understanding me, she reaches out to me, hands stroking at my skin, many hands, not just hers, stroking, caressing me gently, and then tugging at me, slowly urging me closer and closer towards the water.

"We can be together again," she promises, and I let her take me, let them take me.

Until I feel something else in my stomach. The bonds, pulling me just as hard in the other direction, back towards my mates.

Azlan's words ring in my ears.

It isn't real.

I push back against the pull towards the water.

"Not yet," I say, "I'm not ready to leave just yet."

At my words, the grasps become stronger, more violent and more biting. They drag me now and I fight them, swiping at my skin, struggling in their grip.

"No!" I scream. And then I have other hands, warm hands, solid hands, strong hands, gripping my arm and my shoulders, hauling me back.

My mates.

The ghouls hiss at me as I'm snatched from their grasp but not before one swipes forward and rips the locket from around my neck, sinking with it into the water.

"My locket!" I cry, diving forward.

"No, Rhi, No!" Tristan yells, his hand the one gripping my arm. "Let it go!"

"But it's the only thing I have," I cry, swinging my head to look at him through the thick fog.

Azlan crouches next to his cousin, holding onto my shoulder.

"No, Rhi, you have us now, all of us."

My aunt's voice calls to me in the distance and I close my eyes.

He's right. I have them now. My mates, my family. I'm no longer alone.

I take a deep inhale, grounding myself.

"They're too strong," Tristan says. "You need to drive them away."

I stare at him. Me?

I shake my head. "I'm not strong enough."

"You are," Azlan says.

I shake my head more adamantly, tears freezing on my cheeks. I'm not. I nearly succumbed. Nearly let them drag me down into the water.

"Then we do it together," Tristan says. "We combine our magic. Just like before. You remember how?"

This time I nod.

And it's easier. Even easier than before. My magic has always been eager to play with Tristan's, to twist around his and become one. Now it seeks his out, prompting his to come play and my body thrums as our magic spins around one another.

But it doesn't stop there, it nudges at Azlan's too, urging his magic to stream from his hands, and soon all three of our magics twine together.

"How do we do this?" I call out. "How do we make them stop?"

"With light," Tristan says. "We drive away the shadows with light."

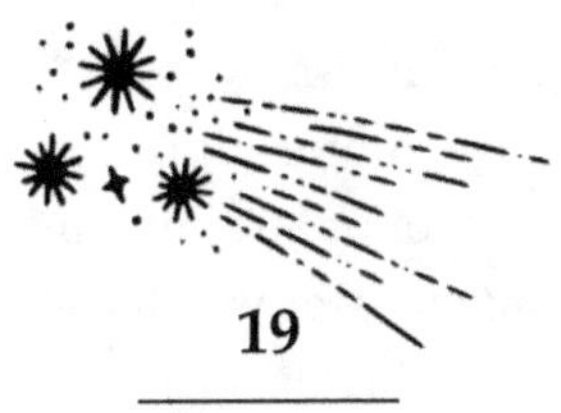

19

S pencer

"RHIANNA!" someone yells. "Rhianna."

And then there's light, white dazzling lights, streaming through the mist and chasing away the shadows and all they contain. I squint against the light, raising my hand to shade my eyes and see just where that light is coming from.

Rhi.

Standing in the boat, the wooden planks white like the ribs of a skeleton, the light pouring from the palms of her hands. Her face is locked with determination, the man in black's palm resting on her right shoulder and Tristan's on her arm.

"Well, fuck me," Barone says from behind me, clutching the rucksack with the pig in his lap, "now ain't that something to behold."

It is, but it doesn't last long. The light races away and Rhi slumps forward.

"Come on," Tristan says, grabbing her hand. "Who knows how long that will last."

And this time we motor the boat forward like it's a fucking speed boat, all of us straining our magic to push the boat through the water, water that feels thick and heavy like treacle, cold water slapping over the sides and lashing at our arms and legs, catching on our legs as if the water itself is trying to catch us and entrap us, but finally, finally, the mist thins and the Gray Isle itself looms above us, ragged and cragged, the convent – weathered and bare – stretching up from the rocks.

We stop the boat again, catching our breaths, Rhi hunched over her knees and Professor Stone spitting into the ocean.

"That was fun!" Barone says, grinning like a maniac.

I consider smacking him right in the mouth.

"You like being harassed by the dead?" Tristan asks, his face still pale from whatever came for him out there on the water.

"It was like a little reunion with all the people I've ..." he glances towards Rhi, "sent on their way. Good times, man. What a trip!"

"Whatever," I say, eyes scanning the ragged rocks, the sea pounding against them. I can't see any obvious place for us to moor a boat on this island, not without being smashed to smithereens. "How do we reach these books?" I ask.

"There should be a passageway through the rocks. It leads right under the convent," Stone says.

We all scan the rocks and the ocean and finally I spot a slight gap between two high rocks, almost invisible to the naked eye, the flow of water between them the only real giveaway.

"There," I say, pointing, and slowly, with caution, we maneuver the boat in that direction, the gap in the rock suddenly materializing more obviously as we approach it. The gap is narrow though, barely wide enough for our boat, but once we're there a current whips us along, through the rocks and then right under the convent into a cave covered in seaweed and slime, the light tinged green.

Here the water laps gently against a mooring and stone steps reach up from the water.

I swallow, trying once again not to think of that damn dungeon. Of the walls crowding in on me, of the pain and the shame and ... It smells the same down here, damp and dank, the walls lined with cool stone.

"Spencer?" It's Rhi's voice.

The others have moored the boat and tied it to a metal ring driven into the stone. Tristan and Azlan are already out of the boat and on the steps and Stone and Barone are following.

"Okay?" she whispers, concern in her eyes as she offers me her hand.

"Yeah," I say, taking her hand gladly.

Together, we follow the spiraling stone steps upwards. Soon the weak daylight can't penetrate this far and we're plunged into more darkness. Stone forms a ball of light and names, dates and patterns carved into the stone walls are suddenly revealed. I can almost see the past magicals, carving their names before they made their way in or out of the convent.

The staircase is small and narrow, wide enough only for one person and the ceiling so low I'm forced to duck my head. We climb upwards and after a while we can hear noise from above, the wind and the waves.

Stone stops.

"The stairway leads into the heart of the convent. I very much doubt there's going to be anyone here but .... Rhi?"

"I can't feel any magicals," she says.

"I suggest we proceed with caution anyway."

We all nod, a tension stirring through the magic I can feel in the air. Then Stone extinguishes the ball of light and pushes on the door ahead. It's stiff and heavy and he has to use his weight against it before it gives way. We pause. Beyond is what once must have been the chapel of the convent, the ceiling high and carved into great arches, although it's no longer neat and orderly. The pews are all overturned, prayer mats strewn across the floor, tapestries fallen from the walls and goose downing scattered every-where. It looks like a chicken pen after a visit from a particu-larly hungry fox.

The place is empty, although candles flicker from holders on the walls.

I point to one. "Someone's been here."

Stone shakes his head. "They're enchanted. Ever-burning."

"Where are the prophecies?" Rhi asks.

Stone scratches his head. "It's a long time since I visit-ed." He thinks some more, then he motions for us to follow him to the back of the chapel, past the altar and to the back wall. Here the tapestry still hangs, all the way from the high ceiling to the cold stone floor. The light here is so poor, the embroidery on the tapestry is as vibrant as I'm sure it was the day it was weaved – the pictures of magic and magicals, dragons and ghouls, knights and battles, kings and queens.

Stone pushes the heavy tapestry to one side and behind lurks a solid stone door.

"That's the Sacristy," he explains.

"Is that where the prophecy books are kept?" Rhi says, looking anxiously at the heavy door and its giant lock.

"Yes and only scholars can open the door." He lays his palm against the woodwork. "Let's hope I'm still considered one."

He whispers an old incantation, his magic humming, the door eventually doing the same, and then it clicks and he swings it open.

A light flickers on as Stone steps through, but it's dim and the air magically cooled. Given the state of the ancient-looking volumes housed inside elaborate glass cases, I'm not surprised.

"Wow," Rhi says, stepping in after Stone and bending her head to inspect the books. "How old are these?"

"The manuscript of spells is over one thousand years old. Handwritten by a family of witches who formed the first commune. A commune that eventually became this convent." He points to the case with a scroll, a portion unraveled and on display, black elaborate writing framed by the swirl of gilded patterns.

"It's beautiful," Rhi gasps, staring transfixed.

"Where are the books of prophecies?" Azlan asks.

"Here," Stone says, walking toward a wooden case. He tries the doors and finds them locked and when they won't open to his touch, he turns to his friend, I assume to smash the thing to pieces. Instead the man in black rests his fingertips and then his ear against the square door and closes his eyes.

"What's he doing?" Rhi whispers to Stone.

"Azlan has the ability to read other people's spells,"

Stone explains. "He's finding a way to undo or break through the magic."

Whatever magic is keeping the book locked away, it's obviously complex because it takes the man in black almost a quarter of an hour before the doors finally pop open. Behind them lies a thick book, its cover a burgundy leather with golden lettering, bound shut with leather twine. Spilling from the cover are yellowing pages of different sizes and ages, some of the writing visible – a mishmash of different handwriting and styles.

"This book," Stone says, lifting it with much care from its shelf, as if it were a newborn baby, "is a collection of every prediction the ancient seers of the past made. Some are minor, of little importance, and some are considered much more critical. It includes the six prophecies." He unwinds the twine and then lays the book on top of the only desk in the room, clicking his fingers so that the candle above it flickers alight. Then he draws back the cover and peels over the first, second and third pages. "These are the early premonitions. There is one that predicts the Great Flood and one the fall of the Hallian Empire."

"Shit," I mutter, "are they genuine? I mean, they could have been written after the event, or altered to fit the event."

"No, they've been verified. Far greater minds than mine devoted their lives to the study of such premonitions, hoping to reveal how the gift works, how it could be taught and better refined."

He flips over one more page and then he stops.

"This is the one," he says, his blue eyes scanning down the page.

Automatically, we all draw closer, even Barone who I doubt can actually read.

The text is similar to the one on the scroll – handwritten

in a curling calligraphy, the first letter illuminated in scarlet, a small drawing of a crown hovering above the letter, and a gold border framing the text.

"How old is this?" asks Tristan.

Stone flicks the page, behind the manuscript another page has been added to the book, this one typed out. Stone runs his finger over the paragraph. "It was believed to have been written after the reign of Queen Æðelflæd had come to an end. That was the legend associated with this particular prophecy. But no one has been able to verify this and obviously whether Queen Æðelflæd was a real figure or not is much disputed."

"You don't believe she was?" Rhi says.

"I'm an academic, Rhi. I can give you my studied opinion but I'm telling you there is no definitive proof either way."

"Except the story itself."

"Stories can be both true and untrue."

"And somewhere in between," Barone adds.

"What does the prophecy say, Phoenix?" the man in black asks, hovering by the doorway, his eyes flickering out to the chapel like he wants to be away.

Stone turns back to the manuscript but instead of leaning over the page and reading the words, he waves his hand over it instead, his magic sprinkling like snow down onto the words. One by one the words light up gold like the border and a voice rings out from nowhere, a female voice, solemn yet wistful as if the speaker is talking in a trance.

"And she will come again,
    She that fate has anointed,
    She bound with the devotion of five.
    Born a second time.

When the world is dark,
The light hard to find,
She will come again,
From the womb of the future
and the seed of the dark.
She will rise
with power in her veins.
And when the moment strikes,
She will seize the crown,
Where all must go to learn,
Drive away the shadows and the night,
And she will bring the dawn again."

THE VOICE FADES away and the gold lettering fades back to black.

"That's it?" I say, astounded. "That's the damn prophecy we risked our necks to come find? What the hell does that even mean?"

"Apart from the legend of Queen Æðelflæd," Professor Stone says, "there has never been another woman or man who had five known fated mates. One, yes. Two, sometimes. Very, very rarely three. Queen Æðelflæd was the only magical ever known to have five. Most scholars agree that this prophecy predicts there will be another. Another woman."

"And all that crap about dark and light and a crown?" I say with irritation.

"Isn't it clear?" Barone says, his eyes twinkling with awe. "Little rabbit's destined to rule the world."

"That isn't what it says," Rhi mutters, her eyes flicking back and forth over the words.

"It's what it means though," Barone says. "It's your fate to drive out the fuckers in power and rule instead."

Rhi laughs like that's the craziest thing she's ever heard. Part of me can't help agreeing with her. Fuck, I'm head over heels about this girl, but, even if we somehow managed to take out Christopher Kennedy, there is no way all the other powerful magicals in this country would stand back and let an unregistered girl from the wasteland install herself as the next chancellor, or protector, or whatever else she might want to call herself.

And yet there's another part of me that doesn't think that's crazy at all.

Those words made my skin prickle, made my magic buzz, made the beast stir, like it was awakening something inside me, an awareness. As if I was hearing some crucial truth – a truth I'd always known – for the very first time.

"I'm not some queen reincarnated. A few months ago, the magic I knew was limited to growing vegetables, feeding chickens and fighting scumbags."

"Wasn't Queen Æðelflæd just some girl from a back-water village?" Tristan whispers. "You're powerful, Rhi, we all know that and we all feel it too, and when we're together that power seems to amplify. Look what we did just now out on the water! You've seen how my dad is terrorizing the republic – and that's just the stuff we know about. Imagine all the shit he's getting away with in secret. That's the dark-ness and you are the one who is meant to end it."

"You truly believe that?" Rhi asks him.

"Yes. I believe it. I believe that is why fate has brought us together."

To my surprise, Rhi turns to me next. Not to the man in black, or the professor or even the assassin. Me. Perhaps because I am the most skeptical. Being locked and tortured in a dungeon will make you damned cynical.

"What do you think, Spencer?"

I'm leaning against the wall, and I shift my weight from one foot to another.

"I think you're the girl in that prophecy, Rhi. Something in my blood tells me you are. I just wish it was damn clearer, that's all."

She smiles at me. "That would make things a hell of a lot easier, wouldn't it? But what I'm learning is that nothing is easy. Ever."

"No," I say, "it isn't. Not when it comes to you, anyway. I'd say my life has gotten a lot more complicated since you showed up." I smirk at her.

"You ever had dreams about this?" Barone asks her. "When you were young, little rabbit. You ever dream about us? About being powerful?"

She screws up her forehead thinking. "I think I did. I think I did dream of you. I remember this strange sense of déjà vu when I met each of you. Like I'd met you someplace else before."

"That would be the bond," Tristan says assuredly.

"And how about the prophecy? Did you dream about that?" I ask. I've heard about the dreams she had just a few days ago – about needing to heal a beast and a monster. The dragon was that beast. And that monster? No one's said it out loud but I know we're all thinking it was Barone. "Did you dream about being a leader, a queen, someone in charge?"

"No," she says, disbelief in her voice as she shakes her head.

"One of those dreams of yours would be helpful right now, little rabbit."

She chews on her thumb and am I imagining that or is she keeping something back from us?

"Let's go," Azlan says finally. "We've learned all we can from this place. Let's get somewhere safer."

Nobody disputes that idea and we walk the route we've just come, closing the sacristy door behind us and making our way back through the chapel and down into the stairwell. Below us is the green light of the cave and it provides a dim sort of beacon, edging us onward. Stone's the first to climb back into the boat, followed one by one by the rest of us. Then we untie the rope and push away, propelling the vessel back out into the open water.

We're ready for the mist the second time, holding our magic alert and ready, not succumbing to the temptation of the call from the dead.

As the boat emerges from the mist, and the violent surf hurtles us back towards the beach, Rhi swings her gaze around in alarm.

"Someone's here," she hisses as the bow of the boat hits the sand.

"Yes," a voice calls out, "someone is here."

A cold, emotionless voice I've come to know so well by now.

Christopher Kennedy.

20

R^{hi}

Almost on instinct, I reach for the cloaker around my neck. It isn't there. The ghouls snatched it from me out there in the mist and it's lost forever now under the water.

Another part of my past torn away from me.

With another kind of instinct, my five mates stand and form a tight circle around me, removing me from Kennedy's path – wherever the hell he is. I can sense he's nearby but I can't see him at all.

Then he steps silently over the sand dunes ahead of us and I can see he's flanked by others – not ordinary guards or soldiers this time but magicals dressed with that emblem of the fist. Fierce looking – the magical aura around them strong. Kennedy's face remains cased in shadow but none-theless, it's clear he's sneering at us.

"You know, I had a feeling – one doesn't have to be a seer

to perceive these things actually – that you would end up here eventually, Rhianna Blackwaters. I had a feeling you wouldn't be able to resist seeking out this prophecy some among us seem to believe applies to you – the chancellor, Moreau's friend the mutt. It truly is gob-smacking the things that will fall from people's mouths with the right ..."

"Torture," Spencer snarls, his body straining as he struggles to keep the beast contained.

"Encouragement," the Lord Protector corrects with a slight smile. "Of course, the chancellor always was a fool and as for the mutt," he snorts, "those prophecies are not worth the paper they were written on, and this girl is nothing special. Never was. Never will be."

"Then why don't you leave her and us alone," Stone growls. "She's no threat, of no interest. We'll take her over the ocean to Aropia and you'll never have to hear from us again."

"I don't think so, Phoenix Stone. Hope is a very dangerous thing. I'm sure you are aware of that. And if people get the idea in their heads that this girl is someone special, someone who is going to save them from their miserable existences, who knows what that might lead to." He smiles slyly at us. It makes me fucking nervous. "Can you imagine? No, I think it better that she remains here with me. Where I can keep a watchful eye on her. So hand her over and it will save me from having to kill you all."

"Not going to happen, Uncle," Azlan says. "She's staying with us."

"Your disobedience has grown rather wearisome, nephew. How fortunate that your sister shows more promise than you do. Far more obedient. Far more compliant and malleable – especially receptive to corrective punishment."

Azlan takes a step forward, jumping down from the boat,

both his hands curling into fists, his magic all of a sudden dangerous.

"You touch one hair on Ellie's head..."

"You'll what?" his uncle laughs. "You're outnumbered and if you think you're going to simply disappear into thin air again like you did before, I will have to disappoint you."

Without warning, he flings his magic forward. I'm ready for his trick this time and so are Stone and Renzo. All three of us deflect that magic that had encased our hands and locked away our magic last time. No way will it ensnare us a second time. It boomerangs back in Kennedy's direction, but with a simple flick of his wrist, the magic falters, tumbling to the ground.

The Lord Protector huffs in annoyance.

"Let me make myself abundantly clear. You are either with me or against me. You will either hand the girl over and pledge your allegiance to me, or you will be treated as traitors and executed immediately."

"Ha!" Renzo says. "The only person who's popping his clogs LP, is you. Didn't you read the prophecy? She's," he points at me, "your one-way ticket out of here. And I don't think that ticket is taking you any place nice."

The Lord Protector growls and flings his arms forward a second time, the many magicals at his side all doing the same so that a torrent of magic comes blasting our way.

"So be it!" I hear him yell over the thunder of magic. "You've chosen your path. Prepare to meet your end."

I watch that assault of magic blasting towards us as if it's moving in slow motion and for once all my optimism and perseverance whistles away like smoke on the breeze. This man is prepared to kill his own son simply because of an old verse written out on a piece of yellowing paper. He's that twisted. I don't see how we can escape this. We are doomed. The magic is too vast and too powerful. There are too many of them. And they aren't like the gang members in the woods, or the soldiers who tried to kidnap me at the graveyard. They aren't even like the ghouls out there in the mist.

These magicals are better trained and more skillful, the force of their magic scorchingly hot against my face, much of it dark; I can sense it – magic that was meant to be outcast along with those magicals in the West.

The prophecy was wrong. Or maybe it never applied to me in the first place.

I close my eyes, ready to accept my fate, ready to feel that magic melt the skin from my bones.

It doesn't come. There's a flash so bright I see it behind my closed lids and when I open my eyes I find my mates are not frozen in terror like I am but fighting back.

"Rhianna," Stone calls, "we need you."

I step closer to them and I set my magic free, let it flow through my body and out through my fingertips, let it hunt out the magic of my mates, seeking it out like it was always meant to be combined. Our magic spins and twists together in a cacophony of colors and it hits the incoming magic with such force all of us are blown backwards.

"Shit," Renzo says, the colors of the magic reflected in his wide, excitable eyes.

"You aren't going to take Rhianna," Tristan calls out to his dad over the hiss and crackle of magic. "You aren't going to take any of us." His face is more determined than I've ever seen it before, his brow already caked in sweat, the fair hair on his forehead turning damp. I've always known Tristan Kennedy was powerful, now I see just how powerful he is as his magic soars against his dad's. "So fucking stand down, resign your post. Concede!"

"More!" the Lord Protector roars to his followers and their magic pushes against ours.

My own magic strains at the edges and I'm aware I have more in me, more to give, that dark magic of my own. I think of my aunt's message, of Pip, and I think of Spencer, my only mate not to have sealed the bond.

Have I been a fool? Clinging on to Pip despite my aunt's warning, failing to make all of us as powerful as we could be by claiming Spencer completely as my own. Will we fall now because of my stubbornness?

Beside me Tristan grunts and grits his teeth, straining with all his might, his magic streaming from his hands.

On my other side, Spencer's form flickers and flutters, sometimes appearing more beast and sometimes more human.

But despite our efforts, despite the considerable force of our magic, it isn't enough. Their magic gains on us, creeping ever closer and closer, pushing ours back into retreat.

"There are too many of them," Stone grunts, anxious eyes flashing to Azlan.

"No!" Azlan shouts, finding more magic from somewhere, and for a moment it appears to work, our combined magic lunges forward against the assault, sending theirs backward. It only lasts a moment, though, and then we're ceding ground again.

"Barone," Azlan shouts, "grab Rhianna and get the hell out of here. Now!"

"Don't you even think about it," I spit, glaring at Renzo. "I'm not going anywhere. I'm not leaving anyone."

"He's going to kill us," Azlan says.

"If one of us falls," I say, "we all do."

I don't know about any prophecy. I'm not sure I even understand fate. But what I do know more than anything else is we were meant to be together. Living while they are not would kill me anyway.

"Fuck, little rabbit," Renzo tuts, "can't you ever do as you're told?"

I shake my head defiantly. "And don't you think about knocking me out because–"

"Here!" Renzo says, reaching into his pocket as he continues to blast chaotic, erratic magic with the others. He pulls out the knife, tossing it towards me. It spins and twists in the air and the handle lands firmly in my palm as if it were seeking me out.

"What am I meant to do with this?" I ask, even as the metal hums invitingly against my skin.

"Don't know, just had a feeling it might help," Barone says, as the opposing magic inches closer to us.

I stare down at the knife, run my thumb over the engraving and then on instinct I fling it towards the Lord Protector and his supporters.

The knife soars through the air into the chaos of magic and hangs there suspended, caught between the two forces. I hold my breath expecting something, anything.

Nothing happens. Nothing at all.

If that was meant to save us, it didn't work.

I'm tired, my magic waning.

Do we keep fighting to the end? Or do we surrender and accept our fate?

Several thoughts flash through my mind at once; several memories too, all of it in a rush like a wave hitting me.

I come from a line of women who never gave up, who kept fighting, and that is what I will do.

I smile to myself. I gave it a good try. I lasted on the run far longer than Stone ever gave me credit for. I've done things some people could only dream of. Soaring on the back of a dragon for one.

It's as that last thought somersaults through my mind and the knife glows in the flow of magic that I hear her. High above us in the sky, somewhere lost beyond the clouds. The whistle so faint I wonder if my desperate mind imagines it.

But then I hear it again, a second time.

I meet Renzo's eyes and he glances upwards.

Yes, I think in my mind, *yes, come, please come.*

And she does, swooping down through the clouds, her vast size whipping away my breath. The knife radiates with light, reflecting off her golden scales and everything stops and stares. The magicals, the magic, the very air we are breathing. Everything stops to stare at her in wonder, and the knife tumbles to the ground.

She glides low over our heads, her wingspan so wide, we're all plunged into darkness and she whistles again, calling to me.

"What?" Christopher Kennedy says. "What is this? Where is her rider?"

"Right here." Renzo grins, thumbing towards me.

The Lord Protector lowers his gaze from the sky and stares at me with disbelief.

"Then you really are your father's daughter," he sneers at me.

The dragon lunges down towards his supporters and there are screams as men and women drop to the floor, covering their heads with their hands. The dragon does nothing though, simply skims over them, her long talons tucked into her body.

The Lord Protector calls out to his supporters. "This dragon is theirs. Attack her."

I gasp, willing her away, and she spirals up into the air as the scores of magicals fire their magic up into her belly. She howls as it hits her scales, the magic splintering and sparking as if hitting thick metal shields.

"Leave her alone!" I yell, flinging more magic of my own their way. Some of the magicals divert to attack us again and then the dragon is twisting in flight and whistling again.

But this time it isn't me she's whistling to. Other dragons appear – one, two, three – out on the horizon and heading this way. Each of these dragons with a rider on their back.

The large golden dragon sweeps towards the ground. A fierce rumble issues from her chest and it seems to glow even more golden in the dull cloudy light, then a stream of fire bursts from her nostrils, cooking ten magicals at once. I avert my eyes, the smell of burned flesh strong in my nostrils, the cries of the dying magicals loud in my ears. Wings crack above my head and when I open my eyes again, the dragon is looping back up into the clouds as the remaining magicals pelt her with magic. For a moment she's lost behind the thick blanket and then she reappears behind Christopher Kennedy's people, blasting them again, several of them scattering and diving to try and avoid the jet of fire.

Chrisopher Kennedy spins and launches magic so dark it seems to suck the light from the sky. It sears towards the dragon, hitting her square on the jaw. Immediately her fire extinguishes, clouds of smoke billowing from her nostrils instead. She thrashes her jaws in anger, grabbing two men in her front talons and taking off into the sky, dropping their squirming bodies when she's almost to the clouds.

Christopher Kennedy, the self-imposed Lord Protector, spins towards us, his eyes wild with madness like the assassins. He laughs as the dragon circles above his head – the other dragons not far away now, almost at the Gray Isle.

"You think this is the end?" He laughs manically. "You poor deluded, stupid fools. So naïve, so clueless. You don't know who she really is. You don't know who he is."

He glances towards the coming dragons and then back to his remaining supporters.

"Away!" he yells. And suddenly we're all consumed in a thick dark blanket of smoke, so thick I can hardly see, the vapors choking me so I'm coughing and spluttering for air.

"No!" Tristan cries out and then he lunges forward, crouching down to pick up my discarded knife. He flings it through the air, the metal singing as it flies through the thick smoke in the direction of his father.

I wait for the thud of metal against skin. I wait for the retaliation of magic.

Nothing.

The cold wind sweeps away the black smoke and the sand in front of us is empty.

Christopher Kennedy and his followers are gone.

21

R^{hi}

"HE'S GONE!" I pant, spinning my gaze around.

"Yes, but who the hell is that?" Stone says, shielding his eyes and watching as the three dragons fly closer, finally joining the golden dragon in the sky. They circle us three times and once again my mates are crowding round me and lifting their hands.

Then together all four dragons swoop towards the beach, the ground shaking as they land in front of us.

Renzo's rucksack – the one he's been carrying all this time – now lying discarded on the sand, begins to wriggle, and then Pip squirms his way out of the top, squawking angrily as he does.

The others pay him no attention. They bristle ready for another attack, but the three riders – one man and two women – simply stare at us. These three dragons are smaller than the one I healed, with duller coloring. The women riding smaller green dragons and the man a larger brown one.

They are dressed in tight-fitted suits of leather, dark helmets on the women's heads.

"You may lower your hands," the man says, his accent thick with the West. "We are not here to harm you."

He clicks his tongue and the brown dragon lowers its head to the sand. The man slides down the dragon, landing deftly on his feet. Closer now, I see how well his suit is cut, how well the leather has been buffed, and spy the heavy gold rings he wears on his fingers.

"I see you have found my dragon," he says. "Gwenhwyfar."

His voice is quiet but full of authority. The man clasps his hands in front of him as the golden dragon watches him, her lidless eyes unblinking.

"Your dragon?" I say, scowling at him automatically, thinking of the cuffs around her neck and ankles and the scars on her body I'm sure were made from whips.

"She was, although perhaps she has changed her allegiance, daughter. Dragons have always favored female riders."

I stare at him, my mouth falling open, even Pip stops snorting by my ankles.

Daughter?

"Yes, daughter," he says.

The scowl on my brow deepens. Can he read my thoughts? I draw up my defenses like Stone taught me. I may think I know who this man is but I don't know for sure. I don't want him wandering through my mind.

"I have been looking for you. Looking for you for a long, long time." He smiles, a warmth in his eyes. "I sent men out looking for you." Those men? The ones that came for us over and over again? I always thought they were lowlifes taking their opportunity to abuse women who lived on their own, or possibly gangs hoping to capture magicals they could use for their own purposes. Was I wrong? Was it this man's men all along? Is that why my aunt fought them so hard over and over again? And if so, why? What was she so afraid of?

"I even came myself when the rumors began to circulate about a powerful girl – risked the start of a new war, daughter, to find you. And now, here you are at last."

I peer up at the man, my heart thumping in my ears. Tears glisten in his eyes.

"I should have known it would be this way," he continues. "That you would call to me, Rhianna."

"Call you?" I say, confused. "I didn't call you."

"You did," he says, pointing to the knife, blade down in the sand by his feet. He holds out his hand, palm upwards. The rings on his fingers glint in the pale light and his fingertips are worn and calloused. "Come, we have so much to discuss. So much lost time to make up."

I look past that hand and up into his face. He's handsome, despite the lines of time that have marked his face. His eyes are dark and beautiful, his jaw sharp, his build solid. He is the man in the locket. The man I saw when I held my father's knife. Is this the man my mom loved, then? The man who seduced her?

Is this my father?

I want to take his hand. I want to be welcomed with arms wide open. But something holds me back.

"How do I know I can trust you?"

"You don't," he says simply. I nod. I should know that by now. "Come. It's time to go home."

22

R hi

"HOME?" I say. Pip butts his snout against my ankles and I reach down and scoop him up.

"Little rabbit is going nowhere," Renzo growls.

The man examines him with shrewd eyes.

"Ahhh, Lowsky's hunting dog. I've heard of you."

"No longer Lowsky's hunting dog. I'm hers now." Renzo points towards me, his chest puffing with pride. "We all are," he adds, tilting his head towards my other mates this time.

"Five mates," the man says. "So it is true."

"Yes," I whisper as butterflies flutter in my stomach. Is he my dad, really my dad? "Five fated mates."

"Then there is even more for us to discuss. It is not safe here. Let us leave. We have enough dragons to take you all." The golden dragon rumbles and his dark eyes flick to hers. "Gwenhwyfar will carry you." The man watches her, his face unreadable. "The connection between you is strong," he comments.

"I healed her," I say, an accusation in my tone.

He lowers his gaze back to mine.

"Healed a dragon." His gaze falls back to Pip squirming in my arms. "And this is ..."

"My pig."

"Your familiar. I have not seen such practice for some time. May I?" He reaches out his hand and before I have a chance to tell him no, or to snatch Pip away, he's pressed his fingertips to the crown of Pip's head. Pip's eyes dart to mine in desperation and he squeals. But nothing happens and the man simply withdraws his hand.

"Her magic," he says cryptically. "You have her eyes. That same shade. Beautiful. And your magic is like hers. Do you dream like her?" And am I wrong, or do I see a spark of something, something almost like excitement, in those shrewd eyes?

He took my mom for her powers. That's how it started even if it didn't end that way. Does he think he'll use me in the same way?

I don't answer his question.

"Who are you?" I ask him.

That smile again, charming.

"You don't know?"

"I have an idea. But I'd like to hear you tell me."

"My name is Caspian Moray. Although some call me the Black Prince. I am ruler of the Western Kingdom and I believe I am your father."

"The Black Prince is dead."

He looks down at his body. "I may be incorrect – it happens very rarely – but I appear to be well and truly alive."

"The Black Prince?" This time it's Azlan who growls, laying his hand on my shoulder.

"We are wasting time," the Black Prince says, spinning suddenly and strolling back towards his dragon. "Sopherina and Portia will take your mates. You will ride on Gwenhwyfar."

His dragon lowers its head again, and he climbs up onto its back.

"I don't think this is a good idea," Azlan says, his brow knitted with concern.

"You never think anything is a good idea," I whisper with a smile.

"The Black Prince is our enemy."

"He's my dad."

"So he says," Stone snarks from behind me.

"He is," I say with more confidence than I really feel. "He's the man from my locket. The man who owned this knife." I glance at the assassin and he nods his agreement, then kneels down and plucks the knife from the sand, sliding it back into his pocket.

"It doesn't mean we should go with him," Tristan says.

I look at them all. Too often I know I've been a brat, storming off and leaving them no choice but to follow me. I know it's not only brattish, it's also pretty selfish. I peer towards the golden dragon and back to my mates. I'm going to try and do this the reasonable and grown up way.

"You saw how close we came to dying back there. If the dragon hadn't intervened, we would have died – Christopher Kennedy would have killed us." Tristan snorts and I glare at him. "I'm just facing facts here. We have no chance up against him – we all know that. But maybe we would with his help." I glance towards the Black Prince, watching us from the top of his dragon. "He has dragons and fighters.

You saw the damage they did to the academy and the council."

Spencer nods in agreement and Renzo looks eagerly towards the dragons. I've won two of them over.

"And I called him," I say to Azlan, Stone and Tristan, "without even meaning to, I called my dad to come help us. That must be fate. It must be fate intervening to help us."

"You really believe that?" Tristan asks.

"Yes," I say. Because that must be right. Why else would it have happened?

"I don't like it," Azlan says sternly.

"Me neither," Stone adds.

"Seems like we've run out of choices, though, my dudes," Renzo says.

"And you know she's going to go whether we like it or not," Tristan adds.

I pout at him. "I want us to be happy with this decision."

Azlan stares into my eyes. "I'm not going to be happy with it, but I will go along with it. Just ..." he lowers his voice, "be careful, Rhianna."

I think that's asking a lot – when am I ever careful? – but I make the promise anyway, and then we're all trudging over the sand towards the dragons.

The golden dragon watches me come and when I reach her, I lay my hands on her cool scales.

"Hello again, Gwenhwyfar," I say, testing out her name and smiling at her, Pip giving his own little squeak, "thank you for rescuing me. I guess we're even now." She rumbles a second time, lowering her head to the sand. She's too big for me to climb up onto and there's no Renzo here to help me now – he's too busy climbing onto one of the smaller dragons with Stone, who is looking mighty unhappy about being the one stuck with the assassin as his travel companion.

Furrowing my brow with concentration and with Pip in my arms, I manage to lift myself up into the air with my magic, just like I'd done that time in the gym with the rope. When I reach the top of the dragon, I grab ahold of her scales and scrabble up onto her back.

The butterflies continue to flutter around my stomach and I don't know if it's excitement at the prospect of riding her again, or nerves that I'm making another bad decision.

The other dragons lift up into the air. Spencer whoops with excitement and even Azlan appears to be struggling not to grin.

I screw up my eyes and steady my nerves. This is the right thing to do. It has to be.

The dragon spreads her wings and drags us high into the sky, sweeping after the others, until the convent is a mere dot in the distance and the Gray Isle is far far behind us as we fly out towards the West.

It takes us most of the day and into the night, but I'm not even a little bit tired, buzzing too much as we soar across the countryside, past all the places we passed weeks and weeks ago on the motorbikes and in Winnie's car. Up here the wind is fierce and cold and would be keeping me awake even if the adrenaline wasn't.

Pip isn't loving the ride as much as I am. In fact, I think he hates it even more than he did Winnie's driving. His body quakes like it did when he was unwell, and he screws up his eyes and buries his face in my lap. I try to comfort him, stroking my hand down his back and narrating everything there is to see from up here, but he's having none of it, and in the end I give up and enjoy the flight. It's a million times better than flying the broom, even if my thighs and my core ache and my eyes water. The dragon is graceful and the way she moves through the air is incredible.

Renzo said my dad was descended from dragons themselves and I begin to believe it. It's like I belong up here, far away from all my problems on the ground, the wind sweeping through my hair and the stars sparkling around me.

The other dragons soar alongside us, taking turns to lead us, swooping in and out of position and my mates call to me with delight, our bonds thrumming with excitement.

As day breaks, bright golden light racing along the crack where the sky meets the earth, we fly over the border. A huge barracks stationed right below us, tanks, trucks and other equipment parked in neat rows, soldiers like tiny ants swarming between them. They must see us up above, and one or two magical bolts come tearing our way. The dragons dodge them deftly and then we pass over land I don't think belongs to anyone. Empty like a ghost town, dead trees like skeletons staking the scorched earth, great craters pock-marking the ground.

No-man's-land.

And then, as the rays of light chase up into the sky, hitting the dragon's body and turning her golden, we pass into the west. More barracks, more soldiers. No difference. Except no one seems to notice us here, or at least if they do, they don't care. No bolts of magic, no warning shots. The busy little ants continuing their duties, until we're beyond them all and out into the west.

I don't know where I'm going from here. The West is a huge mass of unknown land. I don't know where the people live, how they live.

We fly over desolate land, dry and bare, only dust and sand in all directions, not a single scrabbly bush or even a lone cactus in sight. No trickling streams or racing rivers. Nothing. Nothing at all.

This is the West. Desolate and dangerous. Where men struggle to survive. Where the dark magicals were exiled in punishment.

The winter sun bears down on the cracked earth, roasting further and we fly onwards until finally we spy something in the distance. The first signs of life.

First a farm, cattle chewing on spindly grass, sparse yellowing crops clinging to the earth.

Then a town. Rundown like so many in the republic. Empty and boarded up.

Then another and another, becoming bigger, packed closer together until they spill into one another, one continuing urban sprawl across the land, the tall towers of a city out on the horizon.

This is where we're headed, I feel it in my bones, and I wish Pip would stop sulking and talk to me.

This isn't the West I expected. The desert land, yes. But towns? A city?

The city is packed tight with tall dark towers, nobody visible on the narrow streets below. It seems newer, more sophisticated even than the capital back home. Smarter, cleaner, in a way more intimidating. These people aren't struggling. They aren't struggling at all. They are thriving.

I scan my gaze over the huge mass of city, looking for any sign of where we might be headed, and then I spot it, right in the center of the city itself, slightly raised above the other buildings on a mound: a large compound with dark walls of metal ringing its buildings, inside what can only be described as a grand palace, manicured gardens – the first green we've seen in miles and miles.

The dragons swoop around in a circle, spiraling lower

and lower, and I see just how grand the castle is. No sandy-colored mansions here or grand white pillars, all dark sleek metal and black-paned windows; even the plants in the gardens are a dark shade of purple. There are also guards hidden among the buildings and the gardens and they step out forming a ring as the dragons circle lower and lower until we land on a flat patch of grass right in the center of that ring.

The soldiers are not like the ones that tried to ambush me. No grotty uniforms, no balaclavas. They wear grand sweeping cloaks that remind me of the one Christopher Kennedy wore, long leather gloves and black pointed helmets. They all stand with their heads bowed, waiting.

"We have her," the Black Prince calls from on top of his brown dragon. "My daughter has returned." The guards lift their heads in unison, thrusting their fists into the air and stamping their feet. My dad lifts his hand and they fall quiet. "Tonight we feast."

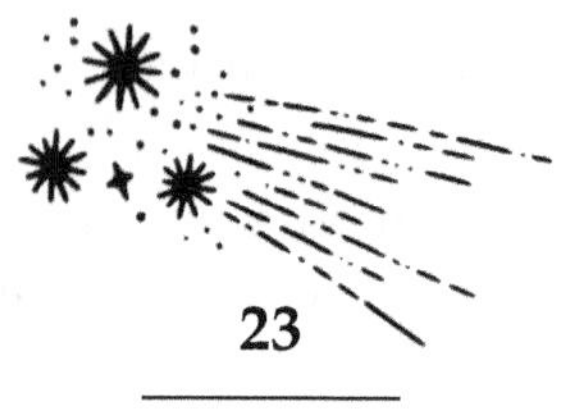

23

R enzo

I SLIDE down the dragon's back and land in the garden of some snooty-looking palace.

Me? Renzo fucking Barone in a palace? I snort and shake my head, my brain unable to compute it.

You spend your whole life as an outsider. Never fitting in. Different. Knowing other people don't work the same way you do. Peering in windows at other people's lives. Banned from fucking places because they'll arrest you and lock you up.

And now here I fucking am, strolling straight through these fancy gardens and towards the palace itself.

How the fucking tables turn.

I have what Lowsky used to call my 'shit-eating grin' stretched across my face. The way my face would look every time I fulfilled an assignment in record time, or with special enjoyment.

I'm wearing this grin for a different reason today, because I belong here now. No matter what all those snotty motherfuckers with their long last names may think. I belong.

Never minded not belonging. Never bothered by it. But now I do – now I belong with her and to her – I realize how much I've been fucking missing out.

Not that my little rabbit's grinning. She's chewing on her thumb, eyes darting all around the place like they used to do when we first met. I'm guessing that means she's scared. Of what? She's a fucking princess. Literally. If what they're saying is true. What does she have to be scared of?

I wrap my arm around her neck and tug her towards me, an action that rewards me with pissy looks from her other mates. They don't like me manhandling her. But she likes it. She has a side they can't see. And I may be shit at reading most things but I don't miss the way her eye lights up with excitement whenever I touch her.

Little man is peaky from our dragon-flight but trotting alongside us nonetheless.

"Little rabbit," I whisper into her ear as we pass through an archway made of dark steel and into a courtyard, the high shiny walls of the palace on all sides, "you wanna get out of here, you just say the word and I'll shoot us somewhere far away."

"If we go," little rabbit says, "we all go together."

"Seriously?" I say. I mean I'd blast them all out of here if she asked me to. The whole dying thing was a fucking trip. I'd do it again if it didn't make her sad. Then again, I don't want to die without fucking her some more. That would make *me* sad.

She looks up at me. Fuck, those eyes of hers. They do things to my insides. Jumble them up. On second thought, fucking her is much better than the dying.

Much, much better.

"I don't mean ..." she says, "I'm just saying, we're all sticking together from now on."

I glance over to where the man in black and the professor are talking, all serious like, together.

I think things would be more fun with just her and me, without the others, and maybe once upon a time I'd have done something to ensure it was just us. No other dudes hanging about, diverting her attention away from me and my dick. But there you have it. I haven't and I won't – and not just because it makes me hard every time I imagine one of them with her – something I'm chewing my fucking right leg off to watch – but because I know this is how things have to be.

Look at me, accepting things. My mom is probably turning in that shallow grave I buried her in.

"Whatever you want," I tell her. "Just know, I'm on your side, little rabbit, and your side only. I don't give a shit about fate, or prophecies, or parents or anything like that."

"I know," she says, and rests her head against my shoulder in a way that has the useless heart in my chest pounding.

I take secret little gulps of her scent. Fuck, I love the way she smells – not so sweet and floral it makes your nose hurt, not so subtle you have to strain with all your might just to smell her. No, she's like Goldilocks – just right, just perfect.

A door slides back and we walk inside, the air immediately warm, the air fragranced, the wide corridor sleek and bare. We stride along this too and though I see no one else, I can sense their presence all around, out of sight. Then we stop.

The Black Prince steps towards us and little rabbit ducks under my arm and steps forward too. The Black Prince smiles at her and takes her hand in his, an action that has all the dudes bristling around us. Seems they don't like *him* touching her either.

"I am so glad you have returned, my child. It is the greatest possible gift – one I feared might never happen."

"I have so many questions," she says.

"I know you do. Later. First, we feast. Sopherina and Portia will show you to your rooms, where you can wash and change in preparation for the feast. Garments will be provided for you."

I glance down at my body. My boots are all fucked up from the seawater and my jacket's covered in sea salt. I'm not taking them off. I don't care where we are.

I look at little rabbit next. Her sneakers are hanging off her feet, the bottom of her pants soaked with seawater. Her cheeks are ruddy from the wind and her hair tangled. She looks like a sea goddess stepped right out of the ocean. Fucking amazing.

"I will send my man to fetch you in an hour," the Black Prince continues. He bends low, kissing little rabbit's paw, and then we're being hustled away.

The professor steps in close to us as we walk down more hallways, this palace like a fucking maze. There's something swirling all over his face, the way he used to look as a kid when some other kid pissed him off.

"What's up, prof?" I ask him.

"Stone," he mumbles, "could you just call me Stone?"

I stare at him. We both know that's not his name. He's named after that bird. The one that rises from the ashes. I fucking hated him for that name when we were young, wanted so badly to steal it for myself.

"This is strange, isn't it?" little rabbit says to him, "not like I thought the West would be like."

"No," Birdman says, eyes sliding all over the place, "not like it at all."

"Does it matter?" I ask.

"No," she says, "I just ... I just don't understand."

The two dragon riders halt outside another door, one waving her hand so it slides back.

"These are your quarters. There is a room for each of you."

It's the first time either of them have spoken and they have those same thick accents. They don't say any more. They bow and go.

We all wait by the open door.

"We going in?" I ask, "or we leaving?" You can never be sure with these dudes.

"Going in," little rabbit says, "I need to radio Winnie. Let her know what's happened." She steps inside the room, her eyes widening like two full moons in her face as she does. "Wow!" she mouths.

I spin my gaze about. I know fuck all about houses and shit, but this is a palace and I'm guessing it's enough to impress little rabbit. Her eyes remain wide as they spin over the large room. It's jammed with stuff. But all I really notice is how dark it is – they really dig the color black here. Even the windows are blacked out.

Little rabbit pats the pig's head as he snuffles about on the ground exploring, then pulls the radio out of my ruck-sack. She twizzles a button, presses a few more, nothing happens.

"It's not working," she says with irritation.

The enforcer takes it from her hands and uses his magic to bring the device to life. It lights up and static buzzes from its belly. He turns the knobs.

"Can you reach her?" little rabbit asks, hovering by his shoulder.

His brows pinch together and he twizzles the knobs some more.

"No," he says finally, "we're too far out of range."

"But we have to let her know what's happened. She's waiting for us. She'll be worried."

"Rhianna," he says, "Winnie is an intelligent woman. When we don't show up, she'll conclude things didn't go to plan and she'll get herself to safety. You don't need to worry about her. And there's nothing we can do about it right now anyway."

Little rabbit worries at her lip but nods.

Then she spots a rack in the middle of the room, clothes hanging in a row. Suits and dresses and all that shit.

She walks straight there like a homing pigeon and starts running her hand over all the material.

"These are beautiful," she mutters, "how am I going to choose which one to wear?"

"You look good as you are," I tell her. She looks at me like I lost a screw in my head. "What? You do!" I say stalking towards her as I lick my lips. I'd like to lick all that sea salt off her body.

She holds up her hand to stop me.

"They're holding a feast. In my honor!" she says, sounding sort of wonder-struck – same way she sounded when I fucked her. "And we only have an hour to get ready. No time for funny business."

"There's always time for funny business," I mutter.

But she picks up a handful of her hair and scowls at me. "Do you have any idea how long it's going to take to untangle my hair?"

I roll my eyes and click my finger, leaving her hair combed and tangle-free.

She stares at me, eyes somehow even rounder. "How the hell did you do that?"

"My mom." I yawn and fling myself down on the nearest soft chair. "She used to get me to do her hair."

"You?" the were asks, coming to look at the clothes. "Do hair?"

I shrug again. It's hardly a big deal. "Yeah. I can do those fiddly braid things," I spin my finger over my head to indicate my meaning, "and waves and shit."

"Makeup?" the Kennedy boy asks with what I think is a piss-taking grin.

"No, she didn't like me touching her face."

The smile vanishes.

"Will you do my hair for me?" little rabbit asks.

My face screws up.

I haven't done hair for a long time. And I don't like thinking about those times, even if they come barging into my head anyway.

But it's little rabbit asking. And so I can't say no. Especially when I picture her hair wound tight around my fist. Fuck yes!

"Okay," I say slowly. "But what are you going to do for me? Suck my cock?"

"Behave, Barone," Birdman mutters, strolling over to the rack of clothes as well.

The were-boy pulls a hanger off the rack and admires the black suit hanging from it.

"They must have known we were coming. There's one in each of our sizes."

"I'm not wearing one of those monkey suits," I say, swinging my legs. No one's ever cared what I've worn before.

Little rabbit looks up from the puffed-up skirt she's examining, eyes drifting back to me.

"I think you'd look really handsome in a suit, Renzo," she says.

My legs fall still and I stare at her. Is she for real? Is she joking with me?

"You think I'd look *handsome*?"

"Yes."

"You don't like the jacket?" I pluck at my collar. Me and this jacket have been friends a long time, but I'd happily fling it on the nearest garbage heap if she says she hates it.

"Renzo," she says, lifting an eyebrow, "you know you look seriously hot in that jacket." I peer down at my body. Do I? "I just think ..." she bites her lip all seductive like, "you'd look pretty good in a suit too." She sighs. "I think you all would."

"You heard the lady," Birdman says, throwing a bundle of clothes my way, "she wants you all dressed up."

I scramble up onto my feet and start stripping off my clothes.

"Woah, dude!" the were says. "Go do that some place else."

"Why?" I say snapping off my pants. I'm going commando and I let it all hang out there for them to see. I may not have known I was handsome. I did know I have a big dick. "You're jocks. You must have seen his junk, right?" I say to him, jerking my head towards the Kennedy boy.

"He's never given me a freaking strip show."

"You're going to see my junk when we all fuck little rabbit together," I say. "You might as well get used to it."

"Renzo," little rabbit says. "Go use the shower."

"Are you coming with me?" I say hopefully, my cock already stiffening at the prospect and the were-boy grimacing.

"No!"

"But that time with the prof in the shower you–"

"Now!" she says, pointing towards the bathroom.

I scoop up my bundle of clothes and slump off with my tail dragging behind me. Little man comes along for the ride. Seems he doesn't have a problem with me getting naked. In fact, he lies down on the bathroom floor, head resting on his trotters and snoozes while I scrub myself under the shower.

When I'm done I tie a towel around my waist and go examine my face in the mirror, wiping away mist from the plane with the side of my hand.

I've never bothered about my face before. It's been sliced and diced and I didn't give a shit. It's just one other part of my body. Who cares?

But she likes it. I tilt my head one way and then the other. She likes it despite the imperfections. Shit, I think she even likes *me* despite the imperfections.

Crowded around the sink are bottles of all sorts of crap including shaving foam and a razor. I fill the sink with piping-hot water and splash my face with it, the temperature making me wince, excitement shooting down my spine. Then I lather the foam all over my face.

"Gotta look smart for little rabbit," I tell little man, who opens one eye and peers up at me. "Yeah, ridiculous, but it's what she wants."

There's a light tap on the door.

"Hey Renzo," my little rabbit says, "is Pip in there?"

"Yeah," I say, "want me to send him in for a shower too?"

Pip scowls at me like don't you even think about it.

Little rabbit giggles. "Can I come in?"

I wink at the pig. Maybe she's changed her mind.

I open the door and she walks inside, crouching down by little man.

"You know a shower wouldn't be such a bad idea, Pip. You don't want to be the only one stinking out there."

Her hair's wet and she's wrapped up in some silky gown which is begging to be untied. I guess she showered already.

Little man snorts at her and then darts as quickly as his stumpy legs will carry him from the room.

"I'm guessing that's a no then." She peers up at me. "Are you shaving?"

I sweep my hand back through my damp hair. "You wanted me looking smart," I mumble.

"I did," she says and then she stands and locks the door. Are we about to get dirty again?

She points to the razor. "May I?"

"Are you going to slit my throat, little rabbit?" I whisper darkly.

She doesn't answer me, picking up the razor in her hand instead and stepping closer to me. With her left hand, she tilts my head backwards, exposing my throat. And, fuck, maybe she is. That or sink her teeth into my throat.

I take a hold of that tie around her waist and drag her closer.

"What you going to do, little rabbit?" I ask.

She meets my eyes and then presses the razor hard against the soft skin beneath my chin, gliding it firmly down my throat. It slides over the foam and my skin, but there's still a sting. A tantalizing sting, and I close my eyes and sigh. She reaches down and swishes the blade through the water, the foam dissolving away, and then she presses the razor again.

"Harder," I tell her.

"Don't move," she tells me, like she's perfectly aware of what I had in mind.

She presses more firmly, scraping at my throat this time and how the fuck did this happen? How did fate make a girl so perfect for me? Dark like me. Prepared to indulge me in my sick little games. I lick my lips, peering down at her as she drags the razor down my throat a third and fourth time, those pretty eyes of hers focused intently at her work, her pink lips pursed.

She grabs a hand towel and wipes at my throat next, examining her work first, before she lowers my head and inspects my chin next, swishing the razor once more through the water as she does. She tilts my head to one side and drags the blade right down my cheek, over the scars, to the edge of my jaw. She does it again and again, cleaning the razor each time. Then she halts and runs the pad of her thumb gently over the place she's just shaved.

"Soft," she comments.

"And handsome?" I ask, still unable to believe that claim.

"Very," she says, sighing slightly in a way that sends shivers all over my body.

"Me?" I say. "Even with the," I pause, "funny eyes?"

"I love your eyes," she says, observing first my left eye and then my right. "They're really very beautiful."

"Shit," I say, stunned.

She stares right into both eyes at once, like she's peering right into my cold, black soul. And fuck, how can a woman looking at me like that turn me so much the fuck on?

She tilts my head the other way, and shaves my other cheek, then my chin and finally it's just the spot above my top lip.

She hovers the blade right there and bites her tongue between her teeth in concentration. She moves the razor closer.

"No mustache, then?" I ask.

"Jeez!" she says. "Stay quiet. I don't want to nip you."

"But what's the point," I pout, "without a little blood?"

"I don't understand your fascination with blood," she says, cupping my jaw and holding my head still. With concentration, she moves the razor over that narrow bit of skin between my nose and my lip, taking special care around the edges of my lip.

"They're too beautiful to spoil," she explains.

"You like my lips too?" I ask her, when she moves the razor away.

"Uh huh," she says, admiring her work a final time.

I take my opportunity, grabbing the hand she has holding my jaw with and dragging it lower to my neck, forcing her to wrap her fingers around my throat. Then I kiss her, and while I do I encourage her to wrap her fingers more tightly. She takes the hint, squeezing, digging her fingers into the newly smooth skin, so I'm gasping for breath as I kiss her, light-headed and giddy.

However, just as it's getting fucking interesting, she pulls away, that mischief, that darkness sparking in her eyes.

"I don't want to hurt you," she says.

"But I want you to, little rabbit," I growl.

She lays one palm on my chest.

"You're really special to me, you know that," she says,

before stroking the other palm down my cheek. "And you look even more handsome now."

My heart stops beating. I feel like I died all over again as she smiles up at me and walks out of the bathroom, leaving me alone there in the misty room like some kind of startled ghost.

24

T ristan

KNUCKLES RAP WOOD softly and then a voice from behind the
door tells us the feast is about to begin and we are expected.
Are we ready?

Us men are. All five of us lined up looking like penguins
in our matching suits and white shirts.

Well, when I say lined up, that's not quite true. Spencer's
pacing the room and Barone's sprawled over a chair again,
muttering to himself with a big grin on his face. We're all
waiting on Rhi, who disappeared into one of the bedrooms
several minutes ago with her arms full of dresses.

Azlan steps towards that bedroom now and raps his own
knuckles on the door.

"Rhianna," he says, "are you ready?"

"Nearly," she calls back, "give me a minute." Azlan

stomps back towards the suite door and informs the person on the other side we'll be one minute.

I whistle under my breath. "You really don't know a lot about women," I say to him.

"And you do?" he says gruffly, giving me the evil eye.

"I know enough about them to understand that when they say they'll be one minute, they won't. We're looking at half an hour at least."

Azlan scoffs, but Stone, fiddling with his bowtie, nods. "He's right."

Azlan looks at us both, clearly debating whether we're pulling his chain or not. Then stomps back over to the bedroom.

"Is there anything we can do to help, Rhi? The feast is about to start."

I rub at my chin, smothering a smile with my hand. Azlan has never enjoyed being late. He's regimental to the point and always on time. No wonder he never had a girl.

I hear Rhi murmur something the other side of the door and then Azlan disappears inside the bedroom.

"Are we likely to see either of them again this evening?" Spencer asks with a hint of bitterness in his tone. I can't blame him. He still hasn't gotten his hands on Rhi and I know exactly what that feels like.

"No," I say, "Az likes being on time far more than he likes sex."

Stone snorts. "I wouldn't count on that."

My eyes shoot to the door, immediately imagining him throwing Piglet down on the bed and ...

The door creaks open and Rhi steps out.

And fuck, it's like all the oxygen is sucked out of the room. We're all catching our breaths. She looks beautiful. Like she did that night of the Victory Ball – only better. A million times better. Gut-wrenchingly beautiful. So much so my bond is dancing in my stomach.

How? Is it because we're bonded now? Is it the way she's done her hair tonight, the seductive cut of the gown, the dark makeup highlighting her honey eyes?

Or is it because I've fallen that little bit more in love with her?

Heck, a lot more in love with her.

I open my mouth to tell her just how amazing she looks, and goddamn Stone beats me to it.

"You look incredible, sweetheart," he says.

She blushes and I remember this girl never can take a compliment.

"It looks okay?" she asks, smoothing her hands down the scarlet silk that clings to her body like water. "Not too ... you know ..."

"Looks the exact right amount of 'you know' to me," Spencer says with a growl.

"But my ..." she swallows, "dad's going to be there and I want to look right."

A chill seems to pass over my skin, an unease that I haven't been able to shift since we climbed aboard those dragons.

I'm not convinced we made the right decision coming here. I'm not sure I trust her dad. The Black Prince for fuck's sake. How is he even alive? And how ... how is this the West? The piece-of-crap land they always said was some barren country where the people were starving.

"You look perfect," Azlan says, sliding an arm around her waist, but his gaze dashes to mine and I read that same unease in him too. In fact, I'd say the only one who seems at ease in this situation is Barone and frankly, that does fuck all to alleviate my reservations. As if reading my thoughts,

Azlan adds, "Let's be careful tonight. Keep our eyes and ears open. We don't know if we can trust these people."

"They saved us from Christopher Kennedy," Rhi points out. "And he's my dad."

"The same dad your aunt was keeping you hidden from," I say, regretting it immediately as the excitement sparking in her eyes only moments ago, extinguishes.

"I know what you're saying," she says. "And I know we should be careful. I have a lot of questions too."

"Then hopefully you'll get a chance to ask them tonight," Stone says.

I turn to look at the professor. He has one power that could prove pretty useful in this situation.

"Have you been able to garner anything from their thoughts?"

He shakes his head. "Everyone we've met so far has been well trained at guarding their thoughts."

"Keep trying," I tell him and he glares at me. He's never liked me.

"Let's all agree to keep a watch out – especially on Rhianna," Azlan says, and we all nod in agreement, even the assassin.

"You know I can look after myself," Rhi protests as Azlan guides her to the door.

"Yeah, yeah, sure we do, sweetheart," Stone says.

"That does not sound convincing," she protests.

He winks at her and then we're all pacing towards the door, everyone, including the pig.

Azlan pauses, hand on the doorknob.

"Is the pig coming with us?" he says, glancing down at Rhi's pet.

"Oh," Rhi says, crouching down in her heels. "Pip, I think it's best you stay here." The pig grunts like it disagrees.

"I have a feeling feasts are like balls – crowded. I don't want you to get trampled."

"Or mistaken for the main meal," Stone says, winking at the pig. The pig grunts again, this time directing its displeasure at the professor, and then we're all squeezing through the gap in the doorway, attempting to stop the pig from following us as he tries to scuttle between our legs.

Once we're all through, the man who's come to collect us stares at us like we're all nut-jobs.

"The feast?" Rhi prompts and with a jerk he sets off down the corridor.

I follow Rhi, watching her back and wishing it were me with my hand on her waist, me whispering into her ear and me making her laugh.

"It's hard taking turns," the assassin says right by my ear, making me jolt. He looks almost respectable with his baby-smooth face and his tux. Or else he would if it weren't for the ink crawling up his neck and the fact he's insisted on wearing his boots with the tux and refused the bowtie outright no matter how hard Rhi begged.

"What do you mean?" I ask, a frown forming on my brow.

"With the girl. It's hard waiting out your turn."

"I wasn't ... I didn't ..."

"Although you do enjoy just watching her, right?"

"What?" I mutter. The man is hard to follow.

"You like watching her. You spend a lot of time doing it."

"Bullshit," I say.

"Huh," he says, eyes boring into me. "Could've sworn it was you watching her all those nights back at the academy."

I feel a chill judder down my spine. How the hell does he know about that? Should I confess to it? Deny it? Take him by the scruff of the neck and ask how the hell he *would* know that? But before I get the chance, he's fallen back and is attempting to make small talk with Spencer next. I mean, I guess I have to give points to the dude for trying.

Our guide halts at the end of the corridor and the rest of us do too. Then he turns to us.

"Your father will want to announce your arrival," he says before disappearing. We wait in the dark corridor, hearing the chatter of many voices behind the great door in front of us. Then there's the blast of trumpets and those voices fall silent.

"Loyal subjects of the Western Kingdom. I have gathered you all here tonight for a great celebration." We hear the Black Prince's voice boom from behind that door. "Today, the royal princess, my daughter, has been returned to me. She has returned."

There is a stunned hush followed by loud cheers and applause. Whether it's genuine or not, I can't tell. But I'm no fool. I've seen how deftly the cheerleaders could cheer for us, could paw all over us, while secretly bitching us out behind our backs – particularly whatever girl it was who'd had her heart broken or her ego dented.

"Tonight we celebrate!" the Black Prince roars above all the noise and the great doors swing back to reveal a huge ballroom – at least three times as big as the Great Hall back at the academy – rammed with magicals all dressed in dark robes and dark dresses, all their gazes trained our way. No, not our way. Rhi's way – standing among the five of us.

The ballroom itself is vaulted like the chapel at the convent, except here everything is made from dark, slick metal, no stone in sight, with fires flickering in the corners, throwing moving shadows up against the walls. Long tables run the length of the room, along which the magicals sit.

The Prince himself waits at a table on a raised platform

at the head of the room, his chair far bigger and more ornately carved than any of the others and on his head balances a crown of jet black metal. He no longer wears his leather suit, but a long black robe, embroidered with scarlet, the pattern making him look as if the flames from the fire are flickering around his very body.

He holds out his hand in our direction.

"Come, daughter. Come, Princess. Take your rightful place beside me."

Rhi hesitates, eyes darting to us, and then she walks forward, through the middle of the tables, the magicals watching her intently, clapping as they do with all their might.

I'm reminded of that first day she showed up at school. Of how she'd walked the length of the Great Hall, out of uniform, dressed in jeans and a hoodie, her hair all scruffy, not a smudge of makeup on her face, chin raised in defiance, not caring at all about the people gaping and whispering around her.

There's that same defiance now, that same determination. Life will throw all sorts of shit at Rhianna and yet she always remains on her goddamn feet, resolved never to fall. My heart swells with pride for her.

Maybe we are wrong to be so wary. Rhi is a fucking queen. Sitting on a throne is where she should be. Maybe this is exactly where fate intended to take us after all.

The five of us follow after her, those gazes examining us with just as much interest, and when we reach the high table, I see there are spaces for all of us.

The Black Prince points to another elaborate, albeit smaller, chair beside him.

"Sit beside me, daughter," he commands. Then he

points to the chair on his other side. This one perfectly normal. "And you too, Kennedy."

I judder. He knows my name. Knows who I am.

I walk around the table, taking my seat, eyes watching Rhi the entire time. The others take their seats too and I notice from the corner of my gaze how they're scanning the crowd, looking for danger.

When we are all seated, the Black Prince raises his hands. "And now we eat," then he claps his hands, and scores of servers come dashing into the ballroom. Only these servers are dressed in plain outfits and their gazes remain resolutely fixed to the ground. Not like the academy where the dinner staff were just as likely to spit in your face as they were to slap food on your plate.

When the food is distributed across the tables, the gathered magicals wait, eyes locked on the top table. The Black Prince peruses the dishes, then drags a slab of meat onto his plate and immediately the other magicals do the same, scooping and skewering bits of food.

I look down at my own plate, empty.

I don't have an appetite. I'm too much on edge.

I peer to Rhi and see she is the same, fiddling with her cutlery as the man who claims to be her dad continues to pile high his plate.

"It is rude in our country not to eat when offered food," he says, not looking at either of us as he deposits a chunk of meat into his mouth and chews. "I promise you, it is not poisoned. I have a man who checks for that."

I stare at the food, feeling even less hungry.

"Your country, they said ... I don't understand," Rhi mutters. "They said the West was–"

"A hellhole beyond compare." The Black Prince smiles, so charming and yet I can't help but find it unsettling. "Perhaps it once was, but I have worked hard to build a home for our people, a country for them. The land where this city now stands was once as much part of the desolate landscape as the rest of the country. It is through grit and determination that I have molded it to be this great city."

"It seems spectacular," Rhi says.

The Black Prince considers her as he takes a sip of wine from his glass.

"I imagine they told you many things that weren't true." He smiles again, lowering his glass. "I have heard the stories about myself." He leans forward and says in a theatrical whisper, "That I am some great evil force that threatened the very existence of the republic."

He laughs.

"Are you not?" I say flatly.

He cuts a roast potato in half with his knife.

"Unfortunately, every ruler must be ruthless at times – for the greater good. There is often little choice. But I pride myself on my fairness and my humanity. It is your country that attacked mine all those years ago when they learned what I was building here. I simply defended what was ours."

"And now?" Rhi says. "Couldn't you find a way to make peace?"

"Ahhh. I suppose they have told you that we remain great enemies when really we are symbiotic. Neither could survive without the other. Wars keep the people distracted, Rhianna. Give them a common enemy and they will unite. Better the disquiet is with your neighbor so that your own house remains at peace."

"You attacked the capital!" I say. "Burned our academy to the ground!"

He shakes his head. "I was searching for my daughter."

He covers her hand with his. "And, of course, I was encouraged by my ally."

"Ally?" I say. "What are you saying? That–"

"Your father, the Lord Protector, is a shrewd politician. He always spoke highly of you Tristan Kennedy. Always boasted of the leader you would become. I was not surprised when I learned you were one of my daughter's fated ones." He chews the fatty meat in his mouth, his jaw working as he looks at me. "I am surprised you don't know all of this already."

"Y-y-you've spoken with my dad? With Christopher Kennedy?"

"But of course," he says, lifting his wine glass to his lips again. "We have an understanding." He takes a long sip of the wine, the liquid dyeing his lips a blood red. "Or at least, we did. Considering my most recent intervention, that understanding may no longer hold." He lowers his glass and meets my gaze, behind him the great fires flicker and the scores of people eat, drink and talk.

"I still don't understand," Rhi says, the frustration clear in her voice and our bond humming with it.

The Black Prince gestures to her plate. "Eat. There will be time for more talking. For now, we celebrate your return. The people are grateful for it. *I* am grateful for it." He pinches her chin. "You are just as beautiful as she was."

I turn back out and look at all the people. They certainly do look happy. Is that simply the free food and the flowing alcohol or are they genuinely elated at the lost princess's return? Can it really mean that much to them? I gaze along the table at the others, at Azlan, Stone, Spencer and Barone. None of them are eating either – not even the crazy-assed assassin. They are all gazing out at the banquet, as fucking puzzled as I am.

25

R^{hi}

THE FOOD in front of me has more spice, more flavor, more depth than any food I've ever tasted in my life. It awakens every taste bud on my tongue and has my stomach rumbling and yet I pick at my food.

None of this makes sense, and this feast is simply delaying my opportunity to ask all the questions burning inside me, delaying my chance to finally, maybe, receive some damn answers. Unfortunately, those answers don't seem like they're coming any time soon because as soon as all the dishes of food are emptied, those meek servers appear and the plates are cleared. Then as if by magic – heck most probably with magic – the long tables vanish and an orchestra shuffles into the room, laden down with their instruments.

"Ahh, time for dancing," the Black Prince says, taking a

firm grip of my hand and leading me down to the heart of this great ballroom, the many magicals stepping aside to let us pass. At the center of the room, he halts.

"Loyal subjects," he says, addressing his assembled audience once more as he squeezes my hand tightly. "Not only has fate returned the lost princess to us, fate has also rewarded our beloved princess with five fated ones."

Almost immediately there's a rush of excitement that seems to pass through the assembly – I can feel their magic bubbling with it, their eyes alight with it too. Much more excitement than seemed to be sparked by the announcement of my return.

I shuffle a little on my feet, wishing the Black Prince did not have such a tight grip of my hand so I could gnaw on my thumb. After my time at the academy, I should be used to people staring at me, whispering about me. Yet, I still find it unsettling, wishing all those eyes weren't fixed on me.

"Five powerful magicals," he continues, pointing to Azlan, Stone, Tristan, Spencer, and Renzo – all still sitting at the raised table. "Even the son of the republic's Lord Protector himself." There are several gasps, one or two amused chuckles. "And which one of these fated ones will you choose to dance with first, daughter?" he asks me.

Inwardly, I take a mighty big sigh of relief. I was half expecting him to dance with me himself, not something I felt entirely comfortable with when I've barely said two words to this man who is my estranged father. Or worse, I thought he might expect me to dance by myself for everyone to watch – like some sort of terrible anxiety nightmare. Not that dancing with one of my mates in front of all these people will be much better.

They must see the horror in my eyes because all five of them stand to their feet, offering their assistance.

"Perhaps, we could all dance," I say with a hesitant smile, "all of us," I add, signaling to the assembled magicals.

The Black Prince nods and then with another click of his fingers, the music starts and before I know it, there are magicals twirling in couples around me, their cloaks and skirts billowing and many faces flashing past me. My father is swallowed up by the crowd and I feel the press of bodies around me, arms and hands brushing against me.

My head spins. I feel dizzy, lost in a sea of people, a strange fear creeping up my throat, and then I'm scooped up into the arms of Tristan Kennedy.

"Okay, Piglet?" he asks, anxious green eyes sweeping all over my face.

I breathe. "I am now."

He rewards me with one of his smiles – far more charming than my dad's even. The kind of smile that had every girl at the academy dropping their panties. Several boys too if he'd given them a chance.

"I never did get an opportunity to dance with you at the Victory Ball and I was looking forward to it."

"It's probably just as well you didn't. Summer freaking Clutton-Brock would have scratched my eyes out and yanked every hair from my head."

"No, she wouldn't have. You'd have blasted her to hell before she got a foot towards you. And maybe this time you'd actually have hit her," he says, smile widening.

I shake my head. "I still don't understand why she never told on me. She was so desperate to get me kicked out of the academy and that was her perfect opportunity."

"She didn't tell on you," he says, spinning me around, his arms like a cocoon around me, "because I made sure she didn't."

I roll my eyes. "That girl would do anything for you, but

still, she thought I was the one standing between the two of you and so–"

"She was jealous because she saw how much I wanted you – saw it long before anyone else did. In her twisted little world, she wanted us to be together and I knew she could hurt you because of it. And so I made her take the unbreakable vow. I stopped her from telling on you."

"Oh," I say, my feet coming to a stop. "You did that for me?"

He nods. "Anyway," he says, the smile fading, "I guess in her eyes she ended up with a serious upgrade in the end – lost one Kennedy but ended up with the top one."

I scoff. "Your dad's an asshole. You're a million times better than him, Tristan."

"Sometimes I think I am – that my power could outmatch his."

"I'm not talking magic," I say, unaware now of all the magicals moving around us. "I mean in here," I tap his chest, "you're better than him because you're kind – when you want to be."

"I'm trying, Piglet. I'm trying to be a better person for you. Trying to unlearn all the fucked-up bullshit he taught me."

"Don't unlearn it all," I say with half a smile of my own. "We may need it."

"True," he says, whispering in my ear, "I'd be as fucked up as Barone if it came to it, if I had to be." He squeezes me to him as he says it as if scared I'll be ripped away from him. But I'm not and I settle my head against his chest, let him hold me close as we sway together in the sea of people. Maybe it's not the right way to dance – heck, maybe it might not be considered respectable. I don't care.

I'm whisked right back to the Victory Ball, to how things

could have been if we'd both accepted each other like fate wanted us to, if we'd allowed the attraction between us to grow, if we'd acknowledged how desperate our magic was to combine, if we'd relented.

"What's wrong, Piglet?" he asks, sensing my sadness through the bond.

"Do you ever think about how things could have turned out if they'd gone differently?"

"You mean with your dad? You mean between your parents?"

"No, between us."

He stops. "Every fucking minute of every day, Piglet."

I look into those deeply green eyes of his and feel his sincerity, feel it deep inside me. I want to say more to him, but my dad's hand lands on his shoulder and he's being pulled away. I'm alone again, watching as the Black Prince demands his attention.

My mind's a mess of emotions.

Because he's right.

What if my mom had never taken me away? What if she stayed here with him? What if my aunt had never hidden me? What if he'd found me?

Is this what my life would have been like? Luxury. Beautiful dresses and gourmet food, servants and subjects and living in a palace.

I think of all those days of suffering, of fighting to stay alive, scrapping for food, racing to outrun those who wanted to harm us.

It could have been so different. All so different.

My head spins even more and that feeling crawls up my throat again so fast I can't breathe.

I push my way through the tight-knit group of dancers, through the people gathered at the edges, past guards and servers with their bowed heads, out to the corridor and then on and on, going on instinct, crashing through the first door I find and then out into the night, the air cool and hitting my lungs with such relief I almost stumble to my knees.

The garden is quiet and still – blessed relief – except for one lone dragon – a golden-red one circling above.

26

S pencer

THE BALLROOM IS HUGE, but any room feels like imprisonment. No matter how big, the walls creep in on me and I'm scratching to get out. The thick throng of people only makes it worse, hot bodies pressing in on me from every direction.

Soon, I can't bear it anymore. But I have to for her, even if every bone in my body screams for space, for freedom, for relief. I grit my teeth and I endure it.

But then I see her slipping away unseen and so I follow her, her own personal protective shadow. I trail her out of the ballroom, along corridors and out into the cold garden, the frigid air like a slap to the face.

I find her peering up at the sky, wrapped in a blanket she wasn't wearing before. The heavy clouds have cleared and high up among the pinprick stars a shadow is circling.

"I think she's watching over me," she says.

"That's pretty awesome," I tell her, rubbing my hands up and down my arms.

"And sort of terrifying too," she says, catching me shivering and offering me a corner of her blanket. "I found it slung over one of the garden chairs." I step in closer, so close our arms are touching, and wrap the blanket around us both. "I mean, what am I meant to do with a dragon?"

"Ride it, according to Barone."

She grins. "Did you dragon-travel better than the broom?"

So she noticed that, huh?

"I don't think that broom was designed for someone my size."

"You are pretty big," she says.

So she noticed that too.

"Fuck, it's cold," I lie. I'm feeling anything but with her so close. "Come give me a bit of your body heat." I slide my arm around her waist and draw her closer, right in front of me, drawing my arms and the blanket tightly around us. To my fucking delight, she comes without a fight, although not without a little snark.

"You could use your magic to warm up, you know."

"Yeah," I say, feeling dizzy. "But this is more fun."

"Hmmm," she says, "it is." And is that my fucking, screwed-up imagination, or did she rub her butt against my cock?

"I can't believe you rode that dragon alone, Rhianna Blackwaters. You're so fucking amazing."

I'd like her to ride something else. I'd like to seal this bond between us. Make this all permanent. I'm sick of being so far away from her even when she's this close. But I'm taking this slow. I have to.

"Maybe if you are well behaved, I'll let you ride her with me," she teases.

"And what warrants good behavior?"

She's silent and so I take a gamble. One big, big gamble. One I pray on every star up there in the heavens pays off. I deserve some good luck, after all, even if I don't deserve *her*.

I bend my head lower and bring my mouth right before her neck, pausing and letting my clouded breath brush against her skin. She holds her own breath, and I take another gamble and press my mouth against her neck, kissing her throat.

"Does this?" I whisper.

She doesn't answer but I take it as a yes, kissing her some more and then slipping my hand under the straps of her dress, skimming the soft skin of her shoulders and then down to her tit.

"Is this good behavior?" I ask, rubbing the pad of my thumb over her nipple until it crinkles and stiffens. "Does it feel good?"

"Uh huh," she says, her voice a little panty as she tips back her head, making her throat all long and beautiful. I grip it with my other hand and tilt her chin towards me, kissing her mouth this time as I massage her tit and she rubs that ass of hers against me.

I don't feel the cold one bit anymore. In fact, my blood is running hot. If Barone interrupts us this time, I will let my beast take over and I will tear out his goddamn throat.

I kiss her deeply, exploring her mouth with my tongue, sucking and biting at her lips. I let my hand fall lower, over her stomach, feeling the waistband of her panties through the silk of her dress.

"You want me to show you just how good I can be and

make you come?" I say, running a finger along the waist-band, teasing her.

She bites down on my bottom lip and I take that as another yes, gathering up the skirt of her dress and then dipping my hand below the fabric and inside her panties, meeting a fine line of soft curls and then lower to the start of her pussy lips. She's damp and sticky with arousal and the beast growls inside me, knowing we did that. Knowing that she wants us, despite all the massive screw ups. Maybe she wants us just as badly as we want her.

"Can I touch you?" I ask. I'm practically begging. The thought of this was the only thing that kept me hanging on in that hellhole.

"You won't ever leave again, will you?" she asks me softly, peering up into my eyes.

"Fuck, no," I promise, "never. I'm yours now. Both of us. And we're never going to leave." I dip a finger between her pussy lips and she jolts, moaning, eyes fluttering shut. "I'm sorry," I whisper to her as I circle her sensitive nub, "sorry for everything. For every dumb, stupid, cruel thing I ever did to you. Sorry for being a dumbass jerk. Sorry for not seeing how truly fucking awesome you are Rhianna Blackwaters. Sorry for not being able to look past my own hangups and tell you how much you mean to me." My voice cracks a little. "I'm really fucking sorry. I'm going to try my best to make it up to you – every single day."

"I know," she whispers back, color spilling into her cheeks, "and I forgive you."

My goddamn knees nearly buckle beneath me and my head spins so fast I nearly fall. She forgives me. Even though she shouldn't, even though I've been a giant shit. She forgives me anyway.

I kiss her again with passion and gratitude and something far, far stronger. I kiss her damn hard, flicking at her clit, until she's moaning into my mouth, body writhing in my arms and then I plunge a finger inside her. Tight and warm, convulsing in waves around my digit.

"Fuck, I want you so badly," I murmur. I know it's dangerous out here. Any moment someone could notice that the feast's guest of honor is missing and they could come looking for us.

I couldn't care less.

"Yes," she pants, "yes."

I find the spot inside her and rub at it, holding her tight by the throat and using my magic to spark against her clit.

When she falls apart, I draw back, wanting to see, wanting to watch her face. All taut with tension one minute, then her brow unfurrows, her mouth slackens, her eyelids flutter and bliss and color sweep across her face, her pussy going fucking crazy around my finger and the noises she makes damn damn damn sexy.

I consider pulling her to the ground and having her right here and now. If she were any other girl, I would. But something stops me and it isn't the threat of being discovered like this. It's the need for our first time to be special.

I chuckle.

Special?

When has sex ever been special? It's always been an itch that needed scratching. Nothing more.

But with her, I think it could be – I know it will be – a hell of a lot more.

So I'll be patient again.

I withdraw my fingers from inside her, slowly, reveling in the way her pussy clamps around me like it doesn't want me to go, and a long whine issues from her throat. Then I bring that hand up to my face. My fingers glisten with her arousal.

It smells slightly bitter like all girls do. Usually I'd want to wash this shit off me. Usually I wouldn't even be bothering with fingering a girl in the first place. Why bother with a pathetic entrée when you can plunge straight into the main course? But again, this is different. I have a desire to know everything about her – including how she tastes. And so, I place my finger in my mouth and suck on it like a baby with a pacifier.

The taste is tart and a little sweet as it spreads over my tongue and the beast goes fucking wild for it inside me, desperate to break free and fucking lick her himself. I resist him. We may have a better understanding now, but this is my time with her, and fuck if I'm about to give it up.

When I open my eyes again, Rhi has twisted around to face me, right up close against my chest, the blanket still a tangle around our shoulders. For a moment we're just staring at each other and then that girl does the last thing in the world I expect her to do. She drops down to her knees on the cold ground and reaches up to undo the fly of my pants.

"We might be seen," I protest, half-hearted.

"I'll know if there's someone coming."

"But you don't have to," I say, "you're not obliged."

She smiles at me. "Spencer, do you really think I'd do anything because I felt obliged?"

I grin back at her. She has a point. I can't see Rhi doing anything at all she didn't want to.

"So you're going to do this because you think I want it or because you think it will be good?"

She tilts her head. "I'm kind of hoping it will be both."

"So just to clarify, you think sucking my cock will be good?"

She rolls her eyes. "Do you want me to do this because if you do, you're doing a really great job of–"

"I want you to do it," I say, clamping my hands over hers so she can't pull them away. Stars, do I want her to do this! Her mouth. Plush pouty pink lips. I've been dreaming about how good her mouth would look wrapped about my dick. And fuck, I haven't had those kind of dreams since I was a pup. "I just wanted to hear you say it too."

"Spencer," she says, drawing down my zipper, "I want to suck on your cock." Then she gives me one of her defiant looks, like she's challenging me or something. "I like it, okay?"

Fuck, I think she just killed me. I groan and watch in amazement as she draws my stiff cock from my briefs and examines my length, her eyes darkening with lust like she actually really does want to do this.

It's another fucking first. I thought girls were about as into this as I was into the fingering. I thought they said bull-shit about your dick being magnificent and all that crap because they thought they had to. But fuck, Rhianna Black-waters looks at my cock like she really does want to devour it. Nothing fake about it. All genuine.

This girl surprises me every goddamn day.

She shuffles forward on her knees, my cock head bumping against her cheek, leaving a line of silver precome trailing over her skin.

Then she captures my cock in her mouth and sucks and the fucking stars in the sky multiply before my eyes.

"Fuccccckkkkk," I groan. "Fuck that feels good."

She circles her tongue over my cockhead like she wants to taste every inch of me and then she takes a hold of my shaft in both her fists and jerks me off as she sucks again, right into her mouth, hollowing out her cheeks. And this girl must really like sucking cock, because fuck she's good at it.

My balls are aching something chronic. It's been a long, long time since I've fucked a girl, since they've got down on their knees for me like this, since I've even touched myself. At first, Rhianna was buzzing around in my head too much for me to even want to think about another girl, let alone fuck one. And then, then everything else happened, and once the pain had died away, there was nothing left. No more feelings.

Numbness. Only numbness.

Now every part of me feels alive. Like the way she's sucking on my cock is bringing me back to life. Every nerve tingles. Every sinew snaps.

I don't know how long I'm going to last. I want it to last forever. For her to never stop. She looks like a queen, a goddess, kneeling before me, her cheeks pink, her eyes dark, her lashes wet. I reach down and tangle my fingers in her dark hair, as soft as her silk dress to the touch.

I groan again, nothing ever felt this good. Nothing at all.

I want to last. But I can't. I'm too freaking sensitive, too turned on. My balls tighten and I grunt, spilling my junk into her mouth and watching as she swallows it all down.

"Good girl," I mutter, not even fucking aware of what I'm saying, so high I'm no longer sure my feet are even on the ground. "Good fucking girl."

I close my eyes and revel in the bliss, suspended somewhere between heaven and earth, not sure I ever want to come down.

I'd begun to think I'd never feel like this again. And that she's given me this. Something so many would consider dirty, depraved. The fact she wanted to. Me a mutt, a cursed. It's too much. My body shakes and it's not the beast attempting to break free. It's something else. All the emotions I've been holding back, caging inside. They all come flooding out.

I drop to my knees before her, sobs wracking my body, my face wet with salty tears.

"Spencer?" she says, laying a hand on my shoulder. "Spencer, what's wrong? Did I do something wrong?"

I shake my head, unable to speak.

"Then what is it?"

There's the smell of arousal in the night's air. Hers and mine and when I look at her through my wet lashes, there's a dribble of my come running down her chin. It guts me, guts me completely.

"I don't deserve this," I say, truthfully, none of the good-old Spencer fucking bravado. The truth. Clear and simple.

"Don't say that," she says sternly.

"It's the truth."

"I disagree. You know how many guys want to be you, Spencer Moreau. How many girls want to be with you." She raises an eyebrow.

"That's before they knew the truth about me."

"You don't think being a werebeast makes you a million times hotter?"

I snort. "No, it makes me a freak."

"A hot freak," she teases. "I think the werebeast thing is incredibly hot, actually."

I smile at her, blinking away tears.

"I think that makes *you* the freak."

"Well, duh?" she says. "Five mates, pet pig. I'm a way bigger freak than you."

"I like how freaky you are. I like it even more when you're being freaky with me," I say, wiping away that dribble of come from her chin and offering it up to her mouth. She catches my gaze and licks it off my thumb, tongue swiping over her lips afterwards.

"Well, shit," I mumble. "I like it a lot."

She smiles widely at me.

"I want to seal the bond between us," she says and my heart goes fucking ballistic in my chest, beating so hard I think it might explode. And then it stops, screeches to a halt. Because I can read it on her face, that smile waning. There's a but coming. A big fat-assed but.

"But ..." I prompt her. It's coming anyway, what's the point in delaying it. "You haven't really forgiven me."

She shakes her head. "It's not that. It's ..." she peers up towards the sky and the dragon circling high above our heads, "what if I'm not who you think I am?" I frown. I don't know what she means. "The crimson magic, Spencer? What if I'm not good?" She lowers her voice. "I'm the Black Prince's daughter."

"Rhi, I'm a giant idiot. You know that. But one thing I do know that I've learned, there are no good or bad people. We do good things; we do bad things." I close my eyes, thinking about how I shut her in that locker, wishing over and over again that I'd never done it. "We just have to hope we do more good things in our lifetime than the bad. That shows us who we are. And I know who you are, Rhianna Blackwaters. A whole lot of freak."

She smiles again, giggling, and I take her hand.

"Wanna go get freaky with me now?" I say, my voice lowering about ten octaves with lust.

She's going to say no. This is the wrong time. We should be back at that feast, mingling with all those people, attempting to find answers in this strange place.

She nods her head, looking up at me all seductively through her lashes.

I pull her to her feet and lead her inside.

"You know which way to go?" I whisper to her as we creep inside.

It's dark and quiet here in the corridors, the sound of music and voices distant. Have they even missed us yet?

She peers along the corridor to the left, then beckons me that way and we stumble together, both of us with cheek-splitting grins on our faces, my heart hammering in my chest, my cock somehow already hard again.

Outside, one of the closed doors, she pauses.

"I think it's this one," she whispers.

I draw it open and poke my head inside. Yes, this one. Thank fuck for that. I drag her inside the suite and then the nearest bedroom, flicking on a side light with my magic and then locking the door with a spell I hope none of the others will be able to infiltrate.

And then we're facing each other, those grins still wide on our faces. It lasts a second before we're ripping each other's clothes off. Actually ripping them, I take the neckline of that dress and rip it right down the middle, the pieces of material falling to the floor and leaving her in just her panties.

"Hey," she says, laughing, "that isn't mine. And I don't have many clothes, Spencer."

"Shit," I say, smiling back at her sheepishly and rubbing my hand over my short hair. "Here you can rip mine."

I offer her up my chest. She yanks the bowtie from my neck and takes my shirt collar in her hands, tugging with all her might. Nothing happens.

"I can't do it," she pouts.

I shake my head. "We are going to work on that, strengthen you up."

I cover my hands with hers and help her to rip my shirt right down the front, buttons popping everywhere.

"Jeez," she says, her eyes swim all over the contours of my chest and my abdomen. "That was insanely hot."

There's no pause, though. Next, she's back at the zipper of my suit pants as I'm toeing off my shoes and my socks. Then she's standing in front of me in just her panties. Some silky lacy pair, a serious upgrade since the last time I saw her in her underwear all those weeks ago in the locker room.

"Fuck, Rhianna. You look fucking amazing. You should have been on the cheering squad. You have the fucking body for it."

"Me? A cheerleader?" she scoffs.

I chuckle, kicking off my pants and my briefs. "I can just see it, bouncing up and down with your pom-poms, cheering out my name."

"Spencer Moreau, take that back," she says, hand on her hip in a way that emphasizes all her curves and has my cock dribbling precome.

"Uh uh," I say, grinning at her. "I like the idea."

"Never going to happen," she says.

"Yeah, but I bet I can make you scream out my name." I stalk towards her.

"You're very sure of yourself."

I grin at her. Then I bend down and go to town on those tits of hers, sucking and licking at her pert nipples. All those doubts and insecurities I was feeling moments ago out in the garden are gone. Being with Rhi is the most natural thing in the world. I don't think I ever smiled, laughed so much with a girl before. Never had this much fun.

As I French-kiss her tit, I slide her panties down her

backside and she gives it a little wiggle, the globes of her ass jiggling. I take them both in my hands and squeeze. Hard.

"Jeez, Spencer!" she cries out.

And I swing up to standing and grin again.

"Bingo!"

"What?" she says.

"Made you cry out my name."

She whacks me on the left pec. "I was hoping you meant it some other way."

"You did, did you?" I say, pulling her right up against my body. "In what way exactly?"

"You like me saying this stuff, huh?"

"Yep."

"In the cock-deep-inside-me, fucking-me way," she says, eyes locked to mine.

"Fuck," I mutter. "I really fucking love it when you talk dirty. That fucking mouth of yours."

I push her backwards onto the large bed behind her, take a thigh in either hand and open her wide, staring down into the glistening folds of her pussy.

"I better do as the lady asks, then, hadn't I?" I step forward, lining myself up with her hole.

"Barrier spell!" she yelps and I mutter the damn words as quickly as I can. Then with a deep breath, eyes locked between us, I step forward and watch my cock thrust inside her pussy.

She moans like a thing possessed, her spine arching.

"Fuck, yes," I mutter. I want to fuck her into actual oblivion. But there's also the desire to make this special. To make this good for her. So I grind into her teasingly, slowly, hitting all those parts inside her, warming her up nice and good. She writhes around on the bed, pussy throbbing around me, moaning some more.

I've watched a lot of porn, seen a lot of girls put on an act. But this is erotic and I could tease her for ever, except soon she's pleading with me.

"Spencer," she moans, "Spencer, please?"

"Please, what, little mate? What do you need from me?"

"Need you to fuck me. Hard."

I chuckle. There it is again. That dirty mouth. Not afraid to ask for what she wants. I love that about this girl.

I grind inside her a couple more times, partly because teasing her has always been a lot of fun. Partly because I love the way her pussy feels around my cock.

Then when she's starting to spit and hiss at me, I fuck her hard, pounding my body into her over and over again, making the bed crash against the wall and the floor creak beneath us.

Maybe I should be concerned about someone coming to find us, especially when she gets louder and louder, but I've had to endure listening to this myself. Now it's my turn.

"Come on, Rhi," I say, "come for me and say my fucking name."

Her hands fist the sheets, a tangle under her body, and she bites down hard on her lip. She's close, so close.

I lift her legs higher, so they're resting against my chest, shifting the angle, hitting her right where she needs me, and now she comes. Noisy as hell, screaming my fucking name louder than any damn cheerleader. It's the biggest ego boost of my life, and I come right after her, spilling my shit a second time, only this time deep, deep inside her pussy as it squeezes around me.

"Stars," I mutter as all that ecstasy sails through my body and that bond in my body soars and tightens, locks inside me and I feel all her emotions, all that bliss she's experiencing reflected back at me. "Stars, Rhi, stars."

It's done. The bond is sealed and the beast purrs inside me, the most content I've ever, ever known him.

27

R^{hi}

A HUGE SMILE cracks across Spencer's face as he tumbles into the bed beside me, pulling me towards him.

"Fuck," he says with elation, "fuck, that feels incredible."

"The bond?" I ask him.

"The bond, your pussy, your pussy coming around my cock. All of it." He rolls me towards him and kisses my mouth. I don't think I've ever seen Spencer Moreau this happy – not even when he won that dueling cup.

He pulls back and looks down at me.

"Was it good for you too?" he says, still grinning, because the dude has never exactly been modest and he knows it was. "Do you feel all right?"

I smile back at him. "Yeah, I feel fine." He beams at me and then settles down on the mattress, hugging me tight to his body and soon, his breathing mellows and I can tell he's passed out.

I lie there.

I didn't want to tell him, didn't want to shatter his good mood. But something feels different. Not simply the new – the final – bond, alive and vibrant deep inside me. My magic too.

With each sealing of the bond it's grown that little bit more, swelled in power. This, however, is different. That dark magic, the one they call crimson, scarlet, soars through my body, stronger than before, hissing in my veins, potent and powerful, drowning out my other magic.

What can it mean?

Christopher Kennedy's words have been eating away at me – the fact I'm the Black Prince's daughter making me uneasy. My dad's explanation had made me feel a little better about that and Spencer had calmed my concerns. Now they come flooding back. Fear churning with the dark magic inside me.

I stare up at the ceiling afraid. I want to stay here with Spencer, snuggled in this bed. His presence is a comfort and I'm scared that if I crawl out of this bed, my fears and this dark magic will consume me. But I need to get back to that party. I'm bound to have been missed by now and stars know what people will think of me.

Carefully, I remove Spencer's arm from around me and roll up to sit, shuffling across the mattress. I've just reached the edge of the bed when Spencer jolts.

At first, I think I've woken him, but then his entire body jerks violently. He's changing and I sit there transfixed as his body transforms painfully into the beast's.

In a matter of minutes, my gaze meets the beast's eyes, glowing that chestnut brown in the darkness.

"Are you afraid, little mate?" he asks me, his gaze intense.

"No," I say, rolling back down to lie by his side. "I just wasn't expecting you."

His tongue slides along his jaw. "I couldn't resist it," he says, his gaze sliding down my naked body. "He's had you," he says, growling. "Seeded your cunt."

My cheeks flush. I was maybe okay with the dirty talk when it comes to Spencer, but the beast is another matter.

"We used a barrier spell," I tell him, predicting what he has in mind. The beast snorts, obviously displeased with that bit of news. "Babies are not on the agenda."

"But you sealed the bond. You are ours now. Bound to us for this lifetime."

I don't know why but the way he says it makes me shiver hard. The beast lifts one of his great paws and glides it down my body, the pads on his paw hard and calloused, his claws withdrawn. I shiver even harder.

"Such a pretty little thing. So sensitive. Did he make you fall apart?"

I nod.

"*I* would like to make you fall apart, little mate. Over and over again."

I swallow hard. I don't think that is in the cards. I have a clear view of what hangs between the beast's legs and it is pretty darn monstrous.

"Or perhaps you could suck on my iron like you sucked on his?" He draws out a claw and hooks it under my chin, lifting my gaze more firmly to his. "You looked so beautiful drinking down his seed. A hungry, needy little thing, aren't you?"

I open my mouth to answer him. I can't deny that the beast stirs something inside me – because no matter what

Winnie says I am clearly a deranged slut who is horny for every one of my mates no matter what they have done or ... what they are. And yet ...

"How about we just lie here and talk," I suggest.

"Too fast, little mate? No matter. I have waited an eternity to find you again. I can wait that little bit longer."

"What do you mean?" I ask, my brow furrowing.

"We have been fated together through the ages, across the times," he says, stroking his great paw back up my body, his fur brushing against my skin. "In different forms. In different places. Sometimes our time together has been fleeting. Sometimes it has lasted a human lifetime."

I remember what Ellie told me about fated mates being destined for one another over and over again. Is that what he means?

Winnie seems convinced I'm Queen Æðelflæd reincarnated. But maybe that was simply one time – one moment in time we were all brought together by fate. Maybe there were others too.

It seems so fantastical. I can't wrap my head around it. And yet here I am lying in bed with a werebeast, brought to this palace on the back of a golden dragon.

Perhaps anything is possible.

"Just us or–"

"All six of us, little mate."

"And every time we have met have you always taken the form of a were?"

He doesn't seem to hear me. Instead he draws that claw down my body next, the faintest of scratches against my skin. At my belly, he pauses and tilts his head. His eyes flash.

"Something has changed inside you, little mate. Something is different."

I go very still on the bed next to him. I want to swallow a

second time, but I daren't and I keep my eyes locked on his, refusing to flinch, refusing to give anything away.

He can't know, can he? He can't possibly tell.

He rings his claw around my belly button.

"Something dark lurks within. It always has. Dark, sinister, powerful. It has grown – although something keeps it contained." My eyes drop to my belly, red scratches now run over my skin and I can almost see the dark magic swirling beneath. "You could destroy the world if you wanted to, little mate. Crush it all. Like you chose to before."

The furrow on my brow deepens. "Queen Æðelflæd? She saved the world. She was a good ruler."

"Were you?" he asks me, searching deep inside my eyes.

"You think I'm her." I screw up my brow. "Or she's me."

"You are you, little mate. Each time we have met." He inhales my scent. "Always two sides to the coin, which way it lands is anyone's guess. Different every time. How will it fall this time, I wonder?"

"Is that what the prophecy means?" I ask him.

He cups my breast in his paw, squeezing it, his eyes flashing.

"The prophecy," he purrs. "Do you need a prophecy to tell you of your fate?"

I push off the bed, more disturbed by his words than his request to suck his giant cock.

"Little mate, now I have scared you," he says, with some concern.

"I don't understand what you're talking about." I scoop my panties and the ruined dress off the floor and hurry to the door. "I need a glass of water," I tell him.

The door is locked, but somehow I manage to remove Spencer's spell and tumble into the suite, the pain in my newly formed bond acute.

Pip comes scuttling towards my feet, snorting away. I'm too distressed to even acknowledge him, tugging on my clothes and mending the dress with my magic.

This secret I've been harboring, this fear that's been growing in my chest, is true, all true. There's a darkness inside me, one that's always lingered there. One that only Pip's presence has held back and now I can feel it, stronger and more dangerous than ever.

I want to talk to Azlan about it or Stone or, stars, I wish Winnie were here. But I can't tell them. I can't tell them the truth.

That I wanted to kill Christopher Kennedy. I relished the chance to do it. Hell, it made that crimson magic tingle and now that magic is more powerful than ever, threatening to take me over.

I stand in the dark suite, my heart pounding, that dark magic sizzling, struck by indecision. What do I do?

I think on Spencer's words.

It's actions that make us, not where we come from.

But what have my actions been? I've killed and maimed. I'm in love with men who kill for fun, who have each tortured and hurt me in their own ways. And my temper! I blasted Spencer and Summer with crimson magic. I'm lucky I didn't kill them. And oh, there have been so so many times I'd liked to have killed Summer Clutton-Brock and every single member of her little gang. Does that make me a bad person? An evil one? It must do! Does the dark blood in my veins, the crimson magic in my body, make me that way? Is Pip, my ever faithful familiar, the only thing that's prevented me from falling into the darkness completely? From tearing up the world? And now that magic is more powerful than ever, is there anything that can hold me back?

What if I am something more sinister, far darker than the Lord Protector himself?

The beast seems to think I am. Seems to think I have been in the past too.

But they said the Black Prince was a dark magical, didn't they? An evil man? And yet he doesn't seem that way. He seems charming, his kingdom prosperous, his subjects loyal and happy, celebrating the return of his daughter with him.

The pain in my stomach from the freshly formed bond is unbearable and I drop down on my knees and scrabble through our discarded belongings, searching for the triggerwot.

"Rhianna." I look up and find Azlan lurking in the doorway. "I've been looking for– What's wrong?"

"Nothing," I snap, yanking at empty pockets. "I'm searching for triggerwot."

Azlan glances towards the bedroom. "You sealed the bond with Spencer. I felt it. We all felt it."

"Yes," I mutter as the pain makes me hiss.

"Why aren't you in there with him now? There's no need for triggerwot if you–"

"It's complicated."

He strides towards me and crouches down, hooking a finger under my chin and lifting my face to his.

"Are you going to tell me what's wrong? Or do I have to go beat it out of him?" His voice is full of menace.

"It's nothing to do with Spencer. I wanted to seal the bond with him. I wanted to be with him."

"So again, I repeat, why are you out here?"

"I have to get back to the feast," I mutter half-heartedly.

"Fine," he says, standing up, cracking his knuckles and marching towards the bedroom.

"Wait! No!"

He halts but doesn't face me.

"Something's changed." The pain in my gut is fierce and I screw up my eyes and grind my teeth.

"Your powers have grown again," he says. "It happens every time you seal the bond with one of us. It's grown all our powers."

"Yes, but this time it's different."

He comes back to crouch beside me and reaches for his cloak in the pile of clothes, plucking triggerwot straight from his pocket and handing it to me. I chew on the leaves and immediately the pain eases. I sigh and rock back onto my behind.

"Explain," he says.

"The dark magic – the crimson magic – it's stronger than before. Much stronger." I watch his face with anxiety. Is this where Azlan, ever dependable and loyal, finally realizes just how fucked up I am and recoils in disgust?

His face doesn't change.

"It's not surprising, Rhianna. Sealing the bond has increased your powers – all your powers."

"But the beast said–"

"The beast!" he growls.

"Is a part of our ..." I wave my hands around frantically, "whatever you want to call our set up."

"Family."

"Okay," I say, "the beast is as much a part of this family as you or I."

Azlan nods without argument. Maybe a beast and an assassin aren't exactly his preferred choices for this new family of ours; then again his actual blood family consists of a power-hungry psychopath so it's hard for him to complain.

"What did the beast say?"

"He seems to think we've met before – have been fated together in past lives."

"Sounds like Ellie's woo woo shit to me."

"That isn't the bit I'm worried about," I say, wringing my hands. He takes them in his and squeezes them.

"What are you worried about, little mate?" he says gently.

"He says it's always been the same: whenever we've met in these past lives, I've always had both light and dark inside me. And sometimes the light has dominated and ... and sometimes the dark ..." I trail off, watching his face a second time with my heart in my throat.

"Hmmm," he says, mulling over my words. "Spencer ... Spencer isn't the first were I've come across, Rhianna. I found them all to be rather mystical and superstitious. Maybe it is down to the circumstances they find themselves in – maybe they need something bigger to believe in to persevere through the prejudice and persecution." I go to argue with him but he speaks again first. "Or maybe they know more than us. Maybe he is right. What difference does it make what you may have done in past lives? What we all may have done? All that matters is the present and what we choose to do now."

"That's what Spencer said," I mutter, "that who we are is determined by the choices we make."

"I think you are far better off listening to him than his beast," Azlan snarks and I smile. "Rhianna," he says, pulling me closer towards him, "I've spent the last decade chasing down bad people–"

"Bad people like me."

"No, Rhi, you are not bad. If I'm honest with myself, many of them weren't bad people, they'd just found them-selves caught on the wrong side of the authorities. However, several of them were bad people, very, very bad people. And I can tell you, with my hand on my heart, you are not like them. Not like them at all."

I inhale, his masculine scent swimming into my nostrils, and filling my lungs, and then I let that same breath out slowly.

"What if the bad magic takes over? What if I can't control it? I have a temper and I'm not always the most patient of people."

Azlan tugs me right into his lap. "Really, I hadn't noticed that about you at all," he teases. I pinch his bicep. "Or your occasional acts of violence," he says, flexing his bicep where I just pinched. "But, seriously, Rhianna, I believe in you – we all do. And if that ever happened, if you ever struggled to control it, we'd be right here to help you. I promise you that."

I snuggle up against his broad chest. There's something about being in his arms, strong and dependable, that makes me feel so safe, like nothing and no one could harm me.

"Thank you, Azlan," I say.

He strokes his fingers along my jawline and tangles them in my hair.

"I think we're both guilty of hiding our feelings away at times. And I'm not exactly the best at talking about mine. But I think it's better when we try."

"Yes," I say. I feel better for talking to him, the worries dissipating. He's right, I have these five men here to help me – to help me make the right choices. "However," I add, "I happen to think you're very good at showing me your feelings in other ways."

"I am?" he says, voice lowering and his grip in my hair tightening. "How's that, little mate?"

"With your lips," I say, tracing my fingertips around his

mouth, "with your touch," I take his hand from my waist and draw my fingers up his, "with your body," I glide my hand down that broad chest of his, "and with your cock." I grip him through the front of his pants, stiff and hard.

"You forgot my tongue," he growls, licking up my throat and then sinking his tongue into my mouth. I wriggle around until I'm straddling his lap as he kisses me. I grind against him.

I bet Winnie would be rolling her eyes at me. I seriously can't keep it in my pants. I blame the bond and hormones and the fact that fate has handed me possibly the five hottest men on the planet. I really can't be held responsible for my actions.

I guess Azlan is thinking the same thing.

"You have such an insatiable appetite," he growls into my mouth. "It's going to take five of us just to satisfy it."

His words make me shiver hard with desire and the next thing I know he's rolling me down on the floor and gathering up my dress.

The bedroom was bad enough but now we're doing this right here in the middle of the suite – on display for anyone who comes looking for us.

I should care.

I don't.

All I care about is his hands on my body, his mouth on my skin and him inside me. He swims his fingers through my folds – still sticky with arousal and Spencer – and I rub myself against him, a mewing sound bubbling in my throat.

He doesn't even bother to undress us. He tugs down his zipper, freeing himself of his pants and murmurs the barrier spell.

Then, with his arms braced either side of my head, he thrusts into me.

"I love the feeling of you inside me," I murmur, as I watch him transfixed, the way he uses his powerful body to pleasure me, thrusting deep inside me, knocking against my sensitive clit, making me dizzy with the sensations.

"Because it's where I belong," he says in that deep voice of his, a voice that rumbles in his chest and seems to vibrate through my own body.

Alone in the forest, I used to imagine what this would be like. And it was nothing like this. So vulnerable, yet so cherished. So invasive, yet so intimate. So raw, yet so cerebral. I never realized it was possible to feel this close to another person.

I come, my spine arching and bliss racing through my body. He watches me, eyes locked on me the whole time as I writhe beneath him, and when it's done, he flips me over on to my stomach, pressing my chest down into the hard floor and lifting up my hips. Then he takes me from behind, the angle making it even deeper and even more intense. I stretch my hands above my head, scraping my fingernails into the polished floorboards and arching my back like a cat, forcing him even deeper.

"Fuck," he says, his fingers digging deep into the flesh of my hips, "fuck, little mate. You are so fucking delicious."

He loses his careful pace, slamming into me once, twice, three times and coming deep inside me with the fourth, moaning his pleasure in a way that tips me over the edge a second time. Then he collapses down on top of me, smoothing the hair away from my face and kissing my cheek.

"You're good, so, so good," he murmurs into my ear and then he scoops me up into his arms and carries me back to the bedroom, laying me out on the bed beside a sleeping

Spencer. I wriggle over the bed and snuggle up to Spencer's warm body, peering up at Azlan.

"Get some sleep," he whispers, about to move off. I catch his wrist.

"Don't go," I say, patting the sliver of mattress beside me.

"There isn't room," he says gruffly.

I give him my most determined look. "There's plenty." I pat the mattress again.

He shakes his head, but slips out of his jacket, his shirt and his ruined pants, and slides into the bed next to me.

Snuggled with my back against Spencer, I wrap my arm over Azlan's waist and one leg between his.

"You know, Phoenix says you are a brat and I'm beginning to think he may be right."

"You just said I was good," I purr.

"Yeah," he says softly, stroking my face again. "You're my good little mate."

I close my eyes, a smile hovering on my lips and soon I'm sound asleep. All my worries, for now, silenced and sedated.

28

R enzo

I CAN'T SLEEP. My mind's too wired, a thousand voices jabbering away inside my head all at once. I sit in an armchair, my legs hanging over the arm, slinging my magic silently across the room.

The voices won't stop. Not if I try and make them. No use arguing with them. I have to wait for them to run out of steam. Or wait for little rabbit. All the voices go quiet when she's around as if they want to pay attention to what she's doing.

It's the middle of the fucking night though. Little rabbit asleep herself.

I toss another ball of magic across the room and fling back my head.

Upside down, I see the professor walk across the ceiling towards the windows. It's dark. He hasn't seen me.

He's wearing tight boxers. The prof's cock is as big as the rest of him. Not surprising. I've heard the way he makes her scream. Bet she loves the feel of that cock.

"Hey," I say. "Your cock's bigger than I remember it."

The prof jumps. Yeah, even after all that's past, I can still scare the shit out of him if I want to.

Good to know.

"What the hell," he mutters. "What are you doing sitting in the dark like that?"

"Couldn't sleep," I say, tossing more magic up into the air and then catching it in my palms.

"Yeah," he says, rubbing his hands through his beard. His eyes slide to me and then he walks over and slumps down into one of the other chairs. He rests each hand on the armrests and taps his fingers against the leather. "Why can't you sleep?"

I flip upright, so I'm looking at him straight on, and tap the side of my head.

"Too many voices."

He looks straight into my eyes. "There are drugs for that, you know."

I snort. Yeah, I know about those. My mom spent a lot of her time trying to shove various drugs and potions and other shit down my throat.

"You ever taken those drugs?" I ask him.

"No."

Didn't think so. Anyone who had wouldn't be recommending them.

"They make your mind fucking sloppy. I'd rather stick with the voices."

"What are the voices saying?"

I sigh, and lean forward, resting my forearms on my knees, legs still jiggling.

"Shit, well, there's this little old lady," the corners of my mouth tug, "she's my favorite. She's always rattling on about the weather and her cakes and whether her dog's got diarrhea or not."

"Right." The prof's brow creases.

"Least favorite's this dude. He's a real fucking asshole. Likes to remind me about all my fuck ups. Constantly encourages me to, you know ..." I mime wrapping the rope around my neck and tugging.

"Fucking hell."

"Yeah, he's a cunt. There's a couple of voices that sound like my mom used to. One that sounds just like Lowsky's pa. Then there's this one," I shuffle forward on the chair, "that's talking in this language I don't understand. Never even heard it before. He's always fucking insistent but I don't know what the fuck he's saying."

"That sounds ... rough."

I slump back in my chair. "You get used to it." My eyes slide towards the bedroom door. "And she, she silences them." He nods. "So, how about you, prof? What keeps you awake?"

The speed at which he's tapping those armrests increases.

"I have a bad feeling about this place."

"A feeling? I thought you were academic or something. I thought you only dealt in facts and proof and shit?"

"That's the problem. I don't have any proof or shit right now. Only a feeling." His hands freeze and he leans in. "These people are hiding something. They're excited about something. I can read it in their minds. I just can't understand the words."

"Their lost princess."

He shakes his head. "I don't think that's it. But she's so

happy to be here, to find her dad. I don't think I can go and destroy that for her just because I have a 'feeling'." He starts tapping all over again and I consider him.

"Can you read *my* mind? All those voices."

"Yes."

"Then why'd you make me say all that shit, man?"

"I was curious." He scratches at his beard, considering me in return.

"You ... you changed that dude's thoughts before, right?" I ask. He nods. "You think you could stop the voices in my head?"

"Would you want me to?"

I think about it, all those voices rattling on as I try to anyway. "Nah," I say. "It's just who I am."

The prof nods again and then stands to his feet.

"I'm going back to bed. You should try and get some sleep too."

"Sure," I say, but I stay where I am and watch him go. There's no point. I'm not sleeping tonight.

After a while I pace the room a bit, then I play with the knife. Flicking the blade up and down, and finally I retreat back to the chair.

Morning arrives, but the room doesn't get a whole lot brighter, the window's darkened. Some dude knocks at the door and then proceeds to place all kinds of breakfast food out on the giant table without saying one word to me.

The smell of all that food wakes all the other dudes up until they appear one by one. First the prof again, then the Kennedy boy, followed by the enforcer, and finally the were and little rabbit together. Instantly those voices in my head go quiet. Like someone slammed off the radio.

Her hair's all tangled and her skin has that flush which tells me he's already made her come this morning.

I'm chewing some pastry shit with a ton load of chocolate and I watch them tiptoe over together, hands linked, little rabbit wearing his shirt.

"Morning," the were says, looking exactly like a dude who just got laid.

He pulls a chair out from the table for her and she sits down.

He takes the chair next to her and as his backside hits the seat, a magic sweeps through me.

"Shit," the Kennedy boy says. "You feel that?"

"Yeah," the were-boy says, "like electricity is passing through my body. What is that?"

"The bond," the prof says. He has dark circles under his eyes and I guess he didn't get that sleep he wanted after all. "All the bonds are sealed now."

"You fucked?" I ask them.

"You know they did," the enforcer hisses. I shrug. I wanted to hear them say it.

"What does it mean?" little rabbit asks.

"It's our magic, linked and entwined together now. The circle complete," the prof answers. I dart my gaze around the table. He's right. A goddamn circle. He rests his hand on the tabletop. "I reckon there's a good chance it'll be even stronger if we link hands."

"I'm not holding hands," the were snorts.

"You were just holding her hand," I point out.

"She's a girl."

"You've got a problem holding boys' hands," the prof asks, his hackles rising.

The were, darts his gaze towards little rabbit and shifts on his chair.

She rests her hand on the table like the prof. "Come on, let's give it a try."

The were takes her hand and then the prof's – I'm pretty sure the prof must squeeze it because he winces.

I stuff the rest of the pastry shit in my mouth and then lick the crap off my fingers, offering my hand out to the Kennedy boy and the enforcer.

With his eyes on little rabbit, the enforcer hesitates, pulls a slight face, then takes my hand. And now there's only one break in the circle. The one between me and the Kennedy boy. I shake my hand at him and he looks at it like it's diseased.

"That is gross."

"What is?" I ask.

"Your hands got your fucking saliva all over it."

"You know what else my saliva's been all over," I say, winking at him and snatching his hand in mine. He mutters under his breath.

But almost immediately that magic swoops around us, so fast it's like it's on drugs.

"Shit," I say, feeling it swoosh through me again and again.

"It's strong, right?" little rabbit says, "really strong. I feel like we could blast a hole in the sky itself."

"Or torch the world," I mutter.

Little rabbit snatches her hands away and reaches for one of those pastries. She doesn't like that idea. But I can taste that dark magic inside her, even stronger than it was before.

29

R^{hi}

"Your father, the Black Prince, wishes to see you."

I've been expecting the summons all morning and now here it is. Finally, we are going to talk, just like he promised.

"Rhi," Stone says, as I go to follow the young woman who has been sent to fetch me. "Be ... be careful."

"Of what?" I ask, frowning.

His eyes flick to the woman and he lowers his voice. "We don't know these people and we don't know if we can trust them."

"He's my dad," I point out. What is Stone going to tell me? That these people are bad, full of dark magic just like me. I'm not sure I want to hear it.

He lowers his voice even further, resting his fingertips on my elbow, "The same dad your aunt hid you from."

"I need to talk to him," I say, attempting to push past

him, Pip at my ankles. He's right. But, in my heart, I'm hoping that my aunt was wrong. That it was all a giant misunderstanding.

Pip and I follow the young woman down the dark corridors, around corners and down steps.

"Jeez, this place is like a maze," I say to the girl, hoping to strike up a conversation. I've barely spoken to anyone but the Black Prince since arriving here. "How do you not get lost?!"

The girl doesn't respond, keeping her eyes fixed to the ground. There were students like this at the academy, so painfully shy they were unable to make eye contact. Sometimes they just needed a little encouragement to emerge from their shells, although most of the time they simply didn't want to talk to an unregistered magical like me.

Pip begins to snort, scuttling around my feet in agitation and I reach down and pick him up. Then I try again with the girl. I'm curious about this place, about my father. I have a million trillion questions I want to ask her. "I'm Rhianna and this is Pip." I lift Pip slightly. "Short for Pipsqueak."

Her eyes slide from the floor to the pig and back again, but she says nothing.

"Do you work here?" I ask, which is probably a very stupid question but I don't know what else to say.

Nothing again.

I sigh and finally we reach a grand door. That strange feeling of déjà vu, of recognition, rings through my body. My father's room. I'm certain of it. The girl knocks lightly against the door and it slides back, the Black Prince standing in the doorway, dressed in another regal gown.

"Come in," he says.

I enter a grand study, far bigger than the principal's at Arrow Hart, and designed in dark metal colors, two large paintings of dragons flying through night skies hanging on the walls, and the windows blacked out and obscuring the view.

The Black Prince clicks his fingers and a fire roars into life in the center of the room, the flickering flames reflected on every gleaming surface, including the black pupils of his eyes. The door slides closed. I hug Pip tight to my chest.

There are so many questions I want to ask. So many things I want to understand. I swing my gaze around the room, grand and sophisticated beyond anything I've seen before.

The Black Prince points to a dark leather couch.

"Let us sit and talk. There is much for us to discuss. Much for us to learn about one another."

I nod and, clutching Pip, come to sit beside him on the couch. Up close, I see just how handsome he is, just how disarming. I guess I shouldn't be so surprised my mom fell for a man like him. It must be in the genes.

"Where to begin," he says, smiling at me with affection. "I would like to know all about you, Rhianna."

I shrug. "There isn't a whole lot to tell."

He chuckles. "I don't think that is true. I rescued you from Christopher Kennedy who seemed to want to kill you. I'm sure there is a lot to tell."

I chew on my cheek. This man may be my father but I hardly know him and, though I really hate to admit it, Stone is right. I don't know if I can trust him. Do I tell him about the prophecy? I decide it's best to keep that to myself for now. "He sees me as a threat."

"Because of your five fated ones?"

"I think so, yes."

He takes my hands in his. His are surprisingly cool despite the roaring fire.

"You are safe here. I will protect you."

"Th-thank you," I say, realizing in that moment what a relief it is to feel safe. "I have lots of questions for you too. Lots of things I don't understand."

"What did they tell you?"

I think. So many things. So many conflicting stories.

"My aunt said the authorities couldn't be trusted," I say at last.

"She was right." His face darkens. "They killed your mother."

"How do I know that wasn't you?" I whisper.

"I adored her," he says, shock adorning his features. "She was ..." he squeezes my hands, "the love of my life. We were so happy together."

"Then why did she run from you? Why did she hide me from you?"

Something flickers in his eyes and I sense his magic swell in the air. It's dark like this room and I recognize it. My magic may be like my mom's, but that other magic, the crimson magic that's grown inside me, that is all his.

"We argued – a stupid, stupid disagreement I have spent all this time regretting. When I realized my mistake, I went after her, tried to find her, hoped to beg her for forgiveness and mend the quarrel between us, plead for her to come back to me." He dips his gaze. "But I was too late. He had already found her. Already killed her."

"Who?" I say, my spine straightening. The chancellor said a dark magical had killed my mom.

His face doesn't alter. "Your fated one's father."

"Christopher Kennedy?!"

"Yes."

The room spins and my stomach plummets and yet, for some reason, I am not surprised.

Although, should I believe him?

"And yet now he's your ally?" I say in disgust, snatching my hand from his.

"You are young and still have so much to learn." He sighs. "Sometimes we must make alliances with our enemies for the greater good. I do not want war for my people."

I rub at my forehead trying to make sense of this all.

"And if he asks you to hand me over, will you do it, for the good of your people, to prevent a new war?"

"No," he says simply. "I will not."

I'm not sure how the hell that makes me feel. A new war? Because of me?

We are both silent, Pip snuffling in my lap and the fire flicking in the grate.

"What was the argument about?" I ask. "Between you and my mom."

"I forget." He shakes his head, his gaze disappearing off into the distance as if he's remembering it all. "Something small that seemed so very important at the time. A quarrel I wish with all my heart I could go back and undo. Both of us lost our tempers and said things we didn't really mean."

I think of all the times I've fought with Stone, with Tristan, with Azlan. Those rows had seemed so important in the moment, and then afterwards so small and trivial.

"Let us not dwell on the past," he says next. "Let us think on the future."

"I want to understand my past. To understand myself."

"What is there to understand? You sense that greatness in your veins. We all do. You wish to grow it."

I frown. "I don't want–"

He leans forward, his face suddenly eager. "I've been

waiting, Rhianna, ever since the moment your mother saw your future, waiting for you."

That dark magic seems to sizzle in my blood, awakening with every word he says. Pip squeaks and butts his snout against my hand. I push him gently away. My aunt gave him to me as a way to leash my powers, to stop me from becoming whatever I was destined to be.

And I want to know what that is. I need to. Maybe my dad is the one to show me.

"What did she see?" I say my gaze sinking into his dark eyes.

"A girl with a power that would know no bounds. A girl who could not be stopped, who could not be contained. A girl who could both see the future and bend it to her will." He peers deep into my eyes. "My daughter."

My magic crackles, pushing against the constraints that hold it tight, straining to break through and rip everything apart.

"They told you all sorts of lies, Rhianna." I can't look away from him, his words igniting an anger inside me. "They told you those who lived in the West were evil. That they'd been beaten into submission. They told you the only thing keeping those evil forces from consuming your country was magicals – trained to protect their lands, sacrifices to the cause. And they told you I was dead."

Yes, lies, lies, lies. So many lies.

"But why?" I cry out. "Why did they tell us all this?"

"Why else?" he says. "To control you."

I frown. It can't be that simple.

"Tell me, how do matters work in your great republic? Do the people live in peace and harmony? No one hungry? No one poor? No one sick? No one suffering? Each bearing equal burden and equal reward?"

"No," I say, the anger growing in my belly, hot and rampant. "It's not like that at all."

"No, of course not. The lies ensure the rich and powerful remain that way."

I think of the chancellor, of Christopher Kennedy, of Tristan and Spencer, of Summer fucking Clutton-Brock. I think of my stupid room at the academy. I think of all the laughter and ridicule I endured just because I was poorer than them. I think of my life with my aunt, scraping to make ends meet.

The anger rages through my veins and I can't control it. It's hot and burning and if I don't let it go, it's going to burn me alive. In desperation, I fling it against the nearest wall, my magic exploding against one of the paintings. It bursts into flames, as if the dragon has come alive inside the picture, the fire curling across the canvas, and then the heavy picture crashes to the floor.

Pip whimpers, and buries his face in my lap.

The man seated next to me doesn't bat a single eyelash though. He sits there watching the fire eat away at the painting.

"You see the injustice and you want to change it, don't you?"

"I th-think," I stutter. "I think that's my destiny." That is what the prophecy must mean. I am the one, along with my five mates, destined to change things.

My shoulders slump, the enormity of that realization too heavy to bear.

"Let me show you," he says. "Let me show you how things can be."

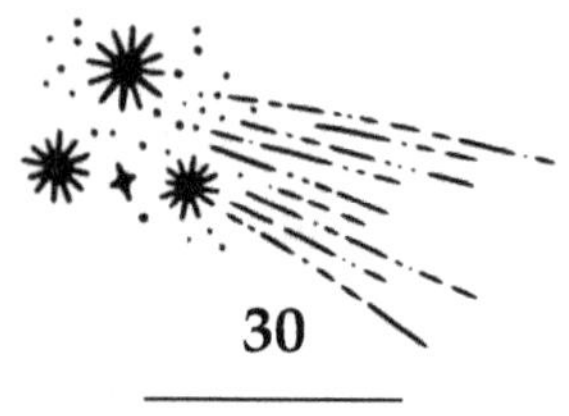

30

S tone

AZLAN IS SITTING at the table fiddling with the radio Trent gave us while we wait for Rhianna to return. He presses buttons, turns knobs and occasionally a hiss of static pierces the air.

"Can you stop doing that?" I snap from where I'm pacing in front of the windows.

I'm irritable as fuck. I don't like Rhi being away from us. Especially in a land full of people we've been fighting for the last several decades. Especially with a father rumored to be a vicious, dark, evil fuck. I scrub my hand through my beard. Why the hell did we let her go off on her own?

Azlan looks up at me. "I'm worried about Ellie."

"And how is molesting that radio going to help with that?"

"If I can reach Winnie, maybe she can tell me what's

going on with my sister." His eyes are full of concern and I remember the words Kennedy sneered at us only yesterday.

I let out a puff of air, and lay my hand on my friend's shoulder, massaging the taut muscle.

"Ellie will be okay. Your father may be a jerk-wad but he loves your sister and he won't let anything bad happen to her."

"My father's under my uncle's control. He's complicit with him."

"It doesn't mean he'll let him hurt Ellie."

Azlan looks unconvinced, but he lowers the radio anyway.

"Rhi's been a long time," I mutter.

"They've got a lot to talk about," Tristan says, from the other side of the table.

"Should we go find her?" Azlan asks.

I'm beginning to nod my head, when there is a smart rap on the door.

Spencer sprints that way and flings it open.

Rhi stands in the doorway along with the Black Prince, tall and elegant in another embroidered cloak. It's hard to reconcile this man with the one we were told about as kids – the dangerous, evil villain who would murder us all in our beds. The man who stands beside Rhi is handsome and oozes charm. He looks more like a hero than a villain.

"I am taking the princess on a tour of the city," he announces. "I invite you to join us. I would be honored if you would."

I try to read Rhi's face, trying to decipher her emotions through the bond – avoiding the temptation to read the thoughts in her head. How did the conversation with her dad go?

Her emotions seem mixed – excitement, reservation, confusion.

Next, I try the Black Prince's thoughts instead, but his are well guarded and it would take considerable force to penetrate them.

"Come," the Black Prince says. "There is much to show you."

I can't deny the tour is impressive. We're led through the streets of the city – wide sweeping avenues with the dark signature of the West fluttering on flags that line the route. Everything is new, well constructed, sleek, clean.

However, I also note that we're heavily guarded wherever we go. Is it to stop us from fleeing? To stop us from snooping around? Or is it to protect the beloved leader from his people?

Many have come out on the streets to watch the procession of the Black Prince, his long-lost daughter and her five fated mates. People stop their everyday routine to stand and watch us pass. Others gather in places they hope will allow them to catch a glimpse of us.

I hear their thoughts, all jumbled and jabbering together. They're not as well shielded as the guards but they are in the language of the West – a language I learned a little of back in the academy. Certain words jump out at me, but I can't make sense of them, not in this context. What do they mean? I search for the memory but it's out of reach.

There are words in those thoughts that stir something inside me. I may not understand them but they make me uneasy.

If the Black Prince hopes to convince us that the West is not a run-down shackle of a country, he's made his point. But he also seems keen to convince us that his kingdom is better than the republic – fairer, kinder, more just. He leads us round the hi-tech clinic – available to all – magicals and non-magicals alike. He takes us to a school brimming with books and computers and eager students. He takes us to a shelter where those unable to work are given a bed and food.

The show seems to have Rhi convinced. She asks many considered questions and as the day progresses I can feel her doubts weakening and her admiration for her father growing.

By the time we return to the palace it's nightfall.

"So," the Black Prince says as we pass through the palace gates, a teasing smile on his face. "What do you make of this dilapidated and desolate kingdom of mine?"

"It's wonderful," Rhi says, giggling, clearly a little giddy. "I still can't believe this is the West."

"Things aren't always as they seem," I say, gaze lingering on the Black Prince's face. "But the truth always outs in the end."

"It does." The Black Prince bows his head with a sense of seriousness. "It has been a pleasure to show you this kingdom, but it has been a long day. Perhaps a quiet dinner in your quarters would be best tonight. We can meet again in the morning." He snaps his fingers and the young girl from earlier comes scurrying out of nowhere. "Charmaine, show the princess and her fated ones back to their quarters."

On the way back to our rooms, Rhi sidles up to me and pinches me hard on the bicep.

"Jeez," I mutter, rubbing my arm. "What was that for?"

"Being rude to my dad."

I lift my eyebrow. *Dad*? Is that what we're calling Daddy Dark Prince now?

"I was not."

"Humph. What was all the," she lowers her voice, "'the

truth will out' business then? You basically called him a liar to his face."

I flick my eyes towards her. I don't want to hurt her. I don't want to pour water on her hopes or squash this excitement she's feeling. I also want to protect her.

"Because, maybe he is, Rhi? Your aunt–"

"He showed us the city. How was that a lie? You think he magiced up some incredible illusion and really the place is falling down and full of rats?" She sniffs.

"No," I say, "but we didn't speak to anyone, did we?"

"We spoke to the doctors at the hospital and the kids at the school."

"We didn't talk to any *real* people, Rhi. How do we know they are as happy as your father is making out?"

"You're such a cynic, Stone." She tuts her tongue in annoyance. "You never trust anyone or anything."

"That isn't true," I say, feeling a little hurt.

"You didn't trust me!"

"That was ... this is ... different."

She snorts and I grab her arm and swing her around to face me.

"You are the most precious thing in my life, Miss Blackwaters. You can't blame me for being a little cautious."

"And he has promised to keep us safe. Safe from Christopher Kennedy." Her face softens as she stares up at me. "You can't blame me for being a little excited about this place. It's so much ..." she draws in a breath, "better than back home." I manage a half smile, reluctant to pour any more scorn on her beliefs. "Stone, it's okay to believe in people," she whispers.

"I believe in you," I whisper right back, and then I slide my hand into her soft hair and kiss her mouth, not caring that I'm keeping all the others waiting.

When she pulls away, I catch the eye of the young woman. She was obviously watching us, awe on her face, but now she averts her gaze. I am unable to penetrate her thoughts either, although I sense an unease about them. Is that because she's in the company of people she would consider enemies? Or is there another reason?

I slide my hand down Rhi's arm, making her shiver slightly under my touch, and grasp her hand in mine. Despite all my suspicions and wariness, a contentment floats through my blood, one I've only ever felt when I'm with her. The entire world could be burning to ashes around us, and as long as I'm with her, as long as I'm with her and she's safe and happy, then I wouldn't give a shit.

I smile to myself as we continue our walk along the corridors, swinging our hands like we're two school kids.

Fuck, this could be the world's stupidest trap, and yet I'm so freaking happy.

And then it hits me.

Cloudpuff.

It hits me like a freight train. Now I remember what that stuff is for.

My blood runs icy cold and my heart pounds in my chest.

As soon as we're back in our quarters, I swing her into the nearest bedroom and slam the door shut behind us, ignoring all the outraged protests from her other mates.

"Cl-cl-cloudpuff?" I stutter.

"What?" she says, paling in front of me.

"Are you … Rhi, are you … pregnant?"

"Pregnant?!" Azlan says, standing in the now open doorway.

"What?" Rhi repeats. "No! Shhh!" She marches right past the two of us and slams the door closed.

"You're pregnant?" Azlan says again, his voice faltering. He takes a step closer, dropping down to his knees so his face hovers right in front of Rhi's belly.

A very flat belly.

"No, no, I'm not pregnant," Rhi hisses, attempting to drag Azlan back up onto his feet. "I mean, I don't think I am. I hope not. I took the cloudpuff to make sure."

"Why would you need to make sure?" I ask, crossing my arms over my chest as Azlan continues to stare at Rhi's belly.

Rhi meets my gaze head on.

"I forgot about the barrier spell. It happens." She glares at me. "It's actually really inconvenient, Professor Stone, to keep remembering the freaking spell each time, especially when my mates are so–"

"I agree," I say. "As soon as ... we're not on the run, we can get you some less onerous contraception."

"Me? What about you?" she asks, scowling like it's entirely my fault that no one in the entire universe has thought to devise some suitable contraceptive for men.

"You know it doesn't work like that, Miss Blackwaters."

"What kind of contraception?"

"There's a pill you can take every day."

"Great. Not onerous at all!"

"There's also an injection. It lasts a couple of months."

"Oh-kay," she says, sounding more satisfied with that option, "that actually sounds helpful." She glances down at Azlan. He has a hold of her hips and is still staring transfixed at her belly.

"Erm, Az," I prompt.

My friend blinks several times in a row as if coming out of a trance.

"Shit," he clears his throat, "shit, I'm sorry. Just the thought of you ... it kind of hit me out of nowhere."

"I'm not ready to have a baby," Rhi says sternly.

"Yeah, I know, of course," he says, nodding his head rapidly.

She gazes down at my friend and, just like earlier with me, her face softens and she strokes her fingers through his long hair.

"In the future though. If things are different ... calmer. Then, I do want one, a whole family actually. Eventually," she stresses. "Not right away."

Azlan grunts, his grip tightening.

I groan.

"It's ... it's, er, a mate thing, Rhi," I try to explain. "The desire to knock you up can be–"

"Overwhelming," Azlan growls.

Rhi swallows.

"Well, like I said," she says, her voice trembling slightly with what I think is desire and not nerves, "I'm not ready for that just yet. But I do think it would be good to, you know, practice."

"Practice," Azlan growls a second time.

"Uh huh."

"They do say practice makes perfect, Az," I point out.

Azlan stands, and taking a hold of each of Rhi's thighs, lifts her from the floor. "And this little mate of ours, does seem to be undertaking a fair bit of practicing."

"Are you complaining?" she snarks.

"Not one little bit," Azlan says, his mouth pressed against her throat. "I can't get enough of listening to you come, little mate. Of listening to you getting fucked. Of fucking you myself."

"Oh stars," she mutters, legs winding around his waist, head falling backwards as he nibbles up her throat. And I understand what she means. Azlan is always so serious.

When he breaks into the dirty talk, it's fucking hot, especially with our girl in his arms, already shivering with lust.

"Can we share you, Miss Blackwaters?" I ask as my friend lays her down on the mattress, and yanks his shirt over his head. My heart ceases beating while I wait with bated breath for her reply.

We've already had her together once.

One time before. One time only.

She said she liked it. She says the idea of being shared turns her on. But those words were spoken when she was drunk. Has she changed her mind?

She peers over Azlan's shoulder and crooks a finger in my direction. I don't need to be asked twice. I'm stalking right over to the bed.

For a moment, I just stand and watch the two of them together – my fated mate and my best friend. He's so much larger than her, so much stronger, packed solid with muscles that ripple on his naked back as he kisses her mouth and massages her tits hard with his hands. In comparison, she seems so small, so fragile, so soft.

The contrast is beautiful.

I watch as my friend draws back up onto his knees and, eyes locked on our mate, slowly threads each of the buttons of her shirt through their hole, drawing the garment open like a fucking birthday present. He sweeps it down her shoulders and then she's lying there in her bra.

He shakes his head, muttering something about how beautiful she is, then snaps his fingers and the bra and the pants she was wearing are both gone. He bends down to lick at her nipples and I pull off my own shirt and undo the zipper of my pants, freeing my stiff cock. I catch Rhi's gaze as I take my cock in my fist and rub up and down my shaft, my friend kissing down her body. He stops at the waistband of her panties and then yanks them down with his teeth.

Her eyes are still on me, hungry eyes that drop to stare at me jerking myself off.

"You want this cock, Miss Blackwaters?"

"You know I do, Professor," she mutters, spine arching as Azlan presses a kiss to her clit and opens her thighs. "And Azlan's too."

Azlan growls like he is the werebeast and not Spencer.

"You heard her, Azlan, lie out on your back and let her ride your cock."

"But–" Rhi begins to protest.

"Miss Blackwaters, do not be a brat," I say. "Do as you're told."

She glares at me but then Azlan is flipping them over and muttering the barrier spell as he shuffles down his pants and his underwear, kicking them away when they reach his calves.

His cock is as big as the rest of him, hard and stiff and framed by an impressive tuft of dark hair that traces up his groin towards his belly button. He takes his cock in his fist and holds it upright.

"Come on, little mate," he tells her. "Come sit on my cock."

Her gaze swings from him to me, then my cock and finally lands on his. Then she shuffles up his body, her knees resting on the mattress either side of his body, her thighs stretched wide open by the sheer size of the man.

At his groin, she leans forward, resting her hands on his shoulders, and giving me a perfect view of her ass cheeks and everything that lies between them. Lining herself up, she slowly sinks down onto his cock, both of them moaning in unison as she does. And then his hands are tight at her waist again as she grinds on top of him, the friction doing something to them both, making her wild on top of him and him groan beneath her.

"Fuck," my usually mild-mannered friend grunts, lifting the little thing up his cock and then slamming her back down and I'm so transfixed by the sight of them together I forget what the hell we were planning to do.

Forget, until she tosses her hair and twists her head, peering over her shoulder at me.

"Stone," she moans, biting down hard on her bottom lip.

And then I remember.

As I stalk closer, I mutter the incantation, loosening her back hole for me, making sure she's not too tight and all lubed up. Closer, I can see the sweat shining on her body, her hair damp at the nape of her neck, can see the way her tight pussy swallows his thick cock, can see the way she slides up and down his column.

I lean over her, licking my tongue down the back of her neck, tasting salt on my tongue, nibbling my teeth along her shoulder as I reach for her ass, finding her hole between the plump cheeks and tickling at it.

"You want it?" I ask her, sliding my finger ever so slowly inside her.

"Oh fuck, yes," she cries out, as Azlan thrums his thumb against her clit.

The incantation has done its job, but I pump my finger in and out of her anyway, loosening her up that little bit further, feeling how her internal muscles squeeze and flutter inside her. Then, I kneel up on the bed, positioning myself between Azlan's bent knees and nibble at her neck again.

"Relax, sweetheart," I tell her and then push myself inside her.

She's tight and perfect and losing fucking control. She rolls her hips, noises of desire gurgling in her throat, arms stretched above her head, as I thrust into her.

I can feel Azlan through the walls of her channel, feel him moving inside her, moving against my cock.

It feels so fucking good, I lose control myself, dropping my hands to grip his waist beneath her just to find some kind of goddamn purchase.

"I'm going to come," she wails.

"Yes, sweetheart," I pant, "come for us. Come for your fucking mates."

"I'm going to come so hard," she cries.

And she's not lying. She squeezes around my cock and jolts about on Azlan's lap like she's being zapped by a live wire. Her magic shoots through the air exploding in a multitude of colors around the bedroom.

It's too much, feels too fucking good, and I come right after her, Azlan too, both of us pumping her full of our seed just like we promised.

And then all three of us are collapsing down on the bed; sweaty, sticky, satisfied.

Rhi lies out between the two of us, head resting on Azlan's bicep, my own arm hooked over her belly.

"The practicing is good," Azlan says, his voice low and throaty, "but one day we're going to do that for real."

31

R^{hi}

Stone twists his face towards me and grins.

"Barone is going to be so pissed off."

"Renzo?" I say. "Why?"

"Are you kidding me, Rhi? All he's been talking about is sharing you and watching you. It's all he can fucking think about too!"

I let Azlan snuggle the blanket up over the three of us.

"You could try to look a little less happy about the fact he'll be upset," I tell Stone.

He shakes his head.

"Why do you dislike him so much?" He snorts and I give him one of my don't-mess-with-me looks.

"What do I dislike about him?!" he repeats with sarcasm.

"You mean apart from the contract killings and psychopathic tendencies," Azlan says.

"I think all of you are a little psychopathic if you ask me," I mumble, then narrow my eyes at Stone. "What is the deal between the two of you?"

"There's no deal."

"Bullshit, you clearly know each other."

The grin falls from Stone's face. "Not really."

"So you do?"

"Did."

"When?"

Stone rolls over onto his back and stares up at the ceiling.

I peer over my shoulder at Azlan. "Do you know?" He shakes his head, which kind of surprises me. I thought these two shared everything. Including me!

"Phoenix?" I ask.

He sighs, then tilts his head to meet my gaze.

"You know I was a foster kid, right? After my mom got ..." he clears his throat, "taken away."

"Yes, I know," I say softly, reaching out to stroke my knuckles down his cheek.

He captures that hand in his and kisses each of my fingers. Not meeting my eyes as he says, "Not all the foster parents were exactly suited to their role. Not exactly caring in nature."

"I'm sorry, Phoenix."

He shakes his head. "It is what it is." He squeezes my hand. "This one time I couldn't stand it any more, couldn't stand what the fucked-up dude was doing to me so I ran away. For a bit, I was out on the streets. I wasn't the only one. There were a few of us. Safety in numbers and all that." He pauses. "Barone was there too. He was younger than me. Pretty skinny and small. Pretty insane even back then."

"And what happened between you?"

"Nothing. Nothing at all. I think he rather looked up to me. Used to follow me around a lot. I couldn't get rid of the dude. Then I got picked up by the authorities and sent to this older man. One who loved learning, loved books. Made me love them too."

"And that's how you ended up a professor," I say, smiling at him.

"It was the start." He's quiet for a moment. "I was lucky, Rhi. I got picked up by the authorities and not Lowsky Senior. Barone wasn't that lucky and sometimes that fucks with my head. Sometimes it makes me feel a hell of a lot of guilt."

"You were just kids. It wasn't your fault."

"Yeah, but I could have helped him out. Could have been kinder to him."

"You could be now."

He closes his eyes. "He reminds me of things I'd rather forget. But you're right. I could be." He opens his eyes again. "I'll try to be."

"Thank you," I say, kissing his cheek.

I'M the first awake the next morning, woken by cramps in my lower belly. Looks like my period is on its way. I've never been so relieved.

I squeeze out from between Azlan and Stone, trying my best not to wake them. After I've yanked Azlan's shirt over my head – I'm becoming addicted to wearing my mates' clothes and drowning myself in their various scents – and used the bathroom, I step out into the main room to find the young woman from yesterday busy at work, setting up the breakfast things. I'm surprised to see her here so early. I wonder what kind of crazy shifts she must work.

"Charmaine, right?" I ask, yawning and stretching my arms over my head. Then, remembering I'm not wearing any panties and could well be flashing the poor woman, drop my arms abruptly.

She stops what she's doing, stands up straight and bows her head.

"Your Royal Highness. I'm sorry if I disturbed you."

I snort. "I'm not your Royal Highness."

Her gaze sneaks up to meet mine. "You are the Black Prince's daughter. His heir."

I snort a second time. Pip emerges from under the table where I bet he was snuffling for crumbs and snorts along with me.

"I don't know about that. I've spent most of my life on the run, hiding or dodging the punches of others. I've certainly never felt like a princess."

She was awfully shy yesterday, barely able to look at me, let alone talk to me. This morning, her curiosity gets the better of her and she can't help asking me, in a voice so hushed I barely hear: "You lived in the East?"

"Yes."

"What is it like?"

I tilt my head, filled with a curiosity of my own. "What have they told you it is like?"

"A place filled with darkness and pain."

I laugh. I can't help it. "Well, some of the time I guess it is. Just as I'm sure here is also filled with darkness and pain sometimes." Although from what I've seen so far, a lot less often than it is back home. Her eyes widen in horror like I've spoken some heinous blasphemy. "That's what they told us the West was like too," I explain.

I can see this takes her a few moments to compute and then she nods.

"Although," I add, "things in here certainly look more beautiful, better run, fairer."

The girl stares at me with her pale eyes but doesn't say anything.

I smile, ignoring the way Pip is licking at my ankles. The girl's gaze drops back down to my pig and then back up to me. I keep on smiling. I bet she thinks I'm mad.

"The pig is yours?" she asks a little unsure.

"Yep, Pip."

"We have a stable in the palace grounds where livestock are kept."

"Oh, no, that's okay. Pip stays with me." I reach down and pick him up, careful this time not to flash the girl, and Pip licks at my face.

"The pig?"

"Yes, he's kind of my best friend."

The girl stares at me unblinking. "You have five fated ones?"

"I do."

"And you also need a pig friend?"

I frown and decide to change the subject. I take a step closer to her, ignoring the way that seems to alarm her. She probably does think I am mad after all and now I have pig slobber all over my cheek.

"Charmaine, actually, I was hoping you might be able to help me."

She bows her head in response.

"I'm about to get my, erm, period, and I don't have any pads or–"

Her pale cheeks redden. "Of course, I'm so sorry we didn't provide you with this already. How thoughtless of us."

"Oh, stars, don't worry about that. But do you think you could get me some?" Everything has happened so quickly the last few days. I didn't exactly have time to pack a bag, certainly no time to stock up on toiletries.

"Right away," she says, bowing her head and dashing away.

She returns about fifteen minutes later just when things are getting on the urgent side and my mates are circling the breakfast table. Her arms are full with a box and she gestures towards the bathroom.

"Your Royal Highness," she murmurs.

"Please, just call me Rhi," I say following her.

"What's all that?" Spencer says, pointing towards the box.

"Sanitary stuff for my period," I say loudly, giving certain other mates some pointed looks.

In the bathroom, I shut the door and Charmaine places the box on the vanity counter next to the sink. She pulls back the lid of the box.

"I wasn't sure what you needed exactly," she says, "so I brought you a selection. There's also chocolate and a hot water bottle inside."

"Oh my goodness, you are a lifesaver," I say, diving straight for the nearest bar of chocolate. I unwrap the heavenly stuff and break a corner off, shoving it straight into my mouth and groaning. Charmaine gives me another of those worried looks and I remind myself she has enough reasons to think I'm coo-coo. I break off another chunk and offer it to her. "Want some? It's amazing. Divine. Possibly better than sex."

"I couldn't possibly ..." she says, gaze falling to the three squares of chocolate in a longing manner.

"Of course you can." I shake my hand at her. "Here, take it."

A little skittishly, like this action is one of the most forbidden in the kingdom, she reaches out and takes the chocolate from my hand, then brings it to her lips and nibbles. Her eyes fall shut.

"See, told you it was good." I peer back inside the box. There are plenty of other bars and I pluck one out and offer that to her next. "Take a whole bar. There are plenty here."

She shakes her head adamantly. "I really can't. Chocolate is in short supply."

"Chocolate?" I say, shocked. "In short supply? But there are plenty of bars in the box."

"Yes, we have given you the palace's supply."

"All of it?"

She nods.

"Why?"

"You are the princess," she explains.

"Oh," I say, my cheeks heating. "Well, I'd like you to take a bar anyway."

"Please, no," she mumbles, "it could cause me problems."

"Problems?"

I stare down at the half-eaten chocolate bar in one hand and the unwrapped bar in the other. I don't understand how chocolate could cause her problems but I remember how the chickens would turn on one another when we gave them rare treats like blackberries. I place both bars back in the box, the chocolate in my mouth tasting a little more bitter now.

"Maybe this place isn't so wonderful after all if you have to be a princess to land your hands on chocolate," I joke.

Charmaine looks at me blankly

"Would you like me to run a bath for you, Your Royal Highness?" she asks, pointing to the marble tub with its golden taps.

"No, jeez, no, I can run one myself!" I shake my head, feeling embarrassed. I'm used to people treating me like dirt. This sudden turnaround is making my head spin.

"Would you like me to tell your father that you are indisposed this morning?"

"Would you?" I say, rubbing at my belly. "I just want to float in a hot bath for about an hour until the cramps are over."

"They are the worst," Charmaine says, a sympathy on her face.

"Yep," I confirm. "Why is there no spell to help with those?"

"Oh, I know of one that helps a little," her gaze falls away, "I can't perform it for you myself. My magic is a little low right now. But yours ... yours is fine?"

"Yes, I used an awful lot of it up yesterday, but it's regenerated again now."

"Regenerated?" she repeats slowly, examining my face.

"Erm, yes," I reply, confused. "Will you teach me the spell?" I sit down on one of the padded bathroom stools, grimacing as another cramp rips through my stomach.

"Okay," she says, "my mom taught me this one. It's a family specialty." She smiles slightly. "Rest your hand against your belly and let your magic sink below the skin. Then utter these words." She whispers some words in the language of the West – a language I don't know. However, I manage to repeat the words closely enough that a warmth radiates from my hand and into my belly, soothing the cramps.

"Oh, stars, that feels good. Thank you so much."

"It is my honor to be of service," she tells me, bowing. It makes me even more uncomfortable. It doesn't seem right that a woman just like me should be bowing and calling me Your Highness.

The door opens a crack and Pip comes scuttling in, trotting up to me and looking up with his I-need-some-love eyes. I scoop him up, landing a kiss on the crown of his head and place him on my lap.

"We used to raise pigs back home," Charmaine says. "I never saw one so small before."

"He's a runt."

"My father used to drown the runts." Pip growls and a little light sparks in the girl's eyes. "I always thought they were cute."

"Pip can be cute when he wants to be." I lean a little towards her. "I once dressed him up in a halo and angel's wings. He hated it but he looked adorable." Charmaine actually smiles. "He also loves having his ears tickled."

She hesitates and then slowly reaches out a hand and strokes her fingers down Pip's velvety ears.

"Does your family have a farm?" I ask her.

Her hand freezes. "They did." Pip butts his nose against her hand and she tickles under his chin. "I had a pet cat then. He liked to have his chin tickled like this. It used to make him dribble." She smiles again.

"Pip has been known to dribble on occasion – usually when you rub his tummy. Or he's watching you eat." Pip snorts as if protesting such an accusation and she giggles. "Does your family live here in the capital with you?"

"No, it is just me now."

"I'm sorry." I know what it's like to be alone. I hope she has friends at least. Meeting Winnie and Trent and my five mates has changed my life for the better in a way I can't even describe.

"Thank you for helping him," I say. "You really should be resting with your magic so weak."

"My master asked me to help you," she says simply.

"Is he a bit of a hard taskmaster?" I ask, attempting to make the question sound innocent but failing miserably.

Her eyes shift up to mine with suspicion.

"I have to go now," she says. Pip snorts and licks her hand again.

"Of course," I say. "I hope we might talk again."

She bows her head and walks towards the door on unstable legs and I can feel how weak her magic remains.

"Your magic is still weak. You should really rest."

"Of course," she says, gaze not meeting mine. It's clear she has no intention of heeding my words.

"Maybe I could accompany you back to your home. I'd love to see–"

"No," she says. "I'm sorry, but I have work to do."

"You shouldn't be working," I call after her, but she's already scurrying out of the room.

32

R^{hi}

I SPEND most of the day wallowing in the bath, floating in fragrant bubbles, listening to relaxing music, and nibbling on more chocolate. It helps ease the period cramps, but as I mull things over in my mind, I grow more and more uncomfortable. I'm thankful for the Black Prince's offer of protection. I'm grateful for the food and all these comforts. But it doesn't feel right wallowing in a luxurious bath while I know my friends – Winnie and Ellie and the others – could be out there suffering. Who am I kidding? There's no *could be* about it. I bet they are.

I tug the plug from the bath and climb out of the tub, wrapping myself in a fluffy gown that was also in Charmaine's box. Stuffing another square of chocolate into my mouth for courage, I head back into the suite to find my mates.

However, I find the suite completely empty. They've gone. With a huff, annoyed they didn't tell me they were going, I collapse down on one of the sofas. Pip snorts and I pick him up and settle him on my belly. He's always been as good as a hot water bottle when it comes to cramps and it's been weeks and weeks since we've been alone. We snuggle up together, enjoying each other's company.

We must doze off, because some minutes later I jerk awake at the sound of five men entering the suite.

"Where have you been?" I ask, nudging Pip off my belly, and stretching my arms above my head, each of my vertebrae clicking in turn.

"Sopherina and Portia took us to watch a session of training for the young dragon-riders," Spencer says, flopping down on the couch next to me. "It seems pretty intuitive to me. A million times easier than broom riding."

"Sopherina and Portia?" I ask.

"The two dragon-riders who brought us here," Spencer explains. "You should see what they can do on a dragon. They are incredible."

"Oh, they are, are they?" I cross my arms over my chest, my bond snarking with jealousy.

"Yeah, the way they move!" he says, oblivious to the death stare I'm giving him.

"But," Stone says, dropping down on the other side of me, "I bet they had to spend hours and hours of training to get that good. They're certainly not naturals like you are, Miss Blackwaters. Plus," he adds, nuzzling his mouth against my neck, "not … nearly … as … brattish."

"Is it any surprise if I do, on occasion, act like a brat when you come back singing the praises of other women?"

"How are you feeling?" Azlan asks, cutting to the chase. No interest in our flirting.

"Better," I say. "But," I eye them all, "we can't stay here. We can't stay here in the West."

They all stare at me, clearly taken back at my sudden change of mind.

"Why not?" Tristan asks, alarm spilling over his face. "What's happened?"

"Nothing has happened. It's just ... You know what the prophecy says. What I'm meant to do. I can't stay here living a life of luxury," I point back towards the bathroom, "while your dad is out there hunting Winnie and probably all our other friends. And stars knows what's happened to Winnie's grandma and Ellie and–"

"Okay, okay, sweetheart," Azlan says, pacing towards me.

"But we only just arrived. There's still so much to understand. So much to learn," Spencer says.

"There'll be time for that later. Right now our friends are in danger. You said yourself there might not be any weres left by the time Christopher Kennedy is finished. Can you sit back with your feet up and let that happen?"

"No," Spencer says, his jaw tightening.

"You wanna go, little rabbit," Renzo says, holding out his hand to me, "we can go right now."

I'm sitting in a dressing gown, hair soaking wet, dripping water all over the cushions. Is he serious?

"Not right this second!" I say.

He shrugs and drops his hand. "Okay."

"I need to talk to my dad. Find out if he'd be prepared to help us."

"You want to start a war?" Stone says, frowning.

"Not if we don't have to. There might be another way to," I swallow, "remove Tristan's dad from power."

Tristan snorts as if he believes only a full scale invasion will do it.

"I'm going to go get dressed and then I'm going to talk to him," I say, already marching towards the bedroom.

"We'll come with you," Stone calls out.

"No," I say, "This is a conversation I need to have alone."

33

R ^{hi}

Somehow I manage to navigate along the maze of corridors, stopping outside the Black Prince's door some minutes later. It's imposing and grand and all of a sudden I feel very small and very alone.

It doesn't matter that there's a supposed prophecy written about me. It doesn't matter that fate has bonded five powerful men to me. It doesn't even matter that I'm the lost daughter of some prince. I still feel exactly like I did those first few days at the academy. Like a nobody. Like I don't really belong or fit in.

I square my shoulders. Tough shit. Time to put my big girl panties on. Winnie is hiding out there somewhere, Ellie is suffering who knows what at the hands of her uncle and I dread to think what's happened to Rosa.

I knock on the door with a firm fist. I may feel afraid but I can do a good job at not showing it.

There's a long pause and for a moment my heart drops. He isn't there. This is going to have to wait. I'm starting to turn away when a voice from within calls:

"Enter." The door springs open.

Inside, the Black Prince stands talking to two older magicals; one male, one female, both dressed in finely embroidered robes. All their eyes land on me and their combined magic flickers to life.

"Rhianna," the Black Prince says, "we were just talking about you."

"You were?" I say, confused.

"We are so happy you have returned, Princess," the woman says. Her silver hair falls in long braids down her back and her rusty brown eyes are piercing.

"Actually," I say, finding my voice from somewhere, "that's what I have come to talk to you about."

The woman's gaze flicks up to the Black Prince. He nods and then the two other magicals leave, the woman's cold arm brushing against my body as she does and her magic prickling over my skin.

When the door closes behind me, the Black Prince fixes me with his charming smile.

"I hear you were feeling unwell this morning. I take it you are feeling better now? That my servant saw to your comfort?"

Servant? I knew Charmaine was some kind of maid or assistant. But to call her a servant? I shake the thought aside. That's not why I'm here.

"I'm feeling much better, thank you." My gaze flicks around the room and I notice the picture I ruined has already been removed and replaced. "I can't stay here. I have to go back, back to the republic."

The Black Prince considers me.

"Nonsense. It is too dangerous. You are safe here. We will protect you."

"But my friends, they are in danger and I can't stay here while they're–"

"Your fated ones are with you. Your familiar too. You will make new friends here in the Kingdom. I can find some young woman your age, have them sent to you and–"

I take another step towards him. "No, you don't understand. I'm not worried about having no friends. Shit, I spent my entire childhood without them. But I have them now and they are important to me and I have to help them."

"And how do you expect to help them? Christopher Kennedy wants you dead. If it was not for my dragon's interference, you *would* be dead!"

"With your help, we could–"

"With my help?" His eyes narrow. "What exactly do you have in mind, daughter?"

"Christopher Kennedy is a monster. He's terrorizing his own people. We need to remove him from power."

"And seize power for ourselves!" The Black Prince steps forward and his eyes glint red with the firelight.

"No, I mean–"

"I have waited so long for you, my powerful child – with your boundless, bottomless wells of magic," he says, his voice more rapid, more eager, the flames flickering in his pupils, "waited for you to join me."

I take a step away from him, alarmed at his sudden change in tone. He leans forward and grabs my wrist. His hand is cool and my dark magic sizzles vividly to life, surpassing my other magic, driving to the forefront, available at my fingertips.

"Together there will be nothing that can stop us," he says. "Together we can bring a utopia to both lands. We can rule over both."

"What?" I say, trying to tug my arm from his grip. "I don't want to–"

"Daughter," my father hisses, "show me what you can do!"

"I don't–"

"Rhianna!" he snaps. "Show me!"

And my crimson magic rises to the challenge. It's arrogant and proud and it wants a chance to show exactly what it can do. Its black tentacles race up the walls of this room, melting and destroying everything in its path, burning a hole in the ceiling above us and continuing on its path of destruction, climbing higher and higher through the floors above us and then bursting straight through to the roof itself, shooting high into the sky, a deadly bolt of jet black lightning that singes the very air itself.

The lightning bolt strikes the sky with darkness and I scream as my magic soars through me.

Then my father lets go of my wrist and the magic falls back down to earth.

I crumple to the ground, my shoulders heaving as I scrabble for breath. I glare up at my father. The magic is still hot and furious in my blood.

"What the hell did you just do?" I cry.

"My apologies," he bows his head slightly, "my *deepest* apologies. It was not my intention to hurt you. Perhaps I was a little overexcited." His eyes gleam. "Your powers are far greater than I expected."

He looks down at the hand that had gripped me and sparks seem to dance between his fingertips.

I pull myself up to standing, smoothing down my now crumpled clothes, my heart still racing in my chest.

"Perhaps it would be best if you returned to your quarters and rest some more. We will talk more on these matters later." He smiles at me, oozing charm. "I am so pleased you are here, Rhianna. Reunited with me at last."

He gestures to the door.

"I don't need to rest," I snap, realizing I sound exactly like a petulant child and wish I'd phrased that better. He may be my father but we're both adults and he is a stranger to me. He doesn't get to boss me around, even if he rules this nation. "We need to talk about–"

"Yes, but I have other business to attend to. Business that you interrupted." My cheeks heat.

"This is important!"

"It can wait!" he snaps, his eyes flashing with anger and I take a hurried step away from him. Then he collects himself. "Such things should not be hurried. Let me speak with my advisers on the best way to proceed."

I'm not satisfied with this compromise, but I need his help and angering him further doesn't seem the best way to gain it. I tamper down my own anger, swallowing it down, and manage a half smile.

"Thank you," I say and then I leave.

The anger still courses through my veins as I make my way back to our quarters, so much so that twice I take the wrong corridor and am forced to retrace my steps.

Then I stop.

This is bullshit. If he's going to talk to his advisers about how to remove Christopher Kennedy from power, then I need to be there too. I'm not some little girl. I am Rhianna Blackwaters.

I spin on my toes and head straight back the way I've come. However, when I reach the Black Prince's study I find it empty. He's gone some place else to have these important conversations. I hiss in annoyance and decide, tough shit, I'm going to track him down.

I begin making my way through the corridors, knocking on doors and peering around doors. The place is bizarrely empty. Not a magical in sight. Probably all at this very important meeting with the Black Prince.

Then I catch the swish of a skirt rounding a corner in the distance – Charmaine's skirt. I chase after her, running on my tiptoes, down a stairwell, and plummeting into the heart of the palace. I don't know what I'm doing, why I decide to keep myself hidden, but I feel compelled to do so.

At the bottom of the stairs, Charmaine pauses, peering upward and I dive backward, pressing myself into the shadows, wishing I hadn't lost my cloaker. Then she sets off along another corridor. Half way along she meets another young woman, dressed in similar robes. The other girl speaks to her softly, so quietly I don't hear, and they set off together in a third direction. I follow the both of them, lurking far enough away that they can't see or hear me.

At the end of the corridor I realize we're back near the ballroom, although they stop outside another door, slightly ajar.

I can hear the eager chatter of voices from within and the strange crackling of magic.

The two girls wait at the entrance until someone from within calls for them. They step inside and once again I follow.

The room is packed with magicals, dressed in their

finery, and sprawled over chaises and cushions, all fixated at something in the center of the room. I peer that way too, my mind taking a moment to decipher what I see.

The Black Prince – my father – bent over a young man, his mouth pressed to his neck as if he's kissing him. The man is young like me, dressed in the same robes as Charmaine and the other girl. He's chained to a low couch and he's barely conscious.

My scalp prickles with unease. I've intruded into something private. Something a daughter shouldn't see – that much I do understand even if I can't compute what it is I'm seeing. I shouldn't be here. The hum of excited voices and the sucking force of the magic in the air makes me shudder hard; a viscous sucking that seems to tug at the magic in my veins.

And then realization hits me hard.

I stumble backward.

My father isn't kissing that man. This isn't some weird orgy I've stumbled into. Not of that kind, anyway.

No, my father's teeth are buried in the man's neck. He's biting him, draining the magical's magic from his veins – taking it for his own!

I want to turn away and run, run as far away from this place as I can, but my feet are glued to the spot and bile and repulsion slosh in my stomach.

My vision spins.

The Black Prince – the horror of it makes me nauseous – is a drainer.

They all are. All of them.

Nosferatu.

Vampires.

The darkest of all magicals.

I watch as the Black Prince stands up, his mouth

crimson with blood and licks his lips. He clicks his fingers and the chains fall away. But the young man doesn't move. His eyes fall shut and his head lulls to one side. The two girls shuffle forward, slinging the man's arms around each of their shoulders. The Black Prince slumps onto an armchair, his eyes dazed like he's on drugs. As the two girls drag the man away, he catches Charmaine by her upper arm.

"Still so weak, Source," he scoffs, "come see me again when you have restored."

I slam my hands over my mouth to smother a gasp. That's why her magic was so low. The Black Prince has been draining it.

A million thoughts spin in my mind as the strange magic in the room tugs at my veins, and the vision of the Black Prince's scarlet mouth plays in my head over and over. For one awful second, I'm so dizzy, I think I might tumble to the ground.

Charmaine nods, bowing her head to the ground in that same meek manner.

She wasn't shy. She was afraid. Not a worker, a slave.

I've been so stupid. So blind.

Together with the other girl, she heaves the boy away, the other magicals watching intently, their eyes seeming to glow red in the strange lighting of the room.

I shrink into the shadows, my heart racing, my lungs gasping for air. On unsteady feet, I follow the women back down the corridor and to another room. Inside are a series of beds, each occupied by an unconscious magical. I rub at my eyes, unable to believe what I'm seeing. Twenty magicals at least, every single one of them near death, drained of nearly all but a few droplets of their magic. It's horrifying. Truly horrifying. How could anyone do this?

The two women lay the man out on the bed. Charmaine

leans over him, then hesitates, pressing her hand to his chest. She lets out a silent scream of distress, stumbling backward into the other woman's arms. For a moment, they hold each other and then finally, Charmaine turns back to the man, and with a steadying breath draws a sheet over his head.

Dead.

He's dead.

I roll out of the room, back pressed against the wall, emotions and thoughts still crashing through my head. I feel sick. So, so sick. I sink to my knees and dry heave into my hands.

This can't be right. This must be wrong. There has to be some other explanation.

"Princess!"

I open my eyes and standing right in front of me, flanked on both sides by three other magicals, is the silver-haired woman from earlier.

All of their eyes glow red and they glare at me with an undisguised hunger.

34

R hi

"Vampires?" I gasp, my knees buckling as I try to stand.

The silver-haired woman hisses, baring her fangs at me, and snatches my wrist. Her grip is bitingly cold and now, now I understand why. She has no warmth of her own, no magic. The only way she can survive is to leech it from others. From magicals like Charmaine.

"Yes, Beautiful, vampires." Her red eyes glint with excitement. "We hoped you would join us soon. Not quite so soon as this, but now the Black Prince will have no further reason to wait."

She yanks me up right and along, and I struggle to pull my arm from her bruising grasp. I'm already surrounded by more of the dark magicals, swarming around me, reaching out to touch me, to scrape their fingers against my skin. I feel them tugging at my magic, sucking at it.

"Let go of me," I cry. I reach for the light magic I'd used to dispel the ghouls out on the water back at the Gray Isle, but all that comes crackling to the surface is that crimson magic, potent and dark. It seems to send the drainers into a frenzy. They scramble to touch me, dragging me along, hissing and murmuring at each other.

"No!" I scream. "No! Let me go!"

I call through the bond for my mates. Pray they can hear me.

And then I'm being hauled into that same dark room, carried up to the raised platform, slung down hard on my knees before the feet of the Black Prince. My father.

All those stories about him, they were true. They were right all along. His kingdom is not some paradise. It's built on the back of the suffering of others. No better than the republic. In fact, worse, much worse. A million times worse.

No wonder my mom ran from him. She must have learned the truth and fled.

"Rhianna," he says, his voice sounding a lot less charming than it did before. "I had not planned for you to join us so soon. But here you are."

I fling back my head and glare up at him.

"You disgust me," I say.

"So very like your mother. I think those were her words too."

"You killed her!" I say, flinging my magic at him. He meets it with his own, strong from his recent draining of the young boy. The two sets of magic sizzle against one another, like dark sparklers in the air, lighting up the room for a brief moment. Then they fizzle out and fall away to the ground.

"I told you. It wasn't me. I never planned to hurt her." He crouches down in front of me. "Just as I have no intention of hurting you, daughter. You're too precious to kill. Much more valuable alive. Kennedy is a fool for believing any different. You will make an enviable Source indeed."

He stands and faces the crowd of vampires, pointing at me with his hand. "My daughter. I promised you she would be powerful – powerful beyond belief. With her magic, we will be unstoppable. No longer relegated to this barren land. No longer trapped in this wasteland. With her magic, we can seize the republic. It's what she wants, after all." He turns and smiles at me, his crimson eyes cruel, his fangs elongating in his mouth as he stares at me.

I stumble up onto my feet and meet his gaze head on.

"I know what you are," I spit. "And now I understand why my mom fled from you."

"Your mom was very precious to me, but she didn't understand. Didn't understand what the two of us could achieve if united."

"United?" I say. "You mean if you sucked up all my magic?"

"With your power, Rhianna, and my abilities, we could achieve great things. We could conquer not only the republic, but Aropia, too."

"You killed that boy!" I cry. "You took his magic and left him for dead! This place is no better than the republic. It's worse."

"You misinterpreted what you saw. He gave his magic willingly, sacrificed himself for the greater good, for a leader who has united his lands and stopped the attacks from the East."

"Then why the hell was he chained up!" I yell. "You're a liar! And there's no way you're using my magic."

"But it's your destiny, Rhianna. Your mother foresaw it."

"Fuck destiny," I say. "There's no way you're taking my magic."

His smile widens and then he strikes me, hard across the face with the palm of his hand. I wasn't expecting it, the pain stunning me, bringing tears into my eyes and knocking me straight back down on the floor.

He bends over me as I struggle to regain my bearings, my ears ringing with white noise.

"I can smell your blood. So potent with that crimson magic. So delicious." He licks his lips, and then, before I've had a chance to lift my arms, the other vampires are back on me, gripping my arms and legs and carrying me struggling to the couch the boy had lain on earlier, cuffing my hands and my ankles.

Immediately, I sense it. The cuffs are just like those Christopher Kennedy bound my hands in. They restrict and bind my magic and my father leans over me. I shuffle on the couch, leaning away from him but I'm caught by the cuffs and he slides my hair off my neck.

"We will feed on the princess tonight," he says, pressing his thumb painfully against the vein in my neck and making me light-headed. All the other vampires hiss in response.

My heart beats frantically and I imagine he can see the blood pulsing in my neck, can feel it under the pad of his thumb. His fangs grow longer still, his eyes so red they're like blood.

He leans right over me.

But I'm stronger now. Bonded to five powerful mates.

I crash through the magical binds, and smash my magic against his body, just as my mates come racing into the room.

It takes the vampires a second to realize what's happening as the Black Prince falls to the floor and I yank my arms and hands free of the cuffs, jumping off the couch.

I race through the crowd of vampires as my mates barrel towards me, firing my magic as I go so no one can touch me.

As I reach the others, I let the anger and disgust inside me boil and snatch their hands. We form our circle, combining our magic and letting it pound through the crowd of drainers.

They tumble to the ground like skittles. And only then do they compute that something is wrong. They are in danger. They respond, hurtling magic towards us. But their magic is weakened – I interrupted their feeding after all – and they are nowhere near as strong as us.

Behind us there's a commotion at the door and from my peripheral vision I see Charmaine and two of the other servants. Now I understand why Charmaine's magic was so weak. They are the vampires' Sources. Magicals with deep wells of magic that the vampires feed upon.

I take a gamble, remembering how frightened Charmaine had seemed, how she'd refused to answer so many of my questions.

"Help us!" I cry out. "Help us destroy them! Help overthrow them!"

There's a hesitation and then Charmaine comes running into the room, flinging what little magic she has at the drainers. Others follow. There are shouts down the corridor and then more of the servants follow, standing alongside us and fighting against the vampires that have been using and abusing them.

And it's working. The vampires fall one by one. Evaporating into dust.

That is until the Black Prince rises back up and strikes.

He raises his magic into the air, shooting blood-red bolts skyward and almost immediately the scores of Sources surrounding us fall to their knees, clutching their faces as if pain soars through their skulls.

"You see," he yells, "they are mine. Infected with my magic as I drain them, programmed to obey even at their own cost. Noble to try of course – I suspected you would have your mother's feeble sentiments – but nonetheless futile." His eyes glitter with a madness. "No harm done. Return to your quarters and we will think no more of it."

"Fuck no!" Renzo says, wrapping his arms around me and shooting us into time and space.

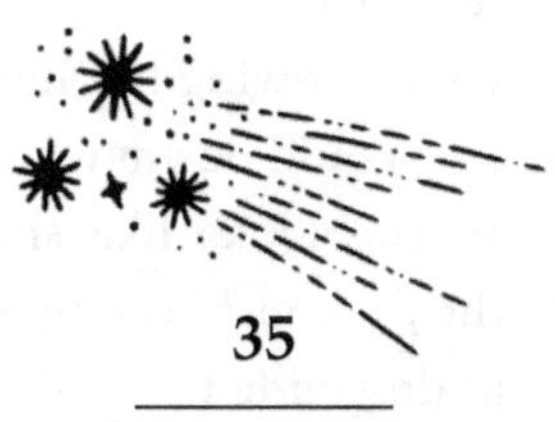

35

R enzo

LITTLE RABBIT WHACKS me hard on the arm.

"What the hell?! You need to warn me before you do that!"

"Wasn't time," I say and her eyes grow all angry with me.

"Why the hell did you do that?"

"Instructions from the enforcer. Ping you away if things ever became a shitshow. And that seemed like a fucking shitshow. Those were–"

"Drainers, I know. The Black Prince is a vampire, and he wanted to drain my magic for himself."

I ball my hands into fists, imagining all the ways I'm going to make him pay.

Little rabbit stomps her foot in frustration.

"I'm going to kill Azlan and then you," she says, but I know by now, disappointingly, she doesn't actually mean it.

"Where are we?" She swings her gaze around in the darkness. "We need to get back to the others."

I scratch my head. "No idea."

"No idea?!" she says, throwing her hands up into the air. "So you're telling me we could be anywhere?!"

"Yeah," I say and she looks like she might strike me again. "But close to the dragon." I tilt my head to one side. "I thought your dad was descended from dragons, not bats."

She ignores me.

"The dragon's somewhere here?" She raises her hand and a spark flickers on her palm. "Stables," she says, "I think we're in the stables."

Under our feet is straw and the wooden roof is high above our heads. Chained to a wall is the huddled form of several sheep, sheep I recognize as the breed Lowsky's men were bundling into trucks. Can't see any dragons though. And those fuckers are pretty big to miss.

"Come on," she says, taking my hand in hers and making me giddy. "I have a sense she's this way."

Little rabbit pulls me through the vast space and stops at a door. It's chained shut, but I blast through it with my magic and then we step inside.

It's a nest. A dragon's nest. The floor knee deep in straw, the skeletons of sheep buried among the strands and five dragons curled up together in the center, sleeping.

At the bottom of the pile of reptiles is little rabbit's dragon, her reddish-gold scales just visible.

Little rabbit steps inside and one of the dragons lifts its head and stares at her, its nostrils rippling like it might barbecue her.

Little rabbit is oblivious. She points in their direction. It makes me wince. Tough fuckers never like it when you point at them. Lowsky never liked it. I never had a problem with it.

A gun pointing at my head, a knife at my throat, that's my kind of fun. I doubt dragons go for that shit though.

"They're chained up."

"So, unchain them," I say, leaning against the wall. I could do it myself, but there's something about watching my little rabbit use her magic that fucking fascinates me – the way her magic flickers with light and dark magic in a way I've never known. It's damn pretty.

She zaps at the metal collars and cuffs, chains falling away and then all the dragons stir, stretching and yawning like cats.

The gold dragon is the last to rise and little rabbit calls to her, using her name now.

"Gwenhwyfar, we need your help. Right now. Will you help us?" she says like she's talking to her little man and not some gigantic dragon.

The golden dragon lowers her head, right close to little rabbit, making me twitch like crazy. She rumbles. Then straightens and swings her huge head from side to side, howling as she does, before she throws her head upwards. She opens her jaws, rumbles, and a stream of fire shoots from her mouth, up into the roof, burning the rafters.

"Could be wrong," I say, "but I think she wants to leave that way."

Females – always so fucking dramatic. Because it's not exactly subtle is it. There's no chance of us slipping off into the night now, not when there's a fire raging.

Then again, I doubt slipping away is little rabbit's plan. She's going to want to go back and help the others, despite what I've been instructed by the enforcer.

Sparks, debris and bits of burning roof come tumbling down onto our heads. The dragon takes no notice, lowering her head to the floor and inviting us to hop on board.

I wrap my hands around my little rabbit's tiny waist and lift her up onto the old girl and then I follow her, securing my spot right behind her.

The dragon raises onto her four legs and peers up at the flaming roof, the fire scorching the top of my head. Too much of the roof remains, we can't squeeze through the gap forming yet. We're going to have to wait.

Little rabbit bites at her thumbnail and my right leg jigs up and down. The temperature rises, which is fine if you're a dragon. Not if you're a human. Trust me, I've seen what happens when you roast a person.

The dragon must read my fucking mind – which give her credit, ain't an easy thing to do – because she spits out more flames towards the roof and the fire burns with more rapidity.

She spreads open her wings and–

"Leaving so soon?" The Black Prince is standing below us, the edges of his lips curled upwards. "But you only just arrived daughter. And things were just starting to get interesting."

The dragon decides she isn't playing games. She blasts that freaky sucker with a jet of fire.

Little rabbit screams in horror – which surprises me because he isn't the first dude she's seen burned alive. Except the Black Prince shields his face with his arms and the flames part around him, not licking him at all. Fireproof. Maybe he's got those reptilian genes after all.

"Gwenhwyfar was always so difficult to train. She has a temper. And after I spent so long searching for her kind – nearly as long as I spent searching for you. After I rescued her from that volcano. Ungrateful wretch."

He flicks his wrist and a whip of magic crashes against the dragon's flank, making her groan.

"Leave her alone!" little rabbit cries out.

"No, I don't think so. She is my dragon after all. They all are."

"Nah," I say, "this one's Rhi's."

"I am the prince descended from dragons!" He peers at the flames burning around him and runs his hand over his skin.

"Then so is Rhi!"

The Black Prince smiles.

"Ah, they say my power comes from dragons – my inability to burn. Such a pretty story. But of course it doesn't. Just another useful piece of magic I borrowed from another source."

"You mean stole!" little rabbit cries out.

"Not stolen, given." His eyes glint. His fangs are sharp in his mouth. "I wonder what powers I'll gain from you, daughter. From each of your fated ones. Pretty little trick this one pulled off."

"Keep wondering," I tell him. "We're leaving."

"I'm not going anywhere!" Rhi protests.

Personally, engaging in conversation with a drainer like him seems dumb. And dull. I say we get the hell out of here. People only use words to deceive you, to entangle you in confusion. Nothing good ever came in talking. Better to strike. Better to flee. Talk and you're dead.

Little rabbit's still learning though. She doesn't know all this stuff yet.

The Black Prince's lips quiver. "Come down from the dragon, daughter. Come down now!"

"Just so you know," I say, leaning in to speak directly into her ear, "that isn't happening."

"It is!" her daddio roars, flicking his wrist violently. This time his magic whips against the dragon's thick neck and coils tightly around it. The dragon shakes her head, nearly tossing us to the ground and scrapes her talons desperately against her neck. "I apologize if I gave the impression that was a request. It isn't. You aren't going anywhere. You will be my power source, daughter, and finally I will seize my destiny. I will become the magical I should always have been! No more bargaining with men like Kennedy and Lowsky. I will have complete control!"

"Uh, no," I say, snatching the knife from my pocket and flinging it directly at his head. Unfortunately, it isn't one of my best throws and he halts the knife with his magic and sends it flying back at me. I dodge it just in time, but not before it scrapes across my face, searing my ear right in half.

"Shit," I mutter, blinking as the pain hits me square between the eyes. The blood roars into my head and leaves me fucking light-headed as it pours out of my ear. The world spins and I lose my fucking balance, slipping straight from the dragon and landing hard on the floor. For a moment, I'm winded, struggling to tear the air back into my lungs. I stumble up onto my feet and feel the press of cool metal against my throat. It's the knife.

My knife.

Her knife.

His knife.

Except this isn't some fun game like with little rabbit. The Black Prince means business. He presses the knife deep into my flesh.

"Don't you touch him!" little rabbit screams.

"Come down from the dragon and I will let him live."

She glares at him like he isn't the legendary Black Prince, a freaking sucker, a vampire, the darkest of all magicals.

Fuck, I love this girl.

I jolt, the blade sliding roughly against my skin.

Love?

Me? Love?

A fucked-up snort comes blurting out my nose.

You have to have a heart to love someone. And I was born with one that does its job. Pumps the blood around my body. Bish bash, bish bash.

That's all it does. It's frozen. It doesn't feel.

Except I have feelings for my little rabbit. Giant fucking big feelings. Ones that make my cock permanently stiff and gives me the desire to stuff tongues down the throats of anyone who hurts her. Plus I like making her happy. And by happy I mean orgasming.

Fuck, perhaps I do love her. Huh, fancy fucking that.

Better rescue her then.

"Go!" I tell her and she gives me one of those fiery looks – same one she gives me whenever I suggest something she doesn't like. But I'm not bowing down this time.

They've always called me a hunting dog. But I'm no dog. I'm one of those mangy alley cats. The kind with his ear sliced in half, his tail bent and most of his whiskers missing. I've been through the wars. Somehow I've survived. How many lives have I lost by now? Surely I've used them all. Surely my time is up.

I take the Black Prince's wrist in mine and push his hand – push the blade – against my throat.

"Doesn't matter if he kills me," I say, that thing that bobs in my throat causing the knife to shave off half my skin. "Little rabbit, go!"

"No!" she yells and I feel that crimson magic soar through her body, even more powerful than it ever was before. It shoots like dark lightning from her outstretched hand and engulfs the Black Prince, forcing the knife from his hand, forcing him down to his knees. He wrestles against the magic, struggling to fight back. But it's no good, little rabbit is too strong for him.

"You are not dying again," she yells at me. "Not until I say you can. Which is going to be when we are both very old!"

"Are you going to kill him?" I ask eagerly, his dark eyes rising to meet mine as he struggles against the magic. "Or do you want me to do it?" I pick up the blood-stained knife and spin it in my palm.

"I-I-I–" She hesitates, but then the choice is taken from her hands.

The stables flood with people – the were, the enforcer, the Kennedy kid and Birdman – plus that other little friend she made today and many others. I guess they're pissed because they see the Black Prince on his knees and they surge on top of him until he's lost under a pile of bodies and the flash of magic.

It reminds me of Lowsky and his brother Joey. That moment they snapped. The moment they turned on their own dad and ripped him to shreds. I'm pretty sure that's what those dudes are doing now.

Little rabbit turns her head away, unable to look.

The hole in the roof is large enough now, the fire racing down the walls of the barn, and little rabbit whispers to her new pet, the dragon spreads its wings and I scrabble up onto her back just in time before she lifts up into the air, out into the night's sky.

Several of the other dragons spread their wings, looking to do the same.

"Come on," I yell at the others. "I'm guessing our girl wants to go."

They scrabble up onto the backs of the other dragons, as

the Sources surge away, leaving the crumpled body of the Black Prince discarded in the blood-stained straw.

The golden dragon whistles again and together all the dragons rise up through the roofless stable.

Below us, the Sources battle the remaining suckers, but it's clear who is winning, who is in control. The Black Prince is dead and with him the control these magicals possessed. The West is in the hands of the people now – for better or for worse.

The dragons circle upwards and when we're high in the sky, I lean forward and mouth right near little rabbit's ear.

"Guess, we're leaving, huh?" She peers down at the chaos and nods.

"I don't belong here," she says, watching the chaos unfold below. Then she blinks and swings her gaze around the others. "Where's Pip?"

I sigh, then shoot myself back into the palace. I find little man snuffling a bar of chocolate on one of the beds, tuck him under my arm and aim back for the dragon. Once I'm seated right behind little rabbit, I lean forward and whisper into her ear:

"So where to now, Princess?"

36

R^{hi}

EVERYBODY LOOKS TO ME, waiting for my answer.

Magical bolts explode below us, as Charmaine and her friends take control of the country that should always have been theirs.

"Back to the republic," Azlan says with a steely determination.

"Are you insane?" Stone asks. "The Lord Protector wants us dead."

"I told you already. We have to go back," I tell him.

"I don't give a shit about the prophecy. We don't have to do anything but keep you safe," Stone says.

"Ellie?" Azlan says.

"Winnie," I add.

The steel in Stone's expression wavers. "We aren't strong enough."

"Then who is?" Azlan snaps.

"We are," I say, addressing Stone. "You know we are."

"Didn't you see little rabbit take out her daddio – a fucking vampire!" Renzo says.

No more running, no more hiding. No, I've had enough of that. There are too many people depending on me. Too many people I care about. Time to meet my destiny. Time to meet it head on. There's only one place to go.

"Arrow Hart," I say, "we're going back to Arrow Hart."

Immediately, Gwenhwyfar lifts her body, catching the warmth of an air current in her wings and expelling us out of the palace compound, out of the city and eastwards.

I spin around and peer past Renzo, straining my eyes to scan the already lightening horizon and catch the city we're leaving for one last time. Like the people, it takes on a more sinister form now I look at it with better-informed eyes. Not so stylish and sleek and modern. Oppressive, soulless and bleak.

I couldn't live in a place like that. I'd miss the chaos, the realness, the honesty of home.

I bet all those things he showed us were a lie. Every single one.

I go to turn back and catch sight of Renzo properly, seated behind me on the dragon, his hands tight around my waist, Pip snuggled between us. Blood trickles from a congealing wound on the assassin's neck and his ear is hanging from his head in two halves. I jolt in shock and shift my body so I'm facing him better.

"Let me heal that for you," I say, raising my hand.

He catches my wrist.

"Nah," he says.

"It'll scar."

"Another one to add to my collection." He winks at me.

"But your ear!"

He lifts his hand and touches it, feeling the two pieces.

"Shit," he says, and his eyes spin in their sockets. The assassin may love pain and gore and things I try my best not to think about, but he doesn't seem to love this ...

"Can I heal it for you, please?" I say.

"You're not touching my ear," he hisses.

I look at it. The scars are one thing – but this, this needs sorting. I try a different tactic.

"I thought you liked me touching you," I say, trailing my fingertips down his chest.

He looks at me with obvious suspicion. "I do, just not the ears."

I consider him. "Renzo," I ask, "do you have a problem with ears?"

"No," he snaps far too quickly.

"Then you'll let me touch your other ear?" I lift my hand to his uninjured ear and immediately he ducks his head to one side.

"Don't touch my ears."

"Why not?"

He stares at me. I stare right back. He relents, leaning in close and whispering so quietly I can barely hear him.

"Ears are like a thing."

"A thing?" I prompt.

His voice drops even quieter. "You won't tell anyone?"

"Cross my heart," I promise.

He swallows. "Ears are my weakness."

I blink and try not to giggle. I can't help it though. After everything that's passed over the last few hours – all that tension, nearly having my magic drained by a roomful of vampires – I can't help a little snort of laughter bubbling out of my mouth.

"It's not funny," he says.

I school my face. "No, totally not funny." Although it totally is. This man who's tortured others, who, I am in no doubt, has been tortured himself. Who willingly walks into the dueling ring one on one with some of the fiercest fighters in the republic, doesn't like having his ears touched.

"They're ... sensitive."

"I agree." I press my fingers to his abdomen. "But it needs fixing, little fox."

"Little fox?" he says, frowning.

"Big fox," I correct, making his lips twitch. "I promise I'll be gentle." He eyes me warily. "I thought we trusted each other ..."

"Fine," he says. I reach my hand out and again he catches my wrist. "Gentle."

I can't help smiling. All this love of pain and hurt but when it comes to the man's ears ...

"Pinky promise." I wiggle my little finger at him.

He nods and lets go of my wrist. As gently as I can – which is pretty damn difficult considering I'm riding a dragon, am facing the wrong way around and have Pip wedged between us – I touch the tip of my forefinger to his earlobe. He flinches, then steels himself.

"Okay?" I ask.

"Yes," he answers grumpily.

I track my finger carefully up his ear to the place where it's ripped in two. Then I concentrate my magic on gluing the two halves back together. It's both harder and easier than the healing I've done before. Harder because that dark magic is still there, pulsating through my body with no interest in healing, dominating my other magic. And easier, because my magic is definitely stronger since sealing the bond with Spencer – much stronger.

Somehow though, despite the way the dragon buffets us about and despite Renzo's frequent whining, I manage to seal the ear together and to my relief it looks as good as new.

"Done," I say and Renzo lets out a great big exhale of air. "Sure, you don't want me to do the wound on your throat?" He tsks at me. I glance at the wound. The blood is clotting and it's stopped bleeding. "It's definitely going to scar."

"A reminder of the day little rabbit was a fucking boss." He grins at me and I shake my head and concentrate forward. We're near the border now.

"Best we avoid the barracks," Azlan calls out to me, pointing out towards the north. The dragons swerve us that way and then east and soon we're flying over wasteland puckered with craters, nothing but scrubland. Spencer mutters that usually there'd be the odd soldier patrolling this area, monitoring the razor-wire fence. But we encounter no one, no soldiers on either side and I wonder if we're so high in the sky we've passed unnoticed.

The sky continues to lighten around us, the late winter sun hanging low near the horizon. We fly over the rundown towns we drifted between when I was younger, the mountains far away in the distance, their ragged tops the first sign the snow may be retreating, making way for spring on their steep slopes. We fly over forests, single-lane roads slicing the trees in half, empty of vehicles, bigger towns beginning to appear. We fly over factories chugging smoke into the air, lakes that glimmer like mirrors, great fields sown ready for the next year. We fly over prairie land with its tall grasses and roaming cattle. We fly over rivers racing towards the coast.

The sun has begun its dip back towards the horizon when the houses and buildings become more frequent, crowding around each other in ever-increasing numbers until there's nothing but buildings in all directions and I know we've reached the capital. We're still so high in the sky that no one blinks an eyelid at us, mistaking us for a small flock of passing birds. Or maybe they would know what we were if they weren't too afraid to lift their heads and look to the sky.

We turn away from the city, over the countryside, Arrow Hart there in the distance, the mansion almost mended on the brow of its hill. The windows flash red with the setting sun and it's as if the school itself has seen us, knows we're coming.

I hold my breath.

Were we right to come here?

"There are guards at the school now," Tristan calls out.

"Then we take them out," Spencer says, cracking his knuckles. Considering how Christopher Kennedy's guards treated Spencer when he was being held captive, I can understand his enthusiasm to impart some revenge.

"You think that's possible?" Azlan asks.

Tristan pats the dragon he's riding. "Yeah, I think we could."

"The students might turn on us, though," I point out. "If the school is full of mini-Summers then–"

"Don't they love those dudes?" Renzo asks, pointing at Tristan and Spencer.

"Not me anymore," Spencer says.

"Then him." Renzo points back at Tristan.

"I don't know ..." Tristan says. But it's obvious he's being modest. It doesn't matter what Summer or his dad or anyone else might say. Tristan Kennedy is popular for a reason and I think most of the student body would follow him right off the edge of a cliff if he told them to.

"Are you sure this is where we should go, sweetheart?" Stone asks.

"Yes," I say. "I think that's what the prophecy means. I just have this feeling."

A feeling and a dream. That dream from way back when. The dream where everything is burning around me. I didn't know what it was, what it meant. But now as it flashes through my mind, I recognize features of the place I'm flying above – the academy. I'd dismissed that dream as a prediction about the attack on the academy all those weeks ago. But it never really fit. The dream signified the end. The end of the story. Of my story.

We're flying towards my destiny. I am sure of that.

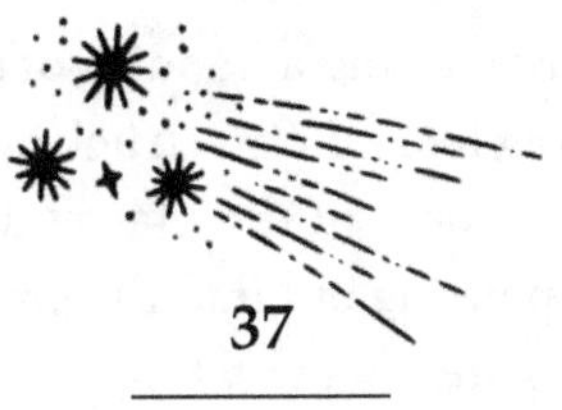

37

T ristan

WE HEAR the first shouts as we swoop down towards the academy followed by bolts of magic firing our way. The dragons spiral back up into the sky again and then downwards, but unlike the night of the Victory Ball, they don't scorch everything to ashes with their fire.

None of us wants the academy destroyed again and either the dragons sense that from us or Rhi has given them some kind of command. Instead, we fire our own magic. It's only the guards my dad stationed here that attack us, the handful of students out on the paths run for cover, hurrying into dormitories or classrooms.

My magic has changed. It's stronger than before and more free flowing. It comes easily when called and I don't even have to form the thought, don't even need to visualize what I want my magic to do, it's already doing it.

I knock one of the guards down easily, despite the way he twists and turns, and I take out another two fighting side by side with one flick of my fingers. In front of me my cousin fights just as deftly, striking a handful of guards at once and sending them flying like tenpins struck by a ball.

Then the great doors of the mansion open and most of the faculty come pouring out into the grounds, heads raised our way, hands moving that way too.

"No," I shout at them, "don't shoot!"

I see York in the middle of the group, her eyes meeting mine and then moving over the others, recognition forming on her face. She hesitates. Then lowers her hands and shoots at one of the guards instead. The teachers around her stand gaping, stunned, and then Coach Hank follows suit, firing his magic at another of the guards and several of the others follow his example.

"What are you doing?" I hear Dr. Johnson screech, her glasses tumbling off her nose, catching on the chain around her neck. "The Lord Protector–"

"Shut up Diana!" Coach Hank yells at her so fiercely, she whimpers and shrinks away.

The guards are outnumbered. Vastly outnumbered. Half of them turn on their heels and run, the other half raise their hands above their heads and surrender.

Coach Hank and a couple of the other teachers gather them up into a circle and then York rests her hands on her hips and shouts up to us:

"Are you coming down or not?"

Stone points over to the meadow and the dragons fly that way, landing in the long grass and slumping to the ground. It's been a long flight and I'm guessing that they're tired. We slide off their backs, our feet landing back on republic soil, Rhi's pig squirming in Barone's arms.

The first person that breaks through the trees and into the meadow is Principal York, followed shortly after by Coach and then Mrs. Holyhill, the old Magical History and Politics teacher (I'm rather shocked the teeny tiny woman can move that fast). Next are several of our old team mates and a handful of cheerleaders, including Summer. I'm surprised to see her here. I assumed she'd be with my dad.

Perhaps he's tired of her already.

Rhi's dragon rumbles but she lifts her hand.

"It's not clear if these people are our friends or enemies," she says to the dragon, "but I'd rather not roast any people alive until we know for sure, okay?"

"And how about you?" Principal York asks us, shrewd eyes lingering on me. "Do you come as friends or enemies?"

"Friends, I hope," Professor Stone replies, stepping forward to take the role as our official spokesperson.

Principal York lets out a long puff of air I reckon she's been holding for some time and her tight shoulders visibly loosen.

"Well ..." she says, "well ..."

"What do you mean?" Summer says, hands on her hips, outrage on her face. "These are enemies of the state!"

Summer never was as bright as she thought she was and it seems she's slow on the uptake.

"Miss Clutton-Brock, be quiet," York tells her. "I don't remember asking for your opinion or your advice and I certainly don't require either!"

"But–"

"Quiet! Miss Blackwaters and Mr. Kennedy are students of this academy. They are welcome here."

"You're making a big mistake," Summer says threateningly, eyes narrowing at me before she swishes her hair and storms off.

"Want me to go after her?" Coach asks. "She's likely to inform the Lord Protector about our arrivals."

York shakes her head. "I suspect she already has."

The students behind them hesitate, some peering anxiously in Summer's direction, and then Al walks forward engulfing Spencer in a tight hug, before stepping towards me and doing the same.

"I'm so glad you're alive, man," he says, "you heard about Will and Samson ..."

I shake my head and curse. Will? Samson? No, I hadn't heard.

The rest of our team members follow suit and while I'm happy to receive the handshakes and the slaps on the back, I notice Spencer seems less enthusiastic. Perhaps he isn't as convinced in their friendship as he used to be. After all, how many of the other students were happy to follow Christopher Kennedy's sick way of thinking, too ready to agree that all weres should be locked away and tortured?

The cheerleaders glance among themselves and look as if they too will come for hugs and grand reunions. But, Rhi stares them down as if to say there's no way she's going to stand there and let them grope her men. I'm guessing the dragon agrees, because she rumbles again and everyone else jumps away.

"She's a beaut," Mrs. Holyhill says, adjusting the spectacles that balance on her nose and gazing at the dragon with her clouded eyes. "A matriarch mother, I think."

"She is?" Rhi says, gaze skimming over her dragon.

"I would think so. She's large enough to be one and she appears to have made a bond with you if I'm not mistaken."

"Little rabbit healed her when she was injured," Barone says with such obvious pride she can't help but blush.

"Really?" the principal says.

"Quite a feat," Mrs. Holyhill adds, as the clearing begins to fill with other curious teachers and students. "I imagine there are not many magicals a dragon would allow to do that, especially a matriarch mother."

"Are matriarch mothers special then, prof?" Renzo says, asking the question I was thinking.

"Well, according to books written in the time of dragons, yes. Dragons are just like elephants – the mothers rule the school."

"School?"

"It's the name for a group of dragons – most often related and living together," the little old lady tells us, smiling up at the dragon as if she were a cute kitten and not a killing machine.

"Is this her family then – or her school?" I ask, pointing towards the other dragons now lazing about in the meadow.

"Most probably."

The principal clears her throat.

"Is it safe to leave your ..." she frowns, "dragons here? I think it pertinent that we go somewhere private to talk."

Rhi turns to the dragon.

"Thank you. For saving us. Again," Piglet says to the dragon, sounding as mad as she does when she speaks to that pig. The dragon stares at her. That same look the pig so often seems to gives her. "You can go now. There's no need to stay. You're free. Only don't go flying straight back to the West, okay? Go to the mountains or the oceans or–"

"I don't think she wants to go," Barone says. "I think that old prof is right. I think she likes you."

Rhi sighs. I can kind of see her point. One pig, five men and now several dragons to add to her collection.

Oh yeah, and a best friend.

A best friend who comes charging through the trees

towards her. Right on her heels is her boyfriend, Trent, and my cousin Ellie.

"Rhi!" Winnie says, pushing through the gathered students and flinging her arms right around Piglet's neck. Ellie does the same, hugging her brother.

"Winnie! Ellie! What the ... what are you doing here?"

Winnie whispers in her ear and I'm assuming I'll find out later.

Rhi hugs her extra tight and then they step apart.

"So you're all riding dragons now?" Winnie asks, still clinging on to Piglet's hand.

"Good to see you again, Miss Wence," Stone says, stepping forward to kiss her cheek.

"Yeah, good to see you, Winnie," Spencer says.

"Miss Blackwaters ..." York prompts.

Rhi turns back to the dragon.

"I'll come back and find you, okay?" The dragon settles herself down on her side as if she understands and rests her great head on the ground.

"Okay," I say, "let's go talk."

"Beryl and Hank," the principal says to both teachers, "I think it wise if you come with us."

Dr. Johnson steps forward from the crowd that's formed. "Perhaps I could be of assistance too, Stella."

"No, I don't think so," Principal York says stiffly, already turning on her heels and walking towards the trees. The crowd parts to let her through and we follow, whispers rippling around us like a breeze through trees as we pass by the students, their eyes brimming with curiosity.

When we arrive back at the campus, there are more students out on the pathways, all having left their classes to watch as we walk towards the mended mansion. One or two students linger in doorways or poke their heads out as we walk up the repaired mansion's staircase and along the corridor to the principal's office, the bronze plaque bearing the principal's name hanging on the new door. She lets us pass inside and closes the door behind us.

"I imagine you are all hungry and thirsty," she says.

I glance at Azlan. We've just turned up unannounced at her school, bringing dragons with us, dispersing the men meant to guard the school and probably bringing a load of shit down on her head. Tea and cakes was not what I was expecting.

"We'd be grateful for something to eat, Stella," Stone says, magicking several chairs into the office and pushing Rhi into the first, followed by me.

Barone lowers the pig to the floor and it goes scuttling toward Rhi.

Mrs. Holyhill takes a seat as well, while Coach Hank leans against the door, his arms crossed over his chest as if he's guarding the entrance – that or preventing our escape.

Principal York clicks her fingers and a kettle in the corner switches on to boil and a tin of cookies deposits itself in my lap. I take two, hesitate then take a third, suddenly so hungry I could happily stuff all thirty cookies in my mouth at once. Then I pass them onto Piglet, who does exactly the same.

"They have magical restorative powers," Principal York explains as she sets several tea cups in a row along her desk.

I sink back into my chair and take a bite into the cookie. We flew straight here, not stopping to eat, and my belly is most definitely empty. I'm guessing Piglet's is too. She moans in pleasure as she bites into a cookie despite the three teachers in this classroom with us. However, despite her hunger, after a couple of bites, she feeds the rest to the pig.

York tips hot water into an ancient-looking teapot and after a swirl of her fingers, pours steaming tea into each of the teacups.

"No milk, I'm afraid," she says, passing the first to Rhi.

Rhi balances her remaining cookies on her lap and takes a long sip, burning her tongue in the process and making her eyes water.

Stone gives her an unimpressed look and accepts a teacup of his own, blowing across the surface of the tea first before gulping a mouthful.

"So," the principal says, once we all have tea, her eyes darting towards Renzo as he slurps down the lot nosily, "I suggest you start at the beginning. And then I think it best that you tell us what you intend to do next."

"Next?" I say, my second cookie hovering in front of my lips.

"I assume you've come here with a plan or a purpose." Her gaze skims across our faces. "I don't know what your intentions are, Miss Blackwaters, Mr. Kennedy." The principal turns to stare Stone right in the eyes. "It seems I have been kept in the dark about certain things. For starters, how on earth did you come by those dragons?"

"The Black Prince," I tell her simply.

"The Black Prince?" Mrs. Holyhill says, spilling her tea all over her lap. "He's alive?"

"He was, and Rhianna's father," Azlan says and this time it's York who chokes on her tea.

"Your father?" Winnie yelps.

"Why on earth did no one tell me?" York asks.

"Because I didn't know myself up until a few days ago," Rhi says.

"Does the Lord Protector know?"

"Most probably," I say.

"And on his way," Coach says from the door. "Only a matter of time. I'm sure he's been alerted to your presence."

York seems unconcerned with this piece of news. "You are … were … his daughter?" she says, seeming as equally unperturbed by this piece of news. "You killed him?"

"He was a drainer. A vampire." Again York takes this piece of news in her stride, although Coach mumbles a series of expletives.

"I always thought that was just some tale," he mutters.

"The dark magicals were expelled," Miss Holyhill says and for once I wish I'd paid more attention in her classes. Maybe we'd have been forewarned about the Black Prince and his inclination for other magicals' blood.

Rhi's gaze swivels around us all. "He planned to drain me of my magic – to drain all of us – to use us as his Sources. We fought back."

"Against an entire coven of vampires?" York says.

"Their Sources joined us – helped us – to fight back. They killed the Black Prince. Not us."

"I see."

"He had plans to use my powers," she adds.

"Your powers?" York raises her eyebrows.

Winnie shuffles forward on her seat. "Rhianna's the girl in the Fourth Prophecy, Stella." Stella? Since when has Winnie Wence been on first-name terms with the principal? Even I was never awarded that privilege.

"The Fourth Prophecy?" Mrs. Holyhill says, eyeing Rhi with even more interest. "*And she will come again.*"

"Queen Æðelflæd?" York's gaze remains trained on Rhi. "And why would you suspect that the prophecy refers to Miss Blackwaters?"

Stone turns his palm skyward and sweeps it around us. "There are six of us. Six fated mates."

"Hmmm," Coach Hanks says.

"These things are very unlikely to be genuine. You have no idea how many students I've had over the years claim they are fated mates. Infatuation," the principal's eyes linger on me, "and lust," they move on to Barone, "can easily be mistaken for more powerful forces."

"This is genuine," I say firmly and Stone and Azlan nod in agreement.

"What do you think, Beryl?" the principal asks, turning back to the Magical History and Politics teacher.

Mrs. Holyhill dips her cookie in her tea and then lifts the sloppy thing into her mouth, chewing as her ancient eyes assess all of us.

"I wonder how you can doubt it. Five fated mates. The Black Prince. Dragons."

Principal York considers the old teacher and then Rhi. Her eyes are just as intelligent as the old lady's and even more piercing. I feel like we're being measured up for some test. I lift my chin and puff out my chest. There's never been a test I've failed to pass.

"Did you find the prophecy?" Winnie asks Rhi and she nods. "What did it say?"

"It wasn't exactly clear," Spencer mutters.

"No offense, Spencer," Winnie replies, "but, erm, could we hear it? What did it say?"

There's a few minutes of head scratching so I place my tea cup on the floor, clear my throat and repeat the entire verse. A photographic memory can come in handy.

"Oh my gosh," Winnie says, grinning at Stone. "I was right."

"Perhaps," he concedes, repressing a smile.

"Yep," Rhi says. "I think you are. I think I – we – are the ones who are meant to stop Christopher Kennedy. That's why I'm here." She stares off into the distance, squaring her shoulders as she does. "I think this is where it all ends. Where the prophecy is realized."

"What makes you say that?" I ask her, a shiver racing right down my spine, my bond thrumming.

She turns, her honey eyes bright and alert.

"*Where all must go to learn,*" she says, repeating the line from the prophecy.

"That could be anywhere."

"Perhaps but I had a dream."

"A dream?" York says, her brow crinkling.

"A premonition," Rhi clarifies. "This is the place where it all ends."

York considers this too, then smoothes down her skirt. "Then we had better prepare."

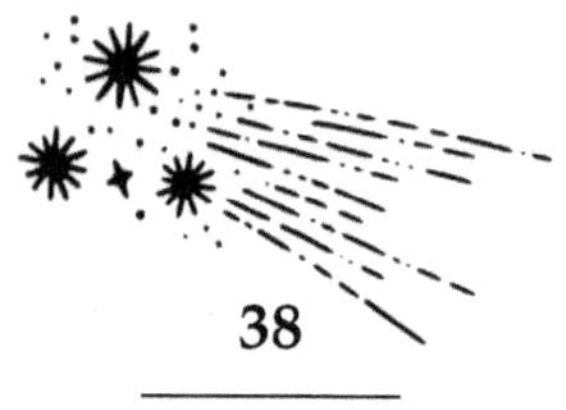

38

S pencer

"Prepare?" I say. Have I missed the memo somewhere? What the hell is going on?

York doesn't answer me though. She addresses Coach. "Hank, you know what to do?"

"All the students?"

"All of them. We'll be along shortly."

Coach nods his head curtly and leaves the room.

"Right," York says, but before she can say any more, a machine crackles and beeps in the corner of her office. She squares her shoulders and glances its way. "That will be the Lord Protector. I advise you to remain quiet."

Then she stands and walks to the corner, pressing several buttons on the device and watching as the blank screen on the machine flickers to life. A grainy picture comes into focus, Christopher Kennedy eventually staring right at her with unblinking eyes.

"Principal York," he says, his voice making my stomach turn and my fists clench.

"Lord Protector," York replies calmly, "how can I be of assistance?"

"We have received reports of intruders at the academy."

"You have?" she says innocently.

"Yes, and our guards are unreachable."

"As you can see," she says, "I am in my office. No such reports have reached my ears." She holds his gaze. "But I am aware your reports are always accurate."

"They are. And the intruders are believed to be wanted fugitives," he pauses, "highly wanted fugitives. You will apprehend them."

"Ahhh," York says slowly, "I'm afraid that won't be possible."

"Not possible?! Why not?" Kennedy spits, frowning so sharply it makes his eyes bulge. "Have the fugitives–"

"No, it's not that. It's simply that I have decided to no longer follow your orders. I will not be apprehending anyone."

Kennedy's entire face reddens with anger. I wait for the explosion.

There is none.

He simply nods his head in understanding. "So be it, Stella. You understand what this means."

"I am aware."

Kennedy's nostrils flare and then the screen goes blank.

"Was that wise?" I ask, unable to help myself.

"You're here to meet your destiny. Is there any point in delaying it?"

I stand up. "And what is our destiny because I'm still in the fucking dark here?" I snap.

"It's us or them," Rhi says.

"Them?"

"The Lord Protector and his followers. They're coming here. They're coming for me."

"Then we should leave," I say, eyes darting to the window. There's time. Especially with the help of those dragons.

"No more running. We fight."

"But there's only six of us against him and his army!"

"Six fated mates. Queen Æðelflæd and her knights. Your powers will know no bounds," Mrs. Holyhill says, her empty teacup still balancing on her knobbly knees, "if you fight together."

"And we will help you," York says, removing her tweed jacket and rolling up her sleeves.

"We've been preparing," Winnie Wence says, bouncing up onto her toes. "Several of us." She nods towards Tristan's cousin, Ellie.

"How are you even here?" I say, shaking my head in disbelief. Winnie is on the wanted list just like us and Ellie has always been heavily guarded by her family. There are obviously Christopher Kenedy's spies in this academy – Summer being an obvious one – as well as his guards. How did either of them sneak into the academy?

"Stella – I mean Principal York," Winnie says, "has been taking in fugitives and hiding us."

"Building a resistance," York clarifies.

"We've been living down in the infirmary in the basement and preparing – thinking of ways to build up the resistance and sabotage the Lord Protector's plans. Trent's come up with some ingenious tech ideas," she says proudly. "And Ellie and I have been brewing special potions."

Ellie smiles shyly, fiddling with the beads that hang around her neck.

"How many of you are there?" Azlan asks.

"About twenty."

I snort. "That isn't enough."

"You will have the support of the staff and the students too," York says.

"All of them?" Stone asks, one eyebrow rising skeptically, obviously thinking of Summer.

"Not all of them, I'm sure. But most. These students have been training for battle all the time they've been at Arrow Hart, Phoenix. Now they have an opportunity to decide which side they will fight for."

"Will they fight for me?" Rhi asks hesitantly.

"Yes, I think they will, especially when they see you have Spencer and Tristan's support," York says, addressing me and using my first name for the first time in my life. "You will need to persuade them that this is the side to fight for."

"Persuade them?" I scoff. "Most of them think I'm some diseased and dirty mutt."

"And they think I'm some mad, untrained girl who speaks to pigs," Rhi mutters, the pig in question, by her feet, snuffling a cookie she's fed him.

"Spencer, you were our most successful dueling captain ever," York says and then turns to Tristan. "And you, our most successful vice-captain. You know how to motivate and coordinate a team between you, so go out and make this happen."

I turn to Azlan. I've come to depend on the enforcer's advice. He is so often the voice of reason.

"What do you think?" I ask him.

"I think Principal York is right."

"Okay," I say, nodding slowly, the idea beginning to grow on me. "And how long do you think we have? How long before the Lord Protector arrives here all guns blazing?"

"I think they'll be here at daybreak," York says.

"You don't think they'll be storming here already?" Rhi asks.

"No, the man is clever and cunning. Christopher Kennedy has no doubt worked out that I'll be leading some kind of resistance here at the academy and he'll know you have dragons. He will need time to gather forces together and consider his attack. We are well defended here, even more so with dragons. It'll take him time. Time we can use to our advantage if we use it now!"

I turn to my friend, gripping his shoulder. "Time to step up, then, buddy."

"Time to step up!" he repeats.

"Coach Hank has gathered the students and staff members together in the gymnasium."

"Do you think you can organize them?" Winnie asks with a little doubt in her voice.

"I may not be as smart as you, Winnie Wence," I say, making her cheeks sizzle, "but I do know how to fight."

Once we're back out on the pathway and jogging towards the gymnasium, Tristan asks me, "Do you actually have a plan, Spence?"

I grin at him. Do I have a plan?

"Same plan we always have, Tris."

"Lure and attack?" he asks.

"Works every time."

He grins back at me. "Shit," he mumbles.

I punch his arm and laugh, a lightness filling me. Maybe that's this bond thrumming like sunshine in my belly, maybe it's being back at the school – my territory, my terrain – or maybe it's because we're going to take action, going to strike back, going to take our destiny into our own fucking hands.

What does it matter what it is, anyway? It makes my feet lighter, my grin wider, and it means I'm going to give those students in the sports hall one hell of a show.

I pick up my pace, crashing straight through the gym doors and raise my fists into the air, as scores of frightened and anxious faces look back at me.

I can't blame them. You can almost smell that battle coming. And though they've all been training for years, the last time they faced actual combat – when the academy was attacked at the Victory Ball – it didn't go so well.

This time, though, this time we'll be ready. And this time I'm here.

"I'm back, motherfuckers!" I yell. Fists high in the air as Tristan skids to a stop behind me. "Me *and* him." I jerk my head Tristan's way and wink at them all.

For a very long, excruciating minute, there is absolute and complete silence. A shocked silence as two hundred-odd faces gape at me like I've lost my mind.

I keep my fists in the air, keep the grin on my face. I won't let them see the doubt. I need to project belief and confidence. Give them someone to follow.

More never-ending silence, so silent, you could hear a pin drop, and then suddenly there's a whoop from the back of the hall and a fist drives up into the air. It's one of the guys from the team. It starts a ripple effect, the other jocks around him following his lead and then those around them, until most of the damn hall is whooping and cheering.

"Hell, yeah," I laugh. Then press my finger to my lips, signaling for quiet again. "Fuck, I love you guys." I spot that little kid I half scared to death several weeks back sitting in among the crowd and give him a nod. "And I missed you."

"We missed you, too, Spence," the dueling team shouts from the back of the hall. Yeah, I'm not convinced that's true but I'm going to play along with all this anyway. "I hear things have been … erm," I smirk, "slightly shit while I've been gone." There's some nodding and murmuring, several gazes fall to the floor. "I can tell you, I haven't had the best of times either. In fact," I hook my arm around Tristan's neck and tug him towards me, "If it wasn't for my buddy here, I'd probably be dead. He risked his neck to come save me." This time there's murmuring and several girls stare at Tristan with actual goddamn love hearts in their eyes. "And now we're here to save all of you."

More murmuring, more eyes swinging nervously around the hall. I'm guessing they really do think I'm mad now.

"Save us how?" asks some girl, chewing gum so furiously I'm surprised her jaw doesn't snap.

"You heard of Queen Æðelflæd? Of the Fourth Prophecy?"

Even more murmuring and several looks of confusion. I guess I'm not the only one who failed to pay attention in history class.

"Queen Æðelflæd had five fated mates and together they drove the darkness and the monsters from the land. The Fourth Prophecy predicts she will return and save us all again," Tristan says, interpreting things in a way I'm sure both Winnie and Professor Stone would argue about. But who cares. It's near enough the truth. It's what these kids need to hear. They need a reason to be brave enough to fight back. To believe they can fight back. "And she has."

The girl stops chewing and the gum nearly tumbles from her mouth.

"Who is she?"

We turn and look at each other. Yeah, this is where things may not go so great. We know how fucking amazing Rhi is, but these guys? Nope.

"Does she have five fated mates?" that small kid calls out, looking amazed.

"Yes," I say. "Five mates. I am one of those fated mates."

"And I am another," Tristan confirms.

The entire hall erupts into chaos and this time it's only Coach lurking at the back and blowing his whistle that silences everyone.

"But who is the girl?" the gum-girl calls out. "Is it Summer?"

Everyone swivels around to stare at someone standing in the shadows at the back of the hall. Her arms are crossed tightly across her body and she's glaring at us with fierce hatred.

I hold her gaze and snort so loud it makes the kids in the front row leap up in the air.

"No," I say. "No, fucking way."

"I would actually die of shame if I was bonded to a diseased mutt like you," she spits, stepping forward.

I laugh like that's the funniest thing I've ever heard.

"Nah, it's not Summer," I say. "It could never be someone so selfish, self-obsessed and cruel." She goes to argue and I cut right over her. "Our mate is someone ... someone who understands what it's like for the world to kick you around, to treat you like shit. Someone who's got back up each time and kept fighting despite her bruises. Someone ..."

How do I even begin to describe what she's like? Why she means so much to me? I don't have the capability with words. Not to make them understand.

Luckily, my friend steps in. One with more charm in his little finger than I possess in my entire body.

"She's funny and smart and caring and ... I'd follow her to the end of the earth and back. I'd lay my life down for her." He scrubs his hand through his floppy locks. "In fact, I already have."

"Who is she?" the girl with the gum asks with annoyance now.

"Rhianna Blackwaters," Tristan says.

I know it's going to be difficult to win people around to this idea. But until the giggles and the scoffs start, I guess I don't realize just how difficult.

"Are you serious, man?" Al says. "Pig girl?"

"Don't call her that," I growl.

"Summer said she'd cast some love spell on you," Fiona sneers at Tristan, "and I guess she was right."

Summer nods her head. "And she tried to kill me with crimson magic. She's evil and dangerous."

The little kid I knocked over pipes up.

"Didn't she save you from that dragon when the academy was attacked?"

"No!" Summer says, with a pout.

"I definitely saw that," the kid says to those around him.

"Summer is never right about anything. Do you know whose bed she's been climbing into?" Tristan hisses.

"Your dad's," someone yells out, and this really isn't going our way. Fuck!

"So, is this like some kind of revenge on her and him?" the girl with gum asks, clearly confused.

"No!" Tristan says, the charm slipping away and his annoyance clear now. I don't blame him. Most of these kids have struggled to keep up with him. It's always been clear to me, his oldest friend, how frustrating that has been. He's never shown it before, though. "We're doing this because the Lord Protector – my father – is restricting your liberties, terrorizing your friends, killing your families."

"And keeping us safe from another attack from the West," Summer says. "And degenerates like you!" She points at me.

"You're on his wanted list!" some other kid says. "That has to be for a reason."

"Really?" Tristan says, the frustration brimming in his features. "You really believe in all that bullshit? You've actually fallen for it? I know my dad better than anyone else in this room." He scowls at the cheerleaders. "Better than fucking Summer. All he cares about is himself. His power and his control. You're fooling yourselves if you believe anything else. And I can tell you, it'll only get worse."

The hall is silent while the other kids take this in. Then someone mutters:

"He arrested my sister because she dated a were. They say she could be infected too," the girl with gum says, her eyes filling with water. "She didn't even know the dude was a were. We haven't heard from her since."

"My best friend is on the wanted list – her entire family are – and they don't even know why," another boy pipes up. "They all disappeared last week."

"I'm sure there was a reason," Summer says, but others around her are mumbling similar stories.

"So you're telling us our only hope is Pig Girl?" one of the cheerleaders asks, ignoring the deathly look Summer throws her.

"Don't call her that," I growl again.

"I'm saying you can have hope because of her," Tristan says. "But one girl, one girl and her five fated mates, even if we are from some damn prophecy can't change things. That takes all of us. All of you. If you want to end this reign of terror, if you want to see a better world, you have to help us fight for it."

"So will you?" I ask, swinging my gaze over every single person in the hall, my eyes landing on Coach last, standing at the back with his hands in his pockets and his whistle hanging from his neck. "Will you fight with us?"

I can't tell what they're thinking. I could see this swinging against us just as much as I could see it swinging for us.

"I don't know," one of the cheerleaders says. "It all seems so far-fetched."

"Far-fetched?" the little kid says. "They flew in here on dragons." That has people talking again. Then that same little kid, the one I terrorized in the corridor, steps forward. "If Tristan and Spencer believe in this girl, believe in this cause, then so do I." He turns and looks me in the eye. "They took my Gramps, just because ..." His gaze falls to the ground.

"I'm sorry, man," I say, resting my hand on his shoulder. "But this is why we have to put an end to things."

"Yes," the boy says, "we do."

And, stars, I could actually kiss the boy, because now everyone is following suit, nodding, voicing their agreement, until my shoulders sag in relief.

We've done it. We've actually goddamn done it. Won them over.

"You're all completely mad," Summer cries, tossing her head in frustration. "And you're only going to get yourselves killed." She turns to her posse. "Come on!"

The posse glance at us and I smile at them. Then they peer back at Summer, her face sour and bitter.

One by one they shake their heads. Summer shrieks and paces away. There are some definite giggles as she goes.

Once she's gone, the others turn their attention back to us.

"So what's the plan?" one of my dueling buddies calls out.

"Ahhh," I say with another of my grins, "Coach, do you think we could borrow your whiteboard?"

39

R^{hi}

"IF SPENCER and Tristan can motivate and organize the students to stand with you, I think we stand a chance," York says once the two boys have left her office.

"Especially with us resistance fighters helping too," Ellie says.

"As soon as Kennedy arrives," Winnie says, "Trent can take out his communication channels."

"And I can release the potion that will disorientate his troops," Ellie adds.

"Thank you," I say, but I'm engulfed in unease.

Stone must read that unease in my mind or through our bond because he asks me, "What's wrong?"

I bite at my thumb considering all the others.

"I can't help feeling that this is my fight, my moment

with destiny, and I shouldn't be asking all of you to get involved."

Winnie tsks and Ellie shakes her head.

"Are you serious, Rhi?" Winnie says. "This fight belongs to all of us. Fate gave you five men for a reason and she also gave you me and Trent and Ellie."

Winnie takes my hand. "We may not be bonded, but we're here to help you and that's what we're going to do."

I can't help smiling at my best friend, my eyes tearing. I've gone from precisely one friend (and he is a pig who can't speak) to so many people that I care about and who care about me too. I may be about to face who-knows-what, but I can't help feeling blessed and lucky and damn, damn happy.

"Thank you," I say again, this time with more feeling. "Thank you all."

"Winnie and Ellie, perhaps you could go and update the other resistance fighters. Beryl, it would be useful if you could dig up any more information that might be of use to us either on Queen Æðelflæd or the prophecy. And Professor Stone, Enforcer Kennedy and ..." She pauses as she looks at Renzo last.

"Renzo Barone," he says, holding out his hand. If the principal recognizes his name and who he is, she doesn't show it, keeping a completely passive face as she shakes his hand, eyes lingering for a millisecond on the blood still staining his throat and his ear.

"I think it would be helpful if the three of you went to see how Tristan and Spencer are getting along."

"I'm not leaving little rabbit alone," Renzo says.

"Pardon?" the principal says and despite everything, I feel my cheeks sizzle.

"It's okay, Renzo," I insist, sensing that the principal wants to talk to me alone. "I'll be along in a moment."

He frowns, but then Stone and Azlan are shoving him out the door.

It closes and then it's just me and the principal. It's been a long time since we've spoken alone and a lot has passed in that time.

I turn and face her. She used to intimidate me in my early days at the academy. I certainly didn't want to end up on her wrong side and even more than that, I found I didn't want to disappoint her. After all, this woman let me keep Pip with me when everyone else was dead set against the idea.

Now, however, I feel differently about her. I still don't want to let her down, but I feel like there's more of a mutual respect between us – especially if she's recognized how great my best friend is.

"Are you going to ask me if I'm sure I know what I'm doing?" I ask her. "Because the answer is no. I can't be sure. But I think you should be more worried if I was. Only assholes tend to believe in themselves and their decisions 100% – that's been my experience anyway. The rest of us have to battle our doubts and weigh up the right thing to do."

"I agree entirely," the principal says, "but I wasn't going to ask if you were sure. Whether you are or not, is almost irrelevant. I think it has to be done. We either take this moment to strike now or we waste years of misery and grief, waiting for destiny to gift us another moment like this."

"You think so?" I ask.

"Yes, Beryl is correct. We have Spencer and Tristan – boys most of my students would follow off the edge of a cliff. We have talented resistance fighters like Ellie, Winnie and

Trent. We have several dragons who appear to be on your side. And then, Rhianna, we have you. You and your five fated mates. If all the prophecy and the tales of Queen Æðelflæd tell us is true, the six of you working together will be truly remarkable." She nods her head. "What I want to say is, don't hold back, if the moment comes, use everything you have, don't let your doubts inhibit you."

I stare into her intelligent eyes. Maybe like Stone, she's been able to read thoughts all along because it's as if she's reached right into my mind and picked out the worries floating there. That I won't be strong enough. Or worse, that I'm twisted and corrupted like my dad and if I let my powers truly take hold of me, who knows what damage I might do.

"I'm going to do everything I can to stop that man," I say, "but you should know, there's a risk–"

"A risk?" She frowns.

I take a deep inhale. "The magic – the powerful magic I have inside me – it isn't all good. Some of it, quite a lot of it, is bad."

"I know."

"You know?"

"Yes, I can feel it. I've always been able to feel it. Although, like you say, it's grown alongside your other magic."

"You could feel it all along?"

"Yes." She tilts her head to one side. "It's a useful skill to have when you're a principal. One of the reasons why they picked me for the job – my ability to seek out talent."

"But I thought you thought there was nothing remarkable about me," I blurt out.

"Well, of course, it depends whether you consider your magic remarkable," she says with a smile that makes me blush. "Which I do, Rhianna. But I have also been principal long enough to see many students with remarkable powers misuse it or fail to live up to their potential. I see that is not the case with you."

"I hope so," I mutter.

"I also know when best to share with others this knowledge and when to keep it firmly to myself."

"Thank you," I say for the third time. "I appreciate it."

"Now," she says, "I've monopolized your time long enough. I'm sure you want to find the others and prepare. I'd advise you to be ready in the morning. The resistance will have lookouts on post to signal to us when there's an approach. You have the night."

I FIND my five mates in the gymnasium, crowded around a whiteboard and listening to Spencer as he waves his arms in the air, occasionally pointing to the board. The others are nodding or asking questions. For once, there is no arguing going on.

I peer down at Pip.

"Are my eyes deceiving me or are they actually getting along?"

"Desperate times call for desperate measures," Stone calls out and the others all look my way.

"Where are all the students?" I ask. "I thought you were trying to persuade them to fight with us."

"We did," Tristan says with a smug grin, "and we briefed them too. Now we told them all to go get a good night's rest and be ready to fight in the morning."

"That's what York told me to do too."

"Well, she's right," Azlan says. "We've been running on adrenaline. We need rest."

"I doubt I'll be able to sleep. I don't see how anyone will be able to."

"Best you try," Azlan insists.

"Not until you've explained the plan," I say, striding up to peer at the whiteboard. It has a rudimentary diagram of the academy scribbled all over it as well as several crosses and arrows.

"It's simple, really," Spencer says, looking way more himself than he has done in days, his excitement buzzing through our bond. "The academy is impregnable to attack. Not only because of the old spells that prevent intruders but also the physical location of where and how it was built."

"Erm," I say, "the Victory Ball."

"Okay, yes," he says, rolling the pen between his hands and bouncing on the balls of his feet. "It's vulnerable to attack from above, but not anymore, not now we have dragons. And this old mansion was built in such a way that it would be protected. We're up here on top of the mound. We can see anyone coming and to reach us they have to climb up the hill, meeting our onslaught from above."

"Or they have to go through the forest," Tristan says.

"Which no sane magical would attempt," Spencer says, grinning at his friend and bumping him with his shoulder.

"They could try tunneling," I point out.

"Sure, but that takes time and also the earth here is chalk – any tunnel they try to build would fill with water."

"They could barrage us with magic," I say.

"Yes, from below. We'd have the high ground and the advantage."

I cross my arms and examine the diagram.

"Okay, this is all very well. But we don't simply want to survive their attack. We want to end things once and for all."

"Yep," Spencer says, "which is why we're going to lure them in – either by dragon or from land– and then ambush them."

"Oldest trick in the book," Renzo says.

"This is what that is," I say, pointing to the board, "luring them in."

"Yep, Kennedy is going to send his foot soldiers first. We lure them in and take them out and then it's just us and Kennedy."

"Us, all of us, right?" I say. "The only way we're going to defeat him is if we fight together." I let my gaze run over these five men. All of them mean so much to me. But would they have each other's backs in battle? Will they fight for one another? "I don't think this works unless we are in it together."

Pip squeaks his agreement from my ankles.

"All of us," Azlan says firmly and Tristan and Spencer both nod.

"Stone?" I say. "I know you have a past with Renzo. I know you have issues with him–"

"You have issues with me?" Renzo asks him, sounding genuinely hurt.

"Of course, I have issues with you. You're a psychopath."

"It's not *nice*," Renzo says, "to call people names. I can't help what I am, Birdman, any more than you can help who you are."

"Yeah, but I don't enjoy killing people."

"I've found something I enjoy even more than killing now," he says, eyeing me up like I'm dessert.

Stone rolls his eyes and shoves his hands deep in his

pockets. "I can live with him," he says to me, "if that's what it takes."

He might even grow on you, I say in my mind. *And remember, you promised me you'd try.*

Stone grimaces, but he's willing to try, and that's good enough for me. Because I'm certain that if we don't stand together, we are going to fall together.

And a hell of a lot of people will fall with us.

40

R^{hi}

IT SEEMS none of the students have taken Spencer's advice. No one is sleeping tonight. The campus is alive with noise as we walk down to Stone's cabin, groups gathered on the pathways, hanging out of windows or crammed into different rooms. They fall silent as we walk past them, staring at us like we're unicorns or made of diamonds or are gods themselves. It makes me a little uncomfortable, but Tristan, Spencer and Renzo lap it up. In fact, Renzo keeps giving little waves or blowing kisses like he's royalty.

I'm relieved when we make it down to the meadow away from everyone else, even if Pip does bitch about the walk through the long grass and I'm obliged to pick him up.

"Seriously," Stone mutters, "that pig gets more love and affection than all the rest of us combined."

"That's because he's special," I tell him.

"And we're not?" Spencer asks with mischief.

"Hmm," I say, shrugging and pretending to be nonchalant.

"Such a brat," Stone says, eyes darkening and I pick up my pace, eager to arrive at the cabin.

Maybe it's seriously morbid, but none of us knows what's going to happen tomorrow, whether or not we'll be successful. We can hope we will be, we can plan and pray and wish to make it that way. But there are no dreams forthcoming to indicate either way. Which means, it's a very good chance that tonight could be our final night together, and I am determined to make it a special one.

However, any plans I may have had receive a large bucketful of ice cold water. The door to Stone's cabin has been kicked in and there are books and possessions strewn all over the front decking.

"Seems I've had one or two visitors while I've been away," Stone says, climbing the porch steps and picking up one of the books, tutting with disapproval as he strokes his hand over the cover with tenderness, as if he's nursing the book. The professor, for all his sarcastic tough guy impressions, is one giant nerd.

Cradling the book in his arms, he strides through the gap in the doorway and then a minute later, strides straight back out, two more books in his arms and a massive frown on his face.

"It's been completely trashed. Sorry, Rhi, we're not staying here tonight."

"Couldn't we do a little repair job with our magic?" I ask.

"I think it best we conserve all our magic for tomorrow," Azlan tells me.

"Then where are we going to go? I doubt my room has fared much better and it wasn't exactly a great room to begin with."

"It was shit," Renzo says, eyeing up the others like that was their fault.

"My room is probably the same," Spencer mutters.

"Then it'll have to be mine," Tristan says, already heading off across the meadow.

"Won't they have trashed yours too?" I ask, trotting to keep up with him.

"I'm still the Lord Protector's son even if I am a traitor. I suspect no one will have dared touch it."

We go back the way we came, past all the onlookers, and inside the more glamorous of the dorm buildings – you know, one of the ones with paint work, light bulbs and curtains. Tristan's room is up on the top floor and we find the door to his room undisturbed. In fact, the entire room appears untouched when he unlocks the door.

Azlan makes us hang back nonetheless, searching for bugs.

"Bugs?" I say.

"Not the insect kind, sweetheart," Stone says, "the kind that listen to you."

"Oh," I say watching as Azlan looks under the bed, underneath the mattress and behind the blinds.

"I can't sense any," he says, "and I can't see any either."

"It probably doesn't matter anyway," Tristan says, tossing his jacket towards the desk chair. "They must know we're here. They know about the prophecy, Rhianna and the five of us." He spins around waving his hands, then halting and changing the hand gesture to something more crude. "If you're watching this dad, you can go to hell!"

"Isn't that where he came from?" Spencer mutters, flopping down on the bed.

"Probably. Only seems fair that we send him back there tomorrow."

"Are you sure?" I ask him, placing Pip on the floor. "He is your dad, Tristan. It's okay to feel conflicted about this."

"I spent my life wishing he was dead," he says, staring into my eyes with a steely determination and once again I'm reminded of all those healed bones and unseen scars inside Tristan Kennedy's body.

Hell, it makes me even more determined to kill Christopher Kennedy.

The dark magic soars in my veins at the very idea, hot and violent, and I close my eyes trying to drive it away.

"Okay, Piglet?" Tristan says, coming closer.

"I ... I just don't like the idea of killing people. Even if they are shitheads." Am I lying? My dark magic likes the idea a lot.

"Yeah," he says. He walks back to his desk and starts to rummage through the contents. I follow him over, intrigued. I think I know Tristan Kennedy much better than I did, but there are parts of him which are still a mystery to me, parts that still seem conflicting. Partly, I realize, it's down to that mask he's always worn, one I've come to understand was necessary growing up with a dad like his.

I peek over his shoulder, curious about what Tristan Kennedy keeps in his desk drawer, somewhere I can tell by the worn-out patch on this otherwise pristine carpet; he must have spent an awful lot of his time here. On one side of the drawer, there is a neat line of rolled-out joints, a bag of marijuana and several scribbled notes and diagrams in Coach Hank and Spencer's hands. On the other side, sits another row, this time of carefully sharpened pencils as well as a pad of sketching paper.

"What's that?" I ask, pointing to the pad. He's printed his name neatly in the top right-hand corner of the cover – it seems at odds with his nonchalant attitude.

"What?" he says as he scrutinizes each joint in turn.

"What's the pad?"

His eyes flick that way and he drops all the joints but one back in the drawer and attempts to shut it. "Nothing," he mutters. Which of course only piques my curiosity even further.

"If it's nothing, can I see?"

"No," he says, positioning his body between me and the desk.

"Why not?"

"It's private," he says, and am I imagining this or is Tristan Kennedy actually blushing?

"It's probably his porn," Renzo calls out from the bed where he's made himself comfortable beside Spencer, Pip splayed out across his lap as he gives him belly tickles.

"It's not porn," Tristan mumbles.

"Then what is it?" I ask, with a frown, attempting to dodge around him, now convinced it's some elaborate plan he was working on to take me out back in the days when he wasn't exactly being nice to me.

"I told you, nothing."

"That's really convincing," Spencer chuckles.

"Tristan," I say, "you can move or I can blast you with my magic."

"You're meant to be conserving your magic, remember what Azlan said."

I place my hands on my hips and glare at him.

"Fuck it," he mutters, rolling his spliff between his fingers and going to drop down on the floor next to the bed.

I'm a little shocked he caved in so easily and open the drawer with caution, half expecting it to be booby-trapped and explode in my hands. It doesn't. It slides open easily and I stare down at the pad. Now I feel guilty. It's his private property. I have no business rummaging through it. That guilt lasts two seconds, then I'm cradling it in my hand and flipping over the cover. I start at the front. The first page is a detailed pencil sketch of Tristan's face. A self portrait. I snigger. I knew the boy was vain, but seriously?

"It's not *that* bad," he mutters, puffing on the joint to get it to light.

"The drawing skills or the face?" I giggle.

"Both."

"They are both very ... striking."

Tristan peers up at his friend. "Is that good?"

"Dude," Spencer says, "I have no idea what either of you are talking about."

I flip over that page and look at the next. Several light sketches of a flower, one I've seen growing by the side of the paths across the campus. The next one is a sketch of one of the suits of armor that stood in the Great Hall and another two of his face, then one of Spencer, followed by the academy mansion from the front.

He's talented, very talented, capturing not only the dimensions and detail of buildings, but the personality and humanity of people too. I settle myself down on the desk chair, resting the book in my lap, completely absorbed as the aroma of weed, coffee and finally dinner fill the penthouse.

I'm waiting for all the pictures of half-nude girls, or most probably completely nude girls. Tristan's slept with enough of them. I'm sure they've been more than willing to pose for him. And if they haven't, I bet he gets sent nudes daily.

I bet they're kept at the back of this book. I shouldn't look. It'll only make me mad or jealous. But once again my self-control is pitiful. I flip to the back. I don't find naked girls. I find myself. My face staring right back up at me.

I let out an involuntary gasp.

"What?" Azlan asks, placing a bowl of noodles down on the desk next to me.

"Look," I say, holding the book up to him.

"That's ... beautiful," Azlan says, "who drew that?"

"Tristan," I say, jerking my chin towards his cousin.

"Let's see," Spencer calls.

I twist the book around and hold it up to him.

"Shit, man," Spencer mumbles, "is there anything you can't do?"

"Travel through space and time," Renzo says, scrubbing Pip's belly.

"Bet I could learn, though?" Tristan says with a lazy smile. Renzo snorts, Pip echoing him.

I turn the book around and flip over the next few pages. That isn't the only drawing of me. There are others. Lots of others. My face full on, tilted to the side, looking down, looking up, a sketch of my entire profile, one of my hands. There's even one of me crouched down stroking Pip's head.

The others have already moved onto another topic – the merits of weight training. But when I peer Tristan's way, I find he isn't listening, he's watching me. I guess he's always been watching me.

Maybe any normal girl would find that damn creepy or disturbing. Not me, I find it ... I find it hot. He wasn't lying. He told me he's been obsessed with me since the day we met and it seems that was the truth.

"I'm keeping this one," I tell him, pointing to the one of me and Pip, as the others chatter around us.

"It's all yours, Piglet," he says. "You can have all of them if you want."

I flick back to the sketch he did of himself and the one of Spencer and decide yes, I will be keeping all of it. I close the book and holding it to my chest, abandon my untouched noodles and go to sit next to him on the floor, our backs resting against the wall. Tristan's penthouse apartment may be big but it has a serious lack of home comforts – like chairs for instance.

"When all of this is over," I say, "do you think you could sketch Azlan, Stone and Renzo too?"

"I'm pretty shit at it," he mumbles, "but if you–"

I laugh. "Are you actually being modest for once, Tristan Kennedy?"

"My dad didn't like me wasting my time with things like drawing," he says, hooking his arm around my shoulder and offering me the spliff.

I shake my head and he passes it on to Spencer.

"It isn't a waste of time," I tell him. "Creating things so beautiful never could be."

"That's lucky," he says grinning, "because I intend to spend a lot of time drawing you."

"You're not eating," Azlan says, from the other side of the room, where he's sunk into the only other available seating option – a beanbag, his knees almost hitting his chin.

"I'm not hungry," I admit.

"You should still eat."

I take the fork from Tristan's bowl, swivel noodles around the prongs and shove the lot into my mouth. "Satisfied?" I ask with a full mouthful.

"No," Azlan says, giving me one of his fierce looks. One

that means I'll be doing exactly as he commands and eating all my noodles. When it comes to Azlan, I have a hard time being a brat.

"Don't they usually give you a really good meal for your final one?" Renzo says, poking the noodles with his fork, Pip watching intently, practically drooling on his lap.

"It's ramen noodles," Stone says. "What's not to like?"

"It's too spicy," he moans and I smile to myself. Ears, spice, me. I'm beginning to gather a list of all the assassin's weak spots. "Do you want some, little man?"

"Do not feed Pip spice!" I say, leaping to my feet.

"Why not? Will he turn into a demon?" Stone says, eyeing my pig.

"No, but he will vomit straight for several hours."

"Remind me why you own a pet pig again?"

I don't answer that question. It's something I haven't been honest about. I'm still too scared to tell them in case they make me give Pip up.

I beckon Pip to follow me and he shuffles off Renzo's lap and follows me through the penthouse to the kitchenette area. I spend the next few minutes nosing through Tristan's cupboards, disappointed to find, just like Azlan's, a serious lack of chocolates and candy. I do find some cereal bars through and I unwrap them and offer them up to Pip.

"Here," I tell him. "Eat these and do not go snuffling after noodle leftovers. Do you hear me?" He snorts as if that would never in a million years occur to him when we both know he's been plotting it. "Pip," he halts his demolition of the bars to look up at me, "erm, would you mind, you know, staying in here for a bit?" My pig glares at me with obvious disapproval. "Don't look at me that way. These might be our last moments together. And they're my fated mates. And, you know, hot." Pip squeaks, clearly disagreeing with that last statement. "Sorry, Pipsqueak, but they are."

Pip huffs and turns his attention back on the cereal bars. He may not be happy about it, but he's going to give us our space and our privacy.

I look back out to the living area and take a deep inhale. My belly is full of butterflies, my nerves ringing with anticipation.

If this is going to be my final night on earth, then I'm going to make it a night to remember.

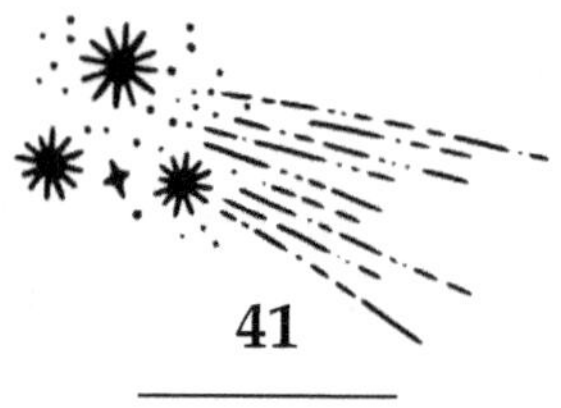

41

S tone

IT'S a lot harder to wander casually into Rhi's mind and her thoughts than it used to be. But occasionally, she'll leave the door right open and I'll catch a glimpse of what she's thinking. And what she's thinking tonight has the fork in my hand clattering to the floor.

"What?" Azlan says, reading the shocked look on my face.

I swallow.

"Rhi," I say as she strides back from the kitchenette, hips swaying, mind brimming with all sorts of frankly smoking-hot ideas. I catch her eyes and I can guarantee mine are shining with lust. A hell of a lot of lust.

Azlan follows my gaze to where Rhi is now standing in the doorway, leaning against the frame.

"What?" he says to her, but her eyes are locked on me. "What?" he tries me next.

"Seems Miss Blackwaters has some ideas about how we should spend our evening."

"I have some ideas," Barone pipes up.

"I'd rather hear Rhianna's," Azlan says, now unable to drag his eyes away from her either.

"Well," she says, reaching up to undo the first button of her shirt.

"Well?" I say, sitting back in my seat, very happy if she's going to provide us with another strip show. The last one is still scorched into my memory.

"It's late and perhaps we ought to go to bed and get some sleep. Tristan, do you have a shirt I could wear to sleep in?"

"You can wear my jersey," he says, gaze as burning hot as mine.

"Miss Blackwaters," I say, standing up and stalking towards her. "Let's not be coy here. Sleeping wasn't what you had in mind."

"What did I have in mind then, Professor?" she asks.

I smirk at her and remove her hands from her blouse, replacing them with mine and carefully threading each button through its hole. I'm sure each one of these men has seen Rhi naked now. They've certainly all slept with her. And yet, there's something irresistible about her, something tantalizing which makes every time just as exciting as the first. Maybe that's the bond. Or maybe it's all her.

When the blouse hangs loose, I ghost it over her shoulders and let it fall down her arms, floating to the floor. She's wearing one of those bras Azlan bought her and, shit, I must remember to thank that guy. I mean, Rhi would look good dressed in a garbage bag – she has the curves. But the bra, the way it frames her tits, the way the material is just that bit see through, giving the hint of her nipples. Yeah, shit.

I trace around the edge of the bra cup with my fingertips, making her shiver, all those ideas spiraling through her mind again, and then I undo her pants and roll them down her legs, following along with them and helping her to lift each leg clear of the material.

She's wearing the smallest, tiniest pair of matching panties and I have to spin her around so I can see her ass – so we can all see that ass. That ass that drove me slightly insane for weeks.

"Goddamn it, Phoenix," Azlan growls, "what does she have in mind?"

I turn her back around so she's facing me, so she's facing all of us and then I look up at her from where I'm kneeling right in front of her on the floor.

"Are you sure about this, sweetheart?"

"More than you could ever know," she whispers and this time I shiver.

Then I nuzzle my face straight into her pussy. There's silk barring me from those soft curls and wet folds, but I can smell her and I press my tongue to the silk anyway, pressing right where I know she's most sensitive. She sighs, her legs buckling slightly and her hands landing on my head to steady herself.

"Stone," she murmurs and, stars, I love my name in her mouth.

"Yes, sweetheart? You want more. You want me to make you fall apart in front of all of them."

"Shit," I hear Spencer mutter from somewhere behind me.

"Yeah, fuck, make her fall apart," Renzo says eagerly.

"Sweetheart?" I ask again because hers is the only

consent I'm seeking. If the others don't want to see this – if they're actually that insane – they can leave the room.

"Yes, Stone, I want that."

I smile against her pussy and then I take a grip of those silly little panties and yank them down her thighs, whispering as I do. "You have to give them a show, though, Miss Blackwaters. I'll make you come, but you be a good girl and play with those tits of yours." She pouts at me, knowing it drives me wild. "Don't be a brat, do as you're told and I'll make you feel damn good with my tongue." I wink at her. "Now part your thighs for me, sweetheart."

This time she does as she's told and I run my hands up her legs, right from her ankles all the way up, stroking that soft, tender inside of her thigh. Then I part her pussy lips, giving all the others a good view before pressing my mouth right against her clit. It's already thrumming and so is her magic, taut and electric. I suck on her and she goes wild above me, one hand tight in my hair, tugging on it so hard it makes my eyes water, calling my name over and over again, and massaging at her tits with the other, squeezing them.

I halt. She curses at me.

"Tell her how beautiful she looks, you goddamn fuckers," I snap.

I'm guessing they were all too busy gaping at the scene with their tongues hanging out. Now they respond though, praise gushing from all of them and I go back to sucking on her. I can read how much she likes the praise and how much she likes to be watched, and I suck on her even harder, sliding two fingers up inside her pussy and making her come right into my mouth.

It's too much for her and she's tumbling downwards, straight into my arms where I catch her, my fingers still in her pussy. I don't withdraw them, I massage that spot inside her as she convulses around my fingers and soon she's coming a second time, this time screaming so loud I bet every student on campus must hear.

Then she slumps, boneless and panting.

"Is that what you had in mind, Rhianna?" Azlan says darkly.

She smiles at him.

"That ... and other things," I mutter.

"What other things?" Barone asks, sliding down onto the floor beside us. "I wanna make you come too, little rabbit." He drags her from my arms and though I don't want her to go, I know it's what she wants so I stay where I am and let him lay her out on the carpet and remove her bra.

"You should draw her like this," he tells Tristan as she arches her back. We all stare at her, drinking her in, until she's scrambling up on her elbows and swinging her gaze around, a line of frustration between her brows.

"Are you all going to just sit there and stare or are you–"

42

R^{hi}

AT FIRST IT'S a little scrappy – five men desperate to touch and taste and pleasure my body. But somehow, among the chaos of it all, we find a way, a way to make it work.

Spencer lifts me up onto Tristan's bed and lays me out. And then all five of them are ripping off their clothes right in front of me, and I am treated to my very own, very hot, private strip show.

I giggle to myself as I watch them – Renzo scrabbling to remove his clothes like his life depends on it, Azlan folding his shirt and pants and placing them neatly on the chair and Tristan undressing with a serious amount of swagger.

"What's funny?" Spencer asks, gazing down at his very perfect body and his very hard cock.

"You're all so different."

"Are we?" Stone says. "Looks to me like you lucked out,

sweetheart. We're all very similar." He winks at me and grips his cock in his hand. And I know exactly what he's implying – each of my mates is very well endowed. Not that I'm going to let them know that.

"And arrogant," I say.

"Not arrogant," Tristan insists. "Realistic."

"Fuck, you got yourself pierced down there?" Renzo mutters, staring right at Stone's cock. "Always wanted to do that."

"Do you not like what you see?" Spencer asks me, ignoring the assassin, rubbing his hand across his chest.

I lick my lips, slowly, and that's all it takes.

Renzo dives between my legs, muttering something about being a tease and being damn ravenous for me. He spreads me wide and licks right from my clit to my pussy. I think the others will hold back and watch like they did with Stone. I huff a little in frustration. I liked all five of them touching me at once.

I've nothing to fear though. Spencer jumps down on one side of me, Tristan crouches on the other, and as Renzo flicks at my clit with the tip of his tongue, my other two mates lick, suck and kiss at my breasts and my nipples, claiming one each.

I sigh and peer up at the ceiling, meeting Azlan's dark gaze. For a minute we just stare at each other and I sink into those dark eyes of his, reading everything I need to know in his expression. Then he lowers his mouth and presses his lips to mine. I part my mouth on instinct and he sinks his tongue into my mouth, just as Renzo sinks his into my pussy.

I sigh again, this time straight into Azlan's mouth, and he kisses me harder, his tongue hungry and persistent.

There's a hand tight on my thigh, another grasping my

waist and another wrapped around my throat. The sensations in my body swirl and swoop, overwhelming me completely.

Azlan pulls back but I've no chance to catch my breath because Stone is there next, kissing me just as hard, just as deep, and then they're kissing me together, both their tongues in my mouth, both their lips caressing mine, both their teeth biting and nipping at my lips.

"Fuck, the view from down here, baby!" Renzo murmurs right against my clit, making me come hard into his mouth, jolting and bucking on the bed as five pairs of hands hold me down.

"You look like a goddess being worshiped by all of us," Tristan says.

"She is a fucking goddess!" Renzo snaps, flicking me so violently with his tongue another orgasm rips right through my body.

"Oh stars!" I cry out, struggling. Because it's too much ... too good ... too damn perfect!

"You want more, little mate?" Spencer growls and I swear, it may be him kneeling beside me, but it's the beast speaking to me.

"Yes," I pant, "so much more. I want it all."

"Fuck," Tristan says, scrubbing his hand through his fair mop of hair, already damp with sweat. "Can Spence and me ... can we share you, Piglet?"

Renzo rolls up to sit cross-legged between my thighs, running the pads of his calloused thumbs over the inside of my thighs as he licks my arousal off his lips. His miscolored eyes flick from me to Tristan to Spencer.

"How? How do you want to share her?"

Tristan looks over to Spencer who's wearing one of his wide grins – the ones that make my stomach spin.

"She sucked your cock yet, Tris? Because she's really, really good at sucking cock."

"Is she now?" Tristan says, eyes darkening.

"Want to find out?" I ask him, scrabbling up onto my hands and knees.

"What do you think?" he says, running his fingers through my hair.

"I think you're encouraging the little brat," Stone says.

"Yeah, damn, encourage her. I want to see that, dude," Renzo says, eyes so bright you think we were offering to show him the meaning of the universe.

Tristan rises up on his knees, his cock bobbing straight in front of me. I shuffle forward and his grip on my hair tightens as I take him into my mouth.

At first, I do nothing but tease him, gliding my tongue around the head of his cock, tasting salty pre-come in my mouth. He lifts his other hand and strokes my cheek gently.

"Such a pretty mouth," someone murmurs.

I hollow my cheeks and suck on him. From this angle, with my arms supporting my weight, I can't grip his cock, but he thrusts his hips forward, moving his cock deeper into my mouth and then out again.

I gag a little. I've not taken any of my mates this deep before and my eyes water.

"Wanna stop?" Tristan asks, the movement of his hips faltering. I peer up at him with a determined look and he smiles down at me. "I'll take that as a no," he says, slamming his cock back into my mouth.

A pair of strong hands land on my hips and the mattress dips behind me.

"Can Spence take you too, Piglet?" Tristan asks.

I pull my head back, his cock leaving my mouth with a pop.

"Have the two of you done this before?" I ask him, looking up at him through wet eyelashes.

"No, we've never shared a girl before."

"But you've done *this* before?" I clarify.

"A spit roast? No, Rhi, never," Spencer says.

I hold Tristan's gaze and he shakes his head. I'm kind of surprised. The rumors about the orgies in the Venus Common Room were pretty wild – what I saw the two of them do was pretty wild too. But they've never done this before – and though I'm sure many would consider it sordid or dirty – for me it feels special.

"Yes," I say, the thought of it making me shiver.

Spencer mutters the barrier spell and then I feel his cock nudge at my entrance.

"Part your thighs a little more for me, Rhi. You're so damn tight."

I do as he says and then he's pushing his way inside me, the both of us moaning as he does.

"Feel good, little rabbit?" Renzo asks from beside me, eyes wide as he soaks the sight of the three of us in.

"Uh huh," I murmur.

"Then keep sucking, sweetheart," Azlan tells me and I capture Tristan's cock in my mouth again and do as I'm told.

Only, it's much harder this time with Spencer thrusting inside me, hitting the spot that sends me kind of crazy. I moan and groan around Tristan's cock, losing concentration, and he takes control, driving his cock in and out of my mouth.

"That looks so freaking awesome, little rabbit. So filthy and dirty and delicious. I love it when you're a little slut."

"You know what would make it even better?" Stone says.

Azlan scoffs like he doesn't think that's possible.

"What?" Tristan grunts, intrigued.

"Barone," Stone says, "think you can ping yourself down there, underneath them, finish eating out our girl?"

My eyes flick to Renzo's and his face morphs the darkest I've ever seen it. Next thing I know, he's disappeared from sight, reappearing beneath me, his body laid out between mine and Spencer's legs.

"The view's even better from down here," he mutters. Then rises up on his elbows so his mouth meets the apex of my pussy lips. He sucks my clit right into his mouth.

And I lied.

I thought it was too much before.

But this, this is too much.

"I'm going to come!" I cry out, writhing between the three of them, the intensity of it increasing and increasing and increasing.

"Fuck, yes, come around my cock, Rhi!" Spencer says, thrusting into me harder, sending me forward and Tristan's cock even deeper into my throat.

For a moment, I can't breathe. No oxygen reaches my lungs. It seems to heighten everything, every feeling, every sensation. Electricity shoots around my body, lighting every nerve into life and I come so hard, for a moment I think I actually pass out.

When I come to again, Spencer's rhythm is faltering. His fingers dig deep into my flesh and he comes with a loud animalistic grunt, hot liquid spilling deep inside me.

Tristan – eyes locked on the two of us, on where his friend is buried deep inside me – comes too. I swallow down the salty taste of his come, loving the way it warms all the way down my throat and into my belly.

And then my arms and legs give way and I fall right down on top of Renzo.

Without missing a heartbeat, he flips me over onto my

back and drags me to the end of the bed, scrambling off the bed himself and standing right between my thighs.

"Always used to like doing it like the fucking hunting dog I am, little rabbit – from behind. That was until I met you. Now I want to see you when I fuck you. Want to see all of you. Your pretty face, your bouncing tits, your fucking pussy."

He lifts my legs, clutching them against his chest.

I smile up at him and then, because I can't help myself, I tickle my toes against his ears.

The skin beneath his right eye twitches and I giggle.

"Little rabbit," he growls, "behave."

Never, I mouth up at him and he groans like I gutted him before driving his cock deep inside me.

I'm sensitive and tender and every thrust he makes feels divine. Soon all that ferocity on his face – the expression that makes him seem so sinister – fades away, replaced by that boyish look. The one that has my heart swelling for him.

The others, lying around the bed, watch as he fucks me. I'm happy for it to be the two of us, for him to show them how he can do beautiful things not just destructive, but soon I'm pining for more hands, more touch. More mates.

"Stone," I mutter. "Azlan, Tristan, Spencer."

"Yes, sweetheart?"

"Don't just lie there!"

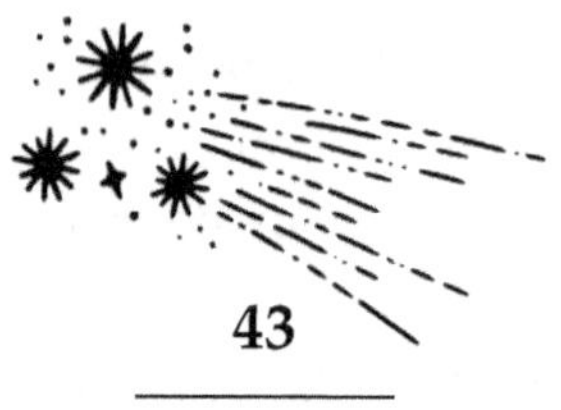

43

A zlan

SHE DOESN'T NEED to finish her words, we're all on her once again and then it's a mixture of all of us, kissing her, touching her, stroking her, pinching her, biting her, sucking her.

I feel her wet arousal on my fingertips and on my tongue; her skin grows damp and slippery with sweat. I taste the salt.

My hand covers someone else's as I squeeze her breast and at some point my tongue slides against someone else's in her mouth.

Our magic shatters and shimmers around us, lighting up the room as the darkness falls and anyone glancing up at Tristan's window will think we're holding our own damn fireworks display.

At some point, someone has the damn foresight to cast

another barrier spell and then I'm kissing her, deep and penetrating as one of her other mates moves between her thighs. Then she's on my lap riding my stiff cock as hands and mouths continue to smother her.

She's wet and sticky now, come on her cheek and on her thighs, her hair tangled, wound around someone's fist. I come, holding her tight against me, kissing her again as someone else claims her from behind.

It goes on like that for most of the night. Us hungry for her, she just as hungry for us, and then we're climbing under the covers, a tangle of bodies and limbs, tumbling into sleep, content, satisfied, floating in bliss regardless of what tomorrow may bring.

44

———

R^{hi}

I FALL ASLEEP COCOONED in the middle of five men – *my* five men – happier than I think I've ever been – okay, sore and tired too. But considering I may be facing death tomorrow, I'm asleep in minutes.

I dream.

I dream of the battle. I dream of the considerable power it's going to take to overcome Christopher Kennedy. All of it streams past my eyes; all of it in such detail there can be no mistaking.

When I wake, the dream doesn't fade like dreams so often do. It's vivid and clear in my mind.

I've seen the future. I've seen what's necessary. Now I just have to make it happen.

I know what I have to do.

Carefully, so as not to wake the five snoozing men curled

around me, I climb out of the bed, pulling on underwear and clothes as I do. Pip's already there waiting for me by the door, sitting calmly, even though I'm convinced he knows what has to happen as much as I do. I find it hard to look at him and I scoop him up into my arms and squeeze him against my chest. He doesn't wriggle or protest. He remains still in my arms, allowing me to carry him out into the hallway and down the stairs.

It's early, the dawn barely creeping across the horizon, but there are already people up and about, whispering to each other, dashing from place to place, or testing their magic, the sound of it echoing off the paths. They stare at me, star-struck, as I pass them by but no one talks to me, not until I'm walking right by the door of our old dorm. Then I hear Winnie call out.

"Rhi, Rhi, wait up!"

I halt, waiting for her to catch up with me, she slows as she sees Pip cradled in my arms and the tears sliding down my face.

"Rhi?" she says, a wariness entering her voice. "Rhi, what's going on here? Where are you going?"

"There's something I have to do – in the forest."

"Pip?"

I nod, wiping my face with the back of my right hand.

"Rhi, you're not.." She takes a decisive step towards me like she might intervene.

"Winnie! No, stars, no." I sniff. "It's just ... I have to ... it's time to say goodbye."

"Goodbye ..." she says, gaze falling to Pip and a sadness filling her eyes. "Is it–"

"Winnie, please don't ask me questions, please don't–"

"Rhi," she says, stepping forward and clutching my arms. "I would never. I trust you. I trust you with my life."

I manage to smile at her. "I trust you too, bestie. And I love you. I'm not sure if I ever told you that before."

"Ditto," she says, "Big time. You're like my girl crush and role model and best friend all rolled into one. Do you want me to come with you?"

"No, I think this is something I have to do alone."

She nods, then strokes Pip's ears, landing a big sloppy kiss on the crown of his head. "I know we had our differences at first," she tells Pip, "but I'm going to miss you. You're one awesome little dude."

I sniffle and next she hugs me, landing an equally sloppy kiss on my cheek.

"I'll be right here waiting for you when you're done, Rhi."

"Thank you," I say, and then I turn towards the forest and walk that way.

As I step underneath the first leafless boughs, I'm struck by how quiet it is and how still, as if every living thing is watching us come. I guess it should feel sinister or spooky or something – Tristan's told me what lurks in this forest, the same things that lurked in those waters surrounding the convent. But I don't feel afraid. A calmness eludes Pip and wraps me in a warm blanket and even though the trees grow closer and closer together, so much so that soon any light is lost behind us, I'm not in the slightest bit deterred.

I know what has to be done. I've known it right from the moment my aunt told me the truth about Pip. He's been here to protect me – as much from myself as others – here to watch over me, but now the time has come. If I want to meet my enemies head on, if I want to defeat them, I have to let him go, just like my mom let me go, even if it breaks my heart.

The temperature drops. The stillness is smothering. And

then I hear that strange calling, like I did out on the water. Except this time it's not me they're beckoning.

I crouch down and place Pip on the cold earth. His dark eyes assess me and for once he's quiet. Not attempting to crawl back into my arms or butt his snout against my legs. I crouch lower so our eyes are level.

"I'm going to miss you," I whisper, my words sounding loud in my ears regardless. "Miss you so so much."

He's been my companion, through thick and thin, during the long, lonely nights, at my lowest those first few days after my aunt had passed and it seemed like the world had ended. He never left me no matter how hard or tough it got, no matter how hungry he was, how frightened, and despite all my stupid mistakes, and crazy adventures.

"Thank you for being my friend."

I kiss him right on the end of his snout and he licks my face, his eyes seeming just as sad as mine must. Then I hug him one last time, feeling his small heart beating against me and inhaling that piggy scent everyone but me seems to hate, but is all Pip, all all Pip.

After a moment, he wriggles out of my arms and this is it. Time for him to go.

He gives me one last steely glare, snorting loudly at me, and then he's trotting off through the trees, not pausing, not looking back. I watch him go, until he's no longer there, until his figure evaporates, and instead of my pig, my aunt appears in his place. Not solid like she was in life, shimmering like the surface of a lake, and behind her my mom, just as beautiful, just as stunning as her photo, and then my grandmother, another woman I only knew from photos, standing between her two sisters. And then more women, more of my relatives, standing in the shadow of the trees, all watching me. Watching over me like they have done all this time.

They've always been there. As long as Pip was by my side, so were they.

The tears come more forcefully, dripping off my chin.

It was them. My aunt, my mom. They've been with me all this time. Protecting me, helping me, loving me.

"I don't want to let you go," I call out.

But they don't answer me. These spirits, these echoes of what once was flesh, they melt away into the trees until they are gone completely and I stand there alone.

Alone but stronger.

The hold on my magic – the cage containing it – has gone too.

45

M abel

I WATCH MY DAUGHTER, Bronwyn's daughter, our girl, walk away. Away from us. No need for us any longer. She is grown. A woman herself now. No longer the girl she once was. A strong woman, full of determination, courage and love. Like her mom, like her grandma, like me, like all of us. Born with this steel in our backbones.

And now it is time for her to end the story. To put an end to what was started long ago.

They will not use her for her powers. Not hunt her. Not abuse her. Perhaps they won't ever use a woman again. That will be her legacy. Her gift to the world. Our gift.

And while she strides out into the world, this girl who has always had both light and dark inside her, we will linger here as all spirits do, waiting one day for the reunion.

And while we wait, we are not gone. She will carry our love in her heart, she will feel it there, even though she will no longer have us by her side guiding her.

Our girl, our precious, precious girl.

Our Rhianna.

46

R^{hi}

I FIND Winnie where I left her, waiting for me by the entrance to the forest, an anxiety crisscrossing her face which lifts when she sees me. She runs forward and engulfs me in a hug.

"Oh Rhi. I'm sorry."

"It's okay, Winnie. I'm fine. I promise you, I'm fine. I understand now."

"But why–"

"Pip was a familiar – just like you said. He wasn't just any ordinary pig."

"You don't say." She manages a half smile, sniffing. "Then why let him go – why let those spirits go if they were here helping you?"

"To unleash the full potential of my powers. I think I will need all of it for what's coming."

"Still, it's hard to let people go," she says, a new sadness filling her eyes.

"Rosa?" I say, not sure I want to know.

Winnie shakes her head.

"What happened?"

"They took her – that's what one of her neighbors told us anyway. We've heard nothing since."

"I'm so sorry, Winnie," I say, wrapping her in my embrace. "She was such an incredibly awesome woman."

"She was," she says.

We stand there, holding each other, both consumed in grief, both thankful for each other.

Winnie's the first to pull away, steeling herself.

"They're serving breakfast in the Great Hall. Do you fancy grabbing some together for old-time's sake?"

She hooks her arm through mine.

I can feel my mates stirring through the bond. They may be wondering where I am but they can feel I'm near, feel I'm okay. I don't think there's any need to dash back to them. Not yet anyway.

"Sure," I tell Winnie, "why not? A breakfast of stale bagels and soggy porridge. I wouldn't miss it for the world."

Winnie pinches my arm. "You can't seriously think they're going to feed you that. Not when you're the 'chosen one'."

"Chosen one?" I say.

"That's what everyone is calling you now. You have to admit, it's an improvement on Pig Girl."

"Pig Girl was starting to grow on me actually."

"Fine, I'll keep using it then. I suspect someone might need to ensure your feet remain on the ground. Oh, and by the way, as soon as people notice the pig is missing, they're going to start rumors."

"I think we're going to have more important things to worry about," I say, spotting the sun hovering right above the horizon and the dragons circling above us in the sky.

"Oh, that won't matter. You should know by now that students at this school won't let a silly little thing like an apocalyptic battle and their impending doom stand in the way of a bit of gossip."

I laugh and let Winnie pull me along to breakfast.

We only make it half way to the Great Hall though when a loud alarm begins to blast, shaking the path beneath our feet. I gape at Winnie about to ask her if this is it, when my question is answered. Chaos breaks loose, people running everywhere.

"Winnie!" I say.

"Yeah, I know, Rhi. You need to find those five men. Go, go, go quickly."

I start to sprint, then skid to a halt and sprint straight back towards my friend, wrapping her in another hug.

"Stay safe, okay? Don't do anything stupid."

"Me? Do anything stupid? You can't be seriously lecturing me on the topic of stupid things, Rhianna 'chosen one' Blackwaters?!"

"Just promise me, Winnie. I've already lost one friend today."

"I'll be careful as long as you promise to be as well."

That's a very hard promise to make, but I cross my fingers behind her back and make the promise anyway, and then I really am sprinting away.

I meet three of my mates out on the path charging my way.

"Rhi, thank fuck," Spencer says, reaching me first. He pulls me into a hug as Renzo and Tristan catch up to us.

"Where are Stone and Azlan?" I ask, my words muffled by a very muscular chest.

"Gone to see who has sounded the alarm and where the attack is coming from. We're meeting them out in the meadows where I'm hoping," his eyes lift to the sky, "those dragons are going to be waiting for us."

"They will be," I tell him.

"Where's the little man?" Renzo asks when I step away from Spencer. "I thought he was with you."

"I ... I let him go."

"You let him go?" Spencer stares at me in disbelief. "But you love that pig and he really loves you!"

"I know but it had to be done."

Spencer and Tristan examine me with curiosity but Renzo nods his head with understanding.

"You had to let him go sooner or later, little rabbit. You did the right thing." He scratches at the healing wound on his neck. "Although I would have liked the opportunity to say goodbye to the little dude."

"He knows you cared about him," I say.

Renzo's eyes widen. "Did I?"

I squeeze his arm. "Yep, you did."

We hurry down to the meadow and I breathe a sigh of relief when I see all the dragons crouching in the long grass as if they've been waiting for us.

Gwenhwyfar rumbles and I walk up to her and lay my hand on her snout. It makes the men with me shuffle on their feet uncomfortably. I don't think even Renzo entirely trusts these dragons and my hand looks tiny against her vast size, like a mere pimple. If she wanted to swallow me whole right now, she could do it with one snap of her jaws.

Her eyes swivel over me and she's looking for Pip.

"He's gone," I tell her too. Did she know who he was?

What he was? She seemed to recognize him all those days ago back in the mountains. Had she known my mom? Did she understand?

The dragon rumbles and is that my imagination or does it sound mournful?

I pat her snout.

"No time to be sad," I say and I wonder where I'm finding this strength. I hear rustling in the grass behind me, my bond tugging, and then Azlan and Stone are here too.

"What did you find out?" Tristan asks them both.

"It's your father," his cousin answers him. "And it's as we suspected. He's brought an entire army."

"Just for me," I say with a smile.

"I'm guessing the Lord Protector believes more of the rumors about the Fourth Prophecy than he's letting on."

"And we're really just going to let them come?" I say, peering down the hill and out across the countryside. There's movement on the horizon. A lot of movement. "We're not going to take the fight to them?"

"That'll be what he expects us to do," Tristan says. "He's always accused me of being rash and reckless. If we head down there to meet them, we lose all our advantage."

"We stay and we wait," Spencer says.

"But we have dragons!"

"Something he knows. Something he'll have prepared for."

I turn back to address Gwenhwyfar.

"We have a job to do. They're coming." She stares at me hard and I know she understands. "But you're going to have to stay here and wait. We will come to you when we need you."

Then I walk back with the others through the academy campus. Students and teachers alike are stationed in strategic positions. Tristan and Spencer give them encouraging nods or a few words of advice as we pass, and then we're walking right around the academy mansion to wait at its front. The drive up to the academy is our weakest point and we have our strongest fighters here. Principal York, Coach Hank and several of the magicals who make up the resistance including Winnie and Trent.

With my five men beside me, I stride right to the front of the small crowd of people and stare straight down the hill. The movement on the horizon has morphed to a grayness that crawls over the countryside like rot. It moves at speed, slithering closer and closer and we can see the tanks and the trucks and the aura of magic around them.

I peer back towards the meadow where the dragons are waiting as ordered. I could climb on Gwenhwyfar's back right now and fly over those troops and that machinery and blast them all away with Gwenhwyfar's fire. But Tristan is insistent that that is what his dad wants us to do. To attack with a recklessness that will see us fall.

I chew my thumb. Winnie's always teased me about my lack of patience. It definitely isn't one of my virtues. But fate gave me these men for this reason. I have to trust in them and their plan.

Azlan removes my thumb from my mouth and grips my hand tightly in his.

"Are you nervous?" he asks.

"A little," I admit.

"You shouldn't be," he says with all that self-assured confidence I love about him. "You have us. We have each other. I felt it last night, how strong the bond between us is. I don't think even a dragon like Gwenhwyfar or a dark magical with an entire army could break that apart. It's more than just magic," he adds with a whisper, causing a shiver of electricity to spiral down my spine. I understand what he means.

Still, it's hard to stand back and watch them come, knowing the danger they bring to all the people I care most about. Especially as a gray cloud seems to spread out in front of the army, racing towards us.

"What the hell is that?" Spencer asks.

"Spider's rot," Tristan answers. "One of his favorite tricks. Brace yourselves! It can penetrate through the shields," he calls out to the others before it hits us a minute later.

It's like a hurricane. The sky darkens above us and the wind whips around us, attempting to knock us off our feet, dust battering our faces. We form our circle, battling to force the wind away up into the sky, although that darkness remains, looming over our heads.

When we look across the landscape again, we find Christopher Kennedy's troops already surrounding the base of the academy's mound, hundreds and hundreds of magicals, some of them soldiers and guards – the like I've seen before – others dressed in those robes with the badge – more skilled magicals like the ones we faced on the beach. Mingled with them is weaponry and machinery. But, though I search, I don't see the Lord Protector himself, although in the next moment I hear his voice, echoing across the campus.

"Students and teachers of Arrow Hart Academy," he says, his voice amplified and intimidating, "among you dwell traitors to our great republic, dangerous fugitives who pose an evil threat to your safety, to this nation's safety, to all our safeties. Hand them over at once and I will deal with them personally. There is no need to be afraid. You will be doing a great service to your country. Several more unsavory degenerates removed with your help." He pauses. "Unless the fugitives themselves would be gracious enough to hand themselves over."

I glance at the others. Azlan shakes his head stiffly and Renzo chuckles.

"As fucking if."

But I can't help glancing behind us at the others, at all the students out here waiting to face battle. Are they as sure? Is this the moment where they have a change of heart and swamp us?

I hold my breath, my heart thumping in my chest.

No one moves. No one even stirs.

Then York's voice rings out. Just as loud, just as determined.

"We shall do no such thing. We will not be complicit in your reign of terror."

"Reign of terror?" Kennedy scoffs. "The only terror you should fear is the chaos that girl will bring on all your heads. You think she is the light. You think she is some sort of savior. You do not know who she really is."

I think he's going to tell them, reveal who my dad is, who I am, the dark magic I have in my veins. He doesn't. I guess he's about as impatient as I am to get this over with, because in the next moment, hundreds of arrows of magic fire our way, glittering like fireworks in the sky.

Spencer is right. The academy is protected with old magic and the arrows shatter against the surface of those spells and wither to the ground. It doesn't deter Christopher Kennedy. More magic hurtles up towards the academy crackling against the old spells.

"How long will they hold?"

"Long enough," Tristan mutters. "Let them use up their magic breaking through. It will only weaken them."

I nod and look up, watching the sky as if I really am at a firework display.

The magic fired towards the academy becomes heavier, denser and more powerful and finally a crack appears in the old spells, a bolt of magic zooming through and hitting the ground behind us. The earth shakes and the grass singes.

"They're through," Azlan yells. "Be alert!"

I raise my hands. Above us great golden cracks appear in the sky, racing towards the ground, and then the old spells are crashing towards the ground in great chunks and we're forced to raise our hands and cover our heads. There are whoops of delight from the troops below and the magic comes streaming towards us. Between us, we deflect and dodge it, sending our own magic down the hill and causing holes in their ranks and soldiers to scatter. But we are outnumbered, vastly outnumbered. Kennedy knew how many people we had here at the academy and he's brought with him twice as many at least.

"This isn't working," I shout to the others.

"It is," Tristan yells back. "This is what we want, Rhi. To weaken them."

Although, as a bolt of magic hits the shoulder of the woman beside me and she staggers to the ground, I can't feel as confident.

Magic crashes against the mansion and behind us into the campus. Great holes appear in the only recently repaired roof, glass windows smash and brickwork tumbles to the ground. Behind me I hear a man grunt as he's hit and a woman scream.

This is too much. It isn't worth it. Why are we fighting like this when I have the dragons? I could break free, run for it and be on Gwenhwyfar's back in a matter of seconds.

"They're coming," Azlan calls. "Retreat. Pull back."

He's right. They're streaming up the hill, plowing right towards the mansion.

Is this still the plan? Is it working?

Stone pushes my shoulder, and then we're running back into the heart of the campus, joining the students there.

"Once they reach the mansion," Spencer calls out to all the gathered students, teachers and resistance members, "they'll be caged and we attack." People raise their arms, grit their teeth, bounce on their toes. "Rhi?" Spencer says.

And now it's time for dragons. I run that way, down the old familiar paths, around the gymnasium and right into the path of Summer fucking Clutton-Brock.

47

R hi

"I KNEW a scaredy cat like you would flee as soon as the fight got real," Summer says, blocking my path. A madness swirls in her eyes. "You've always been pathetic and–"

"Summer," I say, "I really don't have time for this right now. Could you go bother someone else?"

"No!" she says, stalking forward. She's not looking as groomed as usual, which I guess isn't so crazy, none of us are. But this girl could be trekking through hell itself and would still ensure a full face of makeup and a spotless mani-cure. This morning, however, her eyeliner is slightly wonky, her mascara smudged and I notice bruises on her wrists and one on her clavicle. "I'm not letting you go! I'm going to be the one who hands you to him. I'm going to be the one to win his favor."

"Why?" I say, unable to help myself. "Don't you already have it?"

"You've stolen everything from me, Pig Girl," she screams. "You're not stealing this too!"

"Really? What have I stolen from you? You're beautiful, talented, and I assume you must be a good friend when you want to be. Everyone loves you, Summer."

"Not anymore!" she cries. I'm not exactly surprised to hear that. If she has been acting as the Lord Protector's little spy, she's going to be partly responsible for a lot of people's hurt and they are going to hate her guts for it. "They all love *you* now. You've stolen them all from me. You – a smelly little pig girl, with no ass, wonky teeth and a serious lack of manners!"

All those insults would have hurt me a few months back, despite my best efforts, they would have pierced my armor anyway. Now I brush them off as if they are nothing more than cobwebs.

"Summer," I say, sighing. "It's not too late. Go fight alongside your friends. Show them you know you were wrong, show them you're sorry. You're gorgeous and talented. They won't be able to help but forgive you."

"No," she says, "no. You're not fooling me with your twisted logic. I know what you are." Her eyes narrow. "And when I hand you in, he's going to parade you in front of everyone and show them."

"And how exactly do you plan on doing that?" I say, hands on my hips. "You know what I can do. You want me to blast you into oblivion?"

"He's been teaching me magic," she says, her voice faltering slightly, "dark magic. I'm not afraid of you." She lifts her hands and adopts a fighting pose.

My dark magic hisses at the challenge. It hates this girl

even more than I do and in my mind's eye I can see just what that magic would like to do to her – engulf her and blast her into a thousand tiny pieces.

The idea excites me and the crimson magic soars through my veins, engulfing me, taking me over.

She thinks she can match me. She's deluded. I want to make her pay for her insolence and every little hurt towards me, too.

The crimson magic burns, hot and violent. It's so much stronger than it was.

I raise my hands. I am going to destroy her.

Behind me, I hear the first explosions of battle. And in that moment I remember what we're fighting for.

I look down at my hands and then back up at Summer. This is what she wants, some great fight between the two of us, to hand me in to the Lord Protector in some blaze of glory.

Yeah, that's not going to happen.

I battle that crimson magic back down into submission, groaning with the effort as I suppress it.

Then I take a leaf out of Renzo's book, clicking my fingers and watching as the lights go out, her eyes rolling back in their sockets. The head cheerleader crumples unconscious to the ground in a heap. I consider leaving her right there – I'm especially liking the way her tongue is hanging out the side of her mouth in an undignified manner – but there's a chance she could come round and start causing more trouble.

I haul her to the side of the path, propping her up into a seated position against a tree stump, and magic twine around her ankles and then her wrists, tying them behind her back.

"Nice chatting," I tell her. "Talk more later. Bye."

Then I continue on to the meadow, sprinting with all my might. I've already wasted precious time.

I find the dragons pacing, snorting and throwing their heads as if they're impatient to get up into the sky.

I beckon Gwenhwyfar my way, and scrabble up on her neck. If this goes to plan, the battle could be over in a couple of minutes. Kennedy's men will be like rats up a drainpipe, trapped, stuck in a bottleneck with nowhere to go, vulnerable to our counterattack, vulnerable to me and my fire power.

Excitement bubbles in my belly, that dark magic reinvigorated. I lean into it this time. Torching men alive is not what I want to do, but it's for the greater good. We're doing this to prevent further bloodshed and heartache.

I nudge Gwenhwyfar with my heel and she kicks off, her wings stretching wide, her school of dragons following her lead. She lifts me up into the sky, the other dragons trailing after her and we swoop over the campus and down to the front of the mansion – just where the trapped army of Christopher Kennedy's fighters should be.

Gwenhwyfar rumbles, her scales warming beneath me. She's ready to obliterate everything with her fire.

But then I realize, it's not that simple.

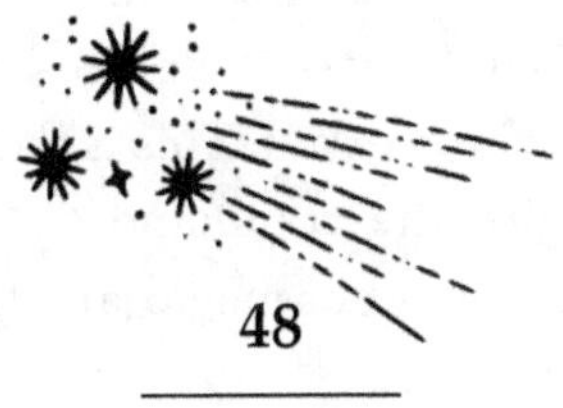

48

Spencer

As THE ACADEMY's protective spells crumble to the ground around us, Kennedy's troops come charging up the slope towards the mansion, just as we planned.

I keep my arms outstretched, signaling to the others to wait, to hold back, to be patient. It's hard when I can feel the thrum of magic all around me, that and anticipation too. It presses against my back and my shoulders and it takes every ounce of my strength and my determination to hold it back.

We can't strike, not yet. We have to wait. Wait until they're right where we want them.

"Ellie," I say.

Azlan's sister steps forward and places a bottle on the ground. Inside, a green mist swirls like angry storm clouds. She yanks off the stopper and with the help of the other resistance fighters casts a wind that sends the mist hurtling down the hill towards the incoming troops.

As the mist curls around them, they falter, coughing and waving their hands in front of their faces.

I smile to myself. It worked. This is our moment. But just as I'm about to give the command to strike, the mist is whisked away by some other magic, and the soldiers reform their ranks.

They surge forward, the first of their soldiers reaching the crown of the hill and sprinting forward, roaring as they do.

I let my vision scan over them, across their angry faces and their armored forms, wondering why the hell they're fighting for a mad man like Kennedy, wondering how they've fallen for his lies and his deceptions, wondering if they had a choice or not.

Then my gaze falters on one face, one face I recognize – that woman from the barracks, the one who showed me around the very first day. I read the fear in her eyes and the terror on her face.

And fuck, I'm not sure I can do this anymore.

The fighting is all I've ever been good at. All anyone has ever admired about me. And fuck, it sparked something inside me too, made me feel alive, unstoppable, like a hero.

What do I feel now? Nothing, nothing at all. I think of all the hits I took in that cell, all the punches and kicks, the stamps and the slaps.

I remember watching them beat Jacob until he lay unmoving. I remember them killing him, striking him down outside the prison.

I remember my brother, the scent of his blood still vivid out there in no-man's-land.

My arms fall by their sides. My knees buckle.

Everyone behind me storms forward.

For a brief moment in time, nothing changes. Both sides rush at each other, but the space between them remains.

Peace. Quiet.

I close my eyes.

The two sides collide. I hear the hiss and the roar, the explosion and the thump of magic.

"Spencer! Spencer! What the hell are you doing?" Someone shakes at my shoulder as I stay immobile on my knees.

I open my eyes.

Azlan.

"I can't," I mumble.

His eyes flicker around my face and he seems to understand, seems to know. I wonder if he's ever felt this way. If the killing, the maiming, ever got too much for him too. Whether he craves it like Barone does. Or whether he simply no longer feels it at all.

"Doesn't matter," he tells me, shaking me harder. "You have to. You have to for Rhianna."

Yes, for the girl!

The beast roars inside me and then he's taking the decision out of my hands, my body transforming into his.

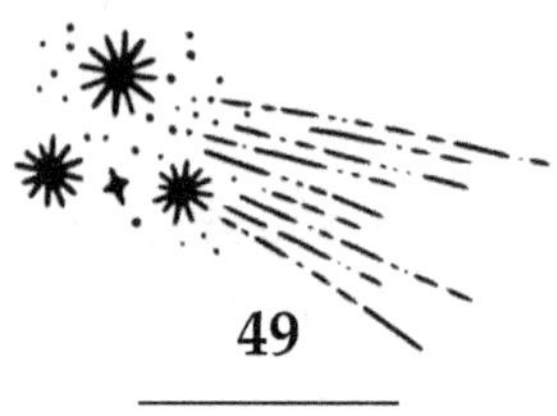

49

The Beast

I LAUNCH my still-transforming body into the throng of magicals.

The boy's plan is disintegrating. The students have failed to hold their ground. Instead of containing our enemy, they battle them hand to hand, magical bolts flying through the sky, exploding on the ground, crashing into bodies and into faces.

I ignore all the magic, ignore the way it singes my fur, stings at my skin. Ignore it and sink my fangs into the throat of an enemy, rip through the body of another, barrel another to the ground, cracking his skull.

The girl is not among us, instead she circles above us on one of the great reptiles, its wings wide and casting us into even darker shadows.

Her other mates are here though.

The enforcer fights with skill and a ruthless efficiency. His face wears a determined expression, his jaw set, his brow furrowed.

In contrast, the madman fights with a wild grin on his face, slashing at anyone around him with his knife, flicking his chaotic magic through the air, disappearing one moment and then reappearing another.

The learned man does not fight alone. He stands in the midst of the younger ones, calling out to them, directing and encouraging them, reminding them of spells as he casts his own and fights to keep the enemy at bay.

And then there's the boy's friend. The boy has always admired him for his strength and his skill and I see it all demonstrated now. His magic is nothing short of magnificent, elegant and beautiful in its power. It cuts through the enemy, scattering and dispersing them and no one and no thing can come close to him.

It is all for nothing though.

I see it clearly. There are too many of them. And as many as we cut down, more race up the hill to replace them. Around me the magicals fall.

First one, then another and another.

Those that remain weaken and tire.

Someone calls out for their mother. Another begs for release. Another weeps as blood seeps from their neck.

The older woman – the one that knew our secret – beckons her students forward. Calls on them to keep fighting. She stands among them wielding magic like lightning, the hair on her head dancing in the wind, her eyes a bright silver.

She is formidable.

And then she too is struck, a bolt of magic from nowhere. It hits her square on the chest. The lightning flickers on the ends of her fingers. Her gaze drops to the gaping hole in her chest. She opens her mouth to cry out, but she's already dead.

I look up to the sky again, to the dragon and the girl.

What will you do now, little mate?

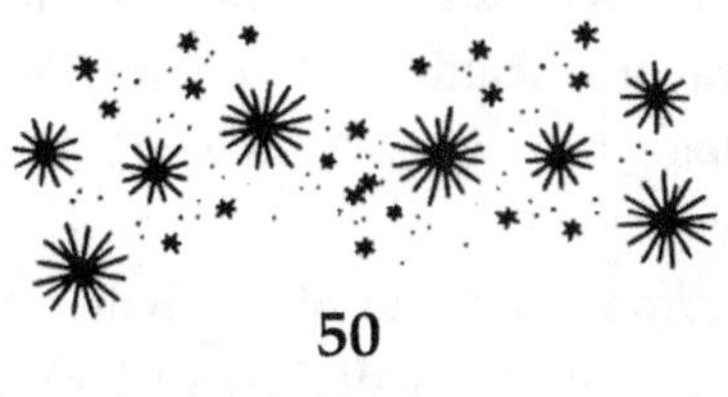

50

R^{hi}

WE'VE FAILED to kettle their fighters as we planned, and the students and teachers and others are fighting one on one with Christopher Kennedy's men, magic exploding above their heads and enemies mingled together with our friends.

Gwenhwyfar's fire is too indiscriminate. If I let her blast fire down below us, she'll take out just as many of us as she will the opposition. I can't risk it.

"Damn it!" I curse, kicking my heels and encouraging her back up into the sky.

We stay there right below Christopher Kennedy's gray clouds, circling, waiting for a chance to strike and I'm just debating giving up on this plan altogether, and flying down the mound to take out the rest of Christopher Kennedy's men when I hear a faint whistling in the air.

I look up but I'm already too late.

Large weapons tear through the sky in our direction, so quick, Gwenhwyfar barely has time to swoop out of the way, one of the great balls of steel narrowly missing her left wing. The other dragons scatter too, diving and dodging the onslaught. I lean flat on Gwenhwyfar's back, willing her back to the meadow.

I'm already too late. One of the balls of steel smashes straight into the body of one of the smaller dragons.

For a moment, it's like time stops. The two great objects collide in the sky and then hang there, joined together, the ball wedged deep in the dragon's side. The dragon wails and then it's spinning, round and round like a maple seed, crashing into the side of the hill.

It flattens several of Kennedy's men who were climbing the bank, and then it rolls, over and over again until it reaches the bottom, its enormous body flopping to a stop. It lies there unmoving and dead.

Gwenhwyfar throws back her head and lets out a mournful wail of her own and I feel her sorrow, raw and immense. She swoops down towards the dead dragon, skimming over its body and her scales heat again as she lets out a breath of fire, cremating the dragon's body in one mighty bellow. Then she swoops up into the sky, her scales boiling hot with anger now, an anger that vibrates through her body.

She sets her eyes on the men below, ignoring more cannonballs as they whizz around her. She's going to scorch the earth, obliterate everything and everyone.

Yes, this is what we need to do. We can take out the rest of Kennedy's troops – the ones waiting at the base of the hill. The reinforcements. Gwenhwyfar and I can weaken his army and give our fighters a chance.

The dragon rumbles in response to my encouragement

and her scales are so hot they burn against my flesh. I grip them anyway, steely determination running through me, that darker magic driving me onwards.

The dragon swoops down, her body casting a shadow over those below.

We are going to do this. She and me together. We are going to kill them.

This is what I saw in my dream. The world burning and we are going to burn it.

My skin sizzles hot like the dragon's. My magic roars in my ears. The anger and the rage spills from my fingers.

Those dark memories from my past come rushing back into my mind. All the times we were forced to run, all the times they beat my aunt, all the times they hurt her. All those times.

The crimson magic inside me takes hold, reacting to all my fear and fury, feeding off the dragon's rage. There's no Pip here anymore to contain it, to cage it, it's running free.

It's more powerful than the light magic. More hungry. More destructive.

Yes, I want to burn them all.

Yes, I want to destroy everything.

Yes, I want to make them pay.

Christopher Kennedy killed my mother. Now I am going to kill him.

Gwenhwyfar spits out her fire, roasting the magicals below us and I let out a torrent of my magic, dark and sinister, strangling and suffocating all those that escape the drag-on's flames.

My gaze, sharper, more vivid, tinged with blood, counts the bodies. One, two, three ... hundreds. Hundreds of them lie dead.

An energy courses through my body. It's eager for more. More death, more destruction.

I flick my gaze up to the academy and more dark memories flood my mind. Newer, fresher ones. Those people fighting up there, they aren't my friends. They despise me. They treated me like dirt. They abused and bullied and hurt me. Over and over again.

And now this is my chance. My chance to make them pay.

Gwenhwyfar loops up into the air, deftly missing the weapons that fly towards her. Her breast rumbles with fire and she swoops down again.

This time towards the academy.

I am going to burn it too.

I lift my hand.

Rhi.

It's a voice from far away. Faint. Muffled. Fighting to be heard.

Rhianna!

It's not one voice. It's five.

My mates. My men. I feel them through the bond. Something bright and good. Something I want to protect and cherish. Not something I want to destroy. Not something I want to harm.

I jolt. The anger melts away, as something warmer, something brighter rears up instead.

But the crimson magic has a stranglehold on me and it won't be so easily suppressed this time. It battles to regain its grip, fights to control me.

"No!" I yell as I struggle against it, struggle to hear those voices, to feel the bond. "No!" I scream and try to push it back down, down into the pit of my gut. I tug on Gwenhwy-

far's scales as she hurtles towards the mansion. "No, Gwenhwyfar, don't!"

She ignores me. Her own rage deafening her to my
pleas.

I press my hands to her scales and try to reach her with
my magic, my lighter magic that's battling to keep the
crimson away. The dark memories swirl in my head, trying
to drag me down into hate and revenge, but I focus on the
good. On my aunt. On Pip. On Azlan and Stone, Tristan and
Spencer, Renzo. I focus on them all and gradually the light
dominates inside me, submerging the dark, and I battle with
the dragon, yanking her upwards away from all those
people.

"No, Gwenhwyfar," I say, resting my face against her
burning-hot scales and stroking my palm down her neck. "I
know it hurts. I know it hurts so much. But this will bring
you no relief. No comfort. Trust me. Trust me."

Gradually as I whisper to her, her rage cools and with it
her scales, her heartbeat slowing and her body skimming
the current up here in the sky.

I'm so focused on consoling her, on calming the situation, I don't see the cannonball.

I don't see it until it's too late. I don't see it until it's
driving right at us. Gwenhwyfar jerks to the side, swerving
to miss it. The movement is so sudden, so violent, I'm jolted
from my seat and thrown loose into the sky.

And then I'm falling.

51

R^{hi}

I TUMBLE THROUGH THE SKY, spinning around and around like the green dragon earlier, the ground hurtling far too quickly towards me.

I'm going to die. Just like that dragon. If I hit the ground, I die.

I'm not ready to die. Not yet. Not like this. If I die, I'm dying in the arms of my fated mates. Not on the ground in some field far from everyone.

I scrabble with my magic, attempting to save myself.

But what can I do? I can't grow wings. I'm too low for a parachute. And no magical has ever been able to make themselves fly. The only thing I can do is to slow my descent and cushion the blow. Despite how dizzy I am, my emotions spinning along with my body, I find a way, focusing all my magic and all my attention.

The ground still comes, hard towards me, but slower now, a little slower, and when I hit, though it hurts – it hurts a fucking a lot – I'm still here, a pile of flesh and bones, still breathing, heart still pumping, brain still thinking. I'm not so sure about my body though. Is *it* still working? I wiggle a toe and then a finger and then I run through my body, each limb, each part of my torso, for signs of damage.

My arm doesn't feel right. It's bent behind me at a strange angle and when I move it, pain screeches through my entire body.

Fortunately, it's the only damage I can find and, hopefully, an injury I can heal myself. With my uninjured hand beneath me, I roll over, more hurt screaming through my body, and open my eyes.

Open my eyes and find Christopher Kennedy towering above me.

His face swims in and out of focus. I'm way more woozy than I realized. From the pain. From the fall. From everything.

But I'm stronger now. Stronger than him. With my fated mates by my side, I'm stronger than anyone. This is my chance. My chance to take him out. But the pain and the throb in my head are too much. I can't find the concentration I need to use my magic.

"Ahhh, I thought fate was meant to be on your side, Pig Girl. And yet it looks like she's landed you right in my lap. It seems that silly little prophecy everyone's gotten so worked up about is wrong. Or maybe it just never applied to you in the first place. Because it seems I am destined to rule, not you," he says, an unpleasant smile on his lips, his dark eyes glittering with amusement. He senses I'm weakened. Weakened and far from anyone who could or would help me. His eyes flicker over my form. "Do you surrender? Have you had *enough*?"

Enough?

That final word triggers something in my mind. Of a night long ago. A star-lit night in the meadow back home. A star-lit night when magic had buzzed in the air like fireflies and the man in black, his eyes dark with wonder, his cape bristling in the breeze, had towered over me too. A night when this story – my story – had begun.

I hadn't surrendered then. Hadn't given up. Even though I was winded and hungry, my magic much weaker than his. Even though I was an unregistered girl with no formal training, no real understanding of the world I was hiding from.

I hadn't given in.

I haven't come this far, endured all I have, to give in now.

No fucking way.

"Enough? No freaking way. I've only just gotten started," I hiss and then, just like I did all those months ago, just like I did in that meadow, just like I did with the man in black, I kick out Christopher Kennedy's legs from underneath him and watch as he sways on his feet and then crashes to the ground. I'm up on mine, despite the pain shooting from my useless arm, and then it's me towering over him, my good arm stretched out in front of me.

Magic sizzles on my fingertips, light and dark. Light and dark together.

"You killed my mom," I say calmly.

"I've killed many people, Pig Girl," he says calmly, like he doesn't believe I'll actually harm him. "Care to jog my memory?"

"Bronwyn."

"Ahhh, the seer. Yes, of course. The gift of fortune telling can be both a benefit and a nuisance. Beneficial while we could see how things between us and the West would go. A nuisance when she saw my rise to the top. I couldn't let her live then. Couldn't let her tell others of the plans, and the deals, the corruption, and all the general unpleasantness it would take to ensure I earned my place ruling this country."

"The chancellor said a dark magical killed her."

"It's what I told him," he smiles. "And it was only half a lie. Just like you, Pig Girl, I have both dark and light magic inside me. Surely, you've understood as much," he says, his eyes drifting up to that gray cloud that lingers over our heads. "Of course, I have been much better at hiding it than you have. Although, I have no need to hide it any longer."

I scoff. "We are not the same. You know nothing about me."

"Oh, I know more than you think. All those little insights my son divulged when he was pumped full of drugs. It was most illuminating."

"You tortured him," I say, stepping towards him. "I've felt the wounds inside him."

"I was teaching him," he snaps. "Making him the man he should be."

"I'm going to make sure you never hurt anyone ever again!" I say, my magic soaring through my body. This is it. My moment.

"What are you going to do? Kill me?" he sneers and then he fires his magic my way, right at me. It's what I expected. What I knew he'd do. And I am ready.

My magic soars through my body, more strong and more powerful than it's ever been. The dark and the light mixing together. It hits Christopher Kennedy's magic head on and then with all my might and my power, though it chills me to the bone, though it sickens me to the stomach, I pull his magic towards me, all of it, all he's firing at me and all he's holding back.

I drain his magic. I drain all his magic from his body, taking it inside me.

Immediately that darkness lifts. Sunshine breaks through the gray clouds, illuminating us both.

I fall to my knees. His magic is like a poison in my body; I retch, spitting bile onto the grass.

"What have you done?" I hear him screech. "What have you done you stupid girl? My magic! My magic! It's gone! Gone!"

"I drained it," I hear myself say, collapsing onto the floor, the grass soft against my cheek. "I guess you didn't know everything about me, after all. My father – the Black Prince – was a Nosferatu. Oh, and by the way, I've no interest in ruling anywhere."

"No!" he screams, and I feel his fists gripping my sweater, shaking my body. But I'm drifting away, drifting into the abyss.

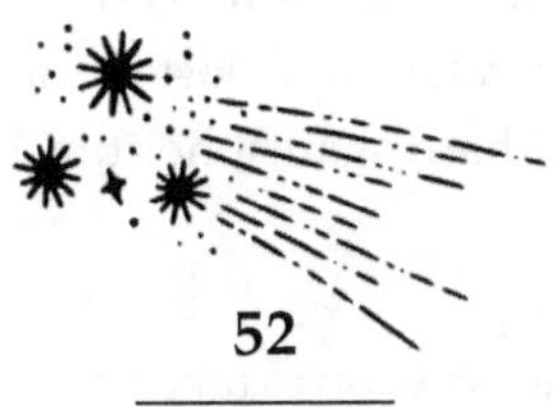

52

zlan

"RHIANNA!" I cry out as I watch my little mate tumble from the dragon high above us.

I lift my hand, driving my magic through the sky, attempting to catch her.

She's too far, too far away.

I start running, crashing through those that lie in wait in front of me, striking at them indiscriminately, running as hard as I can as if I hope I can catch her, as if I hope I can reach her in time.

But I know I can't. She's too far away. And I am too slow. Too damn slow.

I'm resigned to watch her fall, hopeless and useless.

I watch the woman I love, the person I care most about in all the world, the most precious thing in my life, fall through the sky and there is nothing I can do to save her, to help her.

I run anyway, run as she falls and when she hits the ground, I don't see it, her body lost in the distance, but I feel it. I feel the impact hard against her tiny body and I stumble to my knees.

"Rhianna!"

Please no, please don't take her from me. I'll do anything, anything at all. Take me, take me instead.

I stare at the grass beneath me. The world spins. Noise roars in my ears. Oxygen burns in my throat.

And then I feel her, feel her through the bond.

Not dead.

Alive.

I drag myself back up onto my feet and I'm running again.

She's hurt, I can feel it. Hurting and in pain. I need to get to her.

I don't know exactly where she landed but I follow the pull of my bond, so familiar, so comforting it's hard to remember a time when I begrudged it. And yet I did. Stupid fool.

It is – Rhianna is – the best thing that's happened to me in my life and I won't lose her now.

I sprint down the hill, skidding and stumbling in my haste, blasting anyone in my way, desperate to reach her and as I do, the gray clouds – that dark magic – my uncle conjured melt away and rays of light pierce the sky, catch the golden scales of the dragon in the sky high above.

I don't know what it means. And I don't care. All I care about is reaching her.

The bond pulls me out to the east, away from the

scorched land, the dead soldiers and those that remain, and out to the fields I drove her through on my bike.

I crash through hedgerows and out into a field of grass and then I spy them.

Rhianna and my uncle.

She's on her feet, and I sigh in relief, but only for a moment because then she's falling again, that bastard on top of her, shaking at her limp body.

I fire a bolt of magic at him. It takes him by surprise, hitting the side of his body and pummeling him backward onto the ground. He doesn't fire back, doesn't strike out and as I rush closer, I understand why. There's nothing there. His aura of magic – so bold and so strong – is gone.

I tumble down onto my knees beside Rhianna.

Her eyes are closed, her skin pale – too pale.

Not dead though. I can feel her through the bond. I'd know if she were dead, wouldn't I? I'd feel it.

"Rhi?" I choke. "Rhianna?"

She doesn't answer me and I lift her into my arms and cradle her against my chest. Her body flops lifelessly, but she's warm and I can feel her heart beating.

"Fuck, Rhi!" I choke.

I sense someone slump onto the ground next to me and then someone else.

"Azlan?" my cousin says, his voice trembling. "Please ... please tell me she's not–"

"Alive," I whisper, stroking her hair from her face and kissing her soft cheek. There's a gash on her forehead, blood trailing down her face and her arm hangs in a grotesque manner. I don't think those are the cause of this though. "Something's wrong. Something's not right. We need a doctor. We need a doctor right now!" I yank my gaze away from my mate and swing it around, hoping against hope by some miracle there'll be a doctor standing right there. There isn't, just Tristan and Spencer kneeling beside me. Neither of them look in good shape. Spencer – completely naked – hugs his side like his ribs are broken and Tristan's mouth is full of blood, his clothes caked in it too.

"Let me see her, Azlan," Tristan says. I hug my mate tighter to my body. I'm not letting her go. I'm never letting her go again. "I can heal her," he tells me.

I scoff. "There's something seriously wrong with her. We need a trained healer, a professional."

"I can do it, Azlan," Tristan says softly, reaching for her.

I shake my head.

"He's a skilled healer." Spencer pats his friend's shoulder. "Trust me, I should know. He's patched me up innumerable times. Let him see her, Azlan."

I peer into Moreau's eyes and then my cousin's. I can see how concerned they both are, how much they care about Rhianna as well.

Though it pains me, though I never want to let her go, I know I have to. I lay her down carefully, and immediately my cousin casts his hand over the wound on her head and her crooked arm, mending them both, before bending closer to inspect her.

I turn my head away and catch sight of the crumpled form of my uncle five paces away from us. I drag myself up onto my feet and stalk towards him.

He's still alive.

I reach down and fist the scruff of his robe, yanking him towards me.

"What the hell did you do?! What the hell did you do to her?!" I yell in his face.

He's barely conscious from my blast, his eyes spinning in and out of focus. I draw back my fist and punch him hard in the face, feeling the bone of his nose snap beneath my knuckles. Then I hit him again. "I said, what did you do to her, you piece of shit?" I punch him again and again, over and over, feeling skin split, blood spill, teeth crack. I don't care. I don't give a shit.

"Az! That's enough," Stone says from behind me.

I freeze. My friend lands his hand on my shoulder.

I blink, the bloodied, messy face of my uncle coming back into focus. I push him away from me.

"Rhianna," I say, spinning back around.

"She's going to be okay, man."

I collapse forward, into his arms, sobbing with fucking relief. He squeezes me tight.

"I thought we'd lost her," I whisper.

"I know," he says, gripping the back of my neck. "I know. But we didn't. Come on, they're taking her up to the mansion."

I sniff, taking a moment to pull myself back together, then I step away from my oldest friend and point down to the wrecked form of my uncle.

"What are we going to do with him?"

"Is he still alive?"

"Yes ... sort of."

"Damn," Phoenix mutters, "I should have left you for two more minutes."

I glance down at my bloodied knuckles. "She didn't kill him."

"No, seems she took his magic from him. Drained him."

I stare down at my uncle, mulling this over.

"We could dump him in a pond. There's one about a minute's walk away," Stone says.

"No, it's better he's alive. Better he faces justice. Better he ... *suffers*. Dying is too good for him."

"Really, man?" Phoenix says, sounding unconvinced.

I pick up the crumpled body of my uncle and sling him over my shoulder.

"Yeah," I say.

We start the long trudge back up to the mansion, Spencer and Tristan – carrying Rhi – just ahead of us, and I make sure to knock my uncle's head against several tree trunks as we go.

"It's really over," Phoenix says as we reach the mansion.

"Yes," I say, taking in the sight.

Because the fighting has stopped, it's stopped completely.

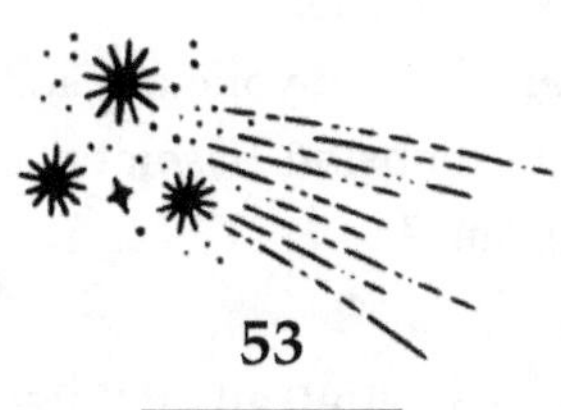

53

T ristan

"PIGLET?"

I rest my hand against her cheek. Her body's warm again now, her magic as strong and as vibrant as it ever was.

Her eyes flicker open and focus in on my face. It takes a moment and then her brow wrinkles.

"Is he dead?" she asks me.

"Not dead. Just, you know, impotent." I can't help smiling. Utterly powerless is probably a fate worse than death when it comes to my dad.

"Wh-what happened?" she asks, attempting to push up onto her elbow. I encourage her back down onto the mattress, stroking back her hair from her face.

"You drained his magic."

"Then why isn't he dead?"

I shrug. "It seems, Piglet, that you have the ability to

drain a magical's magic – drain it completely so it's not coming back – without killing them."

"I do?" she says in wonder.

"Yes, and he can't hurt anyone any longer. He's currently locked down in the mansion basement. Along with his," I make a face, "girlfriend."

"Summer?"

"Yep, someone tied her up and left her on a path."

Piglet's lips twitch and my suspicions are confirmed.

"Are they being guarded?" she says, with a sudden alarm I can understand. My dad is still cunning, even without his powers, although it'll be a lot harder for him to hurt someone now. He may have been magically strong, but he was never physically. I could knock him out with one swing of my fist. I suspect Summer could have a good go at it too.

"Yes, Coach Hank is seeing to it personally. Just until we can work out what to do with him. His army surrendered just as soon as the spider rot spell broke. Although, there will be work to determine who among them remain threats – true supporters – and those who were coerced."

"Why isn't Principal York guarding him?"

"Ahhh," I say, "York ... York didn't make it, Rhi."

"What?" she says, aghast. "You mean ..."

"She's dead."

This time she snaps upright. "Azlan, Stone, Spencer, Renzo?"

"Are all just fine," I lower my voice to a whisper, "although that crazy bastard seems to have gained three more scars on his face. It's like he deliberately walks into oncoming magic."

"Where are they?"

"Right here," several voices call out from behind me and

then her other mates step forward, assembling around her bed.

"Hey," I say, "don't crowd her."

Her eyes skip over all her mates and, seeing them all okay, relief momentarily flickers over her face. Then vanishes.

"Winnie?" Rhi asks, her voice shaking. "Trent? Ellie?"

"They're all just fine. Everyone else is fine. Thanks to you."

She settles back down into the cushions. "I don't feel so good. Did I pass out or ..." She rubs at her forehead.

"All of you out," I say, turning to the others. "She needs her space." They look at me skeptically, probably aware that's only half my motive for throwing them out of the room. "You heard the woman. Besides, someone ought to check what's going on out there."

Azlan ignores me and leans over to kiss Piglet on the cheek.

"I'm glad you're all right, sweetheart. You had me worried there for a moment." She smiles at him weakly. "Get some rest. We'll go check on our ... prisoners."

Stone kisses her next, whispering something I don't catch, and then Spencer wraps her in a big hug. Barone hovers by the end of the bed, fidgeting and looking nervous.

He scratches at his head and then follows the others out.

"Are you sure they're okay?" she whispers, watching them go.

"We're all fine. It's you we've been worried about."

"What happened?" she repeats.

"You drained his magic, took it inside you, and I guess he really is as sick and twisted as we suspected because it poisoned you, made you sick. Nothing I couldn't fix though," I say, unable to help the pride in my voice. I've always been a good healer. "May take a day until you're feeling yourself."

"And the dragons?" she asks, clearly still more concerned about everyone else.

"One got hit – one of the green ones."

"Yeah, I know," she says, "and the others?"

"As far as I know, they're okay. They took off once they saw us arrive and take you."

"How did you find me?"

"The bond."

She nods, her hands resting over her belly. "It's pretty handy."

I rest my hand on top of hers and electricity skates between us at the contact. For the first time, I can see a future. A proper future – one where we're happy and safe and I'm laying my hand over her rounded belly, full with our child. Or maybe Spencer's. Or Azlan's. I can taste that future now.

"Is it really over?" she asks, threading her fingers through mine.

"It is, Piglet. In fact, there's one hell of a party starting up out there."

"A party?" she asks, sitting up straight.

"You're too weak to go to a party. You need to rest and–"

"Tristan Kennedy," she says, "I missed out on a shed-load of parties on account of all the running and hiding from the authorities. I didn't even get to party at the last Founders' Night."

"Yeah, I'm sorry about that," I mumble.

"And so I'm not missing out on another party now, even if you have to carry me around all night."

"Gladly."

She grins at me. "Got anymore of those nice dresses, Tristan Kennedy?"

"Actually, I'm thinking of changing that."

"Changing what? Your name?"

"Yes, my name."

"What to?"

"I dunno, but I kinda thought Tristan Blackwaters had a neat ring to it."

She grins even wider. "You know it does. I like it."

"Sort of cool and mysterious."

"Unlike you, but, hey." She shrugs.

"Hey!" I say, diving in to tickle her. And then I'm kissing her and her arms wrap around my neck and I'm so happy I could fucking explode.

"I haven't forgotten about that party," she murmurs against my mouth.

"Just five more minutes ... resting," I say. I kiss her harder. "Actually, make that ten."

I BEG, steal and borrow and eventually I find a dress worthy of her. Okay, it's not like the one I gave her for the Victory Ball, not like the one she wore at the feast in the West, but damn it looks good on her. Something that scoops down low at her cleavage, nips in at the waist and then floats out in netting and shit.

She loves it. Winnie loves it. Spencer most definitely loves it. Unfortunately there's no hope of actually getting to enjoy the dress up close and personal.

Everyone wants a piece of her tonight. To hug her, to thank her, to talk with her.

The party has spilled out into the academy gardens. The

winter chill has thawed. There's the first hint of spring's warmth in the air tonight, the first buds of blossom on the trees and flowers beginning to poke their heads through the soil.

I follow her around like a love-sick puppy – we all do – just as goddamn entranced by her as we always are.

At some point I find myself next to Coach. He's nursing a bottle of beer and he has a bandage strapped to his forehead.

"Who's guarding my dad?" I ask him. The sooner they've sent him to the Northern Labor Camps – where I'm sure he'll be meeting many of the prisoners he sent up there himself – the better.

"Couple of lads from the dueling team are taking a shift," he says.

"Is that wise?" I ask.

"Why wouldn't it be?" Rhi asks, turning around to join in the conversation and leaning into me. I hook my arm around her waist and draw her close.

"I don't know who we can trust," I say, eyes scanning over all the people out here partying.

It's not like the old dueling parties. Everyone's still clothed – which may be partly because it's still not that warm out – or more likely because tonight isn't about getting wasted and hooking up. People seem genuinely elated, genuinely relieved. There's dancing and singing, quite a bit of hugging and crying and several kids just standing to one side talking to their family on their cell phones.

Yet, I know for some this is performative. They supported my dad. They snitched on their friends and on their teachers. Summer wasn't the only one. They believed weres like Spencer should be locked away for ever –

possibly exterminated. They were convinced some magicals were enemies of the republic and should be dealt with accordingly. It makes me sick to know they are among us.

"People make mistakes," Rhi says simply, looking up at me. She's referring to the way I treated her when she first arrived at the academy. As well as probably all the other stupid mistakes I've inevitably made along the way. "They get sucked into certain ways of thinking, carried along by the masses, or they just, you know, fuck up. We have to find a way to forgive them. We have to find a way to let them show us they are sorry. We have to let them gain our trust."

"I'm never forgiving my dad," I mutter.

Her eyes harden. "No, I don't think I will ever be able to forgive him either. Or my own dad."

"Maybe not right now," Coach says, watching us both, "but give it time. Hate is a heavy burden to carry around in your heart. You may find you don't want that weighing you down. You may find it in yourself to forgive."

I snort. "I doubt it."

Coach chuckles and takes a swig of his beer. "You always were a stubborn bastard, Tristan. It's why you never made it to captain."

"That and Spencer is a better duelist than me."

"You both have your talents. And you kids both did well today. And you too, Rhianna. I'm proud of you all." He pats me on the shoulder and I realize his praise has always meant more to me than my dad's ever did.

"Prouder than when they won the Crosslantic cup?" Rhi asks, teasing the old man.

"Much prouder," he says. He leans in a little. "Don't tell anyone I said this, but dueling's only a game."

"Erm," I raise an eyebrow, "that is not what you said

during countless training sessions. You said dueling was a matter of life and death, of honor and–"

"You shouldn't believe everything I tell you," he says. "What you did out there today, how you rallied the other students," he looks at Rhi, "the bravery and initiative you showed, that was really something. We should have had you on the dueling team."

Rhi grins. "I mean you still could, couldn't you? I haven't technically graduated the academy yet – I don't think I have enough points to."

"Piglet," I say, "you just earned yourself about a trillion points helping those magicals in the West, taking out my dad."

"You think so?"

I laugh. "Of course, you did!"

Some kid from our Practical Magic class taps Rhi on the shoulder and she steps away to talk with them.

"That girl's special. You need to look after her, treat her well," Coach says, peering at me over the top of his beer bottle as he drinks again.

"That's what I plan to do, Sir."

"Good, she's been through a lot. She deserves some happiness now."

I nod and he wanders off, Azlan and Stone coming to take his place.

"What's up?" Stone says, reading the unease on my face. "Did Hank not give you the ego massage you've come to expect?"

"It's not that," I say, distracted, gaze drifting back to Rhi. "She deserves happiness, right?"

"Yes," Stone answers. "Everyone does. Or peace and contentment at the very least."

"Do you think that's possible?" I look up to my cousin.

We were so close before. I hero-worshiped him. Then the distance grew between us and we hardly spoke. That distance has shrunk again now, and while I don't have that same blind-sided awe for him that I once did, I still respect him more than anyone else. After all, he stood up to our shitty family and went his own way – even if that way didn't prove to be much better. He did what he thought was right.

"Why not?" Azlan asks.

"My dad may be out of the picture. Things may be changing in the West. But you know how things go. You cut off the head of the snake only for another five to come slithering out of the woodwork. There's too many powerful people invested in the status quo for things to change."

"I disagree," Stone says, resting one hand on my shoulder and one on Azlan's. "Things can change, if you two force them to."

"Us?" I say.

"Who else?" He shakes us slightly. "You're the two heads of the famous and powerful Kennedy family. Now is your opportunity to change things." He peers Rhi's way. "And I have a feeling that Miss Blackwaters may have a few ideas about how things should change too. Fuck, I think Barone may even have one – just one mind you – good idea as well."

"Ellie too," I say. "She's always understood people better than we have."

"That's true," Azlan says, with half a smile. "Our dads always saw her empathy as a weakness but I think it's her strength."

"They got a lot of things wrong," I say, gazing Rhi's way again. "Time for us to put them right."

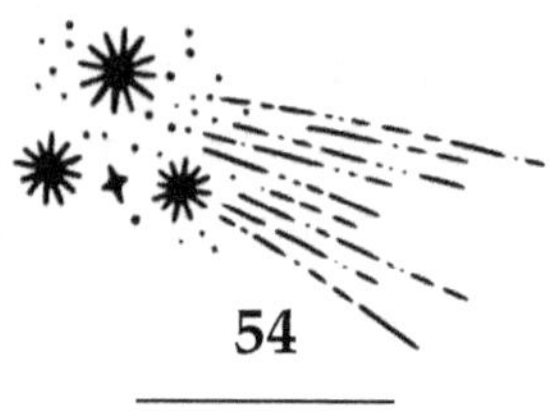

54

R enzo

I HATE PARTIES. Too much noise. Too many people. Too many people trying their best to stay out of my way.

Not this party. This party people actually go out of their fucking way to talk to me. Okay, they're still shaking in their boots when they do it, but they are trying.

Do I like it?

Hmm, not sure yet.

The only person I'm bothered with talking to is my little rabbit. Maybe one of the other dudes when I'm in the mood.

This is different. I guess things are going to be that way now.

The danger's over. People are talking about new beginnings and change. I don't know about any of that crap, but what I do know is she may no longer want me around. Little rabbit can be ruthless. Look what happened with the pig.

They're talking about her like she's some kind of actual angel, descended from the heavens to save them all. And an angel don't need no devil hanging about. Kind of spoils the image.

I find a quiet spot on a wall and jump up with a bottle of beer in my hand, making it clear from the fuck-off expression on my face that I'm done with talking for now. I yank the bottle cap off with my teeth and spit it into the flowerbed.

"Hey!" little rabbit says, appearing out of thin air. She reaches out her hand and the bottle cap flies up into her palm. "Do you know how many hours of work I spent making this garden look as good as it does? No littering."

I swing my gaze around. She may be losing that battle. There are discarded bottles and plastic cups strewn everywhere.

She beckons for me to scoot along and sits down on the wall next to me. I offer her up the bottle and she shakes her head.

"You know I'm not so good with my drink."

I'm gathering this is the 'serious' talk then. Shit. I've had enough of those in my lifetime to know when they're coming even if I can't read people.

Sorry, you're too much to handle.

Sorry, we're kicking you out.

Sorry, but I'm placing a restraining order against you.

It gets old. It's one of the reasons I stopped talking to people. Killing them was a hell of a lot easier.

Both my thighs jiggle and I'm sweating.

She's going to ask me to leave and I can't deny this woman anything. Nah, I can't even deny that. If she asks, I'll leave.

It sucks. Life sucks. Just when you think it's going right –

it slaps you hard around the face and kicks you in the balls. Sometimes it even digs a knife right between your ribs.

"You want me to go," I say. I keep my eyes trained straight ahead. It makes that thing in my chest hurt too much – and not in the good way – to look at her. I'll leave. I'll go. Fuck knows where. Fuck knows what I'll do next.

"Go where?" she says.

"Usually it's more than 100 yards away."

"Why would I want you to be 100 yards away from me?"

I sigh. "I know who I am, little rabbit. You know it too. I'm not like them." I jerk my chin out towards all the fucking normal people. "I don't fit in. You won't want me around."

"Do you usually care what I want?" she mutters.

"I didn't use to care. I care now. I think you made my heart start working."

Beside me she shakes her head. "You think you can say things like that to me and I'd actually be able to send you away?"

"People send me away all the time. They find me ... difficult."

"Because you try and kill them."

"I'm trying my best not to do that. I know you don't like it." I turn my gaze back to her, unable to resist it anymore. She's so ... fascinating. "You didn't kill your dad. You didn't kill Christopher Kennedy. Even though you had the chance."

"If we kill, they kill, then we kill, on and on it goes until there's no one left. It's time to end the cycle of violence. It's too ... exhausting."

"Violence is all I've ever known, little rabbit," I say softly. It's my earliest memory. The belt. The buckle. Because I couldn't sit still.

"But now you know something softer," she whispers, stroking her hand down my cheek, "and you like it."

"I like it," I say, covering her hand and pressing it firmly against my face. "I like it a lot."

"Better than the violence?"

"If you were touching me like this every day, I'd have no need to kill," I admit.

"Then you're staying right with me."

"Even though I'm crazy?" I say, my eyes meeting hers.

"You're not crazy, Renzo. You're ..."

"Different? Special? Yeah, they mean the same thing."

"You're perfect just the way you are. And I love you."

A warmth spreads from the very center of my heart right through my body, along my limbs to the ends of my fingers and the tips of my toes and my bond hums with something I think might be happiness. It feels fucking amazing.

"Shit, you do?"

No one ever said that before. Not even my mom.

No one.

"Yes."

"I love you too, little rabbit."

"I know," she says.

"How? I never told you before."

"Actions speak louder than words."

"Yeah, they do," I say. "It's why I'm going to show you every damn day how much I love you. Gonna start every day by burying my mouth between your legs, licking out your pussy and making you come all over my face."

"Oh, jeez," she says, and I think about dropping down to my knees and doing that right now. Sure there are people about, but I reckon I could hide under the skirt of her dress.

I don't get the chance to enact that idea though. We're

interrupted by the others – her other fated mates, the smart girl with the braids and the enforcer's sister.

"Everyone's going down to the meadow to watch the sunrise," the smart girl says. "Wanna come?"

"No," I say, clinging on to the idea of the pussy eating. "I'm about to make her come."

"Yes!" little rabbit says, giving me one of those looks she does when she wants me to be nice, and jumping down from the wall.

She hooks one arm through the smart girl's and one through the sister's and they walk, heads bent together as they talk so quickly it makes my head spin.

"Nice try, Barone," the were says, slapping me on the back. "But don't worry, there'll be plenty of time for that."

I walk with the others, slam bang in the middle of them, right behind little rabbit. I guess he's right. I belong here now. She says she loves me. She says she wants to keep me. For the first time in my life, I'm part of a family. Which means I've got the rest of my life to be eating her pussy. Heck, I wonder if I'll make it to 50.

There's a crowd already gathered in the meadow, people exploding their magic over their heads creating colors of all sorts in the dark sky. In the distance, I can make out the glow that must be Los Magicos and behind the tall trees are the sleeping forms of dragons.

"Wanna show them how it's done?" Tristan says.

"Yeah, let's show them," Rhi answers.

She holds out her hands. Azlan takes one. Tristan the other. Spencer takes Tristan's hand and Phoenix Azlan's. The circle needs closing. I step forward and take their free hands. There's no flinching, no mumbles of annoyance from Phoenix. We link hands and let our magic flow freely between us, round and round the circle.

"You know your magic would be stronger if you formed a star and not a circle," Winnie calls out.

But we're all too engrossed in this moment, in this feeling of connection. It's the fucking bomb.

I laugh, my cheeks tugging my mouth upwards and then together we shoot our magic upwards, letting it cartwheel and dance high up into the stars, exploding into a million colors.

Everyone around us stops to watch, and the meadow falls quiet as we paint the sky with magic. All of us bringing a piece of ourselves to the picture, knowing it wouldn't be complete without us all.

"The sun," someone calls out.

And we let our magic fall away and watch the sun as it rushes over the horizon, rays of light darting across the sky, the dark melting into light.

"Dawn," I say quietly.

"A new day," Phoenix says, laying his hand on my shoulder. "A new beginning, my friend."

EPILOGUE ONE

S tone

Six months later

We open the door and are greeted by a billow of smoke and the stench of burning.

"Shit!" Azlan says, waving his hand in front of his face. "Is someone trying to burn down my house?"

Behind us Rhi coughs, then whips the smoke away with a twist of her fingers, and wiggles past us all.

"Renzo said something about cooking."

"Jeez," Tristan says, combing his fingers through his hair and yawning. "I was hoping for takeout. Today's round of negotiations have done me in."

"And there's never enough food," Spencer whines.

"Seven hours of peace talks and only a measly sandwich for lunch."

"There was plenty of food," Rhi says, pulling off her boots. "You just have big appetites."

The four of us grin at her, all thinking about what we definitely do have big appetites for.

She rolls her eyes at us, and trots down the hallway, calling as she does: "We're home!"

Immediately, Renzo comes crashing out of the kitchen, his hands encased in oven mitts, a striped apron tied around his waist and what looks like flour in his hair.

I do a double-take. It's been six months and I'm still getting used to the assassin looking so domestic. He has a talent and enjoyment for potion-brewing – in fact, along with Rhi, it seems to have replaced his compulsion for killing. Unfortunately for us, he seems to think if he's good at potions, he should be good at cooking. That hasn't proven to be the case, but Rhi's forcing us to eat all his concoctions with a smile on our faces regardless. Even if the last one tasted remarkably like horseshit.

"Hey, little rabbit, I baked cookies. And there's lasagna in the oven."

She smiles at him and goes to wrap him in a kiss.

I shake my head and pinch my thigh, hard. I have quite a selection of bruises from that action, because it's still pretty unbelievable how everything has turned out and most days I wonder if I'm dreaming.

Six months ago the republic was under Christopher Kennedy's reign of terror. Six months ago we were on the run because he wanted us dead. Six months ago we narrowly escaped becoming the permanent Sources for a coven of powerful dark vampires.

Now, we're living peacefully – well most of the time – at

Azlan's house. It's probably only temporary. The house isn't big enough for five men our size but Tristan isn't keen on claiming his father's house. In fact, he'd like to knock it down.

Maybe we'll move out to the countryside. Set up a farm with a bunch of pigs and chickens. Maybe we'll end up living in the West. They need help out there to re-establish the workings of the city and the wider country now the ones running it are gone.

But for now, we're needed here for these talks. Things are changing. We're no longer at war. The threat from the West has gone. The troops stationed at the border have been disbanded and sent home.

Things are changing.

Of course, some people don't want things to change. There was talk of a new chancellor. A lot of people assumed it would be Rhi – the living embodiment of Queen Æðelflæd, once again taking her crown.

But that's not Rhi, and she's argued adamantly for a fairer set-up, even as other candidates were put forward. We're pushing for a council – one where everyone is repre-sented – weres, magicals, non-magicals alike. Not just the old, rich families.

I tug off my own boots and go to wait patiently while Renzo nuzzles Rhi's throat.

"I missed you, little rabbit," he mutters. "These talks are going on forever."

"Tell me about it," Spencer says.

"I think we made progress today, though." Rhi extracts herself from Renzo's grasp, and taking his hand, leads him into the kitchen. All of us follow, flopping down into chairs around the kitchen table. It's a squeeze to say the least, my elbows knocking against Tristan's on one side and Azlan's on the other.

In front of us lies a plate of objects that look like they've been cremated.

"Are those the cookies?" Tristan asks warily. I guess you never know with Renzo. There's a good chance he may have been torturing mice today as well as cooking.

"Yep, double chocolate chip," he says, proudly. "I'll make us all coffee."

Azlan jerks upright onto his feet. "I'll make it." The last round of coffee Renzo made had us all buzzing for two days straight.

Renzo takes Azlan's vacated seat and pats his thigh. Obediently – because it's only me she likes playing the brat for – Rhi settles on his lap and bravely takes the burned-crisp of a cookie. She takes a big bite at it with a grin.

"Delicious," she says, then glares at us all. We all take one too, nibbling at the edges and murmuring nondescript compliments.

Renzo's gaze spins round us all and you can see the pride dancing in his mismatched eyes. The dude's still as mad as a box of frogs, but he's definitely growing on me. I may even go as far as saying I like his company.

"So what was the breakthrough?" he asks as Azlan places cups of piping hot coffee in front of each of us.

"Did you add sugar?" Rhi asks, peering up at him.

"You know it'll rot your teeth?" he says.

"Yep."

"Two spoons of sugar and cream," he says, handing her a cup.

"You have him well trained," I say, winking at her.

"She has us all well trained." Spencer grins.

"Anyway," Rhi says, drawing her attention back to Renzo and his question. "The representatives from the West were there again today. There was real talk about uniting the two countries."

"You think that's a good idea?" Renzo asks.

"I think so," she says. "It's not those other people's fault what my dad and his cronies were doing. They need our help and I think there are things we can learn from them too."

Rhi swallows down the last of her cookie with a large gulp of coffee and peers towards the back window.

"Have you seen the dragons today?" she asks Renzo.

"Not today, little rabbit."

"That's a week," Azlan says.

Her gaze falls back to her coffee cup. "They've never been away so long. Maybe they're not coming back this time."

"I think they'll be back, Rhi. You know what Mrs. Holly-hill thinks – there's a bond between you."

"She also thinks Gwenhwyfar was stolen from her home. Maybe they've flown back there."

For all her talk of setting the dragons free, of giving them their freedom to fly back to wherever they come from, I know she's going to miss them. She may have five fated mates now – five fated mates who absolutely adore her – but she misses having a pet. It's been six months and she's still grieving Pip.

Which reminds me.

I glance at Renzo and try to say as casually as I can: "Did that ... erm ... parcel arrive today?"

It's no use though. Rhi is too quick. You can't get anything past her.

"What parcel?" she says, gaze shooting up, eyes alert.

"Just a delivery."

"What delivery?" Her eyes narrow.

"I'll go get it," Renzo says, lifting Rhi straight from his lap and onto Tristan's.

"Am I going to like this?" Rhi asks.

"I think so, Miss Blackwaters," I tell her.

"There's no more room for books," Azlan tells me.

"It's not a book."

"Are you sure, Professor? You really do like books!" I can't deny that I may have brought one or two (make that several scores) of books with me when we moved in. I didn't like leaving them behind.

"Know what else I like, Miss Blackwaters?" I say, darkly, leaning towards her.

Seven hours was a long time to be talking, hands to myself, my fated mate all the way on the opposite side of the table from me.

However, I don't get a chance to show her just what I like because Renzo returns with the parcel. The box jiggles slightly in his grasp and there are scuffing sounds from inside. He places it on the kitchen table and Rhi looks at us all with suspicion, reaching forward to undo the big bow and draw back the flaps. She leans forward to peer inside. Then shrieks so loudly we all jump a mile off our chairs.

"A kitten?!" She dips her hands inside and pulls out a wriggling black ball of fluff with a pair of big round eyes. "Oh my goodness, he's adorable."

"She," I correct.

"We didn't talk about this," Azlan says.

I shrug.

"I don't like cats," Spencer says, leaning away from the thing.

"What?" Rhi says, thrusting the fluff ball in his face. "How could you not like an adorable little thing like this?"

Spencer grimaces and the kitten swipes at his nose.

"Feisty," Tristan observes.

"You'll get used to it," I tell the others.

Rhi hugs the kitten tightly to her chest and kisses its little head. "I'm going to call her Coco."

"Is it litter trained?" Azlan asks.

"Probably," I say.

Rhi jumps to her feet. "I have to go call Winnie. And Ellie. They are going to want to come round for kitty snuggles."

I catch her around the waist.

"Invite them round tomorrow," I tell her.

"But–"

"Tomorrow," Tristan confirms. "We want some time alone with you, Piglet."

She nods and then scurries away to find her phone.

"Are these talks really going well?" Renzo says, scratching at his neck. "Little rabbit likes to look at the world through rose-tinted glasses and all that shit. There are plenty of fuckers who won't want to hand over the power they have."

"Several of those fuckers are locked up." I say. "And you know Rhi. She can be pretty damn persuasive."

"Pretty damn insistent," Tristan says. "It was only her pleas to the special tribunal that prevented Summer from being sent to the Northern Labor Camp alongside my dad and all the rest of his supporters."

"I still think she should have been sent there too," Spencer mutters. "That girl will always be trouble."

"She can't cause a lot of trouble under permanent house-arrest," I point out. "And without her powers."

Rhi's special gift has been pretty useful. Removing the powers of those that have abused them. It's seemed a particularly fitting punishment.

Tristan looks like he might argue once again that Summer will always be a danger, with or without her powers, when Rhi returns, the kitten now curled up in her arms and snoring peacefully.

"She's asleep," she whispers.

"Yeah, she spent most of the day doing that," Renzo says, peering down with curiosity at the cat.

"I know she's not Pip. Or a dragon ..." I say.

"She's ..." she hesitates, then giggles, "purrfect."

"When you finally graduate from the academy, do not pursue a career in comedy, Miss Blackwaters. Stick to riding dragons and fighting bad guys."

"You think they'll reopen Arrow Hart?" Spencer asks.

"I'm going to ensure they do. Learning isn't only about becoming a good soldier. We need to make sure the next generation of magicals is well educated, and proficient at spell casting and–"

"Okay, okay." Spencer blows out his cheeks. "I forget you're a teacher sometimes."

"Thank you, Phoenix," Rhi says, stroking the kitten's tiny ears. "She's the cutest thing I've ever seen."

"Erm," Tristan says, raising his eyebrow at her.

"Meh," Rhi teases. "You're the second cutest."

"Are you doing favorites now?" Spencer leans back in his chair and crosses his arms over his chest. "Because I think I'm pretty darn cute."

"You're 6 ft 4 and built like a fridge." Tristan punches his friend on the arm.

"He's still cute," Rhi points out. "You all are. It's one of the many reasons I love you all."

I look at Renzo, scars and tats zig zagging his face and his neck. Then I look at Azlan, dark eyes, square jaw, neck wider than most men's thighs. Not sure cute is the adjective I'd use.

"You know this makes us an official family now," I tell them all.

"It does?" Rhi says.

"Yep. We have a pet. It's a done deal. There's no getting rid of us now. You're stuck with us for life, Miss Blackwaters."

She smiles. Her honey eyes – the ones I've always found so beautiful, so darn irresistible – shine brightly. She's not the girl she once was – scared, alone, fighting for survival, unable to trust anyone. Sure, she's still the same stubborn, persistent and occasionally chaotic brat she's always been, but there's a calmness about her now, a contentment. It radiates from her.

I think we did that. All of us.

I think she did it too.

I bet there are a lot of other people out there too, feeling happier, safer because of her.

"Stuck with all of you?" she says. "I wouldn't want it any other way."

EPILOGUE TWO

R^{hi}

EIGHT YEARS later

"So, remember, class, I want three pages on the fundamentals of broom flying on my desk by next lesson."

As predicted, the class groans.

"Can't we just move on to dragons? We've been stuck doing stupid broom stuff for ever," Stu – the academy's newest dueling hotshot – mutters from the back of my classroom.

"Show me you can master broom flying, and then we'll move on to the dragons." I cross my hands over my front, which is becoming increasingly difficult to do given the giant size of my belly. The baby – who I swear is going to be a dueling star themselves – automatically kicks against my arm. "My dragons are precious and I don't want inexperienced riders hurting them."

I fail to mention I jumped on to the back of a dragon myself with absolutely no training or guidance at all. There are some things the students don't need to know.

"But broom flying is just so," Stu pulls a face, "wussy."

"Coach Spencer says being able to fly a broomstick saved his life," Mae says, glaring at Stu. She's one of the students from the West – more and more coming to the academy each year. When she arrived she was pretty shy, but she's growing in confidence with a little bit of encouragement.

I smile to myself. Spencer on that broom all those years ago could hardly be described as flying. My mate hasn't been back on one since. He likes to call them death-sticks.

"Mae is right," I say, smiling at my student. "Don't be quick to dismiss certain forms of magic. All of it may prove useful at some point in your life."

Stu glares back at Mae and I'm pretty certain they have the hots for each other. Even if they'd never admit it. Love and hate. In my experience, there's a very thin line between the two.

Above me the bell rings out and the students begin to pack up their belongings.

"Be warned, I will know if you've used an auto-writing spell!" I call out as they head for the door. "Trust me, I know all the tricks."

"Do you now, Professor Blackwaters?" a masculine voice rumbles from the doorway as the last student squeezes out of my classroom. It's the end of the day, the end of the week, they're keen to get away – especially as this weekend is the annual Founders' Night celebration.

I peer up from the books I'm collecting and smile over at Stone.

"Well, obviously not as many as an old-crusty professor like you but ..."

He curls his lip down and gives me the puppy dog eyes, stalking over towards me with his hand on his heart.

"I'm hurt. Am I getting too old for you? The age difference isn't that big."

When he reaches me, he rests his palms on my belly, causing the baby to wriggle again and I reach up to stroke my fingers through his beard. There's more white in it than there used to be, more white in the hair around his ears too, plus crinkles around his eyes. It makes him, somehow, more handsome than he ever was.

My tummy flutters and this time it isn't the baby.

"Not too old," I tell him. "Just right."

I fling my magic against the open door, slamming it shut and kiss him. An act that's also becoming more difficult with this enormous baby. Not surprising given the size of its dads.

"Come on," he says, picking up my bag and offering me the crook of his elbow. "I'll walk you home."

It's become our little routine. Ever since I started working at the academy five years ago, he's come to collect me from the classroom at the end of lessons. There hasn't been a day he has missed.

The paths are bustling with students this evening, all buzzing with excitement, and we catch snatches of conversations about costumes and decorations. The themes and creations seem to get wilder by the year.

I lean into Stone. "Let's cast that protective bubble again this year. I want to spend the weekend sitting peacefully on the couch with my feet up."

"No plans to join the festivities then, Professor Blackwaters?"

"Have you seen the size of my ankles?"

"Renzo could probably brew you a potion for that."

"Maybe one to get this baby moving outwards as well." I'm already five days past my due date and am very over being pregnant.

Stone shakes his head. "We've been over that. There's no potion for inducing birth."

"Of course not," I say grumpily.

"You know what else there isn't a spell for?"

"No."

"Finding out who is cheating on their homework."

"I know," I say, shaking my head. "But Winnie likes us to pretend there is. She says it keeps the students honest."

"You know, I'm surprised Principal Wence hasn't found a way to detect cheating. If anyone could, it would be her."

"Nope, you're still our best way of uncovering cheats, Professor Stone."

He groans. His dislike for wandering into adolescent minds and the gruesome things he finds there has only increased the older he's become.

We reach the gymnasium, and I rest on a tree stump. I'm pretty sure it's the tree stump that I tied Summer Clutton-Brock up against. Which makes it one of my favorites. I haven't seen her in years but eventually our paths will cross. I hear she married some older dude and had a bunch of kids. At some point, they'll make it to the academy but I have a few more years of peace before that happens at least.

Stone tells me about his day and after a few minutes, Spencer emerges from the gymnasium, dressed in his usual tracksuit, his whistle hanging around his neck. Hank gave it to him when he retired and Spencer took the job. It's rarely left his neck since.

"Hey, beautiful," he says, leaning down to kiss me, and then the bump. The bump responds with another strong kick. Spencer chuckles. "This baby has to be Renzo's. It's so damn violent."

"Not violent," I say, rubbing my belly. "Active. Which means it could just as well be yours."

"Doesn't matter whose it is," Stone says. "Baby Blackwaters belongs to us all."

Spencer nods in agreement and then together my two mates haul me back up onto my feet.

"I'm so tired," I moan when I'm vertical again.

"Because you should be home resting, not teaching," Spencer says.

"But I love teaching."

Stone smiles at me, kissing the crown of my head. "I know you do, sweetheart."

We continue our walk – although I'm definitely waddling, not walking – towards the meadow, the number of students thinning now until there are none at all. On the edge of the meadow we stop and I catch my breath. Not because I'm that incapable of movement or because the baby is definitely restricting the capacity of my lungs, but because the sight of our home still manages to whip my breath right away.

Is it some magnificent palace like the Black Prince's? No. Is it some grand mansion like Christopher Kennedy's? No. Is it some snazzy pad the like of which Summer Clutton-Brock is probably living in? No.

But it's ours. All ours.

Winnie – the youngest principal to be given the position once Mrs. Hollyhill passed – gave us permission to knock down Stone's old cabin and build something big enough for all of us and our growing family.

And it's perfect. Just perfect.

Feeling my presence through the bond, Renzo steps out onto the porch, lifting his hand to shield his eyes from the setting sun and gazing out at us. He's followed quickly by our daughter Mabel who comes toddling out in the company of Coco the cat, Ryan the rooster and Penny the pig.

We may live on academy grounds and not a farm, but Renzo's been slowly cultivating the meadow, nonetheless, even teaching the odd student or two about growing vegetables and rearing chickens and pigs.

"Mama!" Mabel cries out, lifting her hands in my direction, brightly colored magic zig zagging over the grass.

I pick up my pace and meet her attempting to descend the porch steps which is tough when your legs are so short.

I pick her up into my arms and plant a sloppy kiss on each of her cheeks and then, stroking her dark curly hair from her forehead, plant a kiss there too.

"Yuck, Mama," she complains, furrowing her brow over her dark eyes in an expression stolen entirely from her dad.

"Did you miss me?" I ask.

"No," she says as I place her back on the porch. "Papa and me been playing chase the chick chicks."

I stare at Renzo. He shrugs. "She wanted to."

"And you couldn't say no? Those poor chickens."

The side of his mouth lifts in a half smile. "You know I can't say no to my girls."

He helps me climb the steps, kissing me slow and deep as the others smother Mabel in kisses of their own and then we go inside, shutting out all the animal invaders and the noise from the campus.

"Are Tristan and Azlan back from the council yet?" I ask, as I sink into a couch and kick off my shoes.

"Nope," Renzo calls back.

I peek down at my feet and wince.

"Here, Mama," Mabel says, dragging a foot stool across the room and then struggling to lift each of my legs and place them on the cushion.

"Thank you, sweetie," I say, patting the space next to me and inviting her up for a cuddle.

"Baby not come yet?" she asks, poking the dome of my stomach. The baby kicks back.

"Nope, not yet."

"It's okay. Baby stay there," she tells me. I laugh, running my fingers through her curls. I take it she likes being an only child.

"Don't worry. Being a big sister is going to be awesome."

She looks at my belly, definitely not convinced, and then pops her thumb in her mouth, curling up against my side.

Soon, we're dozing off, and I only stir when someone gently nudges my shoulder.

Azlan.

"Dinner's ready," he tells me before kissing me.

"Did Renzo cook or ..."

"No, I did." He lifts Mabel up into his arms and she stirs too.

"Dinner time. Daddy cooked," he tells her as she yawns.

"S'getti?"

"You bet."

"Up!" she commands, and he tosses her high up into the air and catches her as we walk through to the dining table.

She shrieks with delight, making him do it five more times before she consents to the high chair, still giggling wildly. I've been trying to teach her to use a fork, but she's much happier to use her magic to wiggle the pasta through the air and into her mouth. I'm amazed how much she can do already. I think she'll end up a fearsome magical.

I peer down at my belly. I think this one will be, too. If they ever decide to emerge.

"How was the council today?" Spencer asks Tristan and Azlan, as Stone and Renzo amuse our daughter by turning their own dinners into wriggling plates full of worms.

"Trade negotiations," Tristan says. He rolls his eyes, like he doesn't live for that stuff. No more battling out on the dueling pitch. These days all his battling is done around negotiation and deal tables. "They weren't budging on the custom levels, but we got there in the end."

A lock of his fair hair falls into his face. He doesn't wear it so messy these days, attempts to slick it back. It's a losing battle.

It makes those butterflies in my stomach flutter again.

"Azlan?" I ask.

He twirls his fork around, eyes flicking towards Mabel. Satisfied she's distracted, he says, "We have a lead on the criminals who imported dodo feathers into the republic. We're going to be making arrests."

"Good job, Captain," I say, smiling at him and raising my glass of juice.

Tristan rests his hand on my thigh.

"How about you, Piglet?" After all this time, he still insists on calling me that. Obviously, I pretend I hate it. I don't. "How was your day?"

"Well ..." I say, opening my mouth to tell him.

But then a sharp pain sears through my stomach. I peer down at my belly.

"How about I tell you another time?" I say, because this baby is finally on its way.

The End

The Arrow Hart Journey

THE FIRST ARROW HART BOOK, **Fractured Fates**, released a year to the day of this final one, **Destined Dawn**. But the story, as with all stories, started long before. In fact, probably more than a year before. A year day dreaming and mulling over this story, trying to nail that first book and creating the characters I've come to treasure and adore.

I've never written a series this long before and I've had to be patient. All those mysteries and secrets that couldn't come out until the end when I've been dying to spill them right from the start. Patience is hard, folks – especially for me – but hopefully it paid off. Hopefully, you have enjoyed reading Rhi's story as much as I have enjoyed writing it.

Below, I've shared some little bits of information and writing inside secrets I thought you might be interested to read.

Once again, a massive thank you for following Rhi, her mates and her friends on this journey and for trusting me to deliver this story to you. Without your wonderful support and feedback, lovely readers, who knows if I'd ever finish a story at all 😁

• My dad is a massive Fleetwood Mac fan. Growing up, I loved the song Rhiannon about the witch taken by the wind. I knew if I ever wrote a story about a witch that would have to be her name!

• Of course, I needed a name for Rhi's friend – a second witch. I wanted something a little comical to suit her character. Winnie is totally named after Winnie the witch from the children's book. Look it up if you have kids – they're really funny.

• It was planned long ago that one of Rhi's mates would call her piglet once he fell for her but I had to wait for exactly the right moment for that to happen! I ummed and ahhed about when exactly – hopefully I hit it right.

• I had no idea Spencer was a werebeast – he revealed this to me as I wrote the first book. Lots of the characters reveal things about themselves as I write and get to know them better. Back story and the events in people's pasts that influence their behavior today really fascinates me.

• Renzo is probably the most fun and also the hardest character I've ever written. His way of thinking is so out-of-the-box and different from mine that I have to concentrate extra hard when I'm writing his chapters to stay in his head and in his voice. He is exhausting – good luck to Rhi!!

• I did a poll in my facebook group to see what people wanted to happen to Summer. Overwhelmingly, people wanted her to get her just desserts. I think she did but, I don't know, I still hold out hope for her to be redeemed. I'm a sucker for a redemption.

• My all-time favorite book ever is Pride & Prejudice. I've probably read it at least fifty times and have watched all the adaptations. There are often little P&P easter eggs in my stories. If you spotted them in Rhi's story, well done to you!

So what's next, **Hannah?**

I'll be releasing **deluxe special *Arrow Hart Academy* editions** in 2025 with new covers and beautiful artwork! The Kickstarter campaign will launch in January - you can follow it here!

And, if you enjoyed Rhi's story and want more like it, be

sure to check out my new series, **The Firestone Academy**, coming early 2025. It's going to have everything you love:

- A kick-ass heroine and ruthless love interests
- Magical beings and creatures
- Enemies-to-lovers and a drop of fated mates
- Secrets and mysteries to be solved – not everything is as it appears!

You can read on for a sneaky peek of the first two chapters of book one, **Storm of Shadows**.
And you can pre-order here now!

OH, and if you'd like a steamy bonus scene between Rhi and the beast, check out my website – it's where you can find all my bonus content!

STORM OF SHADOWS

1
____

B^{riony}

SNOWFLAKES SWIRL in the gray sky, catching in my hair and my eyelashes and the cold is biting. I blink them away and hug my bag more tightly to my chest, trying to ignore the stiffness in my fingers, the wetness creeping in through my boots and the ache in my chest.

I can't decide if I'm pleased to be leaving Slate Quarter for the academy or really pretty furious about it.

It doesn't matter either way. I'm going. I don't exactly have a choice in the matter.

I glance down the platform at the other kids my age, surrounded by family and friends – hugging each other close, wiping tears from their eyes, laughing and joking.

There's a sense of anticipation in the air, of excitement. I can practically taste it on the end of my tongue. These kids actually believe this is their ticket out of here. Their tickets to better things.

I snap my head away.

They're fucking deluded.

And, actually, not kids anymore either.

Young adults – that's what they call us when we hit twenty-one and that's why we're all lined up waiting for the train that's going to whisk us away to the Firestone Academy.

The old clock on the wall, its face cracked, ticks another minute.

Monday, January 3rd. 8:57am.

The train will be here in three.

My dad isn't coming to see me off.

Why am I even surprised?

He makes all sorts of promises in the evening, rarely keeps them in the morning. I know that, so why the hell did I think this time would be any different? Just because I'm leaving. Just because he swore on his life. The pull of the tavern has always been more alluring than the pull of his only daughter.

Only *remaining* daughter.

I swallow hard, trying not to think of that. Of the last time I stood on this platform waiting for this train. That day had been filled with glorious sunshine – rare out here in Slate Quarter – and my stomach had been full of that same excitement and anticipation that's buzzing around today.

I don't think it's full of anything today. Mostly because Muriel refused me breakfast. Partly because it's been years since I felt anything at all.

In front of me, the rail tracks vibrate, then rattle and then the station fills with the roar of the train. The people down the platform pick up bags, grab last-minute embraces, and kiss each other's cheeks.

I simply clutch my rucksack and wait as the train slides into the station, halting with a hiss like a giant silver snake, the blacked-out windows of the engine like soulless eyes. It's eerie and, as the doors part and an announcement instructs all young Slate Quarter adults to board, I can't help but feel like we're about to step inside the stomach of a monster.

I've no one to hug. No one to say my goodbyes to. Not even someone to wave to. So I climb on board, walking as far down the carriages as I can until I'm right at the front of the train and there's nowhere else to go. I pick a bench on the far side from the platform and slide along to the window.

I've no interest in watching any more of the spectacle out there on the platform – a reminder that others have people who actually give a damn about them. I'm more than aware of that.

It takes a few more minutes and another announcement over the loudspeaker, and then the others board the train – a trickle at first, just one or two. Then groups of friends, chatting away animatedly, talking over one another, so damn excited. The noise makes me wince.

No one picks the seat next to me on the bench, but I keep my bag on my lap anyway, clinging it tightly to my chest. I lean my head against the frigid pane of glass and close my eyes.

Soon, the train jolts and then slithers forward. I don't bother to open my eyes, to watch my home slip away from sight. It hasn't felt like home for a long time. I don't care if I'm leaving, even if I have no desire at all to go where we're headed.

Around me, the other kids keep right on chattering like monkeys locked in a cage. I wish I had a way to block out all

the noise. I wish I was out in the forest, away from everything and everyone. I've never 'peopled' very well.

Or maybe I did once.

Then things changed.

Unfortunately, like everyone else on this train, I have no
special powers, no remarkable abilities. I don't have a way to
silence all the voices or block out all the sound. Just like them,
I'll endure a year of hell at the academy – tested, assessed,
probed to the extreme. Only for them to find out just how
ordinary we all are and send us straight back to Slate Quarter.

An hour passes and another. Somewhere along the journey, I open my eyes and watch the passing landscapes
outside the window. I can't help it. I've never left Slate
Quarter before. This is the furthest I've ever been from
home, and I am curious.

At first, it's all snow and ragged crops of mountains as far
as the eyes can see, then gradually it thaws and trees and
grass spring up from the ground – so much green it makes
my head buzz. I want to press my nose against the glass and
breathe it all in, pretend this is some magical adventure and
not the start of a year of pain.

Unfortunately, any hope of escaping into a comforting
daydream is interrupted by the slamming open of the
carriage door. I should ignore whoever is swaggering
through the doorway, but that damn curiosity of mine gets
the better of me and I can't help peering over my shoulder.

Stanley Chandlers and his band of merry meatheads.

For a second, I catch his eyes and his top lip – one I've
kissed – curls in disgust. Then I snatch my head back round
and stare straight ahead.

I'm not interested in any of his bullshit.

"Hello, friends," he snarls, and I can almost hear the

others in the carriage shaking around me. Seriously, and they think they're actually going to make it through Firestone Academy? That they'll return home heroes to their families and not in a body bag?

I'd roll my eyes, but I know it'll only provoke a jerk like Stanley.

"You know the drill," he says, striding into the middle of the carriage, hands deep in his worn pant pockets. "Open your bags and hand over your lunches."

There's a menace in his voice, at odds to his laid-back demeanor, and no one argues. There's rustling as people unzip bags and root around for their lunches – lunches their moms probably packed with care.

From the corner of my eye, I watch Stanley's gang move around the carriage, snatching boxes and parcels of food, irritatingly smug grins plastered across their faces.

I turn my attention back to the window.

"And you too, Storm." I feel a hand slap down on my shoulder and then his hoarse voice by my ear. "We all know you think you're special or some such shit. You're not. Give me your lunch."

I'm trapped. My usual method of escape – running as fast as I freaking well can – is not an option. The only place to run to is right off the end of the carriage, onto the tracks, and most probably under the wheels of the train.

I snap my head around and glare at him. "Why? Did your mom forget to pack you one?"

It's a low blow. One I know will hit him hard. I doubt anyone else knows about his mom. Only me.

His brow furrows, his eyes turn cruel, and he shakes me so damn hard I feel my brain rattle against my skull.

It's hard to remember the sweet boy he used to be, the

one I spent that summer with three years ago. The one who was my friend. The one I kissed.

That was before he got tall and big and popular.

"Give me your fucking lunch, bitch," he snarls.

I keep my face blank. I learned from Muriel that if you show nothing, it makes them even madder. They want tears. They want anger. It's best if you don't give them anything at all.

"I don't have any," I say robotically.

He slams me back against the seat. The carriage is silent except for the rattle of the train on the tracks and the wind whistling past the windows. Everyone else is still, watching us.

"You're lying." He takes a fistful of the collar of my thin jacket. "You think you're special."

"I don't," I whisper.

"You think you're going to get to the academy and they're going to see how smart you are and you'll be assigned Granite Quarter. But you're wrong. You're fucking stupid. There's only a handful of us who are going to make it through the academy with enough points to be assigned some better quarter – who aren't going back to that shithole. And you won't be with us."

For once, he may actually be right. Although, I doubt it will be as many as a handful. One or two, possibly. Stanley, though, has a good chance. He's strong and athletic – he certainly won't make it to Granite Quarter with all the nerds and scholars, definitely won't be going to Onyx Quarter with the shadow weavers, but he has a good chance of Iron Quarter with all the other jocks and soldiers.

"Oh - kay," I say slowly, as if what he's saying is the most boring thing I've ever heard.

His expression hardens further. Since his glow up, he's

been used to people treating him with respect. I can sense the blood in his veins boiling.

"Last chance, you little slut."

I snort.

And he slams his fist right into my face. I hear my cheek crack and pain spirals right across my face and into the recesses of my skull. My mouth fills with the warm coppery taste of blood and my vision multiplies.

Despite the pain, I wrap my arms tightly around my bag and clutch it to my chest. He tugs on it, but I cling all the harder, refusing to let it go.

"You're going to regret this," he snarls, swinging his fist into my ribs and then against the side of my head.

I expect him to keep swinging, to beat me until I'm unconscious and he can take the bag from my limp arms. He doesn't. He stops and stalks away with his treasure, the carriage door slamming shut behind him.

He knows I'm not lying.

There may be something hidden in my bag, but it isn't lunch.

2

B riony

I WAIT for everyone else to shuffle off the train, then stand and swing my rucksack up onto my shoulder. The action makes my bruised ribs ache and I wince against the pain, my head still pounding from the two punches I took to the skull.

It's fine. Sure, my reflection confirms my left eye's all puffed up and slowly turning blue, a cut striping across my cheek bone where Stanley caught me with his ring. But it will heal. It always does.

I lift my chin, walk to the train door and descend the metal steps out onto another platform.

This one's not covered in snow, but it's as cold and bleak as home, a frigid wind whipping around all the kids already lined up for some kind of inspection, the sun hanging low in the sky and shadows already descending.

I join the line, standing beside some girl who used to be in my woodwork class back at school. I lower my bag to the ground, positioning it between my feet, and wait.

There must be several hundred of us at least and we're the last ones to join. Not surprising. We had the furthest to travel because, of course, they'd build the academy closest to Onyx Quarter – can't have all those spoiled bastards traveling too far, can we? Plus, I suspect our train was the oldest and most decrepit. In fact, I bet most of the shadow weavers were driven in fancy cars by goddamn chauffeurs.

It's easy to spot who they are and an extreme sensation of disgust, hatred and fear spirals in my empty stomach.

They're furthest down the line from us and dressed in clothes that weren't handed down or retrieved from thrift stores. They're made from bright, expensive-looking materials and they actually fit them. Although, that isn't the only giveaway. There's something about the kids – an air of self confidence and arrogance that's discernible even over the distance.

Then there's the actual shadow magic – some of the kids tossing balls of it up into the air or at each other, making it clear to all of us losers just how special they are.

I run my gaze over the other soon-to-be students lined up along the platform – kids from the white-collar workers in Granite Quarter or the soldiers and athletes in Iron Quarter. They aren't as extravagantly dressed as the shadow weaver kids, but they still look a hell of a lot better than us.

It's why any one of the kids I traveled up with in the train would give their right arm to come out of the academy and all its trials and testing and be designated one of the other quarters, escaping a lifetime of hard labor in the factories, fields and mines of Slate Quarter. A better life for them and their family – if they choose to take them.

Not all do. Some want an entirely clean break. I can totally relate.

These Granite and Iron kids are ordinary, though, not a lot different from me and the others from Slate Quarter, and as a consequence, and to my utter shame, my gaze is pulled back to the shadow weavers.

To the magic. To the bright clothes. To the sense of power.

They are beautiful, all of them. And well fed and healthy.

It makes me hate them all the more.

They have so much — everything anyone could ever dream of — and yet they took the only thing I ever cared about.

Suddenly, my eyes meet the gaze of a boy peering along the line in our direction. For the briefest of seconds, we simply stare at each other – both stunned to be caught gaping.

Everything about him screams strength – from the way his shirt tugs across his muscular chest, to his square jaw and sharp cheekbones. He looks like he could crush me with his bare hands. Even his eyes are intimidating – an unusually pale color I can't make out over the distance, that contrast – startling so – with his dark brows and the dark hair that hangs to his shoulders.

For a moment, it's like everyone else around us melts away – all the noise, all the commotion – and it's just me and him staring at each other across the distance. A strange sensation shivers down my spine and I wonder if we know each other, if I recognize him from somewhere. Is that what this is? Or is it his magic? I've never met a shadow weaver in real life before – although I've heard a fuck-load about them.

But then the spell is broken.

He frowns like I've displeased him and turns his head away.

I shake my own head, annoyed that some guy could make me feel so disoriented, and concentrate instead on the set of guards marching towards us.

I wonder why they're needed. We're all here, aren't we? If we were going to run, we'd already have done it.

It seems no one's getting shot today, though, because the troop of guards halts in front of us, moves aside and the Empress herself steps forward.

She is a tall, willowy woman, with pale skin and pale eyes. A crimson gown drapes across her delicate shoulders, a pink thread woven through it that makes it glow in the dusk. It reaches the ground, her feet not visible and her arms, gloved in red leather, are clasped in front of her. On top of her head, woven into her golden locks, sits the steel crown of the realm.

All my life, I've seen pictures of her – on posters, in frames, in books. She is beautiful in an ethereal way. Delicate, fragile-looking, like the shell of an egg. Yet, this is the woman that controls the realm and all of us in it.

To see her in real life has me just as disoriented as a moment ago.

Or maybe that's just the two hits to the head. I'm not usually so awed. I don't intend to be. That isn't how my time at the academy is going to go. I know who these people are. I know how they treat people like me. I won't be bowing and scraping at their feet.

"Welcome, offspring of the realm." She smiles at us serenely, like we are her very own children. "One thousand years ago, this realm and its people were lost to the darkness and at the mercy of demons. It was only with the discovery of firestones, the taming of dragons and the emergence of those among us able to wield strong magic that we drove the danger away. From the ashes, our new realm was formed where each has their place, every one their role. However, I do not need to tell you that the threat still remains. The darkness encroaches us from all sides, the demons are an ever-present and deadly threat. It is only through the continued efforts and sacrifice of those able to wield shadow magic that we are protected from harm."

The soldiers stamp their feet and knock their fists against their chests.

"Today you become students of the Firestone Academy. Today you join the thousands of others before you in undergoing the year-long learnings and trials that will determine your future." She casts her eyes over us, seeming to take each one of us in. "All of you have talents – whether it be your intellect, your brute strength, the ability of your hands – or the unique and powerful wielding of magic." She points to the shadow weavers, who smirk with self-satisfaction. "You all have something to offer the realm. You all have your place in ensuring the safety of its people and our collective prosperity. Whether that be by providing the food from Slate Quarter needed to feed our realm, or inventing new technology in Granite Technology to aid our fighters. Whether you will become a foot soldier from Iron Quarter supporting our more elite fighters or you are a shadow weaver protecting our realm with your magic." She lifts her hands into the air, sparks of magic exploding from her palms. "By trial and truth, your Quarter calls!"

The guards around her clap and, taking their cue, so do those lined up on the platform.

Not me though. I keep my hands by my side. This is all bullshit. My fate's already written – was from the moment I slithered from between my dying mother's legs and into Slate Quarter.

Stanley is right. I won't be going anywhere but home, where the 'ability of my hands' will be exploited, where there's nothing worth living for, where I'll be worked to the bone until I'm a broken wretch like my dad – unable to make it through the day without a bottle or two of spirits by my side.

Maybe once upon a time I trusted the system. I believed, like everyone else, if we gave our best, we'd be assigned a Quarter that would most suit our talents. Then I learned better.

My insolence goes unnoticed and finally the Empress lifts her hand for silence.

"I will not pretend that your year at the Firestone Academy will be an easy one. You will be pushed to your boundaries, stretched to your limits, driven to your breaking points. We intend to find the best among you – the most talented, the most powerful. And only the trials of the utmost rigor and hardship will reveal your true capabilities, your true selves." She pauses again, although this time there is no clapping. This time I'd say the realization has finally hit. There's a reason one or two students return home in a coffin each year. The Firestone Academy is a dangerous and forbidding place.

I know that better than anyone else.

"And so," the Empress continues, "there will be no delay. Your first trial begins this evening. In fact, it will start right now. You may leave your bags here – they will be transported up to the academy for you." She points off into the distance. Right there on the horizon, just visible above what looks like the dense tree line of a forest, tall castle turrets climb into the darkening sky. "You will make your own way to the academy. Points will be rewarded and, as you know, points will determine to which of the four Quarters you are assigned. Good luck." She smiles again and then, with a whisk of her cloak, she vanishes from sight, along with the guards that surrounded her, all of them melting into air.

What follows is confusion and chaos.

People swing their heads around in panic, others crowd around with their friends murmuring to one another, some call to each other.

Above the commotion, one of the shadow weavers jumps up onto a pile of bags – or did he fly up there?

"Yeah, good luck, you cock-sucking commoners. This is where you learn what real strength is. This is where you learn why we are the ones chosen to protect the realm. This is where you learn your place. None of you are getting any points. Because we're coming for you." He rubs his hands together with such glee it makes my blood run cold.

The powerful always prey on the weak. And tonight the powerful are going to show us just how weak we are.

The voices become more frantic. One girl is already crying. Another boy shaking.

Me, I'm not hanging about. I've heard what happens the night new students arrive at the academy. I've already taken one beating today. I'm not about to take another.

I swing my bag back up onto my shoulder, wincing again with the pain, and jump down from the platform.

"Hey, Slate scum, you're meant to leave your bag behind," some jerk calls out from above me.

I ignore him. There is no way I'm leaving my bag unattended. No way on earth I'm being parted from it.

Instead, I scan the landscape quickly as the sun dips behind the horizon and plunges us all into a black so thick it sucks away all the light. The temperature drops several degrees with it and cold caresses my body. Around us lie open fields and the distant forest. And perhaps the gurgle of a stream or a river. Already there are people running out across the fields – people, I bet, who aren't prepared to wait around and find out what's coming.

I peer up at the academy and then I start to run. Not towards it, away from it. I'm not following the crowd. I'm getting as far away from everyone else as I can. It's the tactic I've always used and nine times out of ten it's worked. Run and hide. Don't let them catch you.

Okay, it'll mean I'm one of the last to arrive at the academy. But so what? It's not like I'm going to ace any of these trials anyway. And if I'm punished? It's nothing I haven't handled before.

I run as hard as I can, although the pain in my ribs slows me down and makes every panted-breath agony.

At least I'm running in the wrong direction, though. At least no one is going to follow me this way. At least I'll escape the sadistic mayhem.

Yeah, so much for that plan.

Turns out, I'm wrong.

Behind me comes the pounding of feet on hard earth.

Loud, fast, determined.

Peering over my shoulder and through the darkness, I discover a figure racing towards me. Moving at a colossal speed.

I can't make them out, can't see their face, or determine their identity. But I'm pretty sure they're coming for me.

"Shit," I mutter, driving my arms and legs faster, even though it makes the pain spike in my body.

I scramble up a bank, then skid down the other side, losing my balance for a second, before I find my feet again.

A cloud of thick fog curls around me, drifts of silvery cobwebs swim past my face.

I keep running.

Maybe they'll get bored. Maybe I'll lose them in this mist. There must be easier prey than me out there. That crying girl for starters. I doubt she's going to last this first night at the academy. And they were all so freaking excited about coming here.

I tut, then berate myself for my smugness. I'm not exactly doing so great myself. The pain in my ribs is excruciating, and the shadow is gaining on me. I can hear them – their panted breath, their solid footfall. Shit, I can *feel* them.

I have no idea where I am. My head aches, my ribs sting and my legs are tiring.

I grit my teeth and keep driving forward through the swirling mist.

But it's no use.

My body lets me down, weakened by that goddamn beating.

Fucking Stanley!

I blink away tears of frustration. I try to keep moving.

My feet slow.

And a silvery shadow hooks around my middle, sliding around me, tightening its grip, and slamming me to the earth.

I land flat on my stomach and the air knocks straight from my lungs as my pursuer lands down on top of me, pinning me to the ground with their immense weight.

I close my eyes and try to breathe.

My lungs don't work, no matter how hard I suck at the air, no matter how much my aching ribs pull. Nothing. No air. No breath. Nothing.

The dark shadows of the world encroach across my vision.

Fuck it, Briony. I thought you were made of harder stuff than this.

I jolt myself back from the abyss.

I am made of harder stuff than this. I fucking am.

I suck more desperately at the air, screaming as my injured ribs expand, pain striking through my body.

Whoever has me pinned to the ground doesn't react. Their mouth hovers by my right ear, and their moist breath whistles over my skin.

They're much, much bigger than me, their scent woody and masculine, like the forest at night. Menacing, dark, enticing.

I attempt to shuffle from underneath them, but they hold me locked to the ground with their sizable frame.

"What's your name?"

A man. His voice is deep and polished, and if I hadn't guessed before, I know it now.

A shadow weaver.

"None of your fucking business," I spit, struggling against him. "Get the fuck off me."

"You think wriggling your ass against my cock is going to encourage me to get off you?" he says, with a hint of amusement.

I freeze.

Don't provoke the monsters. Don't give them what they want.

He curls a loose strand of hair around my ear. "Come on now, tell me your name."

I stare down at the hard earth, drops of moisture clinging to the brittle grass. I can feel the beat of his rapid heart pounding against me.

I say nothing.

He huffs a little, shifts his weight, and flips me right over so I'm lying on my back and staring right up at him, my hands pinned to the earth, his body caged over mine.

I jolt.

It's the boy from the platform.

Up close, his eyes are such a soft, pale blue they're almost translucent, almost silver, like the moon on a cool, clear evening. His skin is pale too and the lines of his face so sharp, so defined, they look as if they were carved from marble.

Around him the air crackles with electricity. His magic.

I wonder what power he possesses. I wonder what he can do.

I wonder what the hell he's going to do to me.

The thought has me struggling under him, attempting to break loose. But speed has always been my asset, not strength. I'm a tiny, pathetic weed compared to him. He pins my hands above my head and leans into me, his face mere millimeters from mine, his breath warm as it dances across my face.

He doesn't ask me my name again, instead he stares right into my eyes, like he did before, like he's trying to read my soul. It's so intense, my cheeks run warm, and I'm forced to turn my head away from him.

"How did you get that?" he asks, his voice less playful than before.

"Wh-wh-what?" I say, unable to help but peer back up at him.

"The black eye," he snarls, "the cut on your cheek."

I nearly add the bruised ribs to his list, but I hold my tongue. It's clear I disgust him. Weak, pathetic, easy prey. He probably saw that on the platform and that's why he chased me. Although, it seems dumb to me. It's a done-deal which quarter he'll be assigned. Only shadow weavers make it to Onyx Quarter. Yet, he's chosen to scupper his chance of securing easy points by following me in the wrong direction. Why?

"Who did this to you?" he asks.

Again, I don't reply. What's he going to do with the name? Congratulate the dude? Ask him to be his best friend? Yeah, Stanley's brute strength and large fists already give him enough advantages in this place. I'm not about to gift him a powerful new friend.

I stare over the dude's shoulder, letting my passive expression swamp my face.

He's going to do what the fuck he wants to me. But I won't give him the satisfaction of a reaction.

"Fine," he says. "I'm going to find out anyway. Your name and the name of the piece of shit that did this to you."

I blink. Confused by his words. Still waiting for the first blow.

Or worse ...

But then he's rolling off me and stumbling up to his feet.

His pale eyes glimmer in the darkness, flickering over my form, lingering on my face.

"Don't hang about, sweetheart. There are monsters out here," he whispers, and then he turns away and disappears into the swirling mist.

Continue reading *Storm of Shadows*

ALSO BY HANNAH HAZE

All available on Amazon and Kindle Unlimited.

Fantasy Romance RH
The Arrow Hart Academy
Fractured Fates
Twisted Ties
Shattered Stars
Burdened Bonds
Destined Dawn

The Firestone Academy
Storm of Shadows
Spark of Sorcery
Taste of Thorns
Lure of Lightning

Contemporary RH omegaverse
The Rockview Omegaverse
Pack Rivals Part I

Pack Rivals Part II
Pack Choice
Pack Gamble Part I
Pack Gamble Part II
Pack Education Part I
Pack Education Part II

In With The Pack
<u>In Deep</u> - Rosie's story
<u>In Trouble</u> - Connie's story
<u>In Knots</u> - Alexa's story
<u>In Doubt</u> - Giorgie's story
<u>In Control</u> - Sophia's story
In Stockings (Christmas Novella)

Contemporary MF omegaverse series
The Alpha Rock Stars
<u>The Rockstar's Omega</u>
<u>Rocked by the Alpha</u>
<u>Fourth Base with the Alpha</u>

Contemporary MF omegaverse standalones
<u>Oxford Heat</u>
<u>The Alpha Escort Agency</u>
<u>Omega's Forbidden Heat</u>

Contemporary MF omegaverse novellas
<u>The Omega Chase</u>
<u>Online Heat</u>
<u>Christmas Heat</u>

Alien omegaverse MF romance series

The Alpha Prince of Astia
<u>Alien Desire</u>
<u>Alien Passion</u>

ABOUT THE AUTHOR

A recovering cynic, Hannah grew up swearing she would never marry. Then in 2001, she met her husband and has been a card-carrying romantic ever since. Despite being an avid writer and reader, Hannah decided to do the sensible thing and study science at university, putting authoring ideas to one side.This all changed when she discovered the joys of a good romance book and came to the realisation that love stories are always the best ones.

She now uses her knowledge of chemical bonds and reactions to ensure her books are full of sparks. In fact the electricity between her characters is sure to set your pulse racing and your heart fluttering.

Hannah loves reading to her three children, including doing all the silly voices, and going for long walks in the country-side (the muddier the better). Her head is always full of new story ideas and you are most likely to find her avoiding the demands of her very naughty cat as she attempts to write them all down.

Sign up to my newsletter:
www.hannahhaze.com/about

Join my reader groups:

https://www.facebook.com/groups/hannahhazehotro
mancereads

https://www.facebook.com/groups/softandsteamyomega
verse

Visit my website:

www.hannahhaze.com

Catch me on TikTok:

www.tiktok.com/@hannahhaze_author

ACKNOWLEDGMENTS

This is the last book in the series — so it's only right I thank all the people who have helped me along the way.

Firstly, to you, lovely reader, thank you for joining me on this journey and embracing Rhianna's story as you have. I truly hope the ending of the story lived up to your expectations. Thank you for all your wonderful messages, comments, reviews and ratings. It makes this writing business so much more enjoyable and I am eternally grateful.

Another a massive thank you to my amazing beta reader team who have been with me from the start, helping to craft this story into the best it can be. Your ideas, feedback and support have been crucial. Thank you Courtney, Sara, Jessie, Leandri, Aimee, Jenna, Melissa, Lili and Kiki.

Thank you to Christian for these beautiful covers and James for editing my smutty words.

And finally, thank you to Mr. D, Stephy, my children and the rest of my family. You guys are the best! Love you all x